THE TEARDROP
STORY WOMAN

潸馬淚下

THE TEARDROP
STORY WOMAN

潸馬淚下

Catherine Lim

THE OVERLOOK PRESS

WOODSTOCK & NEW YORK

First published in the United States in 1998 by
The Overlook Press, Peter Mayer Publishers, Inc.
Lewis Hollow Road
Woodstock, New York 12498

Copyright © 1998 by Catharine Lim

Caligraphy by Wai Yee Yip

Library of Congress Catalog-in-Publication Data

Lim, Catherine.
The Teardrop Story Woman / Catherine Lim.
ISBN 0-87951-901-0
I. Title.
PR9570.S53L484   1998   823—dc21   98-16590

Manufactured in the United States of America

ISBN: 0-87951-901-0

1 3 5 7 9 8 6 4 2

Life is made bearable by the stories we save and tell

PART ONE

CHAPTER ONE

When Mei Kwei was born, the midwife, seeing the despised slit between the tiny, quivering legs instead of the prized curl of flesh, shook her head and clucked her tongue. Crying as she came into the world, the baby girl might have been saying, 'Tell them I'm sorry.'

The midwife laid the newborn on a pile of old sarongs folded to make a soft bed on the hard unmattressed one of the mother, and began to examine her carefully for harelip, club-foot, a supernumerary nipple, a ready-formed tooth, the sign of the devil. The double sin of being born female and deformed condemned an infant to instant death in the ancestral country. The midwife's mother, also a midwife who lived in a village in North China, had, in her time, disposed of such unfortunate female babies, usually by turning their faces into a tray filled with ash. That was the more merciful method. A woman who had given birth to a baby girl with bleached skin and hair had screamed, 'Ghost child!' and abandoned her in the mud of a rice-field, only to tiptoe out later to find her still alive, the umbilical cord wrapped around her tiny body.

Here in the adopted country, fate was kinder. Ah Ban Soh's daughter, who was born with a sixth finger on her right hand, and Ah Kim Soh's daughter, who was born with a badly cleft upper lip, had been allowed to live and were even now getting ready to be married, a matchmaker having found willing husbands for them.

Mei Kwei was a perfectly formed baby. Her teardrop mole, close to her right eye, would be discovered only much later.

'Does he want to be told?' said the midwife, meaning the father.

Ah Oon Koh was in a coffee-shop down the road. He had gone there to escape the fuss of the birth and was now drinking one cup of coffee after another, slumped morosely in a chair in his singlet and pyjama trousers. Some hours before, he had seen the midwife getting ready a basin of steaming hot water and piles of rags and paper, and had immediately rushed out of the house, got on his bicycle and pedalled furiously away.

He remembered with much disgust, invariably expressed in a sharp snort and a violent ejection of spittle, the occasion, just three years ago, when he had been unlucky enough to come face to face with her as she emerged from the confinement room carrying a filled chamberpot. The hot fetid smells of afterbirth struck him in the face. Of all the shameful things that women could inflict on men, this was the worst. Later the midwife had tried to make amends by offering him a basin of cool clean water with a sprinkling of fresh flower petals to wash away the bad luck. But the harm was done already: soon afterwards he lost money in his charcoal business.

Still, it had been a boy, and the mother and the midwife had watched with some relief the look of gratification on his face when the newborn was put into his arms with the wrapping towel deliberately rolled up to the waist to show the small bud of power and promise. As he looked intently at the round, sleeping face, the bud slowly unwrinkled and stiffened to eject a silver spray that hit him in the face. He laughed loudly.

This time, it was only a girl.

'He has to be told, sooner or later,' said Ah Oon Soh bitterly. She had an abundance of long hair, which the thrashing throes of birth had cast in wild wet tangles upon her face and surrounding pillow, giving her an aspect of a ghost woman's beauty.

'Do you want to keep this?' The midwife, imperious and impatient as she snapped out one order after another during birth, became deferential after it, asking for instructions concerning the mother's wishes.

'What's the use?' Ah Oon Soh said dispiritedly, and the midwife threw the newly cut cord, glistening, wet, twisted, into the chamberpot on the floor; that of the son had been preserved in lucky red paper, tied with lucky red string.

Second Grandmother, who had been sitting in a chair all this while quietly fanning herself, said she would do it; Second Grandmother of the tiny bound feet that would surely be incapable of negotiating the potholes and bumps in the long stretch of road leading to the coffee-shop, where the father sat drinking.

'Someone has to do it,' she repeated grimly, and proceeded to unbutton the loose blue cotton blouse she was wearing for the finely starched white one used only for going out. She picked up her black umbrella from behind a door and was ready.

Big Older Brother who was three years old then, looked up from an empty cigarette tin in which he had been rattling some clay marbles, and cried to be taken too for he remembered the row of glass jars filled with sweets and biscuits in the coffee-shop. To emphasise the urgency of his wish, he began to howl and to stamp his feet on the hard earthen floor.

'Stop it,' the midwife said severely, 'or the big red ants will get at your bird,' upon which he immediately gave a loud yelp and cupped it protectively with both hands.

The midwife and his mother laughed. The overloading of the upper half of his stout little body, with vest, shirt, bib and rubber teat hanging on a string around his neck, was unmatched with anything on the lower half, so that teasing adults looked upon his little swinging member as he ran or toddled and threatened it with ants, bugs, lizards and hungry, penis-chomping female ghosts. The exposure was less the mother's strategy for flaunting the fact of her child's maleness to the world than a simple expedient to reduce the daily amount of washing of children's clothes and hence to save on soap.

Big Older Brother was easily placated with a spoonful of the special confinement food, which the midwife put into a bowl and placed on the floor for him. He sat contentedly, bare-bottomed, on the cold earthen floor, picking up grains of steamed rice and shreds of fried pork with his small chubby fingers and yelling for more as soon as he saw that the bowl was empty.

Second Grandmother had never ventured out on such a long walk before. In her starched white blouse and black silky trousers, her well-oiled hair neatly combed into a precise bun at the back of her head, her feet smaller than a child's in their tiny, pointed shoes, replica of a bygone age, she attracted attention by the preposterous act of venturing out unescorted.

'Oh, Old Auntie, you will fall, you will hurt yourself.' In the ancestral country she could have hitched a ride on the stout back of a young man; here she was offered various vehicles – a bicycle, a trishaw, a car – all slowing down in solicitous enquiry and offer of assistance.

'No, thank you, I'm fine.' Second Grandmother continued to totter along bravely, acknowledging with a mere nod the greetings and the offers, determination of purpose written on her face, which still bore traces of a former beauty.

Having successfully negotiated a hole, a puddle and a stout branch that had fallen across the road, she grew braver and swung her umbrella energetically to left and right to ward off a swarm of buzzing insects, a sniffing dog, the rude laugh of a boy by the roadside pointing at the incredibly small, tightly bound feet. The coarse boy, to amuse his companions, all ragged and barefoot like himself, stood on his toes, hunched his shoulders, affected a demeanour of extreme female coyness and began to walk beside her with exaggeratedly small mincing steps.

'You are all impolite children. Didn't your mothers ever teach you manners?' scolded Second Grandmother. She launched into a tirade against the disrespectful behaviour of the young, jabbing the air angrily with her umbrella. The obnoxious boy, playing up to the titters of his companions, began to mimic her in a high-pitched voice, still walking mincingly and now striking the air delicately with an invisible umbrella.

'Go away!' cried Second Grandmother angrily.

'Go away!' echoed the boy, now fully launched upon the day's mischief of teasing old women, dogs and beggars, to escape the day's pain of want and hunger.

Second Grandmother lapsed into sullen muttering and decided to ignore the urchins and concentrate on her progress down the road.

She heard a man's voice say roughly, 'Have you no respect?' and turned to see a trishawman, his gold teeth glinting in the afternoon sun, furiously pedalling his vehicle through the group of young miscreants, scattering them. He said in a kind voice to Second Grandmother, 'Old Auntie, where are you going? Why are you by yourself?'

Her little bound feet, which had miraculously borne her down a long stretch of road, now crumbled under the weight of her mission, just when its accomplishment was in sight: she could already see the shop sign in large red and black characters. She sat down heavily on the road and sighed.

'Get in, Old Auntie,' the trishawman told her, 'and I'll give you a ride to wherever you're going.' All the way to Lam Pin coffee-shop, he rang the trishaw bell happily, in self-testimony to his good deed.

'Everyone will see,' said Second Grandmother, with grim purpose, 'that I will not apologise for the birth of a granddaughter.'

Glumly drinking his fourth cup of coffee, Ah Oon Koh ignored the small commotion that had arisen with the arrival of a trishaw, until he realised that the occupant who was causing the rumpus was his mother-in-law.

Sunk into the depths of the broken trishaw seat, Second

Grandmother was having difficulty getting out; her umbrella, moreover, was stuck in the fender. The coffee-shop assistant, a young man ever attentive to the needs of the old, had rushed forward as soon as he saw her plight and immediately freed the umbrella. Now, with the help of the trishawman, he was trying to haul the old woman up and out of the vehicle. Second Grandmother gave an arm co-operatively to each of the tugging men, never minding the damage to her perfectly starched and ironed sleeves. The vehicle, used to the weight of an entire family, creaked and wobbled dangerously. A half-drunk Indian in a loincloth, with a dirty towel draped over his head, stood by watching and cackling with laughter; he lurched forward to help and was pushed aside. As soon as she was on her feet again, Second Grandmother haughtily stood up to her full height, pulled down the corners of her blouse, smoothed out the creases of her trousers and adjusted a tortoise pin on her bun, before walking purposefully to her son-in-law with her black umbrella.

The announcement of the birth of a daughter by one's mother-in-law in a public place, watched by at least a dozen people, was intolerable, to say the least, and Ah Oon Koh, to his dying day, never forgot the humiliation. His ears a hot red, his knuckles stark white as he gripped his coffee-cup with both hands, he stayed slumped in his chair, staring ahead, saying nothing.

'Never mind, Ah Oon Koh, a daughter can be as good as a son.'

'Mother and child are well, surely that's the most important thing –'

'Go home now, Ah Oon Koh –'

A waggish young man broke through the polite restraints to slap him boisterously on the back and tease him about the acquisition of a flat bun instead of a long cruller. Encouraged by a roar of laughter from a nearby table of coffee drinkers, the wag went on to expatiate on the superiority of stout cucumber over cleft melon, of long eel over moist, bivalved cockle so that by slow degrees, the woman in the long silk *cheongsam* on the wall calendar was divested of her garments and stood in compliant, spread nakedness before a row of searching male eyes. The man would have offered more ribald analogies from coarse eating and drinking if someone had not interposed by directing attention, once more, to Second Grandmother. 'Ah Oon Koh, surely you don't mean to let your old mother-in-law walk all the way home.'

In the end, Ah Oon Koh had no choice but to offer his mother-

7

in-law a ride on the pillion of his bicycle. 'Wait,' said the thoughtful shop assistant, and ran to fetch a gunny sack, which he folded into a square and laid on the metal pillion to cushion the effects of a bumpy ride.

'You are very kind,' said Second Grandmother. In her mind she placed him and the trishawman well apart from the rowdy urchins and the surly son-in-law, who already stood in judgement before the Lightning God, ready to hurl his bolts at the unfilial and disrespectful.

In her last years when she grew demented and forgot many things, she remembered the travails of that afternoon and talked about them repeatedly, embellishing her descriptions with rich details so that the child Mei Kwei, squatting at her feet and looking up at her wide-eyed, would say excitedly, 'Second Grandmother, tell me about the cow dung!' For the old woman would have it that her son-in-law deliberately shook his bicycle so hard that she fell off into a dung heap and ruined her best pair of shoes. Miniature peonies and butterflies, delicately worked in the finest silk threads of gold and red, sunk into vile excreta! A gentlewoman's badge of fine breeding and prestige dishonoured for ever! Her best pair, too, brought all the way from the ancestral country and meant for use on the day of her funeral, when she would be laid out in only her best clothes.

Second Grandmother said she cried till her eyes were swollen and she could not see any more. The child's eyes grew large with astonishment. But even she knew that this story was for hearing only, not believing, for the precious shoes were intact and safe at home, wrapped in a piece of soft red cloth in a corner of a tall cupboard. On several occasions, she had dragged a chair, stood on it and felt the precious bundle, tracing the firm edges of the grandmother's secret pride with her small fingers. Years later there was a rumour, spread by the swill woman as she went on her collecting rounds in the neighbourhood, that on the day of Second Grandmother's death when the shoes, surely the finest in Luping or anywhere in Malaya, were at last brought out and put on her feet, the corpse parted its lips in a smile. Some corpses kept their eyes wide open in restless waiting for a loved one to appear; in Second Grandmother's case, it was the feet that grew impatient to claim union with their magnificent peony and butterfly shoes.

'Tell me about the dead boys.' For Second Grandmother would have it that the urchins who had tormented her were severely punished: the sky opened, the Lightning God appeared in full majesty and chased them with his bolts.

'Here's one for making fun of an old woman's speech!' cried the god, and smote their tongues.

'Here's one for making fun of an old woman's gait!' cried the god, and smote their legs.

Then he flew back into the sky, leaving a row of blackened bodies by the roadside.

But her efforts were in vain. Upon arriving home, her son-in-law banged his bicycle several times on the ground to show his displeasure and went straight into his room.

In the following days, he resolutely refused to look at the new baby. He was not, of course, expected to go into the darkened confinement room, now reeking of the sour smells of a woman's unwashed, lactating body, but at least he could have looked at the child when the midwife brought her out, warmly wrapped in a sarong. There had been the one hopeful moment when he looked up from the newspaper he was reading and saw them in front of him. The midwife made a slight movement of bold expectancy, the sarong bundle gave out a small snuffling sound. But the father instantly repulsed the advance with an angry, snorting return to his newspaper.

'It's as he wishes,' Ah Oon Soh said bitterly, when the midwife returned to the room. 'Nobody can force him, that's all.'

Ah Oon Koh's aversion, over and above that dictated by custom, was due to the peculiar circumstances of his own birth and childhood many years before in a small village in China. Perhaps in its unrelenting vehemence, it was meant to redress the partiality – how strange and unwarrantable! – that his own father had shown. It was a partiality bordering on madness and was the talk of the village. The villagers said that it must have been an illness, in particular a very high fever, that had caused the man's brains to turn into porridge in his head. How else could one explain his preference for daughters? The crazy man beat his wife when she gave birth to a son. When a second son – Ah Oon Koh – was born, the father decided to bring him up as a girl. He was given a girl's name and girl's clothes. His ear-lobes were pierced for decorating with tiny silver ear-rings that the lunatic had bought from a pedlar, announcing with pride, 'They are for my daughter!'

As a little pigtailed boy in a girl's dress, with cheeks sometimes rouged by the now completely insane man, he was laughed at by other children and teased by adults. 'Ah Mui, Ah Mui, where is your little pancake? Let us see.' He watched his older brother, who was allowed to remain male, with a burning envy that narrowed his eyes and hardened his young heart. His father, holding him affectionately by the hand, took him for long walks in the village, and stopped for friends and neighbours to pat his cheek, tug his pigtails and exclaim over his beauty in the exaggerated tones of humouring a madman. He would look back, as soon as they had walked on, to see the group clustered together in uproarious laughter, lightly twirling forefinger against temple to demonstrate a madness beyond the power of gods to heal.

'What are you crying about?' his older brother would snarl. 'You get all the good things,' these being tasty buns and roasted chestnuts that the mad father stuffed into the pockets of the girl clothes.

It was a shame that was all the greater for its suppression in those early confused years. On the day of his father's death, when he was nine years old, he tore the ornaments from his ear-lobes and flung them to the ground, casting off the shame for ever. He never forgave his father. About the time his mother was looking for a wife for him, he vowed that he would have no daughters and was secretly terrified by his dreams at night, in which the sombre grey mists of his future parted for him to see a long, detestable female line forming, and to hear the laugh of his hated dead father.

'Papa! Papa! Look at Little Sister!' Big Older Brother, the beloved and pampered one, could always be bribed with the delicious confinement food to help in the urgent task of securing the father's acknowledgement of the newborn's existence. He co-operated with exuberant energy, dragging his father by the hand to the low wooden bench outside the confinement room, where the child had been laid on its bedding of old sarongs, freshly bathed.

'Enough, enough,' the father said gruffly, broke free of the tugging hand and went back into his room.

Second Grandmother, reviewing an increasingly hopeless situation, said, 'We'll wait for the First Month Celebration,' for whoever had heard of a father refusing to carry in his arms his child, girl or boy, on the happy completion of its first thirty days? Second Grandmother began to work hard towards the event, the despised little newborn girl now the centre of her lonely life, loneliest in her last years in the impenetrable shadows of her dementia. The grandeur of the First Month Celebration of the grocer Poon's daughter, who was carried out of the confinement room in full regalia of red satin clothes, red woollen cap, red boots and mittens deliberately peeled off at the right moment to show relatives and neighbours the gold rings on the baby fingers, nettled Second Grandmother into feverish activity to secure something of that glory for her own little granddaughter. For was she not even healthier and prettier than the Poon child and therefore entitled to a greater celebration of victory over the marauding evil spirits that had conceded defeat after the thirty days and slunk away in shame?

Second Grandmother affected a scornful indifference to the swill woman's breathless description of the Poon celebration, but she listened avidly to the details of the celebration food that the Poon family dispensed to neighbours: nothing had been wanting. But there could be no chicken curry or saffron rice or bean cakes to announce her little granddaughter's triumphant survival of the malignancy of both her father and the evil spirits. Second Grandmother did a quick mental assessment of existing resources and concluded that they could afford two dozen hard-boiled eggs, shells stained lucky bright red, for distribution to immediate neighbours.

My granddaughter is the most beautiful baby girl, she thought, and I will make sure that she wears appropriate celebration clothes when she is taken out to be shown to the neighbours. The swaddling clothes from the torn-up old sarongs should never be seen again.

So she came home the next afternoon, hot and panting, her black umbrella of little use against the scorching heat, her little feet bravely holding up from the arduous trip, only partly by trishaw, to the pawn-shop. 'Here,' she had said, taking out of her blouse pocket a pair of jade ear-studs given her by a relative in the ancestral country, many years ago. For the first time in her life, her ear-lobes were without ornament, but now she had money to buy good red cloth, a child's silver anklet and the celebratory eggs. In the later years, when her mind wandered over past events and she spoke incessantly, she would scold her beautiful, strong-willed granddaughter into sheepish submission by reminding her of the enormous debts due for the dung-ruined silken shoes and for her precious ear-studs.

'I didn't ask you to do it, Second Grandmother,' the little girl would say petulantly.

'Ingratitude! Ingratitude!' the other would mutter, but still the old woman and young girl would come together in a natural gravitation of the lost and rejected.

'Smelly cunt,' said Second Grandmother, echoing the father who had spat out, not merely said, the words. 'I want to show everyone you are no smelly cunt but the beautiful granddaughter of Lee Gek Neo!' For she herself had possessed that rare rich beauty that ought to be perpetuated in daughters and granddaughters. She had wept bitterly to see her firstborn, Ah Oon Soh, sallow and ugly, except for the abundant lustrous hair. Fortunately, the beauty had not disappeared down the line but merely skipped a generation, reappearing in a new flowering in the granddaughter.

A concubine raised to the position of Second Wife, subservient to First but wielding enough power over Third and Fourth, Second Grandmother attributed all the good fortune to her beauty. The luck ended, however, with the death of her husband. Immediately after the funeral, First Wife had unleashed the full extent of a resentment simmering over twenty years, and cleared the huge familial mansion, once and for all, of the old man's entire establishment of three secondary wives and two concubines.

The hurried departure with her small daughter, and no more than a bundle of clothes (Second Grandmother insisted, years later, that she had left behind a treasure trove of jade and gold ornaments that had been the gift of her husband), marked the beginning of a pathetic decline into poverty and obscurity. Living with a relative who was kind enough to take her and her child under his protection, she fed on the memories of past passion and glory, distilled into a pair of tiny shoes that had brought joy to an old man on his bed. In her last years, when only her granddaughter could break through the terrible shadows to reach the quivering bewilderment and despair, she recalled her beauty, and the special pleasure she gave her husband, swaying towards him like a flower on its stalk, with nothing on except her small silken doll's shoes, exactly as he wanted it. He would raise himself on his elbow to look at her, cackling with delight.

Ginseng. Rhino's horn. What were these compared to the power of tiny feet in doll's shoes, to enthral and heat up old blood?

Many years before, when she was a little girl, her mother had said to the footbinder, 'Tighter! Tighter!', then turned to her to wipe the tears from her face and to promise, 'My little Gek Neo, when you grow up, you will be beautiful and please your husband.' Her mother must have visualised exactly this supreme reward for her sacrifice and pain. For even after her husband had taken a third, then a fourth wife, Lee Gek Neo remained his favourite.

'Come,' he would say, putting a whole length of room between themselves, for maximal feasting on the sight of the young, naked white body in small pink satin shoes swaying towards him.

'Don't expect me to use that thing,' said Second Grandmother haughtily, when her daughter, still weak from the birth, pointed to the Singer sewing-machine, kept in a corner of the confinement room. Manual, not foot pedal, it could be easily used by her to make the celebration clothes on which she was now so intent. But she trusted only her fingers, deft despite the years, and over a week, working assiduously in the light of a kerosene lamp in the evenings, produced a magnificent set of baby apparel, shirt, trousers, cap, mittens and socks, so finely sewn that they would survive years of use, bleached to a dull pink but with every stitch intact. Long after Second Grandmother's death, in that time of desperation and sadness when Mei Kwei had to decide which possessions she would take with her in flight, she chose the First Month Celebration clothes.

'See how pretty she is!'

'Such large eyes, such abundant hair!'

'She's indeed the prettiest baby girl!'

The compliments of the neighbours gradually subsided in their extravagance, muted by the awareness that the ever present, ever vigilant evil spirits could be provoked into a new wave of jealousy and malignant power. The swill woman whispered urgently, 'Has her father seen her yet?' to which Ah Oon Soh replied with bitter despondence, 'No, and perhaps never will.'

'You only complain, you never do anything for your daughter,' Second Grandmother said reproachfully. Clearing her throat, she addressed the sleeping newborn loudly for the sole benefit of the father who was in his room. 'So you are a despised smelly cunt, are you? So you come into the world unwanted? Never mind, have no fear. Those who are most despised will grow up to be most successful!' Whether a prediction or a wish, she invested it with the fervour and perfume of a prayer, as she lit a fragrant joss-stick and went outside to stand it in an urn on an altar consecrated to no god or goddess in particular but to any benign power that happened to be passing by and was not disinclined to use some of that power to help the meek and despairing of the earth.

No more, no more, thought Ah Oon Koh, and he meant that he would take no more of the old woman's malice. She had not stopped insulting him since that humiliating day in the coffee-shop, lacing the taste of his food and drink, the very quality of his dreams at night, with the acidity of her tongue. Her rancour penetrated the thin plank walls of his room, making sleep impossible.

He would leave his room and flounce out of the house, get on his bicycle and pedal away, no longer to the coffee-shop, where the humiliating incident was recounted in his hearing, but to a small noodles stall in the market-place where the owner allowed him to sit as long as he liked. In the fragrant smell of steaming noodles and prawn soup, he smoked and plotted. He would not talk to women but he could hurt them. There was no question of chasing his mother-in-law out of the house: the old spiteful one was sure to make a scene and stand bare-headed in pouring rain calling upon the Lightning God or the Thunder God to witness her plight and thus have the neighbours rallying round her in compassion.

'None of our business, none of our business,' they would say, and cast sidelong glances of dark, silent reproach at him.

There would be another way of punishing her.

CHAPTER TWO

When Mei Kwei was six months old, Ah Oon Koh announced brusquely to his wife, 'Ah Beng Koh and his wife are coming for the child in a week's time. Make the necessary preparations. I have told them there is no need for an *ang pow*.' Then he quickly left the house on his bicycle, to avoid questions and remonstrations. Absence would enhance power; he would come back to find the women chastened and subdued.

Such things were normally done by women, but Ah Oon Koh had made the arrangements for the adoption himself. Two more reverses in his small charcoal business together with a bout of bad health had convinced him that the bad luck stemmed from the newborn baby girl and, by extension, the grandmother who was preoccupied with her, even to the point of neglecting the grandson. If the child went, the old

14

one might, too: two carbuncles in the blood expelled with one decisive purgative. Soured by life's failure, needing to strike out in revenge, Ah Oon Koh succeeded in throwing the entire household into pandemonium with his decision. The noisy weeping of his wife and mother-in-law, dependent on him for food and shelter, washed futilely against the solidity of his explanation, 'I cannot afford to feed one more mouth,' and the incontrovertibility of his position, 'I am the man in the house.'

'Then I will go! I am a useless old woman. I will go!' Second Grandmother wailed, meaning she would go to join the destitute old men and women mercifully allowed sleeping space in the nooks and corners of the Kek Lok temple near the market-place. The stigma of sending an old parent into beggary was greater than that of giving away female children; indeed, Luping's households were replete with adopted daughters. Second Grandmother, resented as she was, would have a roof over her head and her three bowls of rice a day as long as she lived.

In the midst of the women's tears, the infant Mei Kwei was prepared for the adoption, in the very same clothes she had worn for the First Month, for Second Grandmother, with a frugal eye to future growth, had made the shirt and trousers several sizes too big.

Second Grandmother said, shaking her head, 'Such a beautiful child,' for the baby, even at that age, had the most winsome smile; the teardrop mole, of course, had not yet begun to show.

Ah Beng Koh's wife came on the appointed day with a gift of two bottles of whisky, a box of biscuits, a tin of coffee powder, four tins of condensed milk, a dozen oranges and a bale of fine cotton cloth, since Ah Oon Koh had proudly dismissed all offers of an *ang pow*. The gifts were put on the floor, a glittering array but redundant, really, for baby girls could be had for nothing.

Second Grandmother had said she would have no part in the business and was now sitting sullenly on her bed in her room, working on a patchwork blanket, while her ears stayed alert to pick out the sounds of that execrable transaction. Ah Oon Koh, too, stayed in his room for, from this point onwards, it was women's business and he wanted none of the fuss. He wanted, when he next stepped out of the room, to be able to look only upon a son, and the promise of more sons.

The little three-year-old, gazing wide-eyed at the richness of the gifts laid before his eyes, began to examine them one after the other with intense fascination. The bottles of whisky were put out of his reach but he was allowed to touch the rest, and he ended up by concentrating on the box of biscuits, trying to prise it open with his small fat hands while the adults watched smilingly and were glad of the diversion; neither the giving nor the receiving of a child could be without emotion.

'Be good,' said Ah Oon Soh to the infant sleeping peacefully in her arms, at the precise moment of handing over. 'Grow up good and obedient. Give no trouble to anyone. Show respect and gratitude at all times.' Tears might choke the parting words of mothers to daughters but they were still words of admonition, not endearment: Be this, don't do that.

The transfer from one pair of cradling arms to the other was made with elaborate care, so as not to wake the sleeping child. It could have been the child suddenly waking up and crying piteously, like a newborn kitten, or Ah Beng Soh's noticeably brisk air of new proprietorship as she took over the child and began rocking her and cooing to her, or Ah Oon Soh's overcharged heart, convulsing her body and communicating its pain. Big Older Brother looked up from the box of biscuits in which he had been foraging with both plump hands and was suddenly seized by a terror that made him abandon his spoils, get up from the floor and rush screaming to Ah Beng Soh. He tugged at her trousers, leaping into the air repeatedly to reach his crying little sister. Red-faced with vexation, he hit Ah Beng Soh's legs with both fists. His mother rushed to him to restrain him, but he broke free and again tried to reach his sister, jumping up and down with both arms outstretched.

He paused in his exertions to bawl lustily, his face contorted with the terror and rage of a child's soul. 'I want Little Sister! Don't take away my little sister!'

The astonished adults tried to placate and quieten him, but their efforts were beaten back by the fury that exploded in a violence of flailing arms, kicking legs and biting teeth. Ah Beng Soh's nervous promise of more biscuits, as well as a packet of sweets and a toy, was met by a roar that sent her to the other end of the room, the baby tightly clutched in her arms.

The boy continued to shout, the veins on his neck standing out in fearful knots. His yells mingled with the frightened wails of the baby, by now wide awake, to bring the father, then the grandmother hurrying out of their rooms in consternation. 'I want my little Sister!'

He was choking in the terror of his loss.

In the years that followed, the tale would frequently be told of how

Mei Kwei was saved by her Big Older Brother. Where the combined tears of her mother and grandmother would only have hardened her father's heart against her, the angry demands of her little three-year-old brother broke him, and in the end forced him into a public capitulation. With the still crying boy clinging to his leg, he rubbed the back of his head sheepishly, cleared his throat, raised his arm to scratch an armpit, looked from left to right to avoid the women's tight faces ranged before him and, finally, began to shuffle towards Ah Beng Soh to take back the child. It was a total acknowledgement of defeat, reached on account of the much-loved only son. The boy had now stopped crying. Still clinging to his father's leg, his face still red and wet, he glared angrily at the would-be abductress.

Ah Oon Koh apologised to Ah Beng Soh in a subdued tone and offered to return the gifts.

'No need, no need,' the magnanimous woman said, but the gifts were returned anyway, taken back that same day by the father in a large box on the back of his bicycle.

Second Grandmother said she would never forget the scene as long as she lived – the father holding in his arms his six-month-old daughter and looking at her for the first time, and the child, decked in her First Month's finery, quietly sucking her thumb and looking back at him, her large unblinking eyes made larger by a watchful timidity unusual in one so young. The gods had surely intervened, said Second Grandmother, to give Big Older Brother the chance to save one sister in order to wipe out the sin of causing the death of another.

For when he was about a year old, there had been a sister, only ten months older, who starved while he grew fat. She was given thin rice gruel, made from broken grains; he had good porridge made from whole grains. He drank milk, she sugar-water. The one egg in the house was kept for him, for mixing in his porridge. She cried for milk and tried to snatch a bottle that was being warmed on the stove, but her outstretched arm was beaten down. His limbs grew stout and sleek, hers were no more than sticks.

When she was born, her father had cried vehemently, 'Let her die!' and had indeed worked systematically towards that end by diverting rare food and milk to the son. She finally expired, aged two, her memory so thoroughly consigned to the mists of oblivion that only a year later, her parents had entirely forgotten how she looked, and shortly afterwards, even the name she had been given. Second Grandmother, who said that the child would never have died if she had been around then, told the story to Big Older Brother when he

17

was seven or eight, as a matter of serious responsibility. He had grown stout and strong at his sister's expense; therefore he was guilty of collusion in her death.

'Don't listen to your grandmother, she talks nonsense,' said Ah Oon Koh.

And indeed, Second Grandmother, in her oddities, stood apart from the gentle, proper old women in Luping. The old should earn the respect of the young; when the Lightning God promised to hurl his bolts in support of the old, he meant old women like Ah Poon Mm, who never told bad stories about her own family, or Chong Tiam Mm, who never quarrelled with anybody in the household. Protected by her grey hair, Second Grandmother was ill-served by her bad mouth. The other old women in Luping did not want to have anything to do with her.

'Who can blame them?' sneered Ah Oon Koh. The old must act like the old.

Big Older Brother began to have bad dreams. He saw himself wresting a large bottle of milk from his sister and, later, looking out of a window through pouring rain to see her dead on the cold wet ground, her thin legs sticking up like those of a dead insect. He ran out but found she had been washed away by the rain.

'Second Grandmother, I don't want to hear your stories,' he pleaded, pressing his ears tightly with his hands, but still the dream of the dead sister persisted.

'You saved Little Sister anyway,' said Second Grandmother.

In that terrible time before the final rupture, Mei Kwei, for solace, turned to the memories of those early years. Perhaps longing invested the memories with a false radiance, but she recollected, always with a warming glow in her heart, the protectiveness of strong arms around her little body, the sturdiness of shoulders to press her crying face upon, the generosity of backs turned into beasts of burden to carry her, screaming excitedly, across a whole length of floor. Indifferent to food, pretty clothes or playthings, she craved love's touch and responded with all the ardour of a sensitive, passionate nature to its slightest promise. Thus Big Older Brother, if he should suddenly be in the mood for carrying his little sister on his back or taking her by the hand to go and see Ah Lau Sim's ducklings, was met with a burst of joy. It was the joy, mixed with gratitude, of the rescued slave, for the tale of how he had saved her at the age of six months, running like a persistent thread in the fabric of their childhood, coloured her actions

18

with deep, reverential awe, and his with an unswerving sense of power and patronage.

'Don't make your little sister cry,' Ah Oon Soh would say, if he snatched a bun from her hand or pushed her off the stool.

'See how he loves his little sister,' she would say, her self-contradictoriness precisely reflecting the vagaries of his affection, as she watched him, half an hour later, take over the feeding, and spoon porridge carefully into Little Sister's mouth, or cover her small face with a splatter of wet, rambunctious kisses. The wild alternations of mood never detracted from the awe and affectionate regard; the child would do anything for Big Older Brother.

His touch, if it was not brutal from the excessive energy that was rapidly coarsening his face and body, could be tender, almost like a woman's. When she fell ill with fever, he insisted on letting her have his bolster, which he brought to her as she lay on a mattress on the floor and around which he arranged her limbs with elaborate care. His generous energy by no means at an end: he looked around for a blanket, found his father's and dragged it across the floor to drape it solicitously over the hot, trembling body. Their mother and grandmother watched, nudging each other.

'Don't disturb me,' Ah Oon Soh would say, as the little girl came running to her with upstretched arms. But she would still pick up the child, settle her on her hip and continue her work of frying vegetables or boiling soup at the large cement stove.

The child loved the mother's smell, even the sour smell of her neck, as she stood perspiring at the stove or squatted at the washing tub.

'Go away, you are a nuisance!' she would say sharply, for Mei Kwei's continual burrowing into her arms in the presence of burning firewood or sizzling oil or soapy water was annoying.

The mother's words could be harsh, but caught in a calmer mood, as when she sat chatting with the swill woman, she would allow the child to sit on her lap, until the discomfort of sweat collecting under her breasts or of a numbed knee forced her to complain, adjust her position and cast off the child's weight.

Ah Oon Soh was not one of those amiably relaxed mothers who would, while chatting with friends or neighbours, stretch out arms to carry other people's children. But she did rock in her arms a crying child, the puny grandson of the swill woman; indeed, she was credited with saving the little boy's life. For one day when the baby was very ill, his mother was told by a temple medium that he could

19

only be cured by being adopted. The swill woman immediately begged Ah Oon Soh to do them the favour.

Laughing awkwardly, Ah Oon Soh had said, 'You should choose someone more blessed with fortune! As everyone can see, I'm a poor woman!' But at last she had consented.

It was a simple enough ceremony: Ah Oon Soh went to the temple with the baby and, there, in front of divine witnesses, tied a piece of red thread round the baby's wrist and her own. Gods could be very accommodating with mortals, accepting tokens in place of the real thing. The baby, taken home by his mother, recovered almost immediately.

He was soon brought on a visit by his grateful grandmother. Ah Oon Soh carried the child gently in her arms, commenting on his tiny, feeble limbs. Mei Kwei who was about five then watched sullenly.

'Oh, my, oh, my, what jealousy!' teased the swill woman.

'Come and look at Tee Tee,' Ah Oon Soh said but Mei Kwei turned away.

A while later, seeing the baby asleep on her mother's bed, she stole into the room and pinched his arm. The baby stirred and whimpered. She caught hold of a toe and tweaked it as hard as she could. The baby cried loudly. She got up on to the bed and hit his stomach. The baby began to scream. She ran out of the room.

And the next time her mother said to her, 'Go away!' when she tried to push herself into her arms or between her knees, she remembered with satisfaction the secret assault on the hateful Tee Tee.

Second Grandmother never said, 'Go away!' or called her a nuisance. In her declining years, the old woman grew irritable and quarrelsome and kept to herself, but always made room on her narrow plank bed for the little granddaughter coming in for the comfort of word and touch.

'Come, lie down beside your grandmother.' She would stretch out her arm for the child to lay her head on, and shift herself around to allow the small body to curl snugly against her.

Second Grandmother had a habit of reciting the rhymes of her childhood; her voice would rise and fall in plaintive singsong and soothe the child into sleep or, richly cadenced, it would discharge a glittering offering of tales. Years later, long after the old woman's voice had been stilled in the grave, Mei Kwei would hear snatches of the rhymes and tales which she would repeat slowly to herself, plucking laughter and tears from forgotten whimsical worlds in which turtles saved lost children, roosters lost then regained their voices upon hearing the clack-clack of temple bamboo sticks, rice-stalks grew tall and heavy with grain to reward filial children, goddesses' teardrops turned into pearldrops that rained from the sky.

It was Second Grandmother who plaited her long hair into two neat pigtails down her back, combed the glossy fringe on her forehead and rubbed rice powder on her face after every bath to make her skin soft and smooth.

'He said I had the softest, smoothest skin of them all!' said Second Grandmother, thinking again of the enamoured old man on a silken bed. She was never without a ready stock of the precious rice powder, in tiny pellets, like a doll's teardrops, scented with shreds of dried pandan leaf, which she kept in a large glass jar.

The child did not mind the roughness of Second Grandmother's palms working the wet white paste on her face in slow circular movements, nor the intrusiveness of the ear-digging pin, which Second Grandmother kept conveniently stuck in her bun, to keep ears free of dirt, for, she insisted, beauty and cleanliness went hand in hand.

One day, the child saw the small feet unshod for the first time and cried at their ugliness. Second Grandmother was sitting on a low stool and cleaning them with a piece of cloth dipped in hot water. The stale smell of the removed shoes and the sight of mutilated toes and nails grown inwards into soft flesh hit her and raised a cry of alarm. She ran out of the room.

The generous, encircling arms, the voice upon which flowed a rich stream of tales and dreams, drew her, but the aging, crippled body with malformed hoofs or pig's trotters for feet, as well as the slack, withered breasts – for Second Grandmother liked to take off her blouse and fan herself to sleep on hot nights – beat her back into a silent, cowering anger.

That night she had a horrible dream. She was at the market with her mother and turned to see the butcher bringing his enormous chopping knife down upon a pair of pig's trotters; only it was Second Grandmother, not a pig, lying upon the hard cold block of cement. The trotters flew off the chopping block and she woke up with a scream.

A stranger offered her his protection. It happened when Big Older Brother, who must have been about seven at the time, took her to a rubber plantation to look for rubber seeds lying among dead leaves and took fright when she fell into a ditch overgrown with thorny bushes. Blubbering, he ran home. She remembered screaming and then experiencing a sensation of immense relief as a pair of strong arms hoisted her up and pulled thorns off her blouse and trousers. A dirty sarong cloth tied tightly around his head, a pair of bloodshot eyes, a mouth vivid red with *ceray* juice, coal-black skin, a voice in a strange language – all these she remembered of the rescuer, the very ogre that mothers threatened upon crying children to stop them crying. 'Hush, the *keleng* man is coming!' The *keleng* man, dark as midnight, frightened little children into silence more effectively than the Malay policeman in uniform, with ready handcuffs. She recalled a total absence of fear as the man made reassuring sounds in a strange language and carried her home. Safe in his arms, she looked down unafraid upon the perils of the world below – a barking dog, a rickety wooden bridge across a stream, hostile, stone-throwing children – and was finally met by her mother and brother, running in consternation out of the house.

The ultimate joy, to throw into shadow the offerings of brother, mother, grandmother, stranger, could only come from the store of the father's heart. But it remained resolutely shut against her, as if that one act of taking her back from the arms of the adopting parent had redressed all the indifference of before and ever afterwards.

'Smelly cunt,' he had muttered once more, when he attributed yet another business reverse to her. Despising women, yet like them in seeking the advice of fortune-tellers, he kept in mind the prediction that no daughter would ever be born who would bring him happiness and prosperity. He had stolen glances at his daughter as she played or prattled, the daughter whom everybody praised for beauty and quick intelligence, and still he could not love her. He was not unkind, merely ignoring her or choosing to notice her only to the extent that she was the other half in a game being played by the beloved son, or the beneficiary of a demand made on her behalf, 'Papa, give Little Sister, too,' when he would feel obliged to search his pocket for another small coin to put in her hand, helpfully dragged out and held out towards him by the imperious boy.

Learning from an early age that females were a dependent class, living on surplus, she first grew timid, then canny, watching out for those occasions when she could hitch a ride on her brother's back to gain entry into the coveted field of her father's attention. Thus when her father brought back on the back of his bicycle a whole box of curly wood shavings and small plank remnants from a carpenter friend and emptied it on the floor for his son to play with, she watched for a while, standing in a corner, then struck. Big Older Brother looked up from play to see her, with shrinking timidity, holding out an empty biscuit tin and some nails. He immediately saw their usefulness for his new plaything and got up to grab them. Receiving the gifts, he had the decency to allow the giver a share of his own. She squatted down happily and began to play, mimicking the brother relentlessly, to merit at least one glance, one smile from their father.

'Papa, see, this is a house!'

'Papa, look at my hair!' Precisely following her brother's example, she pressed a fistful of wood curls on her head and turned to face him.

'Papa, knock this nail for me!' But the father would do it only for the son, not the daughter.

Big Older Brother's energies took a savage turn on the first day of the New Year. His eyes watched closely the dispensing of the gift *ang pow* by the adults, watched a visiting neighbour push a small red packet containing a large coin into his sister's blouse pocket. As soon as the visitor left, he made a rough descent on the pocket. The child resisted. He pushed her down and succeeded in extricating the packet from the depths of her pocket. He tore off the red paper and flung it on the floor, secured the coin and ran off with it. She began to whimper. The pain, not only of the loss of the money but of a recent series of assaults on her little box of prized possessions – rubber seeds, rubber bands, calendar cut-outs, a plastic hair-clip, a string of beads, a pencil – made her crouch in a corner, her face pressed to the wall in a discharge of bitterest sorrow.

'Here, take this.'

It was rare that he spoke to her at all; it was even rarer that he should be offering her a gift. She turned slowly to face her father, who was sitting in a chair a short distance away and holding out a coin in his hand, of exactly the same value as the stolen one. The impossibility of such a situation made her stare at him with wide-eyed wariness. Her father repeated, 'Here, take this,' and his voice was almost kind.

She stood up and walked timidly towards him, towards the outstretched hand. She took the coin slowly, her large eyes fixed fearfully on her father's as she stood before him. 'Come.' The softening proceeded with miraculous speed for he was now stretching out his arms to receive her.

Perhaps he had witnessed the son's plunder and felt sorry for her. Perhaps he understood that the goodwill of the festive New Year season should be extended to all, even female children. Or some passing benign god had whispered, in the manner of a kind-hearted mortal, 'Forgive and forget. Your seed, after all.'

The child approached him hesitatingly, a tense finger lodged deep in her mouth. He leaned forward encouragingly. She moved forward by a few steps. He leaned forward further, pulled her towards him, lifted her upon his knees and enclosed her in his strong arms. A tremor ran through her body.

Then suddenly the child was galvanised into frenzied response. Curling tightly into herself, she snuggled close up to him to ensure a full encirclement by those arms. She made small shifts and adjustments of her body, trembling with joy, for deeper burrowing into the offered warmth. Ever sensitive to the smells of close contact, she absorbed, with mounting excitement, the coffee smell of his breath, the dry musk of his large-veined neck palpitating against her face, the faint sourish staleness of his armpits. Surrendering herself fully to the wondrous sensation of being loved at last, she sank quietly into the embrace with something of a sob. She stayed still for a long time, fearing that the slightest movement or noise would disrupt the fragile magic.

It was a long time, for her father did not say, 'Enough, enough,' and put her back on the floor. He continued to hold her close to himself. Perhaps the benign god's gentle whisper was even now expanding into command: Love her. Your seed, after all.

Father, love me even if I am only a girl. She could not have enough of the warmth and snuggled even closer.

He responded to the ardour, stroking her back and hair. His heart was softening towards her, its hard edges fast melting.

I will love you. Even if.

Then, as he looked at her upturned face, the softening stopped abruptly. His expression and voice changed, and his arms stiffened in cold withdrawal. 'What's this?' he said, looking at the teardrop mole, close to her right eye. He was seeing it for the first time.

Once a god, jealous of a goddess who was so happy she never shed a tear in her life, picked up a brush, dipped it in ink and painted a tear in the corner of each eye.

'Now you will cry,' he said, and true enough, there came storms, earthquakes, floods, famine and unspeakable ruin, to make the goddess go into perpetual mourning. Women with teardrop moles condemned their fathers and husbands to ruin. Women's moles should be near mouths as promise of food, never near eyes signifying sorrow, if they wanted to be of any service to men.

He removed her from her position on his knee, placed her on the floor, and said brusquely, 'Now go to your mother.'

'What's the use?' He snorted, thinking of the many comments on his daughter's beauty, and added, 'No wonder,' recollecting the many reverses of fortune since her birth. She was female and teardrop-moled, doubly cursed.

'Father –'

'Enough,' and he turned away from the malignant feature.

She hated her mole for taking her joy. She cried herself to sleep for several nights.

Ah Oon Koh was reading his newspaper when he became aware of a slight rustling movement and looked up to see his daughter standing in front of him, her face pale with expectation and daring purpose. He looked coldly at her. 'What is it?'

She would say nothing but continued to stand before him, trembling with some mighty secret purpose.

'What is it?' he said again, impatiently, recollecting his earlier revulsion of the blemish on her face that was worse than a blemish for it caused suffering to others. He gave a little start. The mole was no longer there. It was covered over with some sticky substance, perhaps paste made from boiled rice.

The child's eyes said, 'It is gone. Will you love me again?'

'Go away,' said her father. 'Don't disturb me.' He added, in extreme exasperation, 'And don't play tricks like that on me again.'

Big Older Brother, who had stayed to watch, shouted and hooted in derision, jumping up and down and pointing to the covered mole in an exaggeration of merriment.

'Quiet,' said his father sternly. Then he folded his newspaper and went back into his room.

'Devil mole! Devil mole!' chanted Big Older Brother. And now the child was in a seething rage, unseen in one so young. She refused to eat and stayed in a corner, curled up like a solitary insect, her little face white with the intensity of an unutterable anger and grief.

'Come, let me wash it away,' said Second Grandmother, 'or you will have ants getting into your eyes.' But the child angrily shook off her hand, and refused to relinquish her self-confinement in the dark corner, solace for the greater darkness within.

'Here,' said Big Older Brother awkwardly, offering half a bun, but she shook off his hand too.

Their father, drinking a cup of coffee in his room some days later, once again looked up sharply to see his daughter standing in front of him. He looked at her surlily. Then he started up in shock, and said, 'What?' He stared at her. 'You are mad.' He made a lunge at her but hesitatingly, provoked by her daring show of defiance but unsure about what to do, for he was suddenly afraid of the strange burning glow in her eyes. They seemed to be saying, with terrifying energy, 'Look at me! Look at me!' And he looked, with astonishment, upon the multitude of teardrop moles around her eyes, in a mad proliferation of misfortune's omens. She looked like some grotesque character from a stage opera, a monster, a demoness.

It was unclear what substance the child had used this time, probably rice paste again, painted with black ink or blackened with charcoal. But it was no child's play; the challenge to an adult, so unnatural in a little girl, pointing possibly to an accession of power granted to the possessed and the insane, unnerved him. He continued to stare at her, as she stood resolutely before him, her eyes preternaturally shining, unflinchingly fixed on his.

Father, love me even if I have a teardrop mole.

That might have been her plea before the overpowering anger; now she was driven only by the raging torment in her soul, and so she forced her father, once more, to look upon not one, but a myriad mutinous moles.

'Siau! Siau!' spluttered the father, before getting up and leaving the room. He could not bear to look at the child. She was mad and the madness would always shrivel up any effort to love her.

There would be one more searing moment of confrontation between father and daughter, many years later, when Mei Kwei would say, again with a look not words, 'Now, Father, what does it feel like to be saved by a smelly cunt?' and break down, sobbing, under the terrible weight of her own malice. She would recover enough to say, in loud words so that he could hear, 'Father, forgive me.'

Ah Ooh Soh, coming out from the kitchen to see what was going on, saw the child, shrieked, 'Siau!' and dragged her to a bucket of water under a tap to have the monstrous moles washed out. She rubbed the crying face vigorously with a towel and said, in great vexation, 'Why must you behave like that? Now go and ask your

26

father's forgiveness.' There would have to be a visit to the temple, to cleanse the child of this strange behaviour.

The child could not stop crying and went to crouch in her favourite dark corner where she remained motionless for a long time. Big Older Brother squatted down beside her to peer into her face and make some sounds of solicitous enquiry, but she turned away from him.

CHAPTER THREE

Beauty was dangerous – the full beauty of ripe breasts, rounded hips and ready wombs that would have the marauding Japanese soldiers salivating, not that of the flat, uncurved, odourless eight-year-old. They were all over Malaya with their lethal bayonets and, it was said, unbuttoned trousers, ready penises hanging out.

Mei Kwei, her long pigtails untidy from play, watched with intense interest as her mother and a female relative locked themselves in a room and proceeded to erase their dangerous beauty. The women were frenziedly cutting out long strips of rough khaki to tie tightly around themselves. Mei Kwei looked wide-eyed at the two women's breasts, her mother's small and firm, the relative's large and swinging, above the string-belts of their cotton trousers. They had tried to shoo her out of the room and had simply ignored her when she came out of her hiding place to continue watching them. They ignored, too, the scuffling sounds outside the locked door as Big Older Brother searched for peeping slits and cracks.

'Curse them,' muttered Ah Oon Soh, who knew of pretty women taken away in open trucks to the enemies' camp. One who put up a fierce resistance was bayoneted and raped anyway.

'Here, take these,' she said to the relative, for the woman's large breasts, big as melons, required several strips of the cloth. Tightly bound, they put on men's rough shirts and looked into the mirror to examine the effect, running their palms down their hard, flat fronts.

Then they brought out scissors for the next stage of the operation. Mei Kwei gasped to see her mother's rich hair falling to the floor in pelts. The other's was dry, thin and curly and floated about the room like feathers. Neither woman bothered to look in the mirror and, at the end of the deed, merely ran fingers over heads rougher even than street urchins'. If beauty were a risk, it had to be destroyed. Both women were now part of a band of frightened, flattened, ragged females in Luping, who stayed within the shadowed confines of their houses or, if they dared to venture out into the scrutiny of the soldiers in the streets, market-place and shops, did so as ugly, unpalatable females.

The only young woman who dared to roam the streets freely on her own was the mad vagrant from the Kek Lok temple who was so thoroughly mad and smelly, with her unwashed body and lice-infested hair, that even the most rabid soldiers turned away in disgust. The ravishing beauty of one Ong Gim Choo, eighteen years old, served her family better. She had her hair curled and decorated with fragrant flowers and her cheeks rouged, and became the favourite mistress of a senior Japanese officer, thus gaining for her family access to rice, sugar, milk and even chocolate while others ate tapioca and fed their babies diluted sugar-water. When the British finally drove away the Japanese, the supply of good things continued, for the beautiful girl simply switched clientele.

One day Big Older Brother came home in great excitement with a small cloth bundle, which he untied on a table before the wondering eyes of his family to reveal a pile of rice grains, whole, white, clean. His mother, who guarded their small store of broken rice in a brown stone jar under the bed, gasped. His father let out a shout of fear. 'Take it back!' For the punishment for even small thefts was severe: Big Older Brother could have had his hand lopped off. Ah Oon Koh had seen a young man strung up naked by his ankles on a lamp-post in the market-place, probably for something less than stealing food.

It turned out that the precious rice was a gift, not loot. Big Older Brother had befriended a Japanese soldier whose work was guarding a garrison store, a wooden building comprising three rooms. It was Satosan who had initiated the friendship. Noticing the boy hang around the compound on a number of occasions, he had ignored him. Then one day, he smelt, then saw a dead cat on the ground under a tree, covered with buzzing insects. He grimaced, and the boy, who was watching from the periphery of a barbed-wire fence, ran up at once and gestured an offer to remove the offensive object. Satosan gave him a large rag, which he immediately threw over the mouldering heap. Watched by Satosan, who was smoking continuously, the boy soon completed the entire operation of scooping up the remains and taking them to throw into a ditch some distance away. He returned, smiling, making a great show of smelling his hands, wrinkling his nose and emitting little choking noises to indicate extreme revulsion. Satosan laughed and made him wash his hands with soap. The boy, sniffing his now clean, sweet-smelling hands, went through an elaborate demonstration of appreciation and delight. Satosan wrapped the soap in a piece of paper and put it in the pocket of the boy's ragged shorts, indicating that he could have it.

The soap was the beginning of a flow of small gifts exuberantly brought home and displayed – pencil stubs, pieces of paper, half a bottle of ink, a packet of biscuits, a box of matches, a tin mug and, best of all, the rice. Ah Oon Soh picked up the precious grains – not a single one broken! – and let them trickle down through her fingers in a rare display of wonder and joy.

It was rice of the best quality: she could tell by the shape, colour, fragrance. The Feast of the Hungry Ghosts was coming. Uncelebrated during these times of scarcity and fear when no one dared venture out to the cemetery to clear ancestors' graves of weeds and place food on them, it might yet be observed this year by an offering of steamed rice on the ancestral altar at home. She might even throw in some fried vegetables as well, and a bit of pork. The revered dead would thus not be forgotten, even in wartime, and after they had had their fill, the food would be brought down from the altar, heated up and served to her family. Hating the Japanese soldiers, Ah Oon Soh was grateful to one for providing food for both living and dead.

It wasn't long before Big Older Brother brought his little sister to see the Japanese soldier. Mei Kwei clutched his hand excitedly, but became shy as soon as they were within sight of Satosan. She refused to go in, but stood rigidly at the doorway, twisting a corner of her blouse and looking intently at Satosan who was cleaning some knives. He looked up at her and smiled. Big Older Brother tried to pull her into the room, but she resisted, continuing to stare at Satosan, a forefinger in her mouth, pressing down her lower lip.

The man got up, walked to a table, opened a drawer and took something out. It was the most marvellous thing the children had ever seen: perfectly round hard candy wrapped in silver and gold paper. Satosan made an offering of three, stretching out a long arm to the little girl. There they lay, on his open palm, like three jewels. 'Go on!' he said. She moved forward and shyly took one. The brother shifted about in an agony of longing and jealousy, while Satosan made the little girl stand before him and looked at her closely, talking to her in Japanese. Perhaps there was a child at home, of the same soft-haired, rose-lipped luminosity. Big Older Brother fidgeted, coughed and was given the remaining two sweets.

Back home, Mei Kwei carefully smoothed out the beautiful shining wrapper, gazing at its little glints of silver and gold for a long time before putting it among her treasures in the tin box.

Convinced that the presence of his sister elicited a higher order of gifts – he had never been given anything beyond mundane pencil stubs and matches – Big Older Brother soon got ready to take her to Satosan again. Little Sister, glittering cornucopia, had gained immeasurably in his estimation.

They were gone a short distance from the house when Ah Oon Soh, still dressed in ugly man's clothes and sporting the ugly man's haircut, ran after them, calling them back. She grabbed her daughter by the hand and pulled her back into the house.

'Wait,' she said urgently to her son. 'Wait. It will take only a little while.'

Picking up a pair of scissors, Ah Oon Soh got ready to denude the child of her beauty. For she had heard that even small girls whose beauty was yet in bud were desired by the conquering masters if they saw promise of later flowering. Her daughter, who was the prettiest little girl in Luping, would be the very target of desire in waiting. Fearful of letting her out of the house, yet glad of the flow of gifts from the enemy that would come through her, she settled on the compromise of taking away some of the beauty.

Mei Kwei remembered, years later, her screams of protest as her mother came at her with the scissors and snipped off her hair, still in its long plaits. The braids fell and lay on the ground, one forming a circle, the other a straight line, eerily distanced from each other. Shorn, the little girl was still beautiful. Her mother pressed down the top of her head with one hand to steady it and with the other, nicked off parts of her eyebrows, beautiful ebony wings even at that early age. Then she went for the rosy lips, rubbing some charcoal powder on and around them, with the same energy that years later, when the girl had reached marriageable age and was about to be inspected, she descended on her with comb, powder, a new, brightly coloured *samfoo* and a pair of gold ear-rings.

Mei Kwei remembered Second Grandmother shouting, '*Siau!*' at her mother and comforting her, remembered, too, the bitter thought, articulated in its full bitterness only in the later years: her beauty was not hers but for plundering by others. She cried all the way to Satosan's, scolded by Big Older Brother.

'*Woa! Woa!*' exclaimed the soldier in consternation, as he looked upon the despoiled child, still crying from the despoliation. He turned to Big Older Brother in puzzled enquiry, pointing to the child and firing off agitated questions in rapid succession. Big Older Brother shrugged, twisted his body and waved his hands about, disclaiming all responsibility.

'*Woa! Woa!*' said the man, in frowning sympathy, as the little girl's tears burst afresh. He reached out for her hand and drew her to himself. He settled her on his knee, and began to rock her gently. He stared at her shorn head and ran a forefinger over the shorn eyebrows, shaking his head and clucking his tongue. She stared back at him, her eyes brimming with tears, her lips trembling.

'*Woa!*' he cried, meaning, 'Never mind, don't cry.' He continued rocking her and when she stopped crying he jerked up a con-gratulatory thumb for encouragement. He took her to a tap to wash the dirt from her face, wiped it carefully with a towel, then produced a comb to neaten her jagged crop. Surveying her with smiling enthusiasm, he once again said, '*Woa! Woa!*', the exclamation obviously covering the entire gamut of human emotions.

In later years, when she recollected her childhood and tried to soften memory's hard edges, she placed Satosan beside the Indian labourer who had pulled her out of the ditch and carried her home, marvelling at the capacity of strangers to stop tears.

CHAPTER FOUR

The end of the Occupation left some families with bags of worthless Japanese currency notes. Ah Cheng Sim, who was in the middle of a business transaction from which she hoped to reap rich profits, found herself without the gold chain and bangles she had so foolishly pawned to raise the money for the business. She sat among her bundles of money and beat her chest repeatedly with her fists, moaning.

'Serves her right,' said the less charitable of Luping's inhabitants. 'Her husband was too friendly with the Japanese. Let the British throw him into jail.'

'Serves her right. Let her use those Japanese notes as toilet paper.' The departing enemy left behind dereliction, also their revered emperor-god's face for the wiping of backsides.

Ah Oon Koh gave up all pretence of doing business after the occupation, and began the steady slide into opium, that would confine him to his room in languorous ease for the next twenty years, allowing only occasional reconnections with the outside world.

Ah Oon Soh raked up whatever pitiful resources she had to invest in a dozen chickens. She ordered her children every day to go out and look for a plant, growing plentifully in drains and ditches, that she could chop up and mix into chicken feed. Or she would send off the dozen fowls in search of their own food in surrounding dumps, sternly enjoining her children to keep an eye on the precious investment and round them up to take home for safe-keeping in the evenings. There was a marauding rag-and-bone man who picked fruit from Ah Wan Soh's guava trees and stole a tray of beans that Ah Too Sim had left to dry in the sun outside her house. He once stole a duck and stuffed it in a sack, but its quacking gave him away.

'Make sure you don't break any,' said Ah Oon Soh, hanging on the arm of her son a small basket of freshly laid eggs. 'Say they're very fresh. But greet politely first.' Her daughter was to go along too, with a handkerchief for knotting the money in and putting safely in her blouse pocket.

Soon there were duck eggs too, for Ah Oon Soh discovered that ducks were cheaper to raise. Like her neighbour Ah Lau Sim, who every morning went out with a *changkul* to dig up worms for her ducklings, Ah Oon Soh needed to invest only in that implement and to make sure that it had a long sturdy handle and a sharp blade for easy digging in the wet black earth found in abundance in the neighbourhood. Big Older Brother and Mei Kwei had the additional job of feeding their mother's brood of ducklings: the boy would do the digging and the girl would assist in breaking up the clumps of moist earth with small, sharp sticks, to release the wriggling worms, sometimes too deeply embedded in the soil for the baby beaks to tug out.

'I hate it,' said Big Older Brother, and it was not pure accident that the blade of his *changkul* descended on a little yellow duckling and split it in two. Mei Kwei looked at her brother in horror. He watched dispassionately as the other ducklings swarmed noisily over the exposed entrails and tugged at them.

The Yellow House was the most profitable to visit with the chicken and duck eggs, since Mr Tong, the owner, was one of the most prosperous men in Luping. It was rumoured that he had secretly befriended the Japanese during the war, made a lot of money through their patronage, then turned his back on them as soon as he smelt their impending defeat. He then befriended the British, showering upon them gifts of brandy and local girls. Nobody knew what he did for a living; the rumours ran the whole range of criminal activities – illicit *samsu*, prostitution, gambling, protection rackets.

Big Older Brother, with Mei Kwei beside him and the hateful basket of eggs on his arm, stared at a miniature spirit house, painted yellow, which stood in front of the main house and gave it its name. He said, 'We should have one like that, in front of our house,' for it was also rumoured that all Mr Tong's luck flowed from the spirit house in which resided a potent deity to whom he allegedly fed human blood. The deity was all the more potent for being an imported one, having been brought south from Thailand.

The extreme frugality practised at home irked Big Older Brother. Residual rice at the bottom of the cooking pot was soaked in water overnight and removed for making into porridge. Toilet paper was squares of old newspapers. Wooden clogs were worn down to flatness and even then were not thrown away, the remaining wood being used to feed the stove. Second Grandmother trimmed the edges of her palm-leaf fan with cloth to prevent them fraying.

'When I grow up and become rich,' said Big Older Brother to his mother, 'I will buy you ten pairs of clogs for just throwing into the fire,' and to his grandmother, 'I will buy you ten ear-diggers, all made of gold.'

Mrs Tong, one of the few women in Luping to have permed hair and wear lipstick, would come out when the children called, open the gate, select the eggs and then return to the house, carefully closing the door behind her. Today, only the son, a boy of about the same age as Big Older Brother, appeared to be at home. He heard their call, 'Eggs! Eggs!', came out carrying a large toy train in his hand, ignored them, sat down on a patch of grass in front of the house and began to play with the train. It was the handsomest contraption that Big Older Brother had ever seen, with its gleaming black body, tall black funnel, rows of windows, rows of wheels. He drew breath, his jaw dropping in his astonishment. The Tong boy continued playing with self-

33

conscious casualness. He was thin and slight, with a face like a girl's, in its pale smoothness and delicacy of features. He made little chugging noises, casting sidelong glances at the coarse boy beyond the gate, looking in with obvious admiration and envy.

Big Older Brother gulped. The yearning was almost painful. His sister looked up at him and said, 'Never mind, Big Older Brother. When I grow up and have a lot of money, I will buy you one like that.' Ordinarily, he would have turned to her with a derisive laugh and scoffed, 'Who says you will ever be rich?' and been provoked to point to the unlucky teardrop mole, but today was no ordinary day. The magnificent toy drew him, as if he was in a trance; he opened the gate and walked in. His sister followed, matching slow steps to his and looking warily into his face. The Tong boy ignored them and continued playing.

They stood a short distance away, and still he ignored them. Responding to the admiration, he moved the train about more energetically, made louder chugging noises, continued to cast the secretive sidelong glances.

Then Big Older Brother struck. He rushed forward and laid his hands on the train. The Tong boy gave a start. He kept his hands on the toy. But it was weak resistance, which broke down under his abject terror when he saw Big Older Brother's fist about to descend on him.

'Don't!' pleaded the Tong boy, turning away and covering his pale face with both hands.

Panting heavily, Big Older Brother pushed him to the ground, grabbed the toy, shouted to his sister, 'Run!' and himself made a dash for the gate. He heard, to his great satisfaction, a whimpering behind him and turned back to see, to his greater satisfaction, the despised rich boy rubbing away tears. He ran up against a huge body, all restraining arms and legs, and looked up to see the large, fearsome, pock-marked face of Mr Tong himself, peering into his own.

'Not so fast, boy,' said the formidable personage, and led him by the back of his neck, the train still clutched in his arms, to where the Tong boy was still cowering on the ground. From a distance, Mei Kwei watched, trembling, poised for a second flight.

'Idiot. Fool. Coward.' The abuse, strangely, was directed at the son, not at his aggressor. Mr Tong jerked the boy up from the ground and continued abusing him for weakness. No father and son could have been less alike: the man large, dark, ferocious, the boy pale, delicate, timid. Still keeping a firm grip on the back of Big Older

Brother's neck, Mr Tong began to demonstrate, for the benefit of his son, a range of defensive and offensive movements, jabbing, punching, kicking the air, all the time roaring his displeasure, until the veins stood out dangerously on his large, florid face. The easy surrender had disgusted him profoundly and he meant to discharge fully the load of the paternal contempt on his son's bent head.

The pale boy wept silently, then suddenly looked up to stare at his father with something like hatred.

'Don't look at me like that!' thundered the father. 'I have beancurd for a son.' The resentment burned brighter in the boy's eyes.

Turning to Big Older Brother, Mr Tong said, 'You go off home with that damn train. His mother bought it for him.' There was almost wistfulness in the coarse eyes that took in Big Older Brother's fighting limbs, his brown sunburnt chest, the feral cunning of his eyes.

'Wait,' he continued, heaving and panting in the heat of an anger by no means fully discharged. He went into the house and reappeared with a large cardboard box, flinging its contents at Big Older Brother's feet. Out spilled more prized possessions – a red car, wooden soldiers, a coconut-shell money box, a penknife, wooden toy animals, colouring pencils.

'All yours,' said Mr Tong to Big Older Brother. 'You deserve them. Not the Beancurd.'

Watching, Mei Kwei gave a little scream for the Tong boy had flung himself upon Big Older Brother and was hitting him wildly with both fists in an attempt to disengage him from the precious possessions. He kicked and bit, galvanised into a furious display of energy by the threat of loss.

Stunned, Big Older Brother fell backwards onto the ground and felt a foot crashing upon his face. He recovered quickly, got up and went straight at his adversary. The boys locked each other's arms and legs in fearful combat, rolling upon the ground.

'Stop! Stop!' Mrs Tong had come out to investigate the commotion and was now running frenziedly about, wringing her hands.

'Get him! That's right! Over there!' Mr Tong's encouragement was now all for his son. Astonishment, then an upsurge of pride such as he thought he would never experience, lent force to his fists pummelling the air, strength to his voice ringing through the neighbourhood. Mrs Tong ran to separate the boys, but he pushed her away.

'Are you mad?' she screamed.

'Go away,' he roared, but intervened at the appropriate moment to prevent his son from being beaten to a pulp by the egg woman's son. The Tong boy stood up, panting, his shirt torn, his nose bleeding, his lower lip a raw red mass. The real metamorphosis was in the malevolence of his eyes as they fixed themselves on his foe, and might well have fixed themselves on his parent: 'Be careful,' they said. 'Don't push me too far.' His father looked proudly at him, then waved a hand impatiently to dismiss Big Older Brother.

'Run!' cried Big Older Brother to Mei Kwei. But flight was unnecessary. The whole family had already gone back into the house. Only the deity in the yellow spirit house was left to preside over a heap of toys strewn on the ground. Big Older Brother made a dash back for the train, then half-way home, flung it angrily into a ditch.

That evening, Mei Kwei went into Second Grandmother's room and laid her head tearfully on the old woman's knee.

'What's the matter, Little Granddaughter?'

She liked her grandmother to stroke her hair and cheek, but not to move a thumb along the eyebrows, now almost fully restored to former beauty.

'Here, let me clean it. I can see dirt. Dirt and beauty don't go together!' chanted the old woman, raising a hand to her bun to feel for the ear-digging pin stuck there. She found it and, very carefully, probed the inside of the girl's ear turned towards her on her lap. 'One day, I'll dig the dirt out with a gold pin,' she chuckled, 'if your brother keeps his promise.'

'See!' she exclaimed, showing the girl a long twist of wax in the tiny bowl at the end of the pin. 'Why, Little Granddaughter, you're crying! What is it? Tell Grandmother.'

But it was a dreariness of spirit that even in the later years she could not describe clearly. It had to do with the raucousness of her brother's world into which he was always drawing her. She longed for a safer environment in which she had seen little girls like herself reading from books, writing on slates, drawing squiggly lines on the chalkboard, singing songs with their teacher in the foreign language.

Mesmerised by her brother's power, she allowed him to lead her into his rough world which was still infinitely better than the cold, silent one of her father's contempt. In any case, he cared for her. It was still her mother's habit, during a special meal, such as on festive occasions, to dig into vegetables with her chopsticks and search for the rare bit of pork or chicken to put on the brother's plate, and it was still his practice to pass, surreptitiously, a tiny portion of the meat on

36

to hers. Once a prawn, fried to a golden crispness, slipped his fingers and dropped to the floor. When his mother was not looking, he bent down quickly, picked it up, cleaned it against his side and dropped it on her plate.

In the years when the last fragile bonds were about to snap, she recalled the little melodrama of food-passing at table and found it in her heart, once more, to forgive him.

CHAPTER FIVE

Well before the last Japanese left Malaya's shores for ever (not quite the last, for a Japanese soldier was, most amazingly, found in the jungles thirty years later, where he had been in hiding, subsisting on tapioca and river fish, and waiting for the emperor's order to surrender), the women in Luping took off the tight chest bands and breathed freely once more. Some breasts were permanently damaged, some none the worse.

'Don't throw away those bands, we will need them again,' said one of the women cynically, meaning that Japanese oppressors would be replaced by British, now entrenched in the country. Yellow dwarfs with their trousers open were less dangerous than white giants with crowbars for penises. One devil for another; what was the difference? Soon little *kopi susu* would be running all over the country, in various shades of milky coffeeness, testimony to colonialism's rampancy in hot climates.

'No, no,' said another of the women. 'Let's be fair. We have no fear. The British are the people's protectors, not their oppressors.'

But in the end, all the women agreed that, for the time being, the chest bands could be removed and lives rebuilt. For one thing, the trucks did not come for their men any more. Let the British take away the tin and gold from the mines, and the rubber and palm oil from the plantations: at least these red-haired devils did not rape or kill. They might even be depended on to put back some of the plundered wealth into roads, hospitals, schools.

Ah Oon Koh, who had not yet slid into opium and still had the time and inclination to concern himself with improving the family's fortunes, was influenced by a conviction that had suddenly shaken some Luping inhabitants into decisive action. 'Send our children to the English schools,' they declared. 'That's where the future is.'

They should have thought of this before. Boys who went to the Chinese, Malay or Tamil schools still ended up as shop assistants, grocers, fishmongers, rubber-tappers. Boys who went to the red-haired devils' schools later got jobs in government service and earned good salaries. Ah Lau Chek's eldest son was a junior administrative officer in some important government department and was one of Luping's most eligible bachelors. His cousin worked as a translator in the courts and earned a good salary. Somebody knew of a man whose son had been awarded a government scholarship and was now studying to be a doctor in a university in Great Britain. The largesse of Empire. Why had they been so foolish as not to benefit from it?

One Ah Cheng Koh struck the table with a fist and spat out his contempt for traitors: 'White man's running dog. Eater of white man's shit. Where is the loyalty to the mother country? You want your sons and daughters to be speaking the white man's language? You want them to abandon the culture of their ancestors?'

The reference to culture struck a deep chord, for sons and daughters, in embracing the white man's religion, turned their backs not only on parents but on a long line of ancestors, stretching far back into the mists of revered memory in the ancestral country. Ancestral altars were neglected, ancestral tombs unvisited.

When Ah Cheng Koh came to Malaya as a fourteen-year-old to find work, he had brought with him a shirt, a vest, a blanket and a handful of the earth of home. His mother had dug up a clod of hard yellow soil outside their hut and then sewn up five generations of sweat, tears, and lost dreams in a little cloth bag. Tearfully, she had pressed it into his hands before the ship sailed, and it had comforted his cough-wracked chest as he lay on the hard planks of the ship's floor to sleep, huddled among a hundred bodies trembling with fear and hope.

Quandary invited easy compromise: some families sent sons to English schools and daughters to Chinese schools; some simply let the great educational divide run exactly down the middle, with an equal number of offspring on each side. But no degree of compromise could deny the ancestral altar its focal position in the home, or long-dead forebears the special food offerings on the Feast of the Hungry Ghosts.

Ah Oon Koh went out to buy good white cotton cloth for his wife to sew a shirt for his son, as well as a new pair of slippers. He said,

'I'm going to put you in the Sultan Hamid boys' school. You need new clothes.'

But Big Older Brother was a dismal failure. Clumsy and loutish, he stood out even among the over-aged pupils who straggled in from the villages, and invited the contempt of his teacher, a Mr Joganathan, who picked on him continually. Entrusted with the urgent task of teaching a ragtag class of boys the skills of reading, writing and spelling English, Mr Joganathan, who came from a prestigious college in India, vented his frustrations in a fine display of knuckle-rapping and head-knocking, often with the help of a round wooden ruler.

Big Older Brother's face, coarse, sullen, obtruded itself continually upon Mr Joganathan's attention and naturally came in for a larger share of the knocks and raps.

'Idiot! Fool! Shit-head!' hissed Mr Joganathan, and a thousand years of resentment against a pale-skinned race who were stuck in a wet rice culture yet would deride their dusky neighbours flowed in a stream of invective and emptied itself in a rush of slaps on the hateful Chinese face.

Where Big Older Brother had been an eager pupil under the Japanese teacher, belting out songs and picking up words he could immediately test on Satosan, he shrank into himself under the scornful gaze of his English teacher and cringed to hear his own voice aping the *fftt fftt* and *sshh sshh* sounds of the strange English language that he could not bear to repeat at home or in the neighbourhood. The energies that had expended themselves so satisfyingly in unruly escapades on home territory were now concentrated into a savagery of loathing of the English teacher. One day he simply ran away from school, but not before leaving a hard lump of dog excrement in Mr Joganathan's lunch-box.

Ah Oon Koh was angry, but his anger towards his son never expressed itself in more than a shout or a token flick with a length of rope even following a severe complaint from a neighbour. Now he merely aimed a feeble cuff at the boy's ears, and said sternly, 'Don't blame me if you have regrets later.'

But Big Older Brother didn't care. Right now, he was more concerned with not being able to have his own bicycle or his sister not paying him enough attention.

For she was gradually alienating herself from him. She was spending time with Second Grandmother, listening to foolish tales.

39

He felt she ought to be more grateful to him for protecting her from the Bad Boys.

Beauty drew, like a magnet, but had a restraining power, so that the Bad Boys, watching Mei Kwei play hopscotch, stayed well outside the boundaries of the squares and rectangles drawn in the hard earth with a sharp stick. Inside the squares, the little girl hopped happily, ignoring the stares as she concentrated on pushing a piece of broken tile with bare toes. The hot morning sun, which made playing children an ugly, red-faced, bedraggled horde, touched her still incipient beauty into startling radiance: skin, lips, eyes and hair broke out in an incandescence of colour and energy, inviting appraisal from passing adults, 'This is truly a lovely child,' and concession from the passing boys, 'We will pause for a while to look at her.'

These people were of no consequence to her and so merited not a glance as she played with her best friend, Polly, who lived in one of the bigger houses in Luping, went to St Margaret's convent school, had books and toys and therefore commanded respect. The Bad Boys' attention was fully focused on Mei Kwei: Polly, like the other little girls in Luping, was like a dusky slave beside a fair princess, a coarse earthling beside a moon enchantress. The washerwoman Ah Pin's simple-minded daughter might be easily enticed into a shed with sweets and peanuts; this one, with her rare beauty and intelligent look that she sometimes allowed to sweep over their heads in cool disdain, called for a different strategy of entrapment.

The leader once again rose to his position by advancing closer to the lines of demarcation and firing off the first in a series of strategic manoeuvres. He crossed his arms over his bare, thin chest and stuck his hands tightly under his armpits, then raised his voice to remark jocularly to no one in particular, 'How clever some people are at hopscotch. Unmatchable in the whole of Luping.'

The comment eliciting no response either from Mei Kwei, who was still assiduously trying to guide the tile into the next square with her toes, or from Polly, who merely stole a few cautious glances at him, the boy proceeded to the next step, which would surely call for a definite response: he would watch out for a tile inadvertently pushed out of the territorial lines, seize it and compel negotiations for its return. A tile did shoot out, pushed too hard by Polly. The boy dived for it, then stood up and held it out on the palm of his hand, watched with interest by his comrades who were tittering among themselves.

Polly made a movement forward, then stopped abruptly as the boy, ever alert for greater opportunities for fun, sat down on the ground. He stretched out one leg in front and raised the other, exposing loose passage into his tattered black cotton shorts in which, with a great flourish, he placed the tile, in audacious proximity to his testicles. At the same time, he challenged Mei Kwei with his small, narrow eyes under a thatch of unkempt hair: in a timid attempt to retrieve the stolen item, her small hand might be seized and made to touch male power.

Polly looked at Mei Kwei who instantly turned her back upon the interlopers, began to search the surrounding ground, found another piece of broken tile and handed it to her friend, signalling that the game should continue.

Belittled, the leader got up from the ground and hooted derisively. He was soon joined by his comrades. Their attention turned to Mei Kwei's companion, she of the white man's name and school. *'Yah! Yah! Por-lee! Por-lee! Ang moh kooi!'*

The contempt of Ah Cheng Koh, nurtured by the handful of earth from the ancestral country, had worked itself into a dozen boyish cat-calls. The Pollys and Mollys and Annies of Luping, whose parents had been lured by the white man to abandon the names approved by forebears, came in for much vilification. Mei Kwei! Mei Kwei! Why don't you change your name to an *ang mo kooi* one, too? And still the girl's proud beauty and cool demeanour kept them back.

Shouting, the leader pointed to something a short distance away. His yell was urgent enough for everyone to turn in the direction of his forefinger. A pair of fowls frenziedly copulating in the shade of a bush was the very thing to push hot young blood to fever pitch. Hooting, laughing wildly, bent over with the sheer thrill of such deliciously appropriate diversion, the boy continued to draw attention to the sight of the mounting male continually slipping off the back of the squawking female. Encouraged to see the two girls pausing to watch too, he began to make his own copulatory movements, repeatedly thrusting his thin hips forward in their baggy shorts. Again Polly looked for guidance to Mei Kwei, who immediately caught her hand and pulled her away, preparatory to leaving the field of ignominy. Shaken into quick action by the prospect of the loss of his prey, the boy threw off all restraint, rushed forward, caught Mei Kwei by the waist and lifted her off the ground. She screamed and struggled, kicking, beating his arms with both fists. Polly, too, screamed, then ran away.

Perhaps it was the need to cap the assault with a decisive gesture of power, perhaps it was the mere contact with a female body. The boy pushed his face into the girl's for a kiss, and roared, once again, in response to the approving yells from his watching comrades. The more the girl struggled, the more tightly he held her, and would have attempted a second kiss, if he had not felt a violent kick in his back and heard a tremendous roar of rage. He let go of his victim and turned to face Big Older Brother, but was no match for the thin but powerful arms that struck his head again and again, and the powerful legs that never stopped kicking and stomping. He ran away howling, followed by his comrades.

'Don't you ever do that to my sister again!'

In the years before they were put in different rooms to sleep, she with their mother and he with their father, he would proudly remind her of the many times he had saved her, holding up splayed fingers for the counting – thumb, for rescue from cruel adoption, forefinger, from the Bad Boys, middle finger, from a nasty, drunk *keleng* man, and so on, down to the little finger, in a self-congratulatory listing of adventures, real and imagined.

One day, Big Older Brother invited her to go with him to see the tiger that Uncle Big Gun had killed. Uncle Big Gun was Chinese, but went hunting with the Malays and spoke their language fluently, even had a house like theirs, thatched and on stilts, on the edge of a jungle. He was about to skin the tiger that had been laid on a large wooden table outside the house, and he did not at all mind people gathering round to have a look.

'Come and see. A huge, man-eating beast.' Big Older Brother stuck out a hand to touch the animal's mouth, its ferocious teeth, its magnificent whiskers, enjoying the sight of his sister cowering in admiration by his side.

Uncle Big Gun, a huge hulk of a man with a weathered face and a crew-cut, given to hunting tigers and crocodiles and leering at the *kampung* women as they bathed in rivers or drew water from the well, paused in the work of delicately detaching tiger-skin from flesh with a pocket knife to look at the small, pretty girl standing beside her ugly, awkward brother. There was once a rumour of a sultan who, as he was taken through a village, ignored the beauteous women lined up to receive him and fixed his attention on a little girl playing under a tree. 'This is beauty worth ten years' waiting,' exclaimed the sultan, and gave orders for the little girl to be taken away and brought up in his palace. A retinue of women was put in charge of feeding her the finest food, massaging her young body with the rarest oils, teaching her the secrets of pleasing a man. And, indeed, she fulfilled the sultan's every expectation, becoming the greatest, most accomplished beauty in the land at the age of seventeen.

Perhaps Uncle Big Gun was looking at Mei Kwei with the sultan's eyes. She quickly retreated from his gaze and stood behind her brother. After a while, she peeped out and once more withdrew upon meeting that same relentless look.

'You should know better than to go near Uncle Big Gun!' Ah Oon Soh scolded her children, and she was not thinking of lascivious looks cast upon her daughter. Her protective efforts in that direction would begin only with her daughter's first blood: she had already noticed the first signs of budding under the thin cotton blouse and was preparing for the day when she would swoop upon Mei Kwei with the requisite padding of cloth as well as the necessary advice from mothers: 'You are now a woman. Avoid the touch of all men.'

For men readily smelt first blood and were dangerous.

'Nobody wants to marry a damaged woman,' said Ah Oon Soh. 'You have to remain a maiden for your husband.' In the ancestral country, the injured husband could stuff his wife into one of the round closed baskets made for transporting pigs over great distances, and drop her over a cliff into the sea. In the adopted country, he simply sent her back to her parents or, as in the case of Old Man Thio when he discovered that his seventeen-year-old fourth wife was no longer pristine, allowed her to remain in the household, a target of continuous derision by the other wives.

'You have to give your virginity to no one but your husband,' her mother had said severely. Without understanding the nature of that stupendous gift, Mei Kwei had thought defiantly, I will give it to whomever I like.

Mei Kwei seldom liked what her mother told her. She preferred her grandmother's stories: her mother's seemed always to be sharp, puzzling, joyless.

'What –' she began.

'You will know when the time comes,' said Ah Oon Soh brusquely. Once worried about the sinister intentions of the Japanese enemy towards little girls, she now thought less of Uncle Big Gun's reputation for lechery than of the danger of his associations with the spirit world, which could easily spill over into the world of the innocent bystander. The tiger he shot was no tiger but a *datok* who slipped in and out of animal guises, one day a tiger, another a

43

monkey, and still another, a water buffalo. His vengeful spirit might leap from the dead tiger body into that of any of the bystanders, including little children.

'I told you never to go near dead animals!' she said, in great vexation. Unsure about the efficacy of joss-sticks on a spirit from another culture, Ah Oon Soh made the children go back to the spot of the skinning, stand with heads bowed, press palms together and move them rapidly up and down in apology and supplication. The simplicity of gestures, unadorned by the trappings of each separate culture's rituals, would be understood and accepted by all the many gods and spirits of this diverse country. Ah Oon Soh would, on another occasion, force her children to offer the same sign of humble contrition before a richly garlanded cow deity in an Indian wayside shrine.

'Yah! Yah! Coward!' cried Big Older Brother, and he pulled out of his pocket a long white whisker, which he poked into his sister's face. 'Yah! Yah! You are now under the spell of the tiger spirit!'

She screamed. She tried to free herself from his grasp. There was a moment when his face almost touched hers and he paused and brushed his lips against her cheek, remembering the moment of male intensity he had witnessed when the Bad Boy captured her, and again, when Uncle Big Gun paused to look up and fix his gaze on her.

CHAPTER SIX

'Granddaughter, you are always crying,' said Second Grandmother, as the girl went into her room and laid her head on her lap.

How could she tell Second Grandmother – oh, the shame of it! – of her brother's skulking shadow outside the lavatory, and the peeping, to catch her at the most shameful stage, the lowering of trousers and squatting over the bucket below? She had quickly stood up and pulled up her trousers.

'Granddaughter, stop that crying.'

These days, her grandmother's tongue was sharp rather than

tender, corresponding to a new mood of great restlessness, as she paced the house and talked to herself.

'Her time has come,' said her son-in-law, with brutal glee. 'She has given trouble enough.'

'Tell me a story, Second Grandmother,' said the child, thinking of how the joyousness of a tale once banished her misery, and at the same time realising that no talk of magic turtle or golden-voiced rooster or pearldrop-shedding goddess would ever enchant her again.

'I will tell you a story,' said Second Grandmother, her eyes brightening, her irritability gone. But the child did not want to hear the story, told a hundred times, about an old man on a silken bed who loved his second wife above all his other wives, and on his death-bed pleaded with everybody to treat her well. Second Grandmother could get tediously repetitive, talking about gift shoes and a gift hoard of diamonds, jade and gold that even the child knew to be non-existent.

'No? You don't want to hear my love story?' said Second Grandmother, and the child, her eyes filling with vexed tears, buried her small face on her grandmother's lap and said nothing.

'Do you hear it?' Second Grandmother often turned up an ear to catch sounds coming from the distance – the rumble of thunder, the moan of a rising wind, the owl's lonely hoot, as if these were intimations of her death.

The sounds this time were of joyful celebration. They came from the market-place upon the evening air – the faint roll of drums, the distinct clash of cymbals, a woman's voice raised in song.

'Let's go!' The child caught the old woman's enthusiasm and was up in an instant.

'Let's not tell anyone,' said Second Grandmother, with a conspiratorial finger to lips, for the last time she had responded to the sounds, Ah Oon Soh made a lot of fuss and prevented her from leaving the house, saying, 'You will get lost in the crowd. You will fall and get trampled upon.' Adding wearily, 'Old people should know how to behave to earn the respect of the young.'

They slipped out of the house in the darkness, hand in hand.

The opera was magnificent, as always. Staged to honour temple gods, it delighted lesser mortals, who crept out of the greynesses of their lives into a riotous burst of colour and sound. Clutching her grandmother's hand, unmindful of mosquitoes that came out in swarms in the evening and attacked arms and legs, the child sat enthralled through the performance, her eyes fixed on the performers in their dazzling finery. Against the rough wood of the stage and the tawdry backdrop of cheap, faded banners, the costumes stood out in all the unmitigated brilliance of sequinned crimson, green, gold, orange, purple. The extremity of glitter, which caused children to blink and cover their eyes, was matched by the exaggeratedness of coal-black, waist-long beards and whiskers, vermilion mouths against chalk white skin, black-lined eyes with corners lifted into raven wings, bellies big as wine casks. The spectators' ears, like their eyes, luxuriated in extravagance; the drums, cymbals and gongs filled the night air with a deafening din that yet regulated itself to move in fine step with every utterance, every gesture of hand, every glide across the stage. A god-king with an enormous black beard but bushy white eyebrows made a long speech punctuated by majestic cymbal clashes that mesmerised the spectators into breathless attention. He exhorted, with hands authoritatively placed across his ample belly – CLASH! – warned, with severe uplifted forefinger – CLASH! – and punished, with a mighty stamp of his foot – CLASH!

The music stayed in the ears a long time, so that after each performance little children went away and staged their own. They assumed the gravest of expressions, tugged at imaginary beards, and, to the beat of imitative tin cans, pails or coconut shells, declaimed, strutted and pranced to their hearts' content.

God-kings, emperors, eunuchs, demons, warriors, chieftains, princesses, moon maidens – they crowded the stage in the full splendour of their apparel, their makeup, their cymbal-regulated exclamations of surprise, anger, joy and sorrow, their gong-heralded movements of victory, defeat, parting and reconciliation.

'Go away.' Second Grandmother pressed her lips in great displeasure and turned away abruptly from the Mad Temple Vagrant, who made an appearance at every opera performance, moving among the crowd with her smelly clothes and hair, shamelessly pointing to food held in the hands of the more fortunate of the earth, and hoping for crumbs that might be allowed to fall from their table.

Mei Kwei was holding a newspaper cone of freshly boiled peanuts, bought with a small coin that the old woman had extracted from the depths of her blouse pocket. The Mad Temple Vagrant looked longingly at the nuts, and when her grandmother was not looking, the child quickly passed them to her, then turned back to continue watching the opera.

'Why, Second Grandmother, you're crying.'

Each was alert to the onset of tears in the other's eyes: it was Mei

Kwei's turn to notice and exclaim. She watched the tears filling up the old, sorrowful eyes, the taking out of a handkerchief from the blouse pocket to wipe them away. Her quick mind connected the sadness to the scene now playing on stage: a dying king on his death-bed was saying goodbye to his favourite concubine. The king sang a sad farewell, the concubine responded with a song that rose tremblingly and fell sobbingly upon the air enthralling the audience. The concubine was telling her lover that she would remain loyal for a thousand years, that neither fire nor sword would make her yield to another man's embrace.

'Improper,' Ah Oon Soh would have said, of her mother stealing out of the house in the darkness with a child to watch an opera. 'Worse than improper,' she would have said, of tears shed in a public place, to foolish love stories that were for the stage only. Romance is for the young, not the old. You would have done better to have held on to that bundle of jewels you are always talking about. They would have helped posterity much more than dreams of lost love.

Second Grandmother was tight-lipped about the evening's jaunt despite the ensuing noisy confrontation with her daughter. The little granddaughter, loyal to the end, shook her head when asked and also chose to remain silent.

'Let's go to the Kek Lok temple.'

The second expedition was even trickier as it was in the daytime and involved greater cunning to elude pairs of watching eyes and ears alert for departing sounds. But they managed to get out of the house and into a trishaw, Second Grandmother again digging into her deep blouse pocket, an inexhaustible store of coins, to pay the trishaw-man.

Second Grandmother had no need of advice from the gods and goddesses on the altars and in the temple. She brought along no joss-sticks or fragrant flowers but went straight to the Ancient Fortune-teller who had a little space behind the temple where he sat on a stool behind a small table, bare except for an urn in which stood a cluster of lit joss-sticks, and a porcelain saucer in which grateful clients placed coins.

Used to predicting lottery wins, the birth of male children, the end of a season of bad luck, the Ancient Fortune-teller remained silent to Second Grandmother's question: when would she be released from the travails of life, to be united with her dead husband in heaven?

The Ancient Fortune-teller began to talk in riddles, which disconcerted the old lady.

'Let's go,' she said to the child. Disguising ignorance with nonsensical talk. Ever the fraud's ploy. She would have no more to do with him. Haughtily, she dropped a coin into the saucer and pulled the child away.

Departing, she heard an urgent call from the old man to return. She went back and stood before him with the child, in frowning puzzlement, as he talked, in a thin, quavering voice, of love and sorrow, of tears and blood, of lovers tossed upon storm. A man would come from a foreign land, riding across vast tracts of water, to claim her heart and crush it.

Even venerable fortune-tellers had to be put in their place for uttering nonsense, and Second Grandmother, in her haughtiest voice, said, 'Old Uncle, cease this foolish talk,' before she realised that the prediction was not for her but for her granddaughter. The old man was holding the arm of the little girl in one hand and touching her cheek with the other. A great wounding love, he said, to the terrified little girl, and lifted his sightless eyes once more to have sight of the future.

In later years, she recollected with wonder the prediction of that day in the temple with her grandmother, and was provoked, in that time of rare secret happiness with the man she had grown to love so much, to tell him and watch him express the wonder.

'Impossible,' he said.

'True,' she smiled.

At last the Ancient Fortune-teller let go of her arm. She did not understand what he had said, but the urgency in his thin, reedy voice communicated itself to her, and she began to cry.

'Enough! Enough! Let's go home!' cried Second Grandmother, pulling her away.

If the mortals were found wanting, there were always the immortals; the gods and goddesses who would not say, 'You should have come to us first,' but would understand the desperation of old women. The goddess Kuan Yin, who dispensed gentle mercy, would be the most understanding, Second Grandmother thought.

Taking her little granddaughter with her, she went to pray at the altar of the goddess in the Kek Lok temple, apologising for the meagre offering of a solitary joss-stick and a handful of flower petals for so colossal a request: Tell me the exact day when I will go to meet my husband in heaven.

It was the goddess's beauty, more than her magnanimity, that made the old woman single her out from the pantheon of deities in the temple. In a hushed voice to the little granddaughter kneeling beside her, Second Grandmother pointed out the goddess's loveliness – the eyes, the hair, the gracious mouth, the delicate limbs, the flowing robes, the floating nimbus around her feet.

'Improper and irrelevant,' Ah Oon Soh would have hissed in disapproval. 'We come into a temple to pray, not to notice this god's beauty or that god's ugliness.' For hairy-faced monkey gods, black-faced warriors or pot-bellied guardians with grotesque domes for foreheads had no appeal for Second Grandmother.

The child agreed that the goddess Kuan Yin's eyes, mouth and hair were lovely but thought her robes imperfectly painted and the cloud curls around her feet distinctly tawdry, as if the artisan had run out of paint, or patience. But, of course, she did not dare point this out. She shifted her attention from the goddess (after discovering, additionally, that at least half the holy beads in the goddess's hands were rusty) to her grandmother, who was praying with the fervour of tightly closed eyes, visibly moving lips and hands pressed to chest.

The goddess heard. For that very night Second Grandmother had a dream. Kuan Yin, who seldom favoured her devotees with appearances in dreams, not only appeared but spoke, not only spoke but touched, so that on waking up in the morning the old woman quickly took off her blouse, gazed at it reverently and put it aside for the special day of her death, sternly instructing her daughter not to wash it but to preserve the fragrance of the goddess's touch for ever. Sometimes the heavens open and gods and goddesses dispense with the mediation of priest or shaman or fortune-teller to touch directly the lowest of the low on this earth.

Yes, it will be soon, Kuan Yin had promised, and Second Grandmother, in the dream and later in the temple, thanked her with tears.

But the old woman's dreams of immortal love and union shattered fearfully against the reality.

'What?' said her daughter incredulously.

'What?' exploded her son-in-law when told by her daughter. 'Just where does she think the money is coming from?'

For Second Grandmother had demanded that a coffin be bought in preparation for the promised day of release; not any cheap coffin, she

49

had added, but one worthy of the presence of the Goddess of Mercy who would personally come down to fetch her. She wanted it immediately.

Ah Oon Koh opened his mouth wide in a long discharge of ringing mockery. Was the goddess coming down on wings or in a sedan chair? he asked. Would she be accompanied by Tua Peh Kong himself, since it would suit the old one to be welcomed by no less than the Great God? Better still, why not empty heaven of all its denizens to have the largest welcoming party for his mother-in-law? Carried along by rare loquacity, Ah Oon Koh could not stop. His wife stood by, a deep frown on her brow.

Gathering the lines of her mouth tightly together in grim determination, Second Grandmother said, 'I will have the coffin. I want it brought to the house tomorrow. And I want it placed upright on the wall, pointing heavenwards.'

Madness upon madness! That evening, Ah Oon Koh joined his wife at the small table in the kitchen to discuss the handling of the latest in a long line of misdemeanours so unusual in the old. The ancient one was proving totally unmanageable, and that was cause enough to put her in the mental asylum in the local hospital or in the house at Amoy Lane where the elderly and the sick were taken to die.

'But she has a family,' said Ah Oon Soh, her voice faltering a little. Amoy Lane received only the homeless, old men and women who had come from the ancestral country, worked, never married and now expected to die alone.

'Then you find the money for her coffin,' snarled Ah Oon Koh, turning away in disgust. He looked up, startled to see the old woman, her clothes dishevelled, her hair let down, the customary neatness all gone, standing in the doorway and holding a small cloth bundle in her hands. She walked towards them and placed the bundle on the table.

There it was, before their eyes, the gift hoard from a besotted old man, which they had heard endlessly about and scoffed at as just so much empty boasting. Jade ear-rings, diamond ear-studs, jade bangles, gold tortoise and crab pins, ropes of gold for neck and wrists – she had told of the old man's love, expressed not only in the nightly appreciation of the lovely young body in doll's shoes but in a cascade of jewels upon that body. Once no more than froth from an overheated imagination, the old woman's detailed descriptions of bounty were materialising in the solidity of the bundle before their eyes.

Ah Oon Koh looked at his wife. She looked at her mother.

'Open it,' commanded Second Grandmother. Tremblingly, Ah Oon Soh's fingers untied the bundle.

The size, the rich bulges had grossly misled them. Expecting to see the long-vaunted treasure, the couple looked upon balls of crushed white paper and rags enclosing a few pieces of tawdry jewellery, yet another quirk of the old woman. Ah Oon Soh poked and prodded every ragged ball and pulled out one gold chain, two silver bracelets, a pair of ear-rings and a gold ring, which she laid on the table: meagre truth that had at last come out from behind magnificent obsession.

'So. Now what do you want us to do?' Ah Oon Soh felt an overwhelming sense of weariness and powerlessness with regard to her increasingly strange, recalcitrant mother, and thought a speedy death no bad thing.

'Not enough to pay for a coffin!' said Ah Oon Koh, with a derisive laugh.

'With enough left over to pay for a priest from the Kek Lok temple. I want prayers for two days and two nights,' said Second Grandmother sharply and left the room.

CHAPTER SEVEN

'Second Grandmother, Second Grandmother, your coffin has come!' cried Mei Kwei excitedly.

Big Older Brother also ran out to watch, but feigned indifference, saying, with something of his father's derisive tone and mordancy of language, 'What is there to be excited about? We have worse than poison in our midst.' He stayed close to his father and refused any more contact with his sister and the mad grandmother.

The coffin divided the town, too. Standing in readiness, in accordance with the precise order of the goddess, to receive one who was still alive and fussing around it, as if matching her body to its precise measurements, it invited awe as well as ridicule from the many who came to gape and gawk. On one side stood the fervent who were provoked to put hands together in reverential acknowledgement of divine presence; on the other stood the cynics, sniggering. A mother, with a small child beside her, slapped down the child's pointing finger. A full moon, pointed at, would leave a horrible cut behind the ear; a consecrated coffin might do worse.

One of the cynics suspended his disbelief long enough to listen, without smirking, to a similar story of an old man, many years before, who had bought a coffin in readiness and died at the exact hour he had predicted. Another abandoned disbelief for gain, joining a small group that had moved closer to the coffin for the sole purpose of testing its power to confer lucky lottery numbers.

The news of Ah Oon Koh's crazy mother-in-law had spread, attracting larger and larger crowds. The story accreted bizarre details as it passed from mouth to mouth: the old woman was already in her death throes and crying out to the goddess; the coffin was seen to be shaking; the coffin had so far yielded three lucky lottery numbers; someone had seen a bright light enveloping the coffin; another had seen a brighter light enveloping the old woman, now so removed from her former neatness and meticulous grooming as to shock everyone who looked upon her.

As always, imagination had overtaken reality, and the onlookers looked upon an ordinary coffin, with its head-end raised some height above the ground on a few old bricks and wood blocks, in pathetic symbolism of the promised great ascent heavenwards.

Expecting to see a dishevelled old woman with hair let down and wildly floating around her face, they were disappointed to see Second Grandmother no untidier than themselves in clothes, hair, finger-nails, and behaving normally towards the little granddaughter, always by her side. They had heard stories of Ah Oon Koh's towering rages, but saw him once only, coming out of the house and riding away on his bicycle. As for Ah Oon Soh, she went on with her usual activities of washing, cleaning, cooking, feeding the chickens, maintaining life's sane rhythms against madness's onslaught. The son was always by the father's side, in profound unhappiness, glaring at everybody.

United in their curiosity about an event such as had never been seen before in Luping, the onlookers were also united in their sympathy for the beleaguered family. The swill woman tried to be helpful to all, and whispered to Ah Oon Soh, 'Never mind, it will soon be over.' She would recommend one thing immediately after the funeral: take the little granddaughter for a thorough temple cleansing, for she had been too much in the company of madness.

In that terrible time in the distant future, just before her flight from Luping, some people would recollect vividly Mei Kwei's close association with her mad grandmother during those days and shake their heads and remark, 'Just like her grandmother. There is a fever in the brain of such women, which drives them to do unheard-of things,' not understanding the fever of love's dreams.

And, indeed, Mei Kwei never left her grandmother's side in those last days. Bewildered and frightened by what was going on around her, she clung steadily to one belief, and was consoled by it: Second Grandmother would go to heaven and be happy at last. It was an overpowering concern, for Second Grandmother had been crying far too much lately, and only the merciful Kuan Yin could put an end to those tears. Of the grandfather waiting in heaven, she had little notion except, vaguely, of a benign old man with white hair and white beard, not unlike one of the guardian deities she had seen in the temple, who slept all day on a silken couch and showered those he loved with beautiful dolls' shoes and jewels. The terror of loss had as yet no place in love's solicitousness.

'Second Grandmother, don't pay attention to all those stupid people.'

The sight of the onlookers, gazing in, pointing to the coffin, whispering and tittering among themselves, had begun to distress the old woman.

'How can the pure goddess come to fetch me in the midst of so many impure people?' Second Grandmother counted crooks, thieves, gangsters, prostitutes, pimps, beef-eaters.

Mei Kwei, peeping from behind a curtain, studied the crowd of faces for signs of impurity and saw an ugly scar on one face, pock-marked cheeks on another, a scabbed nose on a third, saw also heavy rouge and lipstick which, said Second Grandmother, marked the bad woman. There were two such bad women, reeking of cheap perfume, expertly cracking melon seeds with their teeth and spitting out the husks.

As the crowd grew, she began to recognise some faces, then to wince and retreat behind the curtain, for she did not want to look upon them again. Uncle Big Gun, who was on his way somewhere, paused to look, an amused smile playing around his moist brutal mouth. She trembled behind the curtain and felt again the burning power of the deep-set, staring eyes that could have detached her budding body from its covering clothes as surely as the small, sharp penknife had detached tiger-skin from flesh.

Truly a gathering of Luping's lunatics, someone commented, when the Mad Temple Vagrant appeared, in search of food and friendship, such as even a crowd of coffin-watchers might offer. Someone did, indeed, give her a coin, perhaps in the hope that the good deed would improve the chances of securing a lucky lottery number from the coffin.

There were the Bad Boys who stood in a cluster, talking and laughing together, then looked around furtively for purses left unattended or sweets and toys held in baby hands that could be easily removed.

Big Older Brother came out of the house, then quickly retreated into the shadows of the interior for, at the same instant as his sister, who also gave a start, he recognised the dreaded father and son. Mr Tong, large, sunburnt, aggressive, and his pale-faced, delicate-limbed son were among the curious onlookers. Would they, remembering him, demand the return of the train?

Mei Kwei looked at Big Older Brother and knew what he was thinking. She, too, retreated into shadows with him, linked with him in the crime of theft. She had often wondered about the magnificent toy, flung into the ditch that day in an unaccountable fit of rage: had some child seen it and picked it up, whooping with joy?

Only one onlooker was welcome, because she promised comfort in a time of confusion. Polly, secure in her Catholic faith which was of a piece with her English name, her English education, her disdain of the Chinese-educated and of whom Sister St Elizabeth at the St Margaret's convent school called 'pagans', came with the paraphernalia of holy water taken from church, a holy medal of the Sacred Heart and a holy picture of the Blessed Virgin Mary, to disengage her good friend from the forces of pagan evil, represented most decidedly by the coffin and the urn of lit joss-sticks beside it.

'Sister St Margaret says that those who pray to pagan gods will go to hell.' She advised Mei Kwei, with a grave face, to sprinkle the holy water around the house, which by now must have been fully claimed by the devil as his own. Unsure about her behaviour in the playground, Polly was most confident when imitating adults; the person she was imitating now, right down to the urgent tone of voice, was her own mother, a second-generation Catholic in Luping, as single-minded in her work of converting pagans as in her dream to provide an English education for all her six children. Polly had her mother's persuasive powers. 'Come. I will take you to our church to pray to the Blessed Virgin Mary.'

But Mei Kwei stood loyally by her grandmother who was

54

supported by a tradition that stretched back a thousand years in the ancestral country.

'Then you will go to hell! Sister St Elizabeth says so!'

The threat of eternal damnation was less daunting than the prospect of losing Polly's friendship, and with it all the thrills of looking at her reading books and listening, second-hand, to the stories of Christian saints and devils told by the indefatigable Sister St Elizabeth.

Yes, said Mei Kwei, she would go with her to pray to the Blessed Virgin Mary. But, in the end, they did not go to the church but to Polly's house where there was a large statue of the Virgin in Polly's mother's room.

Mei Kwei thought the Virgin was even more beautiful than the goddess Kuan Yin. Her eyes, lips, cheeks were perfect; like the goddess, she wore a long flowing robe, stood on floating clouds and held a string of beads in her hands. But the clouds were perfectly painted in white and blue, and the beads had no rust in them.

Polly taught Mei Kwei the words of the 'Our Father' and the 'Hail Mary', holding a stern ruler over the head of the learner, to descend in punitive force at the sound of any mispronunciation.

In that precious, secret time with her lover, years later when he said to her, 'Your stories are so sad. Tell me some happy things from your childhood, or some funny things, to make me smile,' she would recount that scene with Polly by her side and the Holy Virgin in front, in which her earnest prayer to be saved from hell was continually interrupted by knocks on the head with a ruler. The 'Our Father' and the 'Hail Mary' were her hard-earned induction into the intricacies of English pronunciation and grammar.

Of course, she never told her grandmother about her kneeling before foreign gods.

'Second Grandmother, how would you know that it is really Kuan Yin who is coming for you?' Mei Kwei was worried that a demon in cunning disguise might carry off her grandmother, and rob her of her dream of seeing again the beloved old man on his silken bed.

Second Grandmother scolded the child for doubting the goddess who had never reneged on a promise. 'I will see her again in a dream. She will be as beautiful as ever, and then I will be gone,' she promised.

No reality of painful parting as yet intruded upon the idyll of the divinely appointed death, the heavenly ascent and final union with the beloved. In those last days, the old woman, chasing her dream, and the young girl, joyfully cheering her on, were borne along on a buoyancy of expectation as together they waited for the coming of the goddess Kuan Yin. By her grandmother's side, the girl could not have been more estranged from her family. Nobody said, 'Siau!' anymore: the madness of the old one and of the child in her power had plumbed depths beyond the reach of advice or blame.

'Let them be,' said Ah Oon Soh wearily. 'It will come to an end soon.'

Lying in bed, Mei Kwei thought she heard a rustle of wind or silk, or perhaps it was both, for she opened her eyes and looked upon the goddess herself, her white and blue robe blowing softly around her. She really is beautiful, the girl thought, then gave a start and said, 'Why, it's the Blessed Virgin Mary.'

But as she looked, and as the apparition looked back at her, she saw that the eyes were black not blue, and caught a glimpse of the hair under the veil, black not golden. It's Kuan Yin, after all, she realised. Mei Kwei craned her neck to peer at the beads in her hand, but they were bright and shiny, not rusty. And then, as she continued looking, she saw, to her alarm, the pure features melting and reshaping into a face garishly painted, chalk white, with vivid crimson lips, bright pink cheeks, eye-whites glittering inside their borders of heavy black paint, eyebrows like a crow's wings in flight. The face was framed by a shimmering headdress of gold and silver beads, which fell in strings on the forehead and shook against one another with the slightest movement. Only when the lady opened her bright red mouth and lifted her hand did Mei Kwei recognise her. In the opera performance she had looked sad, mourning the death of her beloved; here, she shed no tears. In fact, she was smiling.

Virgin Mary, Kuan Yin, Concubine – the images floated in and out of each other, but always there was the kind smile.

'Who are you?' Mei Kwei asked, and the apparition replied, 'I've come for your grandmother, as I promised.'

The shout of joy in the dream coincided precisely with a crash of thunder, and the girl sat bolt upright in her bed, her heart pounding wildly. Her mother, who was beside her, stirred in the darkness and muttered something inaudible, then slipped into the depths of sleep again.

Mei Kwei got up and ran out of her room. 'Second Grandmother! Second Grandmother!' But her grandmother was not in her room and the bed had not been slept in.

'Second Grandmother!'

Then she saw the old woman sitting beside the coffin, her back turned to her.

'Second Grandmother,' Mei Kwei whispered urgently, 'she has come! I saw her!'

The old woman made no reply, but continued to sit with her head bowed.

'Second Grandmother, she's come to take you to heaven.'

It was the last concession to a grand illusion for, from that moment on, when the sitting figure gently fell over and was felt to be cold and stiff, death was stripped of its gentle mask and exposed in the full pitilessness of its power. Mei Kwei saw, in the cold light of the dawn, not a resplendent soul in ascent, but a pitiful corpse soon to be laid in the coffin and consigned to the earth. Unable to speak, she ran back to her mother to wake her, making tiny choking sounds of pure terror.

In the later years, her vivid memories of that day were not of the trauma of the loss – she was ill for a week, tossing and turning in a fever, while the sounds of the priest's intoning and the ringing of prayer bells reached her through the thin wooden walls of the bedroom – but of the tranquillity of her grandmother's expression as she lay in her coffin. The swill woman's story, of the corpse breaking into a smile when the precious silk shoes were taken from their wrapping of cloth and put on its feet, was just so much exaggeration. Mei Kwei remembered, with a clarity all the more startling because she had only a fleeting look at the dead body in the coffin before being pushed back to her sick bed by her alarmed mother, an expression of ineffable peace that made her say to herself, 'Why, Second Grandmother is only sleeping, and dreaming a happy dream.'

Her illness created great concern: was the old one about to take her away? The old, on their death-beds, struggled to bestow blessings of health and prosperity on progeny, but there were the perverse few who carried away the young with them. One Ah Ban Mm died, and exactly a week later, a grandson fell ill with a mysterious illness and died too. Ah Oon Soh rushed to the temple and offered frantic prayers for her daughter's recovery, shedding bitter tears that the old troublesome one should continue to be troublesome after death.

Some time after her recovery, her mother took Mei Kwei to pray at her grandmother's grave in the large cemetery at the edge of the town. A cluster of lit joss-sticks was put in her hand. 'Ask Second Grandmother to make you good. To make you obedient to your elders. To give no trouble to anyone.'

The admonitions remained the same, whether in the hearing of the deity presiding over babies in arms about to be given away or of a dead woman empowered by death to help the living. Be good. Be obedient.

Mei Kwei remembered only a sensation of great numbness, as if all feeling was suspended. A vague thought floated in her mind: how strange that Second Grandmother, considered a nuisance in life, had instantly become a goddess in death, with power to confer virtues on the living.

The numbness broke and allowed the release of tears, which was shared by the mother who, in a rare demonstration of tenderness – she laid her daughter's head upon her shoulder, held her and stroked her back – elicited a different kind of crying. Mother and daughter, in the unmitigated black of their mourning clothes, clung together on their bed and wept.

Ah Oon Soh wept noisily again as she cleaned up the room and touched objects once closely associated with the old one – the small hard pillow, stuffed with sand, which bore the oil stains from her hair, the nipa-palm fan, frugally protected with the cloth edging, the neat blouses, the ear-digging pins. Perhaps it was with a faint hope that Ah Oon Soh dug deep into the recesses of cupboard shelves used by the old one, but no cloth bundle, no covering balls of paper or rags were found to raise any hopes of vestigial bits of jewellery that might be used to pay for the tombstone that would soon be erected on the grave, or the ancestral altar that would soon be set up.

The granddaughter's grief was unmixed with any thought of gain. It was all-consuming and frightening to behold, for it racked her young body and drew from it, night after night, great choking sobs that could not be muffled by pillows. It was a gouging sorrow, hollowing out heart, eyes, cheeks so that she frightened all by her appearance, a walking child ghost. The swill woman, ever solicitous about the family, went to a neighbouring town to pray at the shrine of a deity reported to be more powerful than any in the Kek Lok temple.

The intensity of the sorrow penetrated even the morose indifference that the father had affected since the death. Clad in black mourning shirt and trousers, he neither mourned nor missed the old one, but he began to feel stirrings of pity for the daughter.

'Enough, enough.' His curt first response to the tormented weeping softened into a genuine offer of solace. 'Here, take this.' He was standing at the doorway of the room she shared with her mother, looking at her as she lay curled on the bed, her back towards him, and holding out a large coin. She did not turn towards him or stop her crying. Big Older Brother offered food and then, by a great effort of will, his most prized possession, a penknife with a mother-of-pearl clasp. She turned away from him.

It could have been a dream of Second Grandmother happy at last, or simply the reassertion of youthful hope, but one morning she woke up, the pain dispelled, the energy restored. The sorrow and the illness had run their course and vanished. Her mother watched her finish a bowl of porridge, then another. The swill woman, with immense generosity, went to buy expensive herbs to make into a nourishing brew which she brought straight from the stove, bubbling in restorative power. She also brought along the small grandson, still thin but healthy enough. It was fitting, said the swill woman, that Tee Tee, saved from death by timely adoption, should be brought to share the joy of the adoptive sister, saved from a similar fate by the timely intervention of the powerful shrine deity.

Mei Kwei spoke little, but was aware of returning strength creeping into her limbs, filling her cheeks, putting the brightness back into her eyes. She began to look with hope in a certain direction, began indeed to mobilise all her energies for the fulfilment of her dearest dream.

CHAPTER EIGHT

'Where were you this morning?' Ah Oon Soh said severely. She knew where her daughter had been, but liked to cast the rhetoric of her annoyance in the form of questions: 'Why are you taking so long to have your bath? Why haven't you fed the chickens yet? Have the cigarettes been done?'

The languor of mourning had given way to a burst of purposeful energy, which took Mei Kwei out of the house every morning and brought her back, after several hours, in a flush of new interest. It was not considered proper for young girls on the verge of womanhood, with their buds already showing under their cotton blouses, to be out on their own, for who could tell when male lust, too impatient to wait for first blood, would pounce?

But dishes had not been left unwashed, or chamberpots unemptied, or the cigarettes unrolled.

'I get the work done anyway,' the girl said petulantly, and it was true. She either rose earlier to finish the various chores assigned to her or completed them as soon as she returned home. A large pile of rolled cigarettes stood ready to be collected, in testimony of her claim: her mother let her keep a few cents off each dollar earned.

Big Older Brother shouted, 'White devils' school! White devils' school!'

He had told her the incident of the dog excrement in Mr Joganathan's lunch box many times as supreme proof of his contempt of an English education. Since running away from the Sultan Hamid English school, he had returned on a number of occasions to harass old classmates during the school recess, jeering at them from behind the fence, or taking shots at them with his catapult from the cover of leafy foliage. The boys in the Christian school of St Joseph's came in for even greater scorn, for they included the hated, pale-faced Tong boy, one of the very few boys to go to school in a car. To mix some cow-dung in the rice or noodles in the boy's lunch box and watch him eat it unsuspectingly, to piss into his flask of Ovaltine or Milo and watch him drink it: that would yield far greater pleasure than even the prank on Mr Joganathan.

St Margaret's convent school for girls would not have merited any attention if it had not been for his sister's attraction to it. Now he pondered its despicable nature, for it was not only a white devils' school, but run by a white devil woman in a long black dress.

His scorn slid off the smooth, cool exterior of his sister's indifference, so he attacked her on another point: 'If the foreign devils know what you are doing, they can put you in jail. You can't go to their school and not pay the fees.' For he had secretly, out of great curiosity, followed his sister out of the house one morning and seen her loiter outside the classrooms of the convent school, peeping in through the window, watching and listening to the learning going on inside.

It was the next best thing to being allowed to go to school.

'Second Grandmother, did you ever go to school?' she had asked. Her grandmother had laughed at the preposterousness of the idea, then grown pensive at a recollection. There had been a wise old *si fu* who came sometimes to the house to teach clever things to her brothers, and she had hung around, listening, absorbing knowledge.

The *si fu* told stories too, which Second Grandmother, then only ten, remembered all her life.

St Margaret's convent school was no more than an old wooden building, on the edge of a *kampong*, which the missionary nuns of the Holy Infant Jesus hoped to turn into a proper school with places for all the young girls in Luping. Sister St Elizabeth – who, with her fellow nuns, lived in the main St Margaret's convent in the nearby larger town of Bukit Tuas and came every morning in a small black Ford driven by a Malay driver – already saw in her mind a handsome brick building with a shrine to the Blessed Virgin Mary in the grounds and a chapel inside, receiving a continuous stream of pagan girls and sending out, with great triumph, a stream of the converted to light up the darkness of this strange little Malayan town to which her superiors in Ireland had sent her. All for the glory of God! Ruddy-cheeked and bright-eyed, struggling against the tropical heat in her starched white wimple and voluminous black serge habit, Sister St Elizabeth with her fellow nun, Sister St Agatha, would devote her energies to the education and edification of girls in Luping. If now the roof of the school leaked each time it rained, or snakes appeared from the surrounding thick bushes to frighten the girls, or the *kampung* children, dirty and bedraggled, peeped in through the windows and were a nuisance, she would be patient and pray hard for the fulfilment of her dream. *The harvest is great and the labourers are few.* She would be a humble labourer in Empire's vast fields, sowing the seeds of learning, and reap a bountiful harvest.

Then she noticed a little Chinese girl, neither dirty nor bedraggled, who seemed to be around quite often, peeping in, but since she gave no trouble, Sister St Elizabeth decided to ignore her.

'Does anyone know her?' she once asked her class. They turned to look, but Mei Kwei had already retreated and hidden herself from sight. Polly, refusing to taint herself by association with a pagan, kept silence. On the hopscotch playground near Mei Kwei's house, she did not mind the association, but the school was her territory, brooking no rival presence. Rival turned admirer: she was aware of Mei Kwei's looking on deeply impressed whenever she shot up an arm to answer a question Sister St Elizabeth threw at the class, or stood up to read loudly from a book or went up to the blackboard and wrote words against which the nun put a great approving tick.

'Polly, there's no need to shout,' said Sister St Elizabeth, thinking local children very strange indeed, for Polly was declaiming Robert

Louis Stevenson in a very loud voice, at the same time stealing a glance at the furtive peeper at the window. 'Come, let me read to you.'

Both in school and at home, when she received the ardent visitor who begged to look at her books and exclaimed over her colouring pencils, Polly exploited the privileged status of one sent to an English school; no small compensation for a girl with little promise of future beauty. With an air of supreme importance, she traced each word on each page with a pudgy forefinger and made Mei Kwei repeat after her: 'Here comes the Tick Tock Man.'

The Tick Tock Man, a Chinese itinerant hawker pushing his food cart with one hand and knocking wooden clappers with the other, was a concession to local culture by the colonial education authorities. With the Indian policeman, easily identified by his turban and beard, and the Malay fisherman on the steps of his thatched hut on stilts, in his peaceful *kampong* of swaying coconut palms, the Chinese Tick Tock Man formed the obligatory racial trio in school reading books, a demonstration of racial equality in a mixed society. For too long, said the British authorities, native children had been fed on an unrealistic diet of John and Mary and their dog Woof, of English elves and castles, of woods in springtime they would never see. Little brown and yellow children recited English nursery rhymes and, for their school concerts, paraded as Little Bo-Peep and Jack and the Beanstalk. If political independence were to be granted in due course of time, the people should not lose touch with their own culture.

Sister St Elizabeth went to a great deal of trouble to get simplified editions of *Grimms' Fairy Tales*, *The Water Babies* and *A Christmas Carol* for her pupils, of whom Polly proved the most enthusiastic, clamouring to be the first to read aloud in class, the first to copy out lists of words on the blackboard. Mei Kwei stood humbly by the great table of learning, waiting for the crumbs that might be tossed at her or procured by her with some ingenuity. A pretty plastic hair-clip secured a reading of 'Hansel and Gretel', a bag of rubber seeds a retelling of the life of St Agnes, a compliment a lesson on spelling, for Polly had enough shrewdness not to give something for nothing, and Mei Kwei had a matching shrewdness to resort to flattery once the material resources ran out.

Peeping into the magical world of learning, Mei Kwei ached to be allowed to go to school, carry books, sit on a bench to listen to the teacher, even perhaps to tell stories to the teacher and her classmates.

'Why would a girl want to go to school? A foreign school, at that.' Her mother, washing clothes in a tub, frowned her disapproval. 'If you are so keen,' she added, 'go and ask your father,' knowing the girl would never go to ask her father, by now an opium recluse, his presence marked by a closed door and the small sounds of preparation and ingestion.

The arrangement was beginning to impose special strains, as when Mei Kwei had to complete skinning an entire bucket of soaked peanuts in readiness for the restaurant people to collect by early afternoon, yet felt an overpowering urge to run to St Margaret's convent for a lesson on Peoples of Exciting Lands which Sister St Elizabeth had promised the day before. The lesson, she knew, would be accompanied by pictures, which Sister would hold up for the class to see, perhaps even long enough for her to scrutinize from her position at the window.

'Where is that child gone again?' muttered Ah Oon Soh, and shook her head, for the bucket of peanuts was gone too.

Skinning the nuts and peeping at the same time, Mei Kwei managed to see most of the pictures. She had slipped out of the house with the bucket covered by a piece of cloth. The work crinkled the skin of her fingers and numbed her hands, but it had to be done. Two small Malay children from the nearby *kampong* came to watch her, but she ignored them.

Another day, it rained. There were no protective eaves against the rain beating in; no protective umbrella to be spared from home, which in any case would draw attention to her presence. So she found a large plastic sheet in the chicken yard, dirty and foul-smelling, and cleaned it secretly, well away from the disapproving mother and prying brother. But it was no use. She still got wet from the rain. And the puddles of rainwater that collected so quickly around her feet ruined her slippers. Rainy days were lost days.

'Please teach me to write my name. And the sums. And tell me the story of the princess with the long hair.' Mei Kwei had only caught parts of the fascinating tale and was frustrated not to know what happened after the princess let down her long, golden hair from her prison tower, for her lover to make into a rope to climb up to her.

There was a limit to Polly's bounty. Indeed, she was becoming unfriendly. The threat of brains in league with beauty was beginning to present itself: it would be intolerable if the playmate who attracted looks of admiration from boys and adults also turned out to be cleverer than her.

'Go away, don't come to St Margaret's again,' said Polly, adding darkly, 'If you do, I will tell Sister and she will take you to the police station. We have to pay school fees to go to school.'

Mei Kwei had learned that open opposition was futile. She drew from a small bag she was carrying the largest guava, nursed and protected against birds through a careful wrapping of paper through the weeks of its ripening on the tree behind her house. It was a miracle that her brother had not noticed it and claimed first possession; she had watched it grow, the ultimate gift to buy yet one more visit to the school before her secret broke and the authorities banished her forever.

Polly looked at the beautiful offering, perfect in its size, colouring and promise of pure eating pleasure. 'All right,' she said. 'Just one more time.'

As Mei Kwei handed over the gift, she hoped that her tree would be a never-ending supply of fruit.

Her last visit to St Margaret's convent school was made with much sacrifice of comfort: a swarm of mosquitoes buzzed round her arms and legs, a mangy dog threatened to bite. The discomfort disappeared in the thrill of the discovery of her own powers. Second Grandmother had once said, tapping her forehead with a forefinger, 'You have much up there, more than that useless –' and had refrained from mentioning her brother who, as male grandchild, should have received the most attention and approbation.

Second Grandmother would have been delighted to witness the manifestation of that brightness. Mei Kwei, watching Sister St Elizabeth struggle to elicit the answers to a previous history lesson from a patently dull class, mouthed each correct response silently and longed to shoot up a hand, shout out an answer: 'Ask me, Sister. I know! I know!'

Flustered, Sister St Elizabeth next tried to get the class to recite a poem they were supposed to have learned by heart a week ago. One by one they faltered, some unable to go beyond the first stanza.

Polly stood up bravely, but looked stupid as she racked her brains to remember.

'Come on, Polly,' said Sister St Elizabeth severely. And she waited, almost with grim relish, to put this noisy, boastful child in her place.

I know! I know! thought Mei Kwei. In her excitement, she moved from window to doorway, and began to recite the poem loudly, in full hearing of the class, and perhaps even of the adjoining one of Sister St

Agatha, separated by a low wooden partition. Everyone turned to look at her, but she recited on, her heart pounding inside her, her eyes bright and shining, her voice steady. She would never again, in the course of her life, hear about or read Tennyson, but now, as she stood in the doorway, her legs badly bitten by mosquitoes, her *samfoo* reeking from heat and sweat, she recited, flawlessly, one stanza after another, the much-loved poem of a playful English brook, expressing, in convincing tones, the exuberant love of the English countryside, of the wondrous haunts of coot and hern. It was unfamiliar to her little world of tropical heat, dirty chicken yards, weird coffins, irate parents and lost dreams as the magical refrain, 'Men may come and men may go/But I go on for ever', was to the tension-charged atmosphere at home created by her cursing, opium-smoking father.

When she finished, the class of twenty girls stared at her, then turned, as if on cue, to look at Sister St Elizabeth who, all this while, had stood gazing at the interloper-turned-enchantress.

'Girls, open your books at page twelve, and learn all the Spelling words there.' The nun intended to keep the class occupied for a full ten minutes at least, and was determined to use that time to question the strange visitor.

'Recite that poem again.'

The child complied, her cheeks glowing.

'Recite . . .' The nun raked her memory for more poems she had taught the class. The girl recited Tennyson, Robert Louis Stevenson, Blake without any help.

Tyger, Tyger, burning bright
In the forests of the night.

The girl's eyes, sparkling in her triumph, were brighter than any tiger's.

'Wait!' Sister St Elizabeth had to have a witness. She bustled off and brought Sister St Agatha. She made the girl recite each poem again.

'All learned while she was hanging about outside the windows,' she whispered to her fellow nun.

Sister St Agatha proceeded with her own tests.

'Three times twelve. Spell "apple", "tiger", "woman". Spell "Malaya". Spell St Margaret's. Write your name here.'

It turned out that the girl could not write her own name. But she gave, in flawless English, a brief description of herself, based on the easy formula devised for beginners. 'My name is Oon Mei Kwei. I am eleven years old. I was born in nineteen thirty-four. My father's name is Oon Seng Huat. My mother's name is Chan Poh Choo. I have one brother. His name is Oon Chye Leong. We live at number four, Lorong Hijau . . .'

'Amazing,' said Sister St Agatha. She had not finished yet. She began 'Our Father, who art in heaven . . .' and the girl finished the prayer for her, then went on to say the Hail Mary, having the impression they were one continuous prayer.

Secular knowledge was admirable enough; touched with Christianity's fervour, it was magical.

In the later years, during some of their happiest moments together before the storm broke and they had to flee, Mei Kwei told her lover of the heady victory of that morning. 'Do you still remember those poems?' he asked. She recited them for him, but not the Lord's Prayer nor the Hail Mary, which would have been out of place in that secret, guilty setting.

'Amazing,' said Sister St Agatha again. She always made a fervent sign of the Cross in the presence of good or evil. She made one now in wonder. 'You can never tell, with some of these native children.'

'Can you wait till one o'clock?' said Sister St Elizabeth. Mei Kwei nodded. She had no watch, but knew what one o'clock meant: dismissal time. The nun invited her into the classroom, made her sit on a chair at the back and put a story book in her hand to read, then went back to resume teaching her class till one o'clock.

There was one moment of pure gratification, at one o'clock, when she was led into the black Ford by Sister St Elizabeth, and turned round briefly to see Polly staring stupidly, her mouth hanging open.

After some difficulty the Malay driver found the house, good-naturedly manoeuvring the car along narrow dirt tracks, a muddy puddle, fallen tree branches. Sister St Elizabeth and Sister St Agatha got out with a great flourish of purpose, watched by some of the neighbours' children pointing and giggling, and launched straight into her good work of the day. She asked to see the father, but it was the mother she found herself talking to, a pinched, tired-looking woman, who stood up from a large tub of washing, her trousers half rolled up her calves, her bewildered eyes looking from the white devil women in their strange nun's habits to her daughter standing quietly beside them and back to the intimidating visitors. Sister St Elizabeth graciously but firmly brushed aside all hospitable offers of a seat and a cup of tea, and got down to business. Rosy-cheeked, blue-eyed, in her severe medieval habit of white and black, she seemed to have stepped out of another dimension of time and space, a freak in the service of Empire's noble ideals.

Mei Kwei translated slowly but confidently, surprising her mother with her use of the foreign language. Ah Oon Soh had heard her speaking the language with her friend Polly, but to hear her talk to these important foreign people was a shock indeed. In one of her rare good moods, Ah Oon Soh would imitate the *fftt fftt* and *sshh sshh* sounds for the amusement of her friends. Now she could only stare, a tremendous frown wrinkling her brow. It turned out that Sister St Agatha could speak a little colloquial Malay, enough to convey the purpose of the visit.

'But her father would never allow her to go to your school. You must talk to her father.' Shifting the burden of decision to her husband, Ah Oon Soh went to get him from his room. After a while, he came out reluctantly, not wanting to look at, much less talk to any strange white devil women.

The nuns explained, persuaded, pleaded. Bright child. The brightest they had seen since coming to the country. A great pity if. Great opportunity lost. Education for girls just as important. Parents must understand. Unused to articulate females and increasingly disliking the boldness of these two foreign nuns, Ah Oon Koh finally said he would leave the decision to his wife, and went back to his room. The nuns once more turned to Ah Oon Soh. By this time, Big Older Brother had appeared, watching everything keenly from a corner. Always alert for new situations providing yet more evidence of the foreign devils' misdemeanours that would add to his arsenal of scorn, he took in every detail of the white devil women's appearance, including the crucifixes on their chests and the blueness of their eyes.

'No, no, no, she is needed at home – there is work to do. We are very poor people,' Ah Oon Soh protested.

But Sister St Elizabeth already had an answer to that. There would hardly be any money involved. No school fees, free textbooks. The teaching order of the Holy Infant Jesus would not be true to its noble ideals if it allowed such mundane considerations as school fees to stand in the way of a truly deserving girl. In a country where females were shockingly discriminated against, there was every reason to bear down all parental objections on behalf of this bright, lovely, courageous child.

Ah Oon Soh said, 'All right, all right. Who am I to say anything? I'm a poor uneducated woman,' and in that utterance, found truth and its pain: the poverty and the degradation of her life might have been obviated by education. She turned to her daughter and, for the first time, asked her, 'Would you like to go to school?'

CHAPTER NINE

With the fulfilment of a dream she had not thought possible, Mei Kwei now set about pleasing everyone. The work of peanut-skinning and cigarette-rolling was reduced, but she was prepared to do her best, sometimes falling asleep over the mounds of soaked nuts, sometimes secretly lamenting the smells and stains of tobacco on her fingers from the cigarette-rolling, surely something the holy nuns in St Margaret's convent would not approve of.

'All right, go to sleep now. I'll do the rest.' Her mother proved kinder than Mei Kwei had expected. She had had something saved from her share of the peanuts and rolled-cigarettes money, woefully insufficient for the new clothes and shoes needed for school. 'What to do?' Ah Oon Soh said, but went out immediately and bought the cloth for the clothes, a pair of sandals, and a bag to put her books in. She sewed new blouses and trousers on the Singer sewing-machine, as well as new pairs of knickers.

Mei Kwei could not remember a happier time. Every morning, with well-scrubbed face and neatly plaited hair, and a slice of bread sprinkled with sugar, carefully wrapped in paper, she made her way to St Margaret's convent. There was a classmate who was so timid her mother had to accompany her to school every day, sit through the recess with her and take her home. Another girl cried throughout the torture of adding, subtracting and spelling. Yet a third, a tall, lanky Indian girl with a squint, needed the threat of stern ruler and sterner voice to read correctly from her textbook. Mei Kwei, several years behind them in school, outstripped them all and went on to be a serious competitor to the most advanced in the class. Polly, undecided about whether to make her foe or ally, went through a crisis and resorted to carrying tales about her to the nuns one day, and offering to lend her a favourite colouring pencil on another.

'Very good progress,' Sister St Elizabeth wrote in her report card.

'Father, please sign my report card.'

68

She stood timidly at the doorway of his room, with the card. He ignored her and continued smoking his opium pipe.

'Ask your mother.'

'Father, Teacher says –'

He got up with a growl, looked for a pen, took the one she was holding out to him, wrote his signature, handed back the pen and was once more with his pipe.

'Father, see, no red ink!'

If he had loved her, she would have drawn his attention not only to the absence of the condemnatory red ink, but the rows of laudatory blue and read to him the warm comments in Sister St Elizabeth's neat, flowing hand.

She never missed a day of school. There was a morning of thunderstorms on which very few of the children turned up. No umbrella could have withstood the violence of wind and lashing water. Even the trishawmen, setting up canvas curtains to protect their young charges inside their vehicles gave up and waited out the storm in the shelter of the covered walkways of the town's shops. A teacher, a Mrs de Cruz, who had decided to go home for the day since no pupil had appeared, saw her shivering in a corner of the classroom, drenched, clutching her books, which were safe and dry in a careful wrapping of plastic.

One morning, she went to school and found the gate locked and the grounds empty. There was a moment of panic in which the wildest of fears darted through her mind: had the nuns changed their minds about her and, emptied the whole school to punish her and drive her away for ever? She hung around for a while, miserably. Then the rustling of leaves and branches made her look up. The school caretaker, a scrawny old Indian, given the job more out of the nuns' charity than any belief in his competence, was trying to knock down a bunch of ripe *rambutans* in one of the trees beside the school. Caught by Mei Kwei, he made a lot of fuss over her mistake in coming to school on a holiday, but as he tried to distract her attention from the stolen fruit lying in a neat pile on the grass. He offered her a handful, and she turned away.

Once Mei Kwei was absent from school for three days. But even if she had not felt unwell, she would not have wanted to risk the embarrassment of her swollen cheeks and neck, painted in vivid blue indigo mixed with vinegar, and bearing the Chinese character for 'Tiger', which a neighbour, born in the Year of the Tiger, had been specially requested to write with his finger. Sister would have exclaimed, 'Gracious, what's that?' and she would have had to tell the story of how the tiger, now alive on her cheeks, would gobble up the hateful swellings of the mumps and restore her to health. There were some stories she was ashamed to tell Sister.

She loved all Sister's stories. Sister would either read from a book or tell the tales in simplified language, with the help of a great deal of gesturing and play-acting that she made the pupils do. Thus the girls had to get up from their benches and go to the front to enact scenes of children falling asleep on riverbanks, waking up to the touch of a fairy wand, skipping about to avoid the stout stick of the wicked stepmother, dilating their eyes in astonishment at a frog turning into a prince or a pumpkin into a coach. Sister St Elizabeth became ambitious and embellished action with stage props such as golden crowns made from cardboard and the thin silver wrappers collected from cigarette boxes, and queenly robes made from discarded blankets or sarongs.

One day Mei Kwei breathlessly handed over her contribution of a string of red beads, which she had found among her mother's possessions, and a hat that had once belonged to her father. She begged Sister to tell only stories with happy endings, where tears shed in sorrow became iridescent jewels, rainbows, stars, where a young girl, drowning in a river, was mourned until a beautiful flower magically appeared on the spot where she had died.

My star pupil, thought the nun, in a glow of gratification at having rescued her from squalor and ignorance. One day we foreign nuns will have to hand over the work to the locals. We must begin to nurture them now. For Sister St Elizabeth, whose dreams of advancing God's glory on earth took on the roseate hues of romance, already saw a young Chinese face framed by the white wimple of her beloved order, the small Chinese frame draped by the black robe. Indeed, she saw a long line of Chinese, Indian and African brides of Christ in an ultimate fulfilment of the divine call to plant the Cross on every shore. The dream could begin with this unusually bright girl, who valued education so much she thieved it from under their noses.

Inspiration and edification would be the first step. Mei Kwei loved the stories of saints, sometimes told to her exclusively, since she was the chosen one. The glittering pantheon of holy nuns and virgin martyrs that had irradiated Sister St Elizabeth's girlhood dreams was now brought into her world. For a while, Mei Kwei struggled with difficult, almost unpronounceable names, Barbara, Tryphena,

Philomena, Cecilia, Augusta, Teresa, and difficult, almost inconceivable notions, such as the nothingness of physical pain, of having hands, feet, and breasts cut off, the body thrown to wild beasts, in relation to the glory of martyrdom. Sister showed her a picture of St Agatha looking heavenwards, holding a golden platter on which lay two lovely creamy buns – or were they some exotic fruit?

The saint's breasts, said Sister St Elizabeth. The saint would rather have her body mutilated than defiled.

Mei Kwei stared at the offering on the gold plate, deeply impressed. She recollected the time her mother had denuded her of her beauty for a higher good, and felt ashamed of her unwillingness to make the sacrifice.

These were all brides of Christ, Sister St Elizabeth explained, who saved their beauty, the true beauty of a pure body and soul, for the Divine Bridegroom, Jesus Christ.

Mei Kwei was puzzled by the tremendous value put on virginity, the ultimate gift to a male, recollecting her mother's severe warning to her to preserve it only for her husband and no one else. She knew it resided somewhere in her private body, this precious thing belonging to women, making its existence known to men with the first drops of secret blood. Nuns saved their virginity for a naked, blood-splattered man nailed on a cross: was blood a two-way gift?

Brides found to be unpristine, her mother had once told her, were put in pig-baskets since they had no greater value than low animals. How did the Christian God punish similarly errant brides?

But she refrained from asking Sister St Elizabeth such rude questions, sensing her displeasure at any intrusion, no matter how slight, of the pagan world. No faint whiff of joss scent followed her to school. As soon as she lit the morning joss-stick at her grandmother's altar and stuck it in the urn, she fled that world. No tale of the Lightning God or of Kuan Yin or of her grandmother's visit to the Ancient Fortune-teller at the Kek Lok temple had ever passed her lips during story-telling time since the day her picture of the bright-faced Monkey God during drawing time had incurred the displeasure. But returning home from school, she returned to the old gods brooding in their temples and shrines, who resented the advent of the new, and issued their own warnings.

'Mei Kwei, what is that?'

The sharpness in Sister's voice made her raise a hand instinctively to the object of guilt that all this time she had been trying to hide under her blouse.

'Let me see.'

Sister deftly caught the twisted strand of red cotton thread round her neck and pulled out the offending object. Mei Kwei's fingers reached up to hide it, but Sister brushed them away.

'You must not wear such things to school.' And Sister turned and walked away in cold displeasure.

Mei Kwei wanted to run after the nun and cry out, 'Second Grandmother gave it to me,' but the very next day, she removed the amulet, a small triangular cloth pouch to fend off evil spirits, and kept it in a drawer. Then she went on an energetic campaign of reclamation, working harder than ever at her reading and spelling and arithmetic, to earn back the smiles and nods of approval.

'What was your favourite subject in school?' he had asked her, in that later time of their joyful secret meetings, when the silences, threatening to be awkward, were quickly filled by innocuous questions about childhood. What was your favourite subject? Favourite food as a child. Games you played. Geography was especially innocuous. He asked, 'Does it rain here throughout the year?' And she asked, 'What is snow like?'

She remembered a geography lesson best of all, in that brief, exciting time of school. More than the reading lessons in which she shone, the story-telling sessions in which she revelled, it stayed in her memory with the sweetest of fragrances because it had the aspect of a prediction. Sister St Elizabeth had brought a large globe to class, placed it on the centre of her table and invited the girls to gather round to be shown the countries of the world.

'This is Malaya,' she said. She spun the globe, with its pleasing colours of light blue, red, pink, white, green. This is Ireland where Sister St Agatha and I come from. This is England. The girls took turns, breathlessly, to spin the magical orb of knowledge. When it was her turn, Mei Kwei did a tremendous spin, blurring the globe. She watched for it to come to a standstill, her eyes bright with excitement.

'What's the name of this country?' she asked Sister St Elizabeth, pointing, and was told, 'France.' Sister had added, 'The home of our teaching order of the Holy Infant Jesus,' but she remembered only the name of the country, and she told her lover, in that happy time, adding, 'Now wasn't that strange? Your country.'

72

The enthusiasm in the classroom was continued at home where in the evenings, after helping her mother with the housework, she sat down at the table in the kitchen and did her homework in the light of a kerosene lamp.

'What's that?' Big Older Brother asked, looking over her shoulder, pointing at something in a textbook or copy book.

She stiffened at his approach, sensing mischief in the exaggerated tones of interested enquiry and praise. Ignoring him would hasten the mischief, so she said, quietly and warily, without looking at him, 'Sister says we have to do three pages of handwriting.'

She copied, slowly and laboriously in impeccable script, the irrefutable proverb 'A rolling stone gathers no moss', watched by Big Older Brother who was planning the next move. 'Read it to me. I like to hear the *fftt fftt* and *sshh sshh* sounds of the white devils' language.'

Every morning, the boy went out and sat on a tree-stump along a road that led to St Joseph's school, to taunt the white man's shit-eaters, the schoolchildren walking to school, their hair neatly slicked down with cream or water, their bags of books in their hands. He made appreciative smacking sounds. 'Does it taste good?' The children walked past him, silently and sulkily, ignoring the *ping* of a rubber seed hitting forehead or arm. His sister had stepped over to the side of the enemy and was lost irrevocably to him.

Then teasing turned to savagery.

Mei Kwei had to be careful to hide her school books from Big Older Brother. He searched them out and drew long ugly lines in charcoal across their covers or smeared them with dirty hands. He snatched her *Oxford Reader*, turned to a page, read loudly from it with great contortions of face and voice, then ran screaming out of the house, pursued by her.

'Please, Big Older Brother, please don't.' For he was running up the steps to the lavatory outside the house and threatening to drop the book into the receiving bucket. 'Please don't.' The book fell with a sickening plop into the bucket.

Mei Kwei trembled with fear when Sister St Elizabeth opened her spelling book and saw violent lightning zigzags across a whole page. She said it was her brother's doing and burst into tears. Expecting punishment, she stopped crying in dazed astonishment when Sister took her by the hand to a corner of the classroom and poured her a hot drink of Ovaltine from a flask. From that day, she followed the nun everywhere in the school, carrying her bag of books, cutting paper for her, watching her eat her egg sandwiches during recess. She learned the names of the nuns she had never met, who resided and taught in the main Bukit Tuas Convent. Sister St Ignatius, Sister St Fabian, Sister St Philomena, Sister St Augustine, the unfamiliar names of ancient Roman virgins and martyrs tying her eager little tongue in fearful knots.

Placating, she found, was more effective than protesting. Mei Kwei quickly learned the strategy of placation and raised it to a level of subtlety beyond her years. Her brother, three years older and twice her size, could be induced, in the midst of unruly display, to quieten down enough to respond to the cajoling sweetness of voice she mobilised for the offer of a story. For she had long discovered the power of story-telling to quell unruliness. The power was not the less for depending on gross flattery.

'Teacher told us a story about a boy your age. Just as strong. Fought a giant. Page ten.' She held her breath and sighed with silent relief at the response.

'Show me.' He handed back the book.

She riffled busily and noisily through the pages, telling, with breathless speed, the story, magically concocted on the spot from bits of oft heard and loved tales, of a boy who climbed a magic plant that grew right into the sky, and killed a giant with one stone from his sling-shot. She knew how to fill the story with precisely those details her brother loved – torn-off limbs, a man forced to eat excrement, a strange horse with three penises, so that by the end of the telling, the boy had forgotten about page ten, or his earlier intention to dunk the book in the swill pail. 'Yah! Stupid stories!' he would say, running off, but could be trapped into listening to more.

It was on her brother's account that she experienced the greatest fear of her school life. Her mother gave her some money, in the form of a large note, which she tied securely in the knot of her handkerchief and put into her blouse pocket, for buying some items of stationery. When she had made her purchases, she planned to retie the change, which should amount to several dollars at least, in her handkerchief and bring it home safely. Half-way through a lesson, she put her hand into her pocket: the handkerchief was gone.

Panic-stricken she searched the pocket again, then the other pockets, then her schoolbag. But the handkerchief, with its precious knot of money, was truly gone. She felt the blood drain from her cheeks, an icy chill in her hands. During recess, she returned to the classroom and frantically searched desks, lifting their tops to peer inside. She scoured the floor, peeped behind doors, ran her fingers along window-ledges. In despair, she sat in a corner and cried.

The search continued after school. She retraced her steps of that morning, scrutinising every inch of the dirt road that was a short-cut to the school, beating every nearby bush with a stick to see if the handkerchief had got caught in a branch. She felt little knots and twists of pain in her stomach, and leaned against a tree, whimpering at the terrifying prospect of a severe beating at home because of so much money lost. To her mother's wrath would be added her brother's; their cries of shock were sure to bring out the dreaded father from his room. The ultimate punishment loomed before her and forced out of her little sounds of pure terror. Big Older Brother would gather up all her school things, drop them into the lavatory bucket or make a bonfire of them.

Sister St Elizabeth had once lost some valuable article, a key or a pen, and had searched all over for it, plunging her hand into her deep skirt pockets, shuffling among the things on her desk. Mei Kwei had helped in the search, hoping to claim the supreme satisfaction of turning Sister's frown of anxiety into the brightness of relief and joy.

'Let's pray to St Jude,' said Sister. Like the traditional Monkey, Lightning and Kitchen gods, the Christian deities had their own domains of power and specialised skills: she would remember to pray to St Jude for recovery of lost possessions, to St Christopher for a safe journey.

Suspending dread for hope, she now prayed with all the fervour she could muster for the return of the knotted handkerchief. She walked slowly along the dirt road, her heart ready to jump in grateful joy at the sight of that small square of white cotton with its print of blue and pink flowers. But the saint, apparently, had not heard her prayer or, having heard, had not thought it worthwhile answering.

'Blessed Virgin Mary.' She decided to bypass the saints for the most exalted deity in Heaven, the Mother of God herself, desperation creating boldness. She recited the Hail Mary faultlessly, three times, and looked again. Still no handkerchief appeared. The tears returned and the chill in her heart as, slowly, she made her way home.

'Kuan Yin, please help me.' The request was in her dialect, appropriately, not in English. She remembered the piety of her grandmother in the temple, and the granting of the prayer. Surely the Goddess of Mercy would show some to her now.

In the later years, when she told him about that day, she left out of her story her disillusionment with his Christian deities, fearing to offend him, and had merely concentrated on Kuan Yin. 'What do you think?' she had said, her eyes shining. 'Wasn't that a miracle?' And he, not to offend her, had not derided her gods, but merely laughed. 'You are such a strange, wonderful exasperating, lovable person, you Chinese woman,' he had said, this being his excuse to stretch out his strong arm and pull her to his side.

Even Sister St Elizabeth would have said it was a miracle. There it was at her feet, not the knotted handkerchief, but a crumpled note of exactly the same value. She bent down, pushed aside the dead leaves around it and picked it up carefully. She smoothed it out on her arm. It was faded through exposure to rain and sun, but there was no mistake – a five-dollar note. She held it in both hands, her heart in a flutter of excitement, both at the immediate generosity of the goddess Kuan Yin and the thrilling prospect of going to the stationery shop for a second round of purchases. Lasting allegiances to gods and deities being forged on a single proof of miraculous power, she remained loyal to Kuan Yin all her life.

Mei Kwei now entered the happiest, most fruitful year of her short time in school, cresting a great wave of exuberant energy and hope. Sister St Elizabeth gave her additional private lessons in English grammar, reading, writing, in pursuit of that worthy goal set for her almost from the first day of her astonishing entry into education. She also put in Mei Kwei's hands a little catechism book, to wean her for ever from her dark paganism.

'I have the name you should give yourself when you are baptised as a Catholic,' said Sister. 'Maria!' It was, oddly, not after the Virgin Mary but an obscure little girl saint in Italy who had died at the age of twelve in a heroic defence of her virginity. Mei Kwei loved the story of St Maria Goretti, who chose to keep that jewel in her private body rather than surrender it to a coarse, brutal man.

In her privileged position, she noted, with cool detachment, the jealous writhings of her friend Polly.

'I want all back, give them all back.' Having exhausted all means in class to discomfit her, Polly resorted to the extreme act of final severance by demanding back everything either loaned or given. The next morning, Mei Kwei left on her desk a paper bag filled mostly with discarded textbooks and exercise books. The confused Polly, oscillating wildly in her feelings, was at once enemy and friend, admirer and detractor, confidante and traitor, one morning going to Sister St Elizabeth to whisper that the disreputable amulet from the grandmother was still being worn, not around the neck, but fastened to the inside of the blouse with a safety-pin. Unknown to her, it would be in the role of admirer that she would bring the greatest ruin to her friend.

She had come hurrying in great excitement to see Mei Kwei on a school holiday, with a story book that a relative in Penang had given her. As loan only, the book nevertheless gave tremendous pleasure, Mei Kwei actually writing out an entire story into one of her many copy books, ingeniously made by sewing together the numerous small square pieces of paper that had been discarded, one by one, from the daily calendar hanging on the wall. Every morning, to mark the start of a new day, the father emerged from his room, tore off a piece from the sheaf, crumpled it and threw it to the ground. Every day she picked it up, smoothed it carefully and saved it. She had made a cover for her book and written her name proudly on it. It was a special possession.

Delightedly the girls read their favourite story together, then to each other. Perhaps it was the secret triumph of an acquisition beyond the reach of everyone around them in the house and the neighbourhood, including the obnoxious brother, who hovered around with malicious intent, and the bedraggled neighbourhood children, who gathered to watch and listen to the strange tongue as the girls did a little play in a patch of shade outside the house, one taking the part of Sister St Elizabeth and the other Sister St Agatha.

Whatever the cause, the girls carried their association with the foreign culture to a dangerous degree, for their shrill, giggling voices penetrated the walls of Ah Oon Koh's room and filled him with intense irritation. The opium fumes mingled with the fumes of his rising annoyance to make him snort, then splutter. The foreign sounds were irritating enough; clothed with the superiority which, he was certain, the two girls meant to show non-speakers, they made the blood boil. But still, Ah Oon Koh went on smoking quietly. Then a burst of angry voices made him pause and sit up. He could hear his son's voice, raised in shouts, and the girls' also raised, still in the hateful language. A peal of mocking female laughter was the limit: he got up from his bed, left the room, stood in the house doorway, in full view of the offenders, and bellowed his rage. The girls stopped talking immediately and looked frightened; the boy turned to them with a sly grimace and cocked an obscene finger, to seal his triumph.

Mei Kwei and her classmates were reciting ''Twas the night before Christmas' after Sister St Elizabeth, who had written the words on the blackboard and made the girls copy them. The story of the Magi and the legend of St Nicholas had been told many times, and now a little secularity – in the way of light-hearted poems, a Christmas tree hung with colourful beads that the girls had collected and a cardboard cut-out of a house topped with cotton-wool – was allowable.

'Ask me, Sister! I know! I know!' cried Mei Kwei, ever ready to maintain her position in class as best memoriser. Then she turned and saw her father in the doorway of the classroom. She fell silent and stared, and pairs of eyes, including Sister's, also fixed themselves on the bitter solitary figure at the door.

Ah Oon Koh scanned the sea of faces, located his daughter's and walked straight up to her. 'Get up.' For she had, in a sudden chilling and weakening of limbs, sat down on her bench. 'Get up.' He pulled her up. 'Get your things. You're coming home with me now.'

The tone of finality in his voice allowed for no hope; no domestic exigency such as a sudden illness or accident at home requiring immediate but only temporary absence from school, but an inexorability of will that spelt permanent severance. She made the mistake of looking at him with large, challenging eyes: he had ever hated that defiance. 'GET UP!' he roared, and pushed at her shoulder.

Slowly, methodically, Mei Kwei gathered her small possessions and put them, one by one, into her bag. Stunned into silence, Sister St Elizabeth and her classmates watched her. The last item, a small stump of a pencil attached to a stick for continued use, was dropped into the bag, at the same time as someone, a tall, thin girl whom Mei Kwei did not much like, moved towards her and thrust a picture book awkwardly at her. Not a farewell gift, but stolen property returned: in the last few days, she had been looking frantically for the lost favourite book and had at last given up. Now, when it no longer mattered, the thief turned contrite.

Polly's eyes never left her friend's pale face. Fearful of the father's rage, now filling the room like a malevolent miasma, she recollected its beginnings on that day of her visit and was more concerned to stay outside the orbit of the anger than to question her own part in it. She stepped behind a tall, large girl and watched everything from the protection of the broad back.

In his impatience, Ah Oon Koh took over the elaborate closing of the school-bag, with its numerous buckles, and picked it up himself. Then he took his daughter's hand and jerked it to get her up from the long wooden bench she shared with three other pupils.

78

'Hurry up,' he hissed.

Sister St Elizabeth said, 'Mr Oon, you can't take your daughter out of school like this.'

'HURRY UP!' he roared.

While all watched, he led her out of the classroom, pulling her along so that she broke into a run. Outside the school, he led her to his bicycle parked in the shade of a tree. He hung her bag on the handle-bars, and lifted her on to the pillion. Then he pedalled away furiously in the hot morning sun.

Till the end of her life, Mei Kwei remembered the shame and the loss.

It made her ill immediately. Her mother tried to stem the vomiting and fever with bowls of herbal brews, which Mei Kwei rejected, crying silently into her pillow. On the third day, Sister St Elizabeth, accompanied by a Chinese teacher acting as translator, paid her second and last visit to the house.

Despising the crude, coarse man, she nevertheless marshalled all her resources of gentle persuasion. Ah Oon Koh refused to see her, but in the end came out sullenly because she refused to go away. The intelligence, the brilliance, the rare talent. It was no use, so Sister St Elizabeth, exhausted, tried a different tack. The promise of good jobs, even for girls, especially for girls, in the new world rising from the ashes of war. Sister St Elizabeth was able to give several convincing examples. Never losing her amiability of tone, the nun thought, with unbecoming venom: This man deserves to go to jail for denying his daughter an education. Perhaps hell, too.

Ah Oon Koh's silence was not to be taken for relenting: it was merely to exhaust the nun's loquacity. When Sister paused for breath, he said, very politely, 'It is done. It is my will,' instructed his wife to give the visitors tea and went back into his room, bolting the door noisily.

In her room, under a blanket, Mei Kwei heard the engine of the Ford starting, and listened to the sounds of the departure, and the final collapse of her dream. She thought, Sister knows I'm ill. Why didn't she come to see me? and would not have understood the greater kindness of the omission.

Sister St Elizabeth made a last effort. She contacted the local education authorities but was told parents' decisions should always be respected.

Big Older Brother hovered at the doorway of the room where his sister lay ill, struck less by contrition than the hope that illness might prove useful, as in the early years, for a renewal of ties. When she recovered, he continued to hover round her, meaning to be helpful, to elicit a smile. He went to town and came back with some bean-paste buns, which he offered to her. The next evening Mei Kwei found a brown-paper packet containing a large rice dumpling – her favourite, with minced pork and mushroom filling – on her bed, clearly tossed there by her father from the doorway. Even when relenting, he could not demean himself by going into women's rooms where their underclothes hung from pegs. Angrily, Mei Kwei pushed the brown-paper packet away with her foot and heard the dumpling drop on to the floor.

That night, Mei Kwei waited till everybody was asleep, then slipped out through the back into the darkness. There was a thin curl of a moon in the sky, providing a little light. She untied the bundle that she was carrying and spread its contents on the hard ground. The treasured textbooks were the first to go. She ripped the covers and pages, pushed them into a pile and lit a match. She watched the creamy white paper curl into ash, watched the little bright licks of fire creep along the pink and blue contours of Great Britain, swallow up the smiling face of the Tick Tock Man, crunch multiplication tables, wipe out the entire population of *Grimm's Fairy Tales*. Then she set to work on the exercise books and watched the flames, now greedy and powerful, devour pages of perfect script in the handwriting copy book, compositions decorated with approving red ticks in the margin and glowing marks at the bottom, drawings showing human faces and fruit and buildings in joyous colours. The precious book of the compiled calendar sheets, a massive sheaf, resisted the onslaught but finally succumbed. Pencils, a ruler, an eraser and a pencil-sharpener were the last to go; she put them together in a little pile and pushed them into the flames.

Not quite the last: she slipped back into the house and brought out her little tin box of treasures. One by one, she took them out, fingering each slowly, almost tenderly, before consigning them to the now roaring flames: the pretty sweet wrapper, its gold and silver tints almost all faded, from the Japanese soldier; the coin from her father before he turned virulent and cursed the teardrop mole on her face; the silver baby anklet from Second Grandmother, which her mother had almost taken away to pawn or sell; the holy medal and holy pictures from Sister St Elizabeth. She watched each one crumble and blacken in the flames. Then she put her hand to her neck and pulled from her blouse the red thread necklace, kept in secret defiance of

Sister, who would not have been placated by the sight of the Blessed Virgin's medal dangling in easy conjunction with Kuan Yin's cloth amulet. She dropped both together into the fire.

In the morning, they would all be a blackened, charred mound, inviting questions or sharp words. If it rained, as it was threatening to do, there would be nothing left; every vestige of her dream would have been blown away or washed into the earth.

Mei Kwei stood up, raised a hand to her cheeks and felt the wetness of tears shed for the devastation of her life. In the rising wind, she watched the darkness where the moon had been, and felt another wetness. Shifting about uncomfortably, she put her hand to her inner thighs: a dampness seeped through the thin cotton of her trousers on to her skin. She held up her hand and, in the faint light of the still glowing embers, saw the traces of first blood. A small cry escaped her. It had come, as her mother had said it would. Then, falling on her knees before the smouldering embers, she gave another small, sharp cry, as a new and fearsome world broke upon her.

PART TWO

第二章

CHAPTER TEN

In 1953, Father François Martin was sent from his native Provence to the small Malayan town of Luping to save souls. The saving of lives was already being done competently by the British. The British servicemen and their families did not live in the town itself but outside in special large houses whose high ceilings, open verandas and spacious gardens permitted at least a measure of relief from the tropical heat, and made the carrying out of colonial responsibility less onerous. The townspeople saw little of the onerousness in the congenial evening gatherings of servicemen in the Luping Club, reports of which filtered back through their children who risked the baleful glare of the Sikh watchman to peep through the windows, gasping and gawking at the spectacle of colonial privilege. A spacious wooden building raised above the ground to allow for that free passage of air so desirable to visitors used to cooler climates, the club formed the meeting place of the servicemen, who sometimes brought their wives. The laughter, the language, the clink of ice-cubes in tall glasses, the cool confidence of duty honourably discharged, under the benign gaze of King George VI and Queen Elizabeth on the curtained wall, were of a world removed from the surrounding town, permitting no intrusion from it.

'Look, a native,' whispered one of the ladies, nudging her husband. 'I thought they weren't . . .'

Her husband assured her that it was probably the caterer or electrician, who had come to do business with Ah Hoy and who had blundered as usual through the wrong entrance. Ah Hoy, the bartender, or Jasbir Singh, the Sikh watchman, would tell him to use the right entrance in future.

The lady fanned herself, gathered up her long blonde hair so that she could wipe her neck and face with a handkerchief, then drew her husband's attention to the row of small brown faces peeping in at a window across the room.

'I wish they'd go away,' she said petulantly. 'Ah Hoy says they steal.'

The town children, who came regularly to peep at the *ang moh*, departed with breathless reports of huge sacks of empty beer and whisky bottles and sometimes with the bottles themselves, securely clutched in hands, tucked under arms or stuffed under shirts, which could be sold for three cents each to the *karang guni* man when he came round. They put their money into their ragged pockets and hugged each other in the pure thrill of easy fortune.

The lady listened to her husband and his fellow officers discuss the war they were fighting, which neither Whitehall nor the Malayan government wanted to call a war for fear of making things worse and frightening the locals, who had barely recovered from the trauma of the Japanese occupation. She felt awed by the enormity of the responsibility thrust upon her husband and her friends' husbands. Loyally, she bore her share of the white man's burden, even if it was only at the humble level of a housewife's daily life – the discomfort of the heat and the mosquitoes, the homesickness, the nuisance of the endlessly quarrelling, lying and thieving servants – and was gracious enough, when she took her baby out in the pram in the cool evening, to stop and allow the local women and children to crowd round, exclaim and even touch the small, round, blond head.

The Luping Club and the pretty, talcumed, coolly outfitted wives wheeling prams were not the true reflection of the role of the *ang moh* in Luping, as the local people would be the first to acknowledge. All the proof had to be in the spectacle of the huge military trucks rolling along the town's roads, carrying young British soldiers with their impassive faces and reassuring rifles, on their way to the steaming jungles to flush out and shoot on sight the Communist terrorists. The terrorists had gone too far in their campaign of terror and had alienated even the most sympathetic of the townsfolk; they had taken to murdering innocent people, including women and children.

One dry-goods shopkeeper, suspected (wrongly, it turned out) of being a secret informer for the British, was killed one evening while he was having dinner with his family and relatives. Two terrorists had burst into his house and sliced off his head with a *parang*. It was perhaps unfortunate that, only the week before, he had won a large sum of money in a lottery and decided to throw a lavish dinner for his relatives, ordering from the town's best restaurant a roasted suckling pig, the consummate celebratory item. The pig, magnificently splayed on a platter in the middle of the abundant table, was the first thing the terrorists saw when they burst in. While the terrified guests watched, one of the terrorists, with the bizarre relish of the murderer who would take time and trouble to work the strangling rope on his victim's neck into a decorative bow, did a second decapitation. The suckling pig's head came off with one stroke of the *parang*, was swept off its platter and on to the floor, then replaced by the shopkeeper's amid the delicately carved pink turnip roses. The terrorist did not forget to pull out of his pocket a square piece of white paper with the single word 'Traitor' written in Chinese, and stick it on the head. Then he and his comrade left the house and melted back into the jungle.

A reporter for the local Chinese newspaper was among the first to be at the scene of the murder and promptly took a picture of the head on the plate, its serenely closed eyes in bizarre contradiction to the surrounding savagery.

The boy Tee Tee, his shirt flapping, his chest heaving, ran to Mei Kwei to announce the news of Father François Martin's coming, creating a hurricane path of squawking chickens and flying feathers.

'Oh, do be careful,' said Mei Kwei, looking up from her work of cleaning a basket of vegetables.

The dirt of chicken yards, mean vegetables and meaner clothes soiled and wetted by kitchen and yard work by no means detracted from her beauty. At almost nineteen, she stood above the surrounding squalor like a blooming lotus above its spawning mud, prompting those who looked at her to remark among themselves that it would be only a matter of time before some rich man came to ask for her hand and to pluck her, as well as her family, from poverty and obscurity. For her beauty, it was said, was of that rare kind that benefited family as well, possibly down to some low, opportunistic cousin. In the ancestral country, emperors sent henchmen to scour the mean streets for such a rare jewel, rewarding everyone in the process. In the new country, parental ambitions were somewhat scaled down and if hopes of a sultan's offer were raised by the appearance of royal interest and gifts, they were certainly less realistic than expectations surrounding the many prosperous rubber-plantation owners and tin-miners who came looking for young women as wives or concubines.

If Ah Oon Koh, smoking opium quietly in his room, and Ah Oon Soh, bustling about in nervous energy, had such expectations, they kept them hidden from each other and friends and, most of all, from their daughter, of whose cool hauteur they were beginning to be a little in awe.

'Oh, do be careful.' The coolness melted into a warmth of concern as Tee Tee, to avoid a splatter of chicken dirt, nearly stepped on a sharp pebble. Mei Kwei thought of the time when his hurrying bare feet had picked up a trail of tiny glass fragments. The momentum of eagerness had carried him right through the torment, so that he began to hobble and cry out in pain only when he reached her. Each fragment had to be carefully extracted with a pair of tweezers.

The tenderness was in sharp contrast to the savagery of pinches, tweaks and slaps she had once rained, in a fit of jealous rage, upon the same foot, then only a pathetic assemblage of the tiniest, feeblest baby toes.

'Do you remember?' she had asked him, smiling. Of course he did not, but he had looked at her as if he did, his eyes large and silent with reproach. Now there was only the joy of seeing her again, and Tee Tee kicked the offending pebble out of the way and was ready to give his news.

As tall as a tree, eyes like blue glass, even bluer than Mr Lobinson's, hair all over like a monkey: the child chose to concentrate on the hairiness, the feature best guaranteed to make the newcomer stand out among the scrupulously hairless Chinese.

'As hairy as *keleng kooi*?' Mei Kwei was glad of the reprieve, no matter how brief, from the tedium of washing the mud out of lettuce stalks, pinching off the brown thread-tails of bean sprouts.

The Sikh watchman of the Luping Rest House who was a cousin of the watchman of the Luping Club had a beard so lush it was said to trap enough food after each meal for him to have a second one later if he wanted. Every time his wife ladled out the food during mealtimes, shaking down dollops of rice and curry upon his banana leaf spread on the floor, she would say, 'This one's for you! This one's for your beard!'

'Oh, much hairier!' said the boy, and proceeded to describe the hair growing out of Father Martin's ears. Mei Kwei did not have the heart to rob him of the news-giver's pleasure and privilege of hyperbole. To tell him that she had already seen the priest would have been cruelly deflating.

She got up from her stool, stepped over the basket of vegetables and the bucket of washing water, went inside the house and came back with two biscuits, which Tee Tee received shyly. The last time, it has been a handful of peanuts, and before that, a small coin slipped into his shirt pocket.

A self-appointed vendor of news from the town for a receptive audience of one, he claimed rewards for his trouble. His occupation bore all the marks of careful planning. In the mornings, when the market-place was at its busiest, he wove in and out of the stalls and open-air eating places, as nimble as a monkey, soaking up news and gossip. In the evenings, he went to the town's main coffee-shop where the men gathered to drink and talk, and hovered alertly on the edges of rough adult talk until shooed away.

One of the beer-drinkers dropped a coin. Tee Tee's alert ears picked up the small clinking sound, his alert eyes its final resting place, a crack in the cement floor under the table. As quick to retrieve dropped possessions as news, he wriggled his small body through a formidable phalanx of legs. At the moment of retrieval, a foot descended on his hand, followed by a coarse laugh, drowning his squeal. 'Caught you. Thief as well. You ought to be at school.'

But he was allowed to keep the coin.

Somebody else had called him thief, though he was none. He would have handed the coin back to its owner and not minded if the man had repocketed it and told him to go away. The old vegetable woman in the market-place caught him one morning foraging in her dump.

'*My* dump,' she rasped, and stuck a black umbrella in it. Every day, for twenty years, she had gone to the immense heap of discarded vegetables in a corner of the market and taken away still usable carrots, turnips, cucumbers and onions which, after proper cleaning and slicing, could be sold for a few cents a pile. She shooed Tee Tee off, shouting imprecations in her obscure dialect and shaking the territorial umbrella. She went back, resigned, to her little box-stall in the market-place and lit another joss-stick of supplication to kind gods to punish the transgressions of the young. But as suddenly as he had appeared, Tee Tee disappeared. He didn't like the smell or feel of rotting vegetables.

Never registered for school by his grandmother or mother, he scoured the institutions of learning for both news and good, solid stuff. The news: Ah Kim Soh's son was made to stand on a chair in the sun with his exercise book pinned to his shirt. Later the teacher unpinned the book and hit Ah Kim Soh's son on the head with it, thereby bursting a boil, which ran in a little stream of pus and blood that the teacher quickly cleaned up with his own handkerchief soaked in water. The teacher of the girls' school near the Christian church, a white-haired lady with an unpronounceable *ang moh* name, lined up the girls for a head-lice inspection, pulling out four for the kerosene treatment. Another day, it was a knickers inspection. The teacher's hands felt and found two girls without knickers. The good solid stuff: two halves of a chalk on the ledge of the blackboard as well as a whole pencil from Ah Kim Soh's son's school, an exercise book with five remaining blank pages from the girls' school.

His childhood long ago stolen from him, he had learned to plunder in his turn, venturing back into the child's world of play to scamper away with an unattended toy, a biscuit easily snatched from the inexpert grasp of baby hands.

Tee Tee's store of tales was endless. He pulled them out, one by one, from the marvellous receptacle of his memory, as another child would empty his pocket of a stone, a marble, a piece of string, a half-finished stick of sugar-cane. He used adult words confidently, the shocking language of unspeakable diseases, women's monthly secrets, men's private parts. Birth and death, lust and desire, greed and power, the mundane and the mysterious, the past and the present – all came within the grand sweep of Tee Tee's narrative power, much embellished by a variety of head and arm movements.

He decided to concentrate on Father Martin. For he had noticed a quickening of interest in news about Father Martin. The foreign priest promised immense profit: one sighting could be made to yield several instalments of information, each more engrossing than the last, yielding, in their turn, an endless supply of biscuits, peanuts, coins.

'He is dressed like a woman, in a long white gown with beads around his neck. He wears lipstick, like a woman!' Tee Tee exclaimed, when he came the next morning.

But it was a bad time for story-telling. Ah Oon Soh had just returned from the market with Mei Kwei, lugging three huge baskets of vegetables, fish, prawns and pork. A mangy dog came up and sniffed hungrily at the large slab of meat wrapped in newspaper, atop a pile of vegetables, its fresh blood staining the newspaper. Angrily she shooed the creature away. She was hot and tired. The trishawman had refused to pedal the last stretch, a very narrow footpath, forcing them to get down with their heavy load and trudge the rest of the way home in the hot morning sun.

'Go away!' she hissed in response to Tee Tee's greeting. Unable to free a fist to shake an angry dismissal, she raised her voice in a crescendo of shrieks. 'How dare you – so early in the morning. Thinking other people are as idle as you.'

Big Older Brother came out of the cool shadows inside the house and leaned against the door, blinking in the sunshine and surveying everyone, a toothpick playing between his teeth. A long deep sleep, leaving pillow creases on cheeks and shoulders, produced a pleasing sensation of power as he looked at the sweating women and the frightened boy. He decided to go for the boy.

'A gossiper like your mother, eh? A mother-and-son pair going around town earning a living talking about other people, eh?'

He stood looking down on Tee Tee, swaying with menacing intent. 'Luping's best informer, are you? So you think you know more than other people, do you? Why don't you work for the government and be a big shot in this town?'

Pleased with the hyperbole of his taunt, he stretched it yet further: 'With clever people like you, why, the government will win the war against the terrorists, the British can pack up and go home and everybody will be happy again! So why don't you?'

He punctuated the torrent of scorn with shoves at Tee Tee's thin shoulders. Nursing an impotent rage against the forces of authority and power, he sought to give it potent expression through physical intimidation of women, children, beggars. The hate was rising, as it did almost daily, from its dark, murky depths, tightening the muscles of his face and neck, an anger out of proportion to its convenient target: a mere wisp of a boy who had happened to stray into its dangerous orbit.

Tee Tee fidgeted with a corner of his shirt, sniffed back a thin stream of mucus, lowered his head at the shame of a public chastisement, and then raised it to stare unflinchingly at his aggressor.

'Leave him alone,' said Mei Kwei, with far greater confidence of being heard than if she had said, 'Leave me alone.'

Shrugging his shoulders, Big Older Brother shuffled back into the house.

CHAPTER ELEVEN

In the turbulence of the house, filled with the noise of men eating, of men spitting and burping, of women shrilly ordering tea or coffee above the clack-clack of the mah-jong tiles, Mei Kwei carved out little islands of solitude for herself.

The bathroom should have been one: it had a secure door and, in the late evenings when all the eaters and players had left and the bowls, plates and cups had been washed and stacked away, it had once been a haven for her. Humming the triumphal song of the Moon Maiden and scooping up water from the large cement tank to splash on her face and shoulders, she had been happy. Then, one evening, she turned round suddenly and saw a shadow behind the door adjusting itself around small cracks, testing for maximum viewing. She sensed the solidity of its lust. She snatched up a towel and covered herself. The shadow moved away.

Next morning, she stuffed rags into the cracks in the door but, when she took her bath again, she noticed that they had been poked out.

She took to bathing with her clothes on.

Her anger rose from its dark depths, but she had learned to check it. One morning, when she was sixteen, her father had heard her raise her voice at Big Older Brother. He emerged from his room, walked straight up to her and slapped her across the mouth. Then he had returned to his room, and they heard his opium pipe bubbling once again. Her mother had continued ironing the clothes, a frown of displeasure on her brow. Nobody had spoken a word.

Since then, there had been a kind of peace in the house. Sixteen had marked the end of her father's violence and Ah Oon Koh had never raised his hand to her again.

'Father, here is your medicine.' Mei Kwei intercepted her mother, who was on her way to Ah Oon Koh's room with some herbal brew for his cough. Holding the steaming bowl in both hands, she repeated, 'Father, here's your medicine,' and waited for him to say something.

She was about to speak again when he raised an arm in a swift, impatient gesture to tell her simultaneously that she was to leave the bowl on the table near the door and get out at once.

Later, her mother found her crying. 'I wish Father were dead.'

This time it was her mother's hand that flew across her mouth. 'You stop that! He is your father!' The enormity of the sin of cursing one's own father, punishable by the greater curse of being struck down by the Lightning God, took Ah Oon Soh's breath away. She quivered in her shock, staring at her daughter, who was now calmly looking down and playing with the corner of a handkerchief. 'Why am I so unlucky?' It had become a habit to absorb all the pain in that heaving household into her own general despair.

Ah Oon Soh's shrill responses to life's troubles had cut deep lines into her forehead and turned her voice into a harsh blend of shrieks and rasps, so that on the rare occasions when she laughed she gave the impression of crying.

In the silence of a meal broken only by the slurp of soup, Mei Kwei sensed the violence of hard male stares, above the rims of rice bowls, following her every movement. Their eyes, intrigued by the fullness of her breasts under her blouse, tore it away; tore away, too, the trousers, when they rested for a furtive moment on her taut squatting back as she scrubbed the floor or pounded chillies with the pestle. They followed every small movement: even as she drew an arm across her forehead to wipe off the sweat or brushed up a straying strand of hair, she knew they were watching her. Outside the safety of her house and Big Older Brother's cordon of protective glares directed at every intrusive male visitor, she would have been devoured instantly, suffering the fate of those hapless forebears, way back in the ancestral country, who went to the well or the field and returned home bruised and weeping or who never came back at all, their bodies discovered the next day, hidden in leaves or mud.

One of the men had brushed his hand lightly against her thigh on his way to the lavatory. She pretended not to notice. On his way back, he touched her thigh again. She said, in a low voice, 'Once more, and I'll tell my brother,' knowing she never would. He never touched her again.

Another, who had a dragon tattoo on his right arm, sat on a long wooden bench outside the house, resting and fanning himself after the meal. He had unbuttoned his shirt and, as he fanned himself, picked his teeth and waved away buzzing insects, his small eyes flickered with purpose. In the continual flow of people entering and leaving (there were two separate eating times, as the one large table in the house could seat only eight), one brief moment of opportunity presented itself. He and she were alone, and in walking back into the house after collecting the clothes on the line, she would have to pass by him and face him. At the precise moment, he propped himself up on the bench and struck. He fixed his eyes on hers and gave a low, brutal gurgle; she looked away instantly. By the time someone came outside, he had redone his buttons and put his legs together again.

That evening, she spat three times on the bathroom floor, by way of expunction. Her mother had taught her the ritual of cleansing. When she was about twelve, they had suddenly, on their way home from market, come upon a man standing under a rubber tree with his trousers open, and had hurried home to stand side by side near a drain, where they spat together, three times, into it.

The men were mostly strangers, come in from their hot, dusty worksites for the midday meal. When they laid the payment on the table at the end of each month, in bright crisp notes newly pulled out of their wage envelopes, their eyes, as they followed her, said, 'Ten times this for a chance to sleep with Ah Oon Koh's daughter, talked about so much for her beauty. To strip her of that cold disdain. Or just to peep at her bathing.' Male desire hung heavy in the air, like the smell of rancid soup.

The women mah-jong players' eyes said, 'Who does she think she is? Just because of a little beauty. But look at the unlucky teardrop mole near her eye. Cancels out the beauty.'

The ring of their money on the table was their way of punishing her for her proud beauty. 'Coffee. Tea. Piping hot. The last time you used lukewarm water. Make sure it's right this time.'

With her rolled, netted hair, Auntie Rosie could be particularly sharp, invariably looking up from the mah-jong tiles each time Mei Kwei appeared to stare at a young, blooming beauty that reminded her of what had once been hers but which was now irretrievably sunk into a soft, pallid corpulence and an insipidity of features unredeemed by bright, expensive lipstick or carefully plucked and pencilled eyebrows. Instead, she sought victory through wealth, evident in the stacks of gold bangles on her wrists and a magnificent rope of gold around her neck. Of the mah-jong players, she was the most punctual with the payment, placing the money on the kitchen table before each game and sometimes waving away, with a careless gesture of the gilded arm, the change which, in an effusion of gratitude, Ah Oon Soh would quickly put in her own blouse pocket.

Her daughter would make her return the money. Contemptible mother, proud daughter. Unappeased, Auntie Rosie's vanity dissipated itself in the raucousness of mah-jong tiles.

Coffee was ten cents a cup, tea five. Her mother kept the mah-jong table rent money; Mei Kwei was allowed to keep the drinks money. 'What to do?' asked her mother. Nothing was to be expected of Ah Oon Koh, who had stopped working ten years before and had retreated into his room with his opium pipe, emerging only to scold, punish, eat, go to the lavatory, and ask for money for the next dose. Nothing was expected of Big Older Brother either, whose bad temper made it impossible for him to hold a job. He had fought with a fellow worker in a timber mill and punched out two teeth.

'I will be rich one day and buy a large house for you and Sister,' he promised, in the benign exuberance of beer or the anticipation of seeing the *ronggeng* girls again.

Meanwhile, the midday meals and the mah-jong brought in the money. Meanwhile, too, the interest already expressed by Old Yoong, the well-known millionaire from Penang, who had asked for Mei Kwei's photograph and followed it with a dispatch of his own, together with a generous gift of brandy for the father and sausages and duck for the mother, was promise enough.

CHAPTER TWELVE

'*I have seen him already.*'
She did not like going to the Luping market-place, hating the smell of rotting fowl entrails in the side drains, where they were carelessly flung after each slaughter and of decomposing vegetables in the large dump, always covered with swarms of buzzing insects; or the sight of goats' testicles hanging in obscene ponderousness from iron hooks and overseeing their own dismembered parts on the butcher's cement slab; or the shrill sound of trishaw bells cutting a

carefree path through busy shoppers with large baskets and paper bags on their arms.

The shoppers, no matter how busy, could always be enticed by a megaphone voice in one corner of the large, sprawling market-place, or a growing buzz of people in another, to converge quickly upon the spot to find out what was happening and claim a share of the special excitement that no other place in Luping could offer.

The medicine man was an unfailing draw. In laying out his impressive array of remedies in tantalising little bottles and jars on a large mat on the ground, he collected a sizeable crowd, who squatted down to have a closer look at baby snakes curled up inside jars of murky fluids, powdered rhinoceros' horn, preserved bat's feet, iguana's blood mixed with herbs. The medicine man cleverly mixed comedy with business. At an appropriate point in his delivery, he would announce the testing of his products' rejuvenating powers, bounce up with alacrity, wade into the crowd and drag out, with much aplomb, a confederate – suitably undersized and timid-looking – who would put on a great show of protest.

'For the sake of your wife! You must do it for the sake of your wife!' the medicine man would plead. And the crowd would laugh uproariously.

But this was not the usual crowd collecting around a medicine man's wares or a madman's capers, for a distinct sense of urgency and fear, hushed into silence, gripped the large numbers converging upon someone or something in the main part of the market-place. The ripples of mounting excitement spread rapidly outwards, sucking all in, so that by the time Mei Kwei, who had been hovering on the outermost edges, arrived at the centre, she found herself squeezed into a dense mass of jostling, perspiring, straining bodies.

Bending, she peeped through the first aperture yielded by the dense mass. But for the restraining presence of the local policemen, the crowd might have lost control.

It would not have been to riot or pillage but to look more closely at the four dead bodies lying side by side on the ground. The military truck and the presence of British soldiers, looking on with an intense, straining watchfulness, their hands on the rifles by their sides, marked the scene as part of a deliberate, nationwide exercise to bring home to the people the seriousness of the Emergency.

The public exhibition of the four dead terrorists served several purposes, as the chief of operations, Mr T. C. Williams, was the first to claim. It reminded the people of a sobering reality: after all these years, the war against Communism was far from over. It encouraged the townspeople to take heart: the British would continue to flush out all the bastards from the jungle. And it warned would-be sympathisers who sneaked food, medicine and information to the enemy: you too could end up like them.

In her eighteen years, Mei Kwei had seen only two dead bodies, and even then, very briefly – those of her grandmother and an old neighbour, Ah Mong Peh, whom Big Older Brother had dragged her along to see.

Outside the ameliorating rituals of coffin, joss-sticks, gentle incantations and the respectful tributes of the living, death was ugly and horrifying. Eyes staring in the shock of the moment were left unclosed; limbs twisted in the final throes were left unstraightened. All the four terrorists had frightful staring faces looking up at the open, mocking sky. Their bodies, in the torn, mud-splattered clothes and shoes of their defeat, would soon be tossed into a common grave. They were no different from the myriad dead fowls and pigs strung up on metal hooks in the market-place.

Nobody except herself seemed aware of a tiny ripple of disturbance in a far corner, on the edge of the staring, hushed crowd. In the distance, she saw the foreign priest talking animatedly to a British officer in uniform, his face flushed with anger and the hot morning sun. His hands were moving about rapidly in an energetic demonstration of his feelings. The officer remained unmoved, gazing ahead, even when he felt obliged to say something in response. He was clearly using the strategy of official imperturbability that would eventually wear down and turn away even the most troublesome protestor.

Mei Kwei moved closer to listen. The priest, getting angrier by the moment, was saying, 'This is outrageous. They are already dead – I will complain. Who's in charge?'

The officer turned his head slightly and said, with curt politeness, 'If you like, you can bring up the matter with the chief of operations,' while the small tight smile on his face implied, 'You just try it with T. C. Williams! Good luck.'

The crowd thought it more worthwhile to concentrate their attention on the four dead bodies. They began to murmur among themselves as the terrorist exhibits were studied for distinguishing marks of appearance, age, extent of wounds. Slim, young, Chinese, clad in khaki shirt and trousers, with close-cut hair, they nevertheless began to assume separate identities: the first seemed to be the oldest, the second had a gaping hole in the side of his neck, the third had the darkest complexion, the fourth – the fourth elicited the greatest interest as everyone jostled and strained to look. An officer in uniform, either intoxicated by victory or wishing to drive home a further lesson, had moved up to the body and was standing close to it. Then, with the aplomb of a performer, he slowly raised a heavy, well-polished boot and held it a menacing four inches above its chest. The crowd held its breath as it watched the boot move down in slow, almost graceful, descent then suddenly jerk to one side, to turn over, in one quick, deft movement, a large flap of torn, blood-stained cloth.

Everyone gasped as they looked upon a breast exposed, young, white, rounded, with a grotesque bullet-hole close to the nipple.

The officer seemed to be saying, 'Women, be warned, too.' The face, the legs, the hands, even the cropped hair, were now seen to be unmistakably female. The young woman terrorist could not have been more than twenty years old.

Somebody gave a shout and the crowd raised their eyes to a spectacle within a thrilling spectacle, as the officer, raising his foot a second time to turn the flap of cloth back on the woman's nakedness, was set upon, with the energy and fury of an attacking animal, by someone who seemed to have appeared from nowhere. Mei Kwei caught flashes of the priest's cassock, the vivid red blotches on his face, the quivering of his beard, and the flash of his eyes as he caught the wildly swinging arm of the officer and locked it in his own.

Effortlessly, he spun the officer round to face him fully. 'You bastard,' he hissed, his face white in the intensity of rage. Raising his voice, he continued, 'Have you no decency at all? A woman at that!'

To the crowd, the two men appeared comically locked in an embrace, their noses almost touching. Any fight in the market-place would have attracted attention; the promise of one between two *ang mohs*, one a proselytiser for the foreign religion and the other a member of the governing élite, was especially gratifying.

'How dare –' the officer spluttered, his face a deep purple as he shook himself free of the priest's grip. Deterred both by the clerical status announced by the cassock as well as the impressive build of his adversary, who towered over him, or simply wishing to deny the local people this special enjoyment, he restrained his fury. Adjusting his uniform with appropriate dignity, he glared at the priest and said, in cold rage, 'You will hear from the relevant authority.'

Uniformed soldiers came hurrying up, sensing trouble. The crowd dispersed quietly.

I have seen him already.

Mei Kwei had neither expected him nor herself to be at St Margaret's convent school, but it had happened. She liked to tell Tee Tee stories about the independent life of her bicycle as if there resided in the very wheels or the handle-bars a demon that took her, against her will, to the cemetery where her grandmother lay buried when she should have been on her way to the market-place, or to the Kek Lok temple to see the Mad Temple Vagrant when all the time the Chong family was waiting impatiently for their food. Bicycle Demon had exerted its will yet further: she gave the Chongs' food, already paid for – still warm and delicious-smelling in the tiffin-carrier – to the Temple Vagrant. Like magic, the food brought out from the dark, sheltering corners in the temple the hungry and the maimed, who came with their eyes popping and their tongues lolling and were ungenerously shooed away by one who should have been kinder, as she was one of them.

'I fell into a drain and the food spilled out,' had been her explanation to her mother.

'There's a spirit in my bicycle. It makes me do things,' she explained to the awestruck Tee Tee. Her bicycle now, clearly in a resurgence of assertiveness, broke away from the path that should have been a short-cut to the medicine shop, where a packet of herbs for her mother lay waiting to be collected, and took her on the slow, long road to the old school. More than any place in Luping, the school beckoned with memories of joy, yet repelled, too, with Mei Kwei's bitterest memory, of final loss and shame. She saw again her angry father dragging her out of the schoolroom with one hand and carrying her school-bag with the other; saw herself, once again, pale-faced and as yet tearless, submitting to being hauled up and dumped upon the pillion of the bicycle – the very same bicycle! – intimate companion on the rough terrain of her heart's secret bitter journeys.

She got down at the school gate, which was seldom locked, and paused to look in over the barbed-wire fence. Considerably enlarged and improved, the school was still far from the dream of Sister St Elizabeth, who had either left for another posting in Malaya or gone home to her native Ireland. It was the first time Mei Kwei had seen it since that day of loss and pain. The window of her furtive learning, the door through which she had made the dramatic entrance, unannounced, into the world of English education, were still there, untouched by the renovations. They invited memories, which came in a flood and which, in turn, invited bold re-entry. She wheeled her bicycle slowly through the gate into the compound, moving silently on the gravel path leading towards the school. She caught sight of two pupils coming out of one of the classrooms in their white blouses and blue pinafores, and thought of the two good blouses and trousers that had been her school-wear, infinitely inferior to Polly's frocks with their frills and bows.

She had meant only to stop for a little while and listen to the sounds coming out of the classroom, as she had done so many years ago, and then go away quietly, but stiffened at the sudden appearance of the priest and a nun coming together along the path, talking animatedly. He was a giant beside the little nun who was in the familiar white starched wimple and heavy black serge robes. Neither had seen her. Quickly Mei Kwei leaned her bicycle against a tree, and hid behind some tall bushes.

She saw them go into a classroom, and decided to stay longer, to catch his voice – that thrilling voice of anger and outrage which she had heard in the market-place. Here in a school it was different as it led the pupils in recitation, song or prayer: no solemn sounds floated out, only bursts of laughter, a rich male sonorousness decorated with a froth of girlish squeals.

Mei Kwei peeped in and saw the cause of the merriment: the priest had turned clown. Through an expert command of facial features, vocal cords and all four limbs, the man was producing, in rapid succession, the motions and sounds of a trumpeter, a drummer, a violinist, a flautist, a bassoonist. Then he turned irreverent, dropping Western instruments for the strident gongs and cymbals of Chinese opera, which he mimicked with great comic *brio*, stroking an imaginary waist-length beard and wielding an imaginary sword. Among adults, he might offend: how dare the white-skinned interloper make fun of the local culture? From giggling shyness, the girls exploded in delighted laughter, clapping their hands and jumping about in their seats, while the nun sat by demurely, smiling. The pupils were sure to tell breathless stories, at home, of the crazy new *ang moh* priest.

Clearly only the prelude to, and not the displacement of, serious classroom learning, the music and laughter died down, and the faces, both of teacher and pupils, made swift adjustments to the morning's catechism lesson. With a thrill, Mei Kwei saw that the books the girls brought out for the lesson were exactly the same as the one that Sister St Elizabeth had once placed in her hands, and which had been consigned long since to fire and oblivion. She heard the priest's voice, now full and rich with the earnestness of the dedicated man of God, reading from the little book and asking questions. 'Who made you? Why did God make you? To love Him and Serve Him in this world and be happy with Him for ever in the next.'

She watched the priest single out a shy, intense-looking girl in the back row to repeat the statement of divine purpose and promise. As the child stood up and obeyed, with much timid effort, he helped her along by mouthing each word silently with her, before finally exclaiming, 'Good! Very good!'

With some regret, Mei Kwei thought that happiness in the next world with the Christian God could no longer be hers: she had forfeited that chance with the bonfire of renunciation in which she had watched, with fiercely unrepentant eyes, the holy pictures and medals blacken and crumble, and then gone back to her grand-mother's gods.

Mei Kwei turned to go, and was mounting her bicycle when she became aware of sounds of shrill agitation coming from the classroom interrupting the calm of the catechism lesson. The cries, the alarmed faces suddenly appearing at the window and doorway, and a finger pointing in trembling accusation in her direction, did not tell her what she stood accused of but provoked immediate flight.

She pedalled away with furious energy and, looking back, saw the priest come running out in an attempt to stop her. Despite the long cassock he was very fast, and was upon her in an instant. Panting, he laid a large powerful hand on the bicycle pillion, almost toppling her, as she was about to pass through the gate, then turned round and made a loud sound of alarm, as of one discovering a grotesque mistake. He loosened his hold on her bicycle and she followed his eyes to see another, similar, near the tree where hers had been.

He turned again to face her, to say something, his embarrassed look presaging a sincere apology: 'I'm very sorry – one of the pupils thought you were stealing my bicycle. It had been stolen once before from the school. Please forgive me –'

But she was already pedalling away.

CHAPTER THIRTEEN

Pig Auntie came for the swill which was kept for her in a large kerosene tin in a corner of Ah Oon Soh's kitchen. Pig Auntie herself had two large tins, strung at the ends of a long pole across her sturdy shoulders, for collecting from half a dozen friendly houses in the neighbourhood. Her pigs could choke to death on the massive fish and pork bones that should not have been thrown into the tins and pails, together with the rice and vegetable remnants, but Pig Auntie was too humble to request a separating-out of the bad stuff. As soon as she reached home, she rolled up the long sleeve of her blouse and plunged her arm into the swill, stirring it in slow, patient circles to feel for the bones and remove them.

People said it was a lesser misfortune to smell like a pig than to look like one. By no means fat or coarse, Pig Auntie took great care to keep her fine eyebrows plucked into two delicate arches, her arms and legs thoroughly scrubbed with sweet-smelling soap, and avoided both misfortunes. But not the misfortune of the mean inheritance, perpetuated in the name that was but a variant of her dead mother's, which in turn had come from a long line of swill-collecting ancestors, going right back to the ancestral country. Pig Auntie, Swill Woman, Pig Mother, Swill Girl: the real name given at birth – Siew Choo, Kim Heok, Poh Gaik, Keng Hua – redolent of feminine grace or precious stones or beautiful flowers, had sunk into the slime and squalor of her calling.

'Tee Tee, will you be called Pig Uncle one day?' The boy had grimaced at the taunt, and Mei Kwei had put an arm around him and whispered, 'Tell them that one day you will go to an English school and earn big money.'

Pig Auntie saw Big Older Brother lazing on a bench under a tree by the well and greeted him deferentially. The curl of his lip implied, 'First your son. Now you. As if we'd not had enough of the gossip. Leading the town tattle brigade.'

This was the pain of poverty, Pig Auntie thought. Someone young enough to be your son not only failed to offer the first greeting but rejected yours. An emperor's son knelt before an old beggar for his blessing, mindful of the divinely ordained power of grey hair. But nowadays the young mocked their elders.

Pig Auntie said nothing, lowered her head and made her way into the house. The Almighty sees everything. I will leave everything to the Almighty, she said to herself. It was a sustaining philosophy and saw her through the hurts of a lifetime.

'So, the little fool was here? Well, just don't pay any attention to him.' And with that Pig Auntie dismissed all mention of her son, and prepared to regale Ah Oon Soh with the latest town news, but not before adding, 'What to do? His father left us.' Tee Tee had been six when he was made to earn his keep by helping to care for the pigs, yanked in an instant into hard, bitter adulthood.

What to do? Widows, abandoned women, women whose husbands did not leave home but stayed all day with their opium pipes, or at the gambling tables, first uttered the fatalism, then picked themselves up for the urgent task of corrective action, invoking the example of forebears in the far-away ancestral country, whose broken bodies never stopped nurturing children or pulling ploughs.

Ah Oon Soh made good money with the catered meals and the mah-jong table rent. The widow Lam divided her small house into a warren of tiny rooms, which she let out, keeping one for herself and her four children, all of whom she could afford to send to school. Ah Mui Ee was doing a lucrative business reselling the biscuits sold to her by the young British soldiers, and could expand the business handsomely if they started bringing in foreign ham, milk and butter from their camps' rich stores; it didn't matter that they came knocking on her door at odd hours. Ah Tim Soh was less lucky and had no choice but to go on washing and ironing the mountains of clothes her son collected from a dozen households, her hands as hard and cracked as old wood. Pig Auntie was thankful that she could keep herself and her son alive by rearing and selling pigs. Every year, just before the New Year, she showed her gratitude to the swill-providing households by making each a gift of a pair of fowls, tied together with string, their legs circled by a band of good-luck red paper. Ah Oon Soh received, in addition, a basket of eggs, her year's contribution being the largest. Women could turn endurance into profit.

They could turn their beauty into the greatest profit, if they availed themselves of the opportunity. The trouble with her daughter, Ah Oon Soh whispered to Pig Auntie, was that she had a stubborn nature and would not be guided by adults. Old Yoong had already made the approach with the gifts and the photo, but the girl had remained indifferent to both; Ah Oon Soh had noticed that the photo remained in its place on top of a chest of drawers in their room exactly as she had placed it, untouched and unlooked at.

'He has asked for your photo,' said Ah Oon Soh. She was prepared to spend money on some ornaments such as a pearl necklace or a pair of ear-rings for a good portrait at the Sin Tuck photo studio.

'If you are so keen, why don't you send him yours or Pig Auntie's?' Mei Kwei could be exasperating.

The offers had come in a stream from mothers acting on behalf of their interested, hopeful sons, but she had laughed them away.

'What makes you think you are superior to Hock Leng?' Ah Oon Soh asked.

Hock Leng, the brother of Hock Seng – the hapless dry-goods shop-keeper who had been killed so mercilessly by the terrorists – owned a general-provisions shop. He had gone into hiding after the incident but emerged, as soon as he felt the danger was over, to continue his prosperous business and to spread word that he was looking for a wife. Ah Oon Koh's beautiful daughter was applied for.

'He's got a pock-marked face. And bad teeth. One leg is shorter than the other.' Mei Kwei's irreverence could only be displayed in the presence of her mother, never before her father, who would rasp out a rebuke, or Big Older Brother.

After her fill of merriment, Mei Kwei listened with quiet composure to her mother's tirade, which came in words so precisely anticipated that she could mouth them silently in perfect accompaniment. 'Already eighteen. Stubborn. Wind, not sense, in the head. Will never find a husband.'

But Mei Kwei had not finished with Hock Leng. There was a greater ugliness. He cheated poor Malays. Hock Leng had boasted that he could palm off inferior stuff on the *hwan kooi* and they would never know. Or skim off a few onions or potatoes after weighing and they would not notice. They had no business sense whatever. One of Hock Leng's cousins regularly went to the *hwan koois'* market in another part of the town, bought up the pineapples and mangoes of a woman fruit-seller and sold them for a substantial profit in the Chinese sector. *Hwan kooi, keleng kooi*, despicable devils all. And now, according to Hock Leng, the *ang moh kooi*, the red-haired devils, were invading the town, the Robinsons and Roberts, and that strange, blue-eyed priest, Father François Martin.

'You shut your mouth,' said Ah Oon Soh sharply. 'Who are you to say things like that? Do you think you are so clever?' Among her friends, she shook her head mournfully. 'I don't know what to do with that daughter of mine. There's something wrong with her.'

But her daughter's wilfulness was not at an end. 'I will not marry. I will go to work in Singapore, in a cabaret, and become one of the bad women there who wear frocks and smoke. I will go to live in a temple, like Mad Temple Auntie.' Deliberately, she cited the town's best example of failed womanhood who was allowed to stay in an outbuilding of the Kek Lok temple only because, many years ago, she had been struck dumb by a wrathful deity for some transgression and had to spend the rest of her life in atonement. Mad Temple Auntie, with her pathetic bulging eyes and slack, grinning mouth, ought to strike fear in young girls' hearts. Even the rapacious Japanese soldiers had avoided her.

'Stop your mad talk.' Ah Oon Soh sometimes wished her daughter were not so beautiful. Beauty went to young girls' heads and made them difficult.

The photo remained untouched in Mei Kwei's room. Undiscarded, it allowed hope. In the days that followed, the services of Pig Auntie were utilised in a grand conspiracy of influence.

'Old Yoong is one of the richest men in Penang,' said Pig Auntie loudly. She went on to give details of the wealth, of the coconut and rubber plantations, the large stone house, the many servants, the chauffeured car, casting a sideways glance at Mei Kwei, who was at the other end of the room sprinkling water on shirts preparatory to ironing, watched by Tee Tee.

They were details best repeated for proper digesting, so Ah Oon Soh's deliberately sceptical comment elicited the repetition, in even more ardent tones. One third of the rubber plantations in Penang. Perhaps one half of the coconut plantations. Another big stone house, somewhere along the sea.

Not to be outdone, Tee Tee began to give more news of Father François Martin. He and his mother, talking in different corners of the room to their respective audiences, became locked in a spiral of competitive reporting. The town's most desirable man was pitched against its most intriguing visitor in a dizzying ascent of newsworthiness.

Old Yoong treated all his wives well. Each had a servant and loads of jewellery.

Father Martin ate noodles with three men in the market-place. He used chopsticks expertly. He finished one bowl, then another. He did not pay for the noodles.

Old Yoong was selective. He had only to indicate his interest and the mothers of young girls would come running. The pretty eighteen-year-old virginal daughter of a medicine-shop proprietor in the neighbouring town of Pujong had been offered. Also, the daughter of the proprietor of Tin Peng Goldsmith who was even prettier. But Old Yoong was not interested. Old Yoong was so wealthy that even the Communist terrorists, who resented his donations to the hospitals and schools with *ang moh* names, tried to cultivate him in the hope of diverting some of his substantial wealth to their cause.

Father Martin was so funny that he made all the children laugh. He could make strange sounds with his nose and pull coins and string and beads out of his ears. He rode his bicycle all the way into the rubber plantation to talk to the abusive Indian husband who had beaten his wife yet again. She was taken to hospital and had to have seven stitches in her scalp. Father Martin himself had had to go to hospital for a cut on his arm, inflicted by a swinging *parang*. The wretched husband had finally surrendered the weapon to the priest and promised not to threaten his wife and children again.

Old Yoong let it be known that his next wife would have the biggest diamonds, the thickest gold chains, the finest jade bangles.

Father Martin touched a woman's naked breast.

There was a lull in the chatter, and all turned to look at Tee Tee, whose upturned face looked back confidently, taut with determination to stand by his outrageous claim.

'Don't you talk rubbish!' snapped his mother. 'Where did you hear this?'

The boy averred he had heard it from somebody who had seen it with his own eyes. It was in the market-place. It was a dead woman's naked breast.

'Don't you go round spreading such nonsense,' said Pig Auntie severely. 'Serves you right if the *ang mohs* come after you for saying bad things about one of their kind.'

Father Martin, riding his old bicycle, going into the homes of drunken plantation workers, eating noodles with the local people, was not one of those who lived in a large airy house with numerous servants and gardeners and drank every evening in the exclusive Luping Club. But, still, he was an *ang moh*.

Then Big Older Brother emerged from his room, this time not to abuse but to make his own smiling, sardonic contribution: there was an *ang moh* planter living in the huge rubber plantation ten miles outside Luping who raped his Indian cleaning woman who subsequently bore him a child. Black skin, red hair, blue eyes.

'And we bow and scrape before them!' Big Older Brother returned to his room with a laugh.

CHAPTER FOURTEEN

There was nothing Big Older brother liked better than to go to the *ronggeng* girls, buy his ticket, a pink slip or paper, and make straight for Nee Nee, always the last in the row of girls sitting under the bright multi-coloured lights strung ahead, but always the first to be claimed for the dance, because of her enormous breasts, which were squeezed into a tight red or pink satin bodice. Big Older Brother would leap on to the large wooden stage, to approving yells from the spectators, and pull her from her chair. He liked the loud, strident music of the drums, gongs and flutes, and the tremendous screeching voice of the singing lady at the microphone, with her heavily powdered face, red lips, mascara-ed eyes and huge clusters of pink and yellow flowers in her hair. In the hot night air and the glare of lights, her makeup dissolved into pink and black runnels which coursed slowly down her cheeks, trapping the small petals which had fallen off the blossom-piles on her head and giving her the aspect of a grotesque carnival character.

But the lady never allowed anything to distract her from her singing. Her voice was a rich orchestration of screeches, wails, moans, sighs, quavers and trills to compel the dancers to keep up their tempo, to get closer but not touch, for this was a dance in which, forbidden to touch at all, dancers were soon in a frenzy of desire. At the point when their wildly undulating, throbbing bodies moved close enough for palms or fingertips or knees to brush against each other, the singing lady's voice rose to a shriek that rent the air and forced them to swing round and apart, then turn back to face each other and begin the whole tantalising routine once more.

Each girl carried a colourful flimsy scarf which she used in a hundred alluring ways – holding it tightly at each end to pull it to and

107

fro repeatedly, provocatively, across bare back or shoulders, biting one end, then the other with a great showing of teeth and tongue, snapping it playfully at the partner, throwing it into the air for him to catch, hold, smell, as an extension of her beauteous self.

Big Older Brother claimed he had collected a total of ten scarves, each wrested from his laughing, protesting partner and stuffed into shirt or trouser pocket. He had also collected three pairs of Nee Nee's knickers. She was the most sporting girl he had ever come across, he told his friends, and if he wanted a contrast to the town's pale, sour-faced, ugly, virginal females, she was the perfect example. Some of the townsfolk were highly disapproving of the *ronggeng* shows, claiming that these girls, brought in from the poor Thai villages, gaudy, illiterate, with their revealing frocks and enormous bushes of lice-infested hair, gave the town a bad name.

'First the *ronggeng* girls, then Pearly Chong! What next?' they grumbled.

Pearly Chong was a strip-tease dancer whose brazenness, especially in the grand finale of the Python Dance, put the *ronggeng* girls in the shade. It was said that an old gentleman sitting in the front row fell gasping from his seat and had to be carried out. The reporter from the Chinese newspaper covered every Pearly Chong perform-ance, splashing pictures of the remarkably white and fulsome body, bare except the statutory black square over her pubis.

But Pearly made only one visit to Luping; the Thai girls came several times a year. As soon as they arrived in a bus, they were put in three rooms in a cheap boarding-house. After each show, which would go on late into the night, there was no stopping the men from going back with them to the boarding-house or taking them to cheap hotels. The authorities closed an eye, for no suspicion of Communist connections ever befell the *ronggeng* girls. Besides, remarked a wag in the administration, the terrible privations of first the Japanese occupation and now the Emergency entitled the poor devils in Luping to some enjoyment.

One evening Big Older Brother brought Nee Nee home. It was a bold move. But he had calculated, correctly, the time of his father's monthly meeting with his opium friends in the clan house in town. As for his mother – his mother did not count. His sister could always be depended on to remain in her room and be as silent as a mouse.

Mei Kwei heard the front door open softly, her brother's voice murmuring something and a woman's muffled laughter.

She listened intently and caught the small intense sounds of the act of love between a man and a woman on a bed at every stage of its progression, for the wall separating their bedrooms was but a row of thin planks nailed together. They were rich and heavy sounds, filling the room with their insistence, settling into every crevice of hearing and attentiveness, and inviting the mind of the innocent, while making its heart race guiltily, to shape them into actual images of moving arms and legs, lips and breasts. Her knowledge of the act of love was tentative at best, being derived from disparate sources – men's crude displays which disgusted and distressed her, the daylight wantonness of fowls and stray dogs, which the town's children sometimes pointed to with frank enjoyment, women's stories whispered behind cupped hands and furtive eyes amid giggles.

Mei Kwei expunged the ugliness of male lust by spitting three times, of course, as her mother had taught her, or averted it by wearing an amulet given her by Mad Temple Auntie, and by plugging up peeping holes in bathroom doors. After she had noticed that the rags had been poked out, she had taken a knife and savagely enlarged all the holes. Then, bringing her mother to see, she had demanded that a plank of wood be nailed across them.

Surely a man's loving could be tender and bring joy? Surely a woman need not always have to recoil from a man's touch, but could sometimes turn towards it joyfully? From a distant corner of her memory, there floated up the image of a gentle man on a couch who had loved her grandmother and made her happy.

In the operas, held regularly in the temple grounds, men and women touched, embraced, made love. The Moon Maiden and her lover, at the supreme moment of union, still stood apart, though facing and inclining towards each other. As she watched, her imagination pushed the couple towards each other into a loving embrace, and guided the strong arms of the God-King into a full encirclement of the sobbing girl. She had watched, wide-eyed, and remembered and felt every detail of the hot promise of arms, face, lips.

And beyond the temple grounds, in another part of the town, where the movie-house played interminable romances of desertion and reconciliation, abduction and rescue, the Indian women from the rubber plantations moaned and wept with the lovers and rocked their bodies gently to the rhythm of their pain and exultation. They left the movie-house, still wiping their eyes with the ends of their colourful saris, secure in the knowledge of the ultimate triumph of endurance over injustice, good over evil. In yet another part of the town, the *padang*, a large cloth screen and a movie projector had been set up for the benefit of those too poor to afford a movie-house ticket but who, too, needed to feed their hopes and dreams. They brought their mats, laid them on the grass, sat and munched peanuts as they watched *Tarzan and Jane*, *The Hunchback of Notre Dame* and *Esmeralda*, the swashbuckling Errol Flynn gliding on a rope into a castle to keep a tryst with his lady. What did it matter if the language was foreign? With their babies in sarong cradles strung on their backs or dandled on knees, the crying blocked by rubber teats or sugar-water in bottles, with the bigger children hushed into silence by threats of black-faced demon-warriors or ferocious policemen with handcuffs, the women of Luping watched, mesmerised. The colour of opera shows and movies was solace for the greyness of lives lived out within the confines of the little town.

In a movie that she saw when she was about fourteen, Mei Kwei clung to her seat in a tremor of excitement when the hero entered a room and went straight to the heroine, who was lying on a couch. There was a full four minutes of caressing in the soft glow of candles, during which perfect silence had descended upon the entire audience and hands in the act of dipping into bags of water-melon seeds or pickled plums were immobilised. Somebody sitting behind Mei Kwei, an insolent-faced boy, who had been viciously knocking his knee against the back of her seat, remained completely still. It was precisely at the moment when the heroine sat up to blow out the candles with her soft rounded lips, one after the other, then turned to face her lover again before sinking slowly down with him upon the couch in the swooning darkness, that Mei Kwei felt the wetness and was afraid.

Mei Kwei now heard, quite distinctly, as she leaned yet closer towards the plank wall, the furious panting of a frenziedly quickening tempo, then a roar, as of a sudden, savage twisting together of pleasure and pain, which was so loud and sharp that, even as she was startled into frozen attentiveness, she wondered if the neighbours had heard. She held her breath and listened again. The roar had subsided and melted into a wash of sighs and murmurs, disappearing into silence. She could not hear even the sound of breathing.

Getting up, she went to the wall and pressed her eye to a tiny crack. She saw her brother, huge, naked, glistening, slumped upon Nee Nee, saw part of her famous breasts, crushed under his weight, and their faces nestled tightly against each other under a combined mass of abundant, gleaming black hair. Both lay still, frozen by love's satiety into startling statuary beauty. Mei Kwei stared for a long time, absorbing with increasing fascination every detail of locked limbs, pressed flesh, every manifestation of love's fulfilment, and only moved away when Big Older Brother stirred, sighed and fell off Nee Nee's naked body.

CHAPTER FIFTEEN

'Hurry up, or we'll be late,' urged Mei Kwei, referring to the opera that was to start soon in the Kek Lok Temple grounds. It was not the season for operas but a temple worshipper, in gratitude to the gods for some favour – a large fortune, the recovery of his mother from a serious illness, a safe journey home from a trip – had commissioned the show. But Mad Temple Auntie took her time feeding the temple tortoises in the small cement enclosure at the back.

Mad Temple Auntie knew all six of them by the most obscure markings on shell, neck or head, cooing softly to them as she fed them *kang kong*. Mostly she saved them a weed that grew in wild abundance by the drains, but this time she could afford to buy their favourite vegetable from the market with money someone had given her. The vegetable-seller, knowing her purpose, had reduced his price and sent her away with an armful, wrapped in newspaper.

The tortoises ambled up to her to be fed. Old and grey and smelly, they were nevertheless the sacred temple tortoises that little children were warned not to tease or throw stones at. Their ancestors in the far homeland had been killed for their shells, which were broken and cast into flames to yield patterns of cracks by which mortals could divine the messages of gods. Here they were more fortunate and were allowed to live out their days in peace, and occasionally to receive the obeisance of a worshipper in the form of a joss-stick stuck in a crevice of the cement enclosure.

It was said that the tortoises knew Mad Temple Auntie as intimately as she knew them. Upon her death, they would weep in mourning just as, long ago, according to an old caretaker in the temple, large tears had rolled down the cheeks of two tortoises when the death of a holy monk was announced.

The holiness of Mad Temple Auntie was more to be inferred than witnessed; people seeing her greedily awaiting meal-times and grabbing at food brought by worshippers and by that strange, beautiful daughter of Ah Oon Koh, who was her only friend, forgot the holiness for the coarseness. Besides, her unkemptness – the matted hair, the smelly clothes – was of the kind associated with slovenliness rather than sanctity.

She and her beloved tortoises were linked in a mutuality of dirt and stench. But the pure white doves that were released in large numbers in the temple grounds by grateful devotees gravitated, too, towards her in the strangest of ways. Someone had observed that every time a cage door was opened and the birds, a beautiful white flock, flew out into the blue sky, at least one would fly back to descend upon the head or shoulder of Mad Temple Auntie and remain there a full minute before disappearing into the sky with the others.

Once a python slid into the temple and curled up under one of the altars. Its choice of resting place, under the great Monkey God whose feast was being celebrated, instantly put it outside the pale of destruction that was the invariable fate of the myriad harmful animals and vermin that came in from the untended vegetation near the temple and damaged its property. Yet the python was most certainly evil, casting a beady eye on worshippers who moved nervously to another part of the temple. Many whispered of its emanations of malignant power. Mad Temple Auntie was called in. She did a strange little dance to the accompaniment of odd sounds squeezed out of her pulsing throat, and the python simply slid away and never came back. Sister Tortoise. Brother Python. Only the humility of saints could speak to the lowly in God's creation.

But she had less luck with creatures in the world outside. A dog in a street bit her on the ankle; a cat in a rubbish dump, roused by something in her appearance, arched its back, screeched and sprang upon her, drawing a vicious claw down the whole length of an arm.

The stories of holiness and earthiness entwined to produce a mixed reaction on the part of the temple authorities who would have liked to eject the filthy vagrant from the premises but feared to do so, just in case. The 'just in case' encompassed the entire range of bizarre tales with their implicit warnings: that she had been struck dumb for some transgression but would, once her atonement was over, rise to dazzling heights of oracular power; that the chastisement was in reality a protection, for the woman was possessed of deep truths which could never be uttered; that the dumbness, moreover, disappeared on certain feast days of the gods when she stood at the altars and screamed out the most direful predictions; that anyone who even injured a hair on her head risked divine punishment. A Japanese soldier, it was rumoured, had forced her to take a bath to get rid of the layers of filth that stood between him and his lust but, at the moment of his taking her, something happened to make him scream in terror, pull himself up and run off.

Through all the rumours, Mad Temple Auntie remained as blissful and trusting as a child, her large grotesque eyes wide with the wonder of the world.

Mei Kwei said again, 'Hurry up, Mad Temple Auntie, or we'll be late.' She helped her dispose of the last remnants of *kang kong* and watched her press her hands together and bow her head in a demonstration of utmost reverence for the satiated tortoises, which turned back and ambled through piles of their own dirt to rest in the coolest spot in the cement enclosure.

Among the many women gathered to watch the opera, there were always a few who would recognise the girl, observe her with interest, and at their next meeting with her mother in the market-place, at the medicine shop or the draper's, say in a lowered voice, 'Ah Oon Soh, I saw your daughter at the opera. She was with –' The incongruity of a young unescorted girl, purportedly sought by one of the wealthiest men in Penang, in the company of the commonest beggarwoman, was left unexpressed while the enquirer looked into the mother's face and waited for an answer.

Ah Oon Soh would shrug and say, 'My daughter? Don't ask me about my daughter,' leaving unexpressed, too, both her displeasure about the girl's obstinacy and her unease about the outcome of the wealthy suitor's application.

'I think she's finally looked at it.' The unease became mixed with excitement as Ah Oon Soh pulled Pig Auntie aside to tell her the good news. The evidence was in the new position of the photo on the chest of drawers: previously placed on the right side of a vase, it now lay on the left.

Never meaning to betray any interest, Mei Kwei had, on several occasions, put the photo back precisely as she had found it, but had been careless on the last and thus given her mother the long hoped-for gratification, prelude to that greater gratification shimmering tremulously on the horizon of a hopeful future.

The man in the photo did not displease; instead, there was enough handsomeness in the tall upright figure in the Mao suit, the slightly greying hair at the temples, enough kindness in the eyes under the thick dark eyebrows, to interest and provide matter for thought and feeling. Holding the photo in the light of a small kerosene lamp as her mother lay asleep nearby, Mei Kwei studied every detail. Twice her mother stirred and began talking in her sleep; twice she quickly put back the photo in its place beside the vase and waited for the sounds to die away. She did not look at it again till a few days later.

The man was posed in a setting of opulence, of rich gleaming furniture and tasselled curtains, which connected with the immense wealth so enthusiastically described by Pig Auntie. The second time brought stronger feelings of interest, the third time, again some days later, a distinct desire to meet him, so that when her mother asked her, 'Would you like to go to the Sin Tuck photo studio?', she said nothing, which meant yes.

This was sufficient for Ah Oon Soh to swing into excited preparations with the help of Pig Auntie. Together, they went shopping for a pearl necklace and pearl ear-studs. The photo could not but please its recipient. It did not need the mother's investment in the ornaments; touched with colour at the lips and cheekbones by the photographer's careful brush, it proclaimed a beauty equal to that of Pai Kuan, the famous actress from China.

The suitor, pleased, sent word that he would soon be coming on a visit. The thought of such a great personage in his chauffeured car winding his way to their humble abode through narrow dirt tracks and chicken yards sent a little tremor through Ah Oon Soh.

She was, however, soon calmed by Pig Auntie. 'Why do you worry? The old man will have eyes only for your daughter.'

The worry then focused on new clothes for Mei Kwei. Ah Oon Soh asked, 'Shall we go to Chong Teck's?', the draper being the best in Luping, with bolts of the most attractive cottons and silks that a seamstress, whom Pig Auntie knew well, could sew into the most beautiful *samfoos*.

But the girl steadfastly denied her mother and Pig Auntie any further exultation over the success of their scheme and merely asked what the fuss was all about while her heart secretly beat to its own bold expectations.

She deliberately hung around to listen to her father's reaction, standing close to his closed door. She had seen her mother enter the room and knew her purpose.

'You do as you like. What has that got to do with me?' Indifferent to her birth and marriage, would he utter the same words of repudiation if someone came hurrying to tell him of her death?

Mei Kwei fought back a surge of bitter tears, but not the bitter thought, One day, Father, one day, you will see –

In her dreams, he was different. In her dreams, he called out to her from the doorway of his room and said, 'Come,' and handed her a broom and wiping rag to clean the room of the huge amount of rubbish that had collected over many years on the tops of cupboards, under his bed and on the window-ledges.

'Gracious, Father, look at this,' she said playfully, as she pulled out stacks of old newspapers, paper bags, balls of rope and twine. 'I'm going to make a bonfire of all these.'

'You are going to get married soon,' he said gently, as he watched her at work. 'I am happy for you. You have been a good daughter.'

'Thank you, Father.'

'I have something to ask of you,' he said.

'Tell me, Father! Tell me,' she said eagerly.

But she was unable to catch his words. She saw his mouth open and close, open and close in the voicing of some urgent need, but even as the awful silence swallowed up all sound so a descending darkness swallowed up all sight, and she found herself gazing upon nothing and crying out in mounting panic, 'Father! Father!'

CHAPTER SIXTEEN

'You mustn't go out on your own,' said her mother anxiously, when Mei Kwei insisted on going to the market to get the joss-sticks and flowers for the coming feast of the Goddess of Mercy.

'You mustn't –' Ah Oon Soh looked forward to the time when Old Yoong's wealth would lift Mei Kwei above the meanness of markets and small purchases; when, if she decided to go to the market at all, it would be in the company of a maidservant. Fond wishes overtaking reason, she was already seeing her daughter ensconced in a luxury far exceeding that of his First, Second or Third Wife. Never having benefited from her mother's beauty, she was determined to profit from her daughter's.

'Then you must take along an umbrella.' Her daughter's beauty, of such great worth, had to be protected from harsh sun or rain.

'I've got to get out of the house for a while,' Mei Kwei screamed silently.

It was not only her father's ill-will which like a noxious vapour, crept out of the crevices and slits of his room door to touch her every thought and feeling with a dank sourness, but also the silent, cautious suspicion of her brother. The prospect of Mei Kwei's new position of privilege stung Big Older Brother into a harsh reflection of his own degrading dependence on others or on capricious gods giving out lucky lottery numbers at whim. Pig Auntie's shrill, over-enthusiastic expositions on the advantages of the match had one morning elicited such an explosion of peevishness, expressed in the banging of doors and slamming of furniture, that the frightened woman had shut up immediately and refrained from the subject thereafter.

The most brilliant match in Luping, thought Mei Kwei, with a bitter smile, and here were the father and brother wishing her ill.

In the market-place, the vegetable woman nudged her neighbour, the clogs woman. 'Ah Oon Koh's daughter,' she whispered. Both paused in their transactions of business to watch the girl, inducing their respective customers to turn round and look too.

'Too proud,' said the clogs woman. 'Watch.' She called a cheerful greeting to Mei Kwei, enquiring about the health of her parents. 'What did I tell you?' she said triumphantly to the vegetable woman. 'Proud. And discourteous.' For the girl had just nodded and murmured something, then walked on. 'Just because a rich man . . .' The two women consoled themselves with the observation that rich men who had the pick of the whole town, indeed of half the country, sometimes changed their minds.

Mei Kwei stopped in front of the stall where joss-sticks of various sizes were stacked on shelves and hung from an improvised ceiling. Unlit, they filled the air with their pungent power; lit, they would send giant billows of smoke heavenwards to praise, entreat, thank, cajole gods and goddesses in temples and shrines, and dead ancestors in tombs.

The joss-sticks seller, an old man, had no eye for young beauty but

116

his stall immediately became the focus of intense attention as half a dozen pairs of male eyes converged to fasten on the girl, to roam her face, her eyes, which were determinedly lowered, and her breasts under her cotton blouse. Ah Oon Koh's daughter had been compared to the stunning Pai Kuan and the comparison was by no means exaggerated. A detractor might say, 'But that crying mole near her right eye detracts from her beauty.' Still, there was no denying that the girl's power to attract attention was the greater for her repelling it with her demeanour of cold disdain. The detractor might add, 'Who does she think she is, anyway? Daughter of an opium addict in perpetual debt, sister of the town's greatest wastrel,' but might be hushed into the admission that half the young men in Luping desired her for a wife, half the old men for a concubine.

One of them moved from mere desire into action.

Mei Kwei was leaving the market-place on her way home when she noticed someone following her. A quick glance backwards showed him to be a tall, swarthy young man wearing a white singlet and black trousers, moving with the insolent ease of the confident stalker. Her glance was swift but all embracing. It took in, too, the scar on the left cheek, the piece of water-melon in the right hand, the thin stick under his left arm, which he would use to slash idly at bushes or throw at a dog to reinforce the picture of ease. Perhaps he was a former eater at her mother's table; out of the orbit of Big Older Brother's stern watchfulness, he could afford to be bold.

She changed course and walked in the direction of the town's main street. He followed. She changed direction once more. He did likewise. She quickened her pace and heard the increased slapping sound of his rubber slippers upon the rough gravel, also the sound of seeds spat out. She could see a few people around – a trishawman squatting beside his parked vehicle, an old Indian man walking along with a little barefoot child, a woman carrying a large basket of something on her head. She would not call for help, for he would only feign surprise, shrug his huge shoulders and say, 'What? I was just on my way to . . .' He might even suggest outrage: 'Did I touch her? Did anyone see me touch her?'

She could hear a low gurgle, as of a predator enjoying the growing terror of his prey. Perhaps that was all he wanted – to frighten her and later to boast about it to his friends: 'You know that proud daughter of Ah Oon Koh? Well, I taught her a lesson.'

By now, she was in an unfamiliar place. It was a large patch of wasteground, traversed by a faint footpath. She clutched the string handle of her paper bag tightly, her knuckles white. Yet she would not show her fear. She heard a low voice saying, 'Why are you running away from me, Sister? Don't be afraid, I won't hurt you.'

She thought of that stretch of dirt road leading to her house, lined by trees and bushes, where he might very well harm her. Suddenly she turned in the direction of yet more unfamiliar territory, her face set with grim purpose, her hands growing cold. Her pursuer followed. He went neither faster nor slower, his pace precisely calibrated with hers, the predator performing the last exquisite dance of death with his terrified prey. She heard him chuckle softly again.

The pursuer hesitated a little – she knew this with certainty even though she never once turned round to look – when she entered the grounds of the Church of the Sacred Heart of Jesus. A small squat wooden building, which must have served a less exalted purpose in earlier days, it announced its new dedication by a tall gleaming white cross set atop its roof, and its name in large letters in a graceful arc above the front entrance.

Mei Kwei walked quickly into the building, where a mass was being said, and sat on the first bench she came to, the one furthest away from the altar where the foreign priest was lifting his hands to bless the worshippers, a scattering of men and women, their heads reverently bowed. From where she sat, she saw again the pale skin, the blue eyes, the bushy beard. Not tussling with officers in market-places or chasing bicycle thieves and, clad in his ceremonial robes, he inspired a little awe. He was dispensing blessings with a hand tracing the sign of the Cross in the air, dispensing love with arms stretched wide to embrace, to draw all to his heart. He sang out his benediction and love in a foreign language, but his voice filled the church with warm reassurance: Fear not, you are safe here.

The worshippers kept their heads bowed. She, too, bowed her head to be one with them, yet managed to see that her stalker had brazenly parked himself near the entrance and was looking in.

Women grow eyes at the back of their heads from fear. She was aware of his every movement – he was wiping his mouth on his sleeve, pushing his hands deep into his pockets, looking around with a smile to disarm even the most suspicious. Every muscle in her body twitched to the threat in his: she hoped that by the end of the service, when she would be moving out with the worshippers, he would be gone.

The woman next to her, elderly, grey-haired, bespectacled, with a black net veil on her head and a rosary entwined in her fingers, turned to glance disapprovingly at the paper bag beside her. The Goddess of Mercy's joss-sticks, poking conspicuously out of the bag, were a sacrilege. They were the devil's very own. How dared this girl bring them into the presence of God? The woman's nose twitched at their pungency: only her Christian charity prevented her from asking this pagan intruder to leave the house of God. The girl sensed her displeasure and hurriedly put the offending object under her seat, well hidden from her sight. By no means placated, the woman turned back to face the priest again, and knelt to receive the last blessing and made the sign of the Cross. Mei Kwei hesitated, then decided she could manage both gestures convincingly. She knelt and made the same sign, head bowed, while the pungency of the joss-sticks from under her seat continued their secret defiant invasion of Christian nostrils. Then she stood up, like the rest, for the final ritual of blessing.

It was at this point that she noticed two more men looking at her intently in a flash of shock and recognition: the priest, whose sudden change of expression as he turned from the altar to face the congregation, hands raised in benediction, betrayed distraction; and a young, pale man in the pew in front who had swung round to look at her. Eyes lowered, she could see the priest in a heightened ardour of attentiveness to the closing rituals, as if he was trying to make up for the shameful momentary lapse. The young man, on the other hand, continued to stare at her.

Outside at last, in the bright sunshine, she saw to her relief that her stalker was gone and turned round to see the priest chatting eagerly with a small group of elderly women. He looked up at the same moment and, smiling, detached himself from the group to come up to her. He caught her hand and shook it, laying his other hand on top, warmly. Surprised, she almost dropped her paper bag. Then her body, which had recoiled from the intrusiveness of male rampancy only a short while ago, responded to the protective reassurance of the touch. Her hand settled, tremblingly and gratefully, into the genuine cordiality of the enveloping embrace of his.

'Ah, the bicycle! The bicycle!' he said, in laughing self-reproach, still holding her hand in his. He said something else, which she did not hear for, turning her head slightly, she saw the tall, pale-looking man approaching her. His expression of intense interest, when he had swung round in the church pew had sharpened into something like menacing purpose as he strode towards her.

Seized by the same fear that placed him with the stalker, she broke free of the priest's grasp and hurried away.

CHAPTER SEVENTEEN

The sleek white chauffeur-driven car with its distinguished occupant in the back, making its careful way along the dirt road, crushing fallen twigs and scattering chickens, became an instant focus of interest to the children who, at its approach, stopped playing and fell silent. The haughty disdain of the white-uniformed chauffeur warned against any temptation to pelt the gleaming metallic surfaces with pebbles or rubber seeds, just as the scowls of the black-and-white *amahs* the evening before, wheeling little blond babies in prams, had repulsed these ragged, unwelcome gawkers. A new class of servant, gilded by association, was beginning to look down on its own.

More than any pram with its golden-haired occupant surrounded by tantalisingly inaccessible toys, the sleek car, bearing a heap of gifts visible through the window, drew a trail of small, excited observers who only stopped when it did, smoothly, noiselessly, in front of a house with a thatched roof and a large chicken yard, and stationed themselves in various spots for close observation. They knew the intended recipient of the gifts. But who could know what she was thinking and plotting, this daughter of Ah Oon Koh, whose beauty and artfulness were drawing the wealthy and the influential to her very doorstep? In a favourite opera story, the emperor himself, in full imperial regalia, came to the humble abode of a peasant to woo his daughter, in a blinding clash and flash of cymbals and gongs. There was, however, neither rejoicing nor envy in the sight of the distinguished gentleman in the sleek car at Ah Oon Koh's door, only mild, sceptical curiosity.

Ah Kum Soh peeped from her window, in the middle of pounding chillies, to watch; Ah Cheng Mm, who liked to shake out her long hair to dry in the sun before oiling and recoiling it into the tight neat bun at the back of the head, saw her small grandson among the onlookers and knew she would get the information from a reliable source. All looked at the chauffeur opening the car door for the gentleman, who stepped out with magisterial dignity and purpose.

A lie, a lie, thought Mei Kwei as her mother rushed forward to greet Old Yoong with much nervous deference and he responded graciously. The man standing in front of her was not the man in the advance photograph, which was still lying on the chest of drawers in her room. There must be at least thirty years between the two men; in a flash, the handsome man with the full head of hair, the firm face, the bright eyes, the upright, proud bearing stood beside his own derelict self with sparse white hair, sagging skin, lustreless eyes sunk in heavy webbed bags, and a depleted frame that could never be fully disguised by the handsome Mao suit of finest cut and material. But the aura of opulence was intact, as the old man, speaking graciously, stood against a backdrop of patiently waiting white car and uniformed chauffeur, and momentarily touched the massive gold watch and chain by his side. The perfume of wealth hung palpably in the air, inhaled deeply and reverentially by both hosts and onlookers. Where it was unable to defeat the odours of old age and decline, an old man's vanity took over. Old Yoong would continue to use the photograph of thirty years ago to perpetuate the youthfulness that a regime of nourishing herbs, exotic brews and special ginseng had failed to do, and did not expect the matchmakers and friendly relatives questing on his behalf to ask any questions. In the last and grandest concession to his vanity, the photograph would be used at his funeral, enlarged and solidly framed, propped up against his coffin amid laudatory banners, plaques and flowers, no matter how removed from the ancient corpse within.

But it was with a young man's briskness that Old Yoong dealt with the dark undercurrents swirling beneath the smooth, polite surface of the meeting. It was ever the bad luck of the wealthy suitor, when rescuing a pretty girl from poverty, to have to contend with a family wearing poverty's special badge of smiling obsequiousness and secret envy. The mother's annoying effusiveness was easily countenanced with polite formality; the brother's surly caution and the father's awkward tentativeness were dismissed with a perfunctory nod.

Then Old Yoong moved to the next stage of the visit's agenda. He got his chauffeur to take out of the car and lay before the family the gifts he had brought for them. The small spectators, peeping in from outside, stared wide-eyed at the large gleaming packages of different sizes and shapes and whispered in excited speculation about the contents. They stored up every detail for later re-telling at home to mothers and grandmothers, and wondered at the lack of enthusiasm of the recipients who never got up to examine such a hoard of treasure.

'You shouldn't have – you are too kind,' said Ah Oon Soh, while the father and brother were prompted to murmur something.

Old Yoong dismissed all thanks with a casual wave. He then turned to face the girl, to concentrate on the primary purpose of the visit, which was to establish the justifiability of her photo's claim. On a previous occasion with another girl about a year back, he had suspended judgement until the actual face-to-face meeting; very wisely, it turned out, for the cunning of the photographer's enhancing colour brush had induced false expectations and he found himself looking upon a dull, sallow-faced girl. But this time, he thought, with hardly concealed excitement as he keenly studied the young girl sitting in front of him, her eyes lowered, the reality exceeded the expectations.

First Wife had been chosen for him when he was still a very young man, and he had seen her only on the wedding day itself, politely suppressing his shock at her ugly gash of a mouth. Second Wife was a cousin of First Wife, brought in upon the latter's admission of shameful failure when no child was produced after three years; she was pretty enough, but not nearly as pretty as he would have wished. Third Wife was the prettiest of all, but she had lost her good looks quickly, having a fondness for good food and long hours at the mahjong table. This girl would be the most beautiful of them all, the bold capture by sunset's waning shadows of the firmament's brightest star. It was the supreme acquisition, an old man's gift to himself, to sustain desire more effectively than any diet of steamed rice, fungus, young bamboo shoots, ginseng and boar's blood. The *yang* needed to harvest ripening, virginal *yin*; this girl, with her special beauty and luminosity, was endless bounty.

Turning away from the fidgeting mother and the sullenly silent father and brother, Old Yoong let his cool, practised eyes take in the entirety of the girl's beauty, noting the slim legs and the dainty feet, not shown in the photograph. Satisfied with his first visit, he stood up to leave and be driven home in time for his nap and nourishing herbal brew that Second Wife always prepared for him, and to plan the next visit, and the next, to reach proper union with this rare girl. His standing up was the signal for the rest to stand up also. In his absence the father might snort and the brother scoff, but now, in full view of the gleaming car, the uniformed chauffeur springing to open the car door, the impeccable Mao suit, the gold watch and chain, the pile of gifts on the table which could be the start of a continuous flow of largesse, neither dared give offence.

Ah Oon Soh said, 'Oh, but you haven't yet drunk your coffee,' and settled into shy murmuring as the awesome personage, ignoring her and coffee, made for the door.

But his visit was not quite at an end. He meant it to be capped by the best gift of all, to be handed over personally by him to the girl herself. At precisely the moment of stepping out of the door, he took from his pocket a red box. Handing it to her he said, 'This is for you.' Then with the casual magnanimity of the true benefactor who will not wait for thanks, he was out of the house and in his car.

Ah Oon Soh would always bemoan her sad fate of never being allowed to share in her daughter's triumphs, only in her pain. Not for her now the pleasure, surely a mother's due, of being asked to witness the opening of the red box and comment on the gift. Pathetic in her eagerness to know, she trailed her daughter in the house with beseeching questions. 'So. What is it? Why don't you open and see? Surely you want to know. Why don't you open now?'

Pig Auntie, watching in the background, seemed bursting in the same eagerness. But it was the girl's perverseness to bestow her trust on the least deserving. Tee Tee ran out of her room the next day with a gold bracelet dangling from his thin wrist, shouting, 'Big Sister gave this to me!'

The playfulness was precisely what was needed to lift the pall of unease that had settled on the gift. Out in the open, gleaming on the arm of the ragged friend who, even at his most audacious, would accept it only as play, the bracelet drew the admiring interest of all. Ah Oon Soh touched, examined and did a quick mental evaluation, remembering a bracelet, similar in size and design, that she had seen at Tin Peng Goldsmith. Pig Auntie, with exaggerated care, peeled it off the boy's wrist and was prompted to add to the general light-hearted geniality some of her own, threatening to drag her son to the police station, to be handcuffed for grand theft.

'Go on, put it on,' Ah Oon Soh urged her daughter and, in an instant, proudly demonstrated her knowledge of jewellery by working the clasp expertly on her daughter's wrist.

She was pleased to see it remain on the wrist in the ensuing days. Having gone to Tin Peng Goldsmith one morning on the pretext of buying a comparable bracelet and looked at its price tag, she came home excitedly to her daughter who was ironing clothes, and raised both hands, five fingers spread out on one and the thumb cocked up on the other, by way of announcing the cost of the stupendous gift.

Her daughter thought, It will be yours, Mother. It will give you greater joy. Unwilling to show openly her fascination with the gift, she studied it closely in private. She had never seen, much less possessed, anything like it. Small, delicately shaped leaves intricately linked together, it took her breath away. She remembered once seeing her mother wear a borrowed bracelet to attend a relative's wedding. It was nothing compared to the gift on her wrist.

She put it to immediate use, reaping rich dividends of gratification. At the mah-jong table for the serving of coffee and the taking away of empty coffee cups, she noted, with deep satisfaction, a slow dropping of Auntie Rosie's jaw and a slowing down of her hands shuffling tiles, as her eyes took in the gleaming bracelet and remained fixed on it.

But gift was not promise. No word came from the old man in Penang. No emissary came with a message or more gifts. His silence, possible prelude to a final polite apology and withdrawal, sent little tremors of fear through Ah Oon Soh, who filled the awful void with the tiny incessant noises of her own anxiety, directed both at Pig Auntie and her daughter. 'Why hasn't he called? Do you think something has happened? Do you think we have offended him in some way?'

'Let him do as he likes! He can do as he likes!' Mei Kwei said sharply, but she too wondered about the silence. She reflected long and deeply about the meeting, more than two weeks back, when, without looking up, she had seen the slow stirrings of interest and admiration light up his face, and on raising her eyes for only an instant as she received the red gift box with both hands, had caught the flash of pleasure in his. A sudden thought came into her mind and made her heart quicken: had the spiteful Auntie Rosie gone secretly to the old man on a campaign of malice? Had she fed him lies to make him withdraw?

'The rich, what have we to do with them?' said her mother in aggrieved tones, on the sixteenth day of silence.

'What indeed?' sneered her brother, coming out of silent, surly shadows to share in defeat and anger, never joy.

And then the silence was broken, but not the anxiety. Old Yoong sent word that he needed certain information about the girl, the precise hour and date of her birth. The information was promptly dispatched, and the waiting commenced anew with heightened tremulousness, for many were the stories of negotiations broken off or betrothals terminated on an astrologer's warning.

Ah Oon Soh was on the point of visiting her own fortune-teller to find out the worst, when word came of the decision of a second visit by the august personage who would relay his decision of the betrothal and wedding dates, based on the advice of his astrologers. Ah Ooh Soh immediately went to the temple and offered a joss-stick of gratitude. The second visit required an exercise of cleaning more crucial than the sweeping, dusting and taking down of old calendars from walls. She told the eaters that no meals would be provided for a while, thus clearing the house of low, coarse labourers whose presence would surely displease the visitor.

His decision made, Old Yoong launched himself upon the next stage of the courtship. Having little patience with the proprieties expected of a still only affianced couple, he stood up exactly seven minutes after arrival, looked at his gold watch and invited the girl, with the cool confidence of an old man used to having his way, to take a ride with him in his car.

'But you haven't yet touched your coffee,' Ah Ooh Soh said, blinking nervously. Surely her daughter would have to be escorted if the neighbours were not to gossip?

Mei Kwei got up to go.

The chauffeur's face retained its impassivity as he cast brief glances into his mirror. He could predict each quick stage of the old man's ardour in the presence of young beauty. Unlike the young awkward suitor who would depend on a sudden jolting movement of the car to throw bodies together and allow the accidental hand on the girl's lap to remain there, the old man dispensed with all such help. As soon as the car started, he took up the girl's braceleted wrist and asked her how she liked his gift. His voice had changed remarkably, from crisp curtness in the presence of her family to the silken tones of the confident wooer. As he turned to face her fully and drink in her beauty at close range, he expressed his fervour in a rush of compliments, each attached to a separate feature so that he could, as he spoke, touch, in turn, cheek, brow, mouth, hair, chin. 'You are very beautiful,' he said with ardent sincerity and moved his face to lay it against hers.

Mei Kwei felt a little spasm of terror as the hot dry mouth moved upwards, past the cheek, past the cheekbones, towards the eyes. She held her breath. It did not halt, in its exploration of delight, at the teardrop mole. She relaxed. The terror had disappeared but not the spasm of something like shock, from deep inside, which manifested itself in a slight reddening of cheeks and neck as the old mouth roamed her face and the old hands her body. She gave a little gasp and experienced an involuntary shrinking into herself, as she had as a small girl upon the invasion of hard stares. She feared having given offence, but the old man, withdrawing immediately, seemed pleased at her timid innocence. An uninhibited response would have perturbed him: the brazen, practised one, such as was common among the cabaret girls and songstresses, would have cast her with these and immediately disqualified her for partnership.

His overtures of passion having served as a useful test, Old Yoong leaned back in his seat contentedly, in the certain knowledge that really this girl needed none. For the rest of the car ride, he sat quietly beside her, holding her hand and wishing that the astrologer's date for the wedding, six months ahead, could be brought forward. His mind became busy with many thoughts, all languorously pleasurable: whereas with a cabaret girl or songstress his thoughts would be of the private bed at the end of the car ride in the seaside home well away from the prying eyes of all three wives, here they eschewed coarse anticipation, and concentrated instead on the purer purpose of how to make his new bride happy. He would make clear to the other wives that they were to treat her well and not give her cause for complaint, and that they could expect him, for the first year at least, to go to their beds only very occasionally. Women's petty jealousies and squabbles were matters for amusement only: in any case, they would not be allowed to mar the new bride's happiness. He intended to take her on worldwide travels.

He told her of his plans, always during the car rides, never in the presence of her contemptible family, and experienced the special gratification a man must feel when he succeeds in making a painfully shy, deeply blushing girl turn slowly, radiantly, like a sunflower, to face him with eager curiosity. Mei Kwei had heard of far-away countries, separated by great tracts of water that could only be traversed by big ships. Now, for the first time, she saw them not as mere shapes and colours on a spinning globe in a classroom but as destinations of real journeys in real time.

'After our marriage, we will go to England, China, Australia.' The man's casual tone reduced magical realms to the ordinariness and attainability of Bukit Tuas, the neighbouring town, eight miles away. She looked at him, deeply impressed.

Looking forward to the gift of her pristine body after their marriage, he was prepared to load it with the gifts of his munificence before the event. He instructed his chauffeur to take a long country road well away from all curious eyes but, even before they had passed the main street in Luping, he was already bringing out of his pocket another gift box in lucky red. He asked her to open it and kept his eyes fixed on her face to enjoy fully the delight of her response. She gasped to see a pair of exquisite diamond and jade ear-rings. 'Here, let me,' he said, one of his greatest pleasures being to hang ear-rings on soft ear-lobes, a pendant on a throbbing chest.

The chauffeur, again glancing in the mirror, saw a treasure trove as small boxes appeared from coat and trouser pockets and snapped open to reveal bracelets, necklaces, ear-rings and rings, gifts possibly reclaimed from old loves to please a new.

'I want the Grapes Pendant,' Old Yoong had said. Or, 'Please return the Tortoise Pin.' He gave his gifts names so that he might remember them more easily, and First Wife, or Second or Third, had gone quietly, bitterly, to the safe-boxes in the bank. Now, watching the girl's astonished delight, the besotted old man laughed his own special delight as his hands, with proprietorial zest, roamed ears, wrists, neck to assist in the transference of the glittering cache from its velvet-lined boxes to the beauteous young body. He drank in the hushed exclamations of pure incredulity as her fingers moved to touch, very gingerly, each item; like the peasant girl in her favourite childhood tale, Mei Kwei had stumbled into a magic cave and stood dazed by what she saw.

When the last item had been put on and the overall effect suitably surveyed in a hand mirror that must have been brought for the purpose, the old man asked, with a lover's coyness, 'What about a kiss?'

It was the first time Mei Kwei had kissed a man. If she closed her eyes, she would not have to look upon the eager gluttony of the blotched, mottled hands, the dry, puckered lips, the moving tongue, only feel it. She closed her eyes.

CHAPTER EIGHTEEN

Ah Oon Soh's self-lacerating humility as she hung fearfully around her daughter to catch any sign of the girl's readiness to share her good fortune was amply rewarded.

'Mother, come.' Mei Kwei was sitting on the bed in her room. Ah Oon Soh bustled in, all tight-faced eagerness.

The girl had laid the gifts, neatly and systematically, on the plank bed, in the manner of the goldsmith with his precise, sectioned trays, or the police exhibiting the recovered spoils of a major robbery for the taking of pictures for the newspapers. There were rings, bracelets, necklaces, ear-rings, pendants, testifying to the magnitude of Old Yoong's love, since a rich old man's passion was always measured out in gold, jade and diamonds.

Ah Oon Soh gave a little cry of amazement, and looked at her daughter. Then she went quickly to close the bedroom door. From now on the pre-nuptial gifts would be a secret between only mother and daughter: too rich a hoard, they could never be shown to others without risk. Ah Oon Soh's eyes moved from the jewels to their privileged recipient, then back to the gifts; only then did the enormous success of the enterprise, begun with an old man's request for a photo, sink in. She clasped her hands tightly together, the habitual severity softening into genuine relief and delight on behalf of her difficult daughter as she said, 'Your mother is happy for you.'

With a sudden return to sharpness, Mei Kwei asked, 'How much do you owe that woman?' meaning Auntie Rosie of the cutting tongue.

A note of cautiousness crept into Ah Oon Soh's voice and pinched her features into a frown as she said, 'Not much. Why do you ask?' Then she let out a little cry of protest as the girl jerked up a gold chain and thrust it into her hand, saying, 'Go and sell this and return the money to her at once. There should be enough.'

'You can't, you can't.' Ah Oon Soh was unhappy all over again.

'This will take care of the money you owe Ah Kim Soh,' Mei Kwei fished up another chain with a forefinger, 'and this,' picking up a ring, 'what you owe Ah Beng Chek.' The brisk decisiveness of tone could not hide her pain: Mother, how long are you going to let Father and Big Older Brother make a slave of you? Are you going to prison for their debts? Ah Oon Soh began to cry, but there was now no stopping the girl's recklessness. Her voice rang with mocking laughter and her fingers flew with angry energy to pick up this or that piece of redemptive jewellery and wave it in the air: this for Father's opium for the next six months; this for Big Older Brother's *ronggeng* girls.

The jewellery was now a jumbled heap, bearing the marks of plunder.

'Stop it, stop it! It is not right! Why are you behaving like this?' When Mei Kwei was a child, her mother had responded to her bouts of craziness by shouting, '*Siau!*' and pinching her ear or arm. Something of her old exasperation returned as she bent to retrieve a ring that had dropped to the floor. She shook her head and made little noises of vexed hopelessness. She wished to be taken into the dark depths of the daughter's inner torment no longer. 'You do as you like,' Ah Oon Soh said, with her own return of sharpness.

In that troubled, heaving house, collisions faded into weary resignation as each returned to the private niche of pain and anger and told the other, 'Leave me alone. Do as you like.'

The father left her alone, but not the promise of gain she had brought. In her room, listening listlessly to the small sounds coming from outside, she started suddenly. She peeped through a tiny slit in the door and saw her father's hand shoot out as he was passing a small table to grab at a pair of ear-rings she had left there. She remembered having taken them off the day before, laid them beside an assortment of small objects on the table, then forgotten to return them to their place in a drawer, beside her bed. The sound of somebody coming from the kitchen startled the man into dropping one of the ear-rings. In a second, he was back in his room.

The inner tumult was unbearable, requiring Mei Kwei to press her fingers tightly to her temples as if to contain a crushing headache, as she paced the room. Thieving father, what does it feel like to be saved by a despised daughter? She longed to bang on his room door and scream, 'Father, come out! Ask and you will be given all you need for your opium. This theft is worse than any rejection.'

She lay awake all night, dry-eyed and angry. In the morning, she noticed that the dropped ear-ring had been furtively kicked into a secret safe corner behind one of the table legs, to be retrieved at the first opportunity. A wave of rage broke over her, then gathered into a tight grim knot of resolution.

Ah Oon Koh, coming out of the darkness and blinking in the bright shaft of sunlight that hit his eyes, looked up to see his daughter standing before him. Ever since that time, years ago, when she had challenged him with those unnaturally piercing child's eyes, he had recoiled from any direct encounter with her. His daughter had been born to be his bane. Now he looked at her warily, his brow darkening.

She stretched out her hand on which lay the ear-ring. 'Father, you forgot the other one. The pawnshop will only accept a pair. Here it is.'

Without a word, he raised his fist and struck the offered jewel out of his daughter's hand, making it fly across the whole length of the room. In the old days, he would have struck her too, but now, the growing lustre of her ascent in the world and the taint of his decline, stayed his quivering arm.

'Father –' Mei Kwei longed to ask for his forgiveness. 'Father –' she said again, and made a small movement towards him. He slammed the door in her face. Abruptly, she turned and ran back into her room.

Old Yoong's munificence was not of the amiably careless kind that had no need to keep track of gifts. Instead, its admirable calculus kept every item tagged. He therefore specified in advance what Mei Kwei was to wear. He prided himself on an unerring instinct for fine female grooming, having personally selected for her, on a shopping trip to Penang's best draper, the material for a new wardrobe. Mixed into the endearment of his parting words as he dropped her home would be the reminder to wear this or that dress for his next visit with these or those jewels. Turning round to survey her as they sat in the car before their drive, he told her that he had not seen the jade drop ear-rings for some time or the gold chain with the tortoise pendant. He looked at her ear-lobes, neck, wrists, fingers, and added one more missing item: the gold bracelet with the diamond clasp. He watched her pale expression, the small twitching of the corners of her mouth, and while he held her hands tenderly, felt a sense of pleasing power that in any conflict with this bright, young, beautiful, intense girl, wealth would always transcend the disadvantage of age. For he had guessed at the real circumstances of the missing jewels; the girl would blame herself and even beg forgiveness, but his instincts about that family of hers, especially the idle brother, were correct.

Easily able to afford replacements, he could also afford to be moved rather than angry, to sympathise rather than rebuke. The gentleness could come later; now the stern tone was appropriate, to draw this girl, who could be artful on her family's account, deeper into his orbit of control. His experience with three wives and numerous mistresses had given him insights into the peculiar workings of the female mind and heart under the agitations of guilt and fear, and he had learned to manipulate them, chiefly through a fine orchestration of his own responses, which he allowed to glide up and down an impressive scale, from outright rage to overwhelming tenderness. By the time he had finished, he always had the poor flustered thing sobbing hysterically in his arms and promising better behaviour in the future.

His sternness was working: the girl looked frightened and her hands were cold. Yes, they had all been pawned, to settle debts. No, there had been no choice.

How much? Her mother had trembled at the chilling penetration of her question; Mei Kwei now froze under the ruthless intensity of his. Old Yoon was silent for a moment, while she waited, stealing fearful glances at him. Then he shifted in his seat and stretched out to allow a hand to dig deep into his trouser pocket. The pockets had yielded treasures for the enhancement of her beauty; now they threw up wads of cash for the rescue of her disgraced family. 'Take it,' he said kindly, adding, still more kindly, 'I'm doing it for you,' and closed her fingers, cold and trembling, upon the thick wad.

Mei Kwei sat very still, and he saw the tears forming in her eyes. She had been similarly moved, years ago, when Sister St Elizabeth had offered kind words and Ovaltine rather than a scolding for the exercise book defaced by her brother.

'Come,' he said, and drew her into his arms. In the warmth of his embrace, she began to sob, richly, luxuriously, until the burden in her heart, unbearably overcharged for some time, was eased out upon a last sniffle and she leaned back on the comforting shoulder. He kissed her and stroked her hair, not wanting to spoil the delicious peace by telling her of his decision: after the marriage, she would have as little as possible to do with her family, and especially her brother.

Her mean world would be left far behind for the brilliance of his. Already, in the last months before the wedding, he was inducting her into the glitter of the large gatherings at the exclusive Penang British

Club that he loved. His first three wives had not been afforded the same elaborate induction, but this girl was different and it gave him a distinctly heady sense of achievement as he walked slowly into the Club with her and beamed at the faces turned to watch them. He introduced her to his friends with buoyant enthusiasm and watched their reaction as their eyes, and their wives', took in her beauty, the clothes, the jewellery.

The triumph was especially keen with regard to Old Tang, a long-time business associate, and the most famous racehorse owner in Penang who brooked no competition, either in horses or women. He decked his latest mistress, an extremely beautiful woman who had been formerly a songstress in the Club, with the finest clothes and jewels, and dared any man to do better. Old Tang's keen eyes had narrowed in pique at the sight of a diamond bracelet on the wrist of the young fiancée of that insufferable fool Yoong, and at their next meeting at the Club, he drew attention to a similar – nay, more expensive one – on his own mistress's wrist.

Gifts became weapons in a deadly war of old men's vanities: the two women were paraded with loads of jewellery that increased with each new competitive encounter. They had learned to co-operate with their men's vanity by arranging limbs, moving hands and fingers, twisting necks, for a maximum display of their baubles.

Like schoolboys locked in ferocious combat, Old Yoong and Old Tang would not stop. The competition in the donating of large sums of money to the hospitals and homes under British patronage was far less exciting than that centred on their beautiful women. Then Old Tang began to boast privately that he had won. In the warm glow of brandy and cigar, he pointed laughingly to a jade bangle on his mistress's wrist, a magnificent thick circlet of the purest green translucence. He was coy about the cost but revealed the name of the jeweller's, indisputably the best and most established in Penang, adding archly that there had been only one bangle of the kind.

The race was taken to a new level of intensity. Not expecting to see the white car so early one morning, Mei Kwei was startled to see its owner already in the house and telling her to get ready for a longer ride than usual. She had learned to adjust her demeanour to his; the stern, purposeful set of his face and the slight hint of impatience in his voice with her mother's bumbling effusiveness forbade all questions and demanded instant compliance. In a few minutes she was ready.

It was the culminating gift, found at the end of many hours' drive to the town of Ipoh, in an obscure back-street shop that sold the most exquisite jade jewellery in the country. Old Yoong surveyed the bangles under the glass cases, his expert eye easily picking out the best. The shop assistant complimented him on his astuteness and brought it out with exaggerated care. Old Yoong subjected it to the closest scrutiny. It was the purest, brightest, most exquisite jade piece anywhere in the country, said the shop assistant, and testified to its illustrious history as a relic from an imperial collection.

'Come,' said Old Yoong, and Mei Kwei put out her hand. But the bracelet proved too small; she squeezed her fingers tightly together to allow passage, but to no avail. She laughed the nervous, apologetic laugh of one receiving a tremendous gift and at the same time offering irrefutable proof of her unworthiness of it: The gift is not meant for me. Take it away.

'Here. Let me.' Old Yoong tried to fit the rigid circlet of stone over the bruised bones of her hand, pushing, shoving, tugging.

The gift is hurting, Mei Kwei thought, as the pain brought tears into her eyes. *Tighter, tighter.* But her bones could not come more tightly together, to accommodate the hard gift. *Tighter, tighter.* The small bones in Second Grandmother's feet had yielded to the foot-binder's pitiless crushing bands before they could be slipped into the gift of the beautiful doll's shoes. The bones in her hand refused to be crushed and fought against the invading jade.

The assistant said, 'There's another, slightly bigger bracelet,' but Old Yoong would have no other, and renewed the assault. He asked for some lubricating oil, which was brought immediately, and he rubbed it on the bruised, quivering flesh. He tried to ram home the jade once more, but it was no use. Pausing for breath, he looked around for a place to sit, and was offered a chair, then refreshment. Grimly sipping tea, he gathered his energies for the next stage of the onslaught.

'I can't take the pain any more,' Mei Kwei screamed silently, and her tears, like molten lead, scorched her eyeballs.

There was a final assault from the combined hardness of purpose and jade, which caused a fresh springing of tears and then a little gasp of relief, as the bones, finally reduced to a shivering helplessness, gave in at last.

The circlet of jade, resplendent, triumphant, gleamed. Old Yoong held up her hand, smiling, to gaze upon his trophy, snug on the small wrist.

CHAPTER NINETEEN

Mei Kwei's time was precious because it was her own; his next visit would not be till the following day. Tee Tee, whose alert eyes noticed every shifting tide of emotion under the calm surface, said, 'Big Sister, where are you going?' as she took out her bicycle and prepared to mount it. Her mother, if she had been at home, would have rushed out to protest, 'You can't do that!' meaning that bicycles now had no place in the new lustre of her unfolding life.

'Can I come with you?' Tee Tee asked again.

But Mei Kwei wanted to be alone and was off in an instant.

Every visit to the cemetery was invariably accompanied by a rising wind and the plaintive sounds of some far-away bird, the very sounds to which Second Grandmother's ears had been alerted in her last days. Some people depended on smells for signs: for three years a neighbour, Ah Gaik Ee, waited, nostrils quivering, for the first faint whiff of Six Dragons Embrocation Oil, which her mother-in-law used on her rheumatic legs when alive.

The grass had grown tall and untidy around Second Grand-mother's tombstone, which still bore marks of the red candle drippings from the last visit on the Feast of the Hungry Ghosts, but there was no sign of the ghost money, which had been burned in abundance for her to spend to her heart's content in a kinder world. A tiny blackened remnant floated from somewhere in the cemetery. Mei Kwei watched it spin, like a playful leaf, in an eddy of air, then vanish. Visiting Second Grandmother, she allowed her thoughts to dwell on others, as she sat comfortably on a slab of rock by the tombstone and surveyed the vast, desolate, silent expanse around her. She wondered about those lying unquiet in their quiet graves, the lament of their unfulfilled dreams picked up and echoed by wind and storm. She thought of the countless people maimed and felled by the Japanese: could ghosts travel over water, pursuing their murderers in fleeing ships? She knew of some small children who had died, including her own sister so many years ago, whose name nobody remembered.

Nameless forgotten ghosts elicited a special kindness. An old woman once set up, by the roadside, an offering of a plate of oranges, a bowl of rice and two cups of tea with a bunch of joss-sticks in an empty cigarette tin, for all the ghosts who had nobody to offer them food at the Feast of the Hungry Ghosts. 'Feed my greater hunger,' cried the ghost of an infant, who had died before being named. But the old woman could give it only food, not selfness, and it had slipped back into howling, nameless chaos.

The living sometimes visited the dead only for gain, bringing the ceremonial paraphernalia of cockerel, knife, bamboo stake and candles to facilitate their requests for winning lottery numbers. Mei Kwei would pluck up any such desecration from her grandmother's grave and cast it in anger upon the wind. The daily lighting of the joss-stick to put in the urn before her grandmother's framed photograph was no more than habit; for silent communication and solace, she preferred to come to the grave itself, bringing with her childhood's enduring belief in a heart still beating with understanding and love amid death's mouldering ruins under the weed-covered tombstone.

'Second Grandmother,' Mei Kwei whispered, and believed that the still, sad figure stretched out these many years in the beloved doll's shoes in the dark, dank earth heard and understood. As in childhood, when an unspeakable heaviness of heart was simply brought into the old woman's room and laid, in silence, upon the loving lap, so now she uttered no complaint, made no entreaty, but merely sat quietly in comforting closeness to the loved presence, and surrendered her spirit to its gentle power. The jade bangle on her wrist was hidden from sight, covered over with a tightly twisted handkerchief, having no existence in the absence of its giver. Freed from the sight, she winced at its touch, cold, hard and unyielding upon her wrist.

When she got up to go, it was drizzling. She walked briskly to her bicycle, less afraid of impending storm than of the sudden appearance of a man, at a distance, from behind a cluster of tombstones. His unkempt appearance and the rough bundles he was carrying marked him as the lowest of the low, a rag-and-bone man, reduced to scavenging in cemeteries. He was in the act of picking up something from the ground when he saw her, and stood up immediately, staring. Ignoring him and confident of safety once she reached her bicycle, she broke into a run. Her fear invited boldness: he dropped his bundles and began to move towards her, shouting. In her mounting panic, her eyes still took in the distant serenity of the Church of the Sacred Heart of Jesus, its spire and roof distinctly visible. There she had, not too long before, sought refuge from a stalker: her heart quickened to the hope of a second rescue. But the church was too far away and the intruder within attacking distance. She managed to get on her bicycle and to pedal away with all her might. The man ran after her, shouting even more loudly. Then the bicycle hit a rock and sent her sprawling to the ground. She thought he was already upon her and her terror distilled into a single gasp of surrendering despair, when from a distance she heard a shout – a shout of warning, of rescue. She raised her head, and turned to see a black car roar up and screech to a halt. The intruder stopped, paused, then fled.

The driver of the car was beside Mei Kwei in an instant, helping her up with anxious, solicitous enquiries. In any situation, his pale intensity would have made him instantly recognisable. In the church she had had occasion to notice it twice: once when he swung round to stare at her and again when he approached her after the service.

With elaborate care, he examined the bruises on her arm and picked up her bicycle. The eagerness marked him more as admirer than rescuer, grateful for, rather than perturbed by, the incident. They had not yet exchanged names, but the momentousness of the encounter was already raising, in both, perplexing thoughts and feelings.

The strangeness of her world struck her like a bizarre dream in the extraordinary shifting of its menacing shadows and comforting radiances, where men stalked her with dark intent or rescued her from other men. In her dreams, Old Yoong came with the gleaming power of his wealth, to save her from the despair of her father's and brother's shame, then turned attacker, shackling her in gold. This stranger, too, seemed both stalker and rescuer. She had fled him once; yet now she was turning to him, trembling with relief, not only in the gratitude of a rescue from a derelict in a cemetery, but in the hope – as yet only a daring, shimmering possibility in the desperate corners of her heart – of a far greater rescue. Her grandmother, listening to her wrenching cry only a short while ago, had heard, understood and responded.

As a child, Mei Kwei had sunk with inexpressible relief into the kind arms of a stranger who had picked her up from a ditch, and of another who had put her on his knee and wiped away tears. It would be to strangers that she would always turn. When alive, Second

Grandmother had said, 'Beware of strangers'; dead, she was making use of them.

She allowed her rescuer to lead her to the safety of his car. He was saying something but she was too tired to listen, merely letting the reassuring sound of his voice, like a warm gentle wave, wash over her exhausted body and spirit. Then he fell silent and they remained quiet, each deep in thought.

She could have no idea of the depth or scope of his, which even now, as he drove his car carefully along dirt tracks, induced an overpowering intensity that made his eyes glow and his hands tighten their grip, knuckles stark white, upon the steering wheel.

CHAPTER TWENTY

It has come, it has come, was Austin Tong's exultant thought. In church, he had asked for a sign from God in his despair. It was the kind of pitch-black despair that engulfed the soul and dragged it down to impenetrable depths, but his plea had struggled up, like an enfeebled fish in suffocating mud, and lain gasping at God's feet: Show me a sign now or I go out this instant to kill myself.

He had meant it. He would get into his car and race home to meet his end. Loneliness like his was a slow poison; he would speed up its effect with the more merciful poison in bottles and vials, and nobody would be the worse off for his passing away. 'What a pity,' would be about all that could be said. 'So young, good-looking and wealthy. What a pity.'

God, a sign or else –

Kneeling, his head buried in his hands, oblivious of the sounds around him, the priest's intoning and the congregation's murmuring, he delivered an ultimatum to God. And God had responded instantly. It was almost as if the divine voice had whispered in his ear right there and then, 'Turn round,' for suddenly his head jerked up from his hands and his body twisted to see the girl behind him. She was kneeling, her hands clasped in prayer. He had let out an audible gasp at the sheer wondrousness of God's preciseness: the reality exactly matched the image that he had been carrying, in some tender corner of mind and heart, down to the last detail of gentle face, prayerful downward glance, clasped hands. The only difference was the absence of the soft white veil on the head – but the shafts of sunlight coming in through the church windows cast a shimmering gauze over the girl's hair, making the resemblance perfect.

He had waited impatiently for the end of the service. Outside the church, he did not see her again and, for an instant, experienced a little frisson of terror: had he imagined it all? But it had been no hallucination, for he had turned and seen the priest shaking her hand and talking to her. And then she was gone again. She had vanished from his sight as quickly as she had come into it. But the sign had been irrevocably given, and he could not but be committed to its pursuit. Reckless with excitement, he had decided to test the divine patience further: Give me another, final sign.

God had obliged again.

There was no reason why he should have been driving along a desolate cemetery path. He had later explained it to himself as a divine infusion of independent will so that his car suddenly swerved and took him to the most unlikely spot on earth for a visit, a pagan cemetery – for the most unlikely of deeds, rescuing her from a marauder. The symbolism was profoundly moving: he had plucked her from physical danger as he would surely pluck her from the darkness of her pagan ancestors' ways.

She had told him, 'Please drop me here,' in the midst of a dirt road, and he had an immediate idea of the first of many obstacles in her troubled world. He wanted to delay her return to this world, to talk to her and find out more. The bruises on her arms and legs from the fall became both a subject of genuine concern and an instrument for a purpose rapidly shaping in his mind.

'You must have medicine for them. Let me get some for you,' he said kindly, and turned his car round.

She let the kindness, like a refreshing spring of cool water, slake her parched soul, and was not bothered that, during the drive down at least three roads in the town, somebody was sure to notice and say, 'Isn't that Mei Kwei? Isn't she to be married soon? What is she doing in another man's car?'

She had seen the Britannia eating-house on a few occasions, as different from Luping's numerous eating-houses and coffee-shops in its sleek appearance as in its exclusive clientele, the free-spending British officers and their wives. Austin Tong said casually, as he helped her out of the car and then led her into the restaurant through a back, private entrance, 'My father's. He died some years ago and left it to me.'

He searched the contents of a medicine cabinet in a small back room and then applied himself assiduously to the task of cleaning the bruises and putting ointment on them. She was aware, as she sat quietly looking on, of the sounds and smells of cooking, coming as from a great distance, although the restaurant kitchen must have been very close by: of the distinct hissing sound of furious deep-frying, and of men's voices raised above the hissing in friendly chat. They were reassuring sounds and smells, as were the small neat pieces of protective pink plaster on her skin. What kind hands he has, she thought.

'Shall I drop you here?' He slowed his car at the precise spot on the dirt road she had indicated earlier.

A new defiance crept into her. Why should I be afraid all the time? she thought and directed him right to the doorstep, preparing to meet the frowning enquiries of her mother and brother coming out of the house to see an unfamiliar car – preparing even to see the familiar gleaming white car parked near the door and its owner narrow his eyes in silent displeasure at the sight of another man beside her.

'I will bring round your bicycle as soon as I have had it repaired,' Austin Tong said, seizing upon the first of many excuses to visit her. Looking at her eager, defiant face, he felt a thrill of joy that whispered, 'You will not need excuses.'

'Thank you,' she said, for the first time that eventful afternoon, an expression of gratitude that had the dangerous flavour of complicity.

CHAPTER TWENTY-ONE

'One day it is white. Another day it is black.' Peeping from their windows and fed a continuous stream of information by small sons and grandsons ever alert to the sound of approaching vehicles, Ah Kum Soh and Ah Cheng Mm speculated about the dangerous indiscretion of Ah Oon Koh's daughter.

'Look, it is White Car's turn today. It's that wealthy old man from

Penang, didn't you know?' they would whisper, a cluster of heads at the window or doorway, watching Old Yoong escort her to his car. 'Black Car's turn today. Look, it's that young son of Mr Tong, who owns that *ang moh* restaurant in town. Mr Tong was an ugly man, but look at his handsome boy!'

The whispers carried the severity of judgement against the unscrupulous girl, never the competing men. What was she up to? Ah Kum Soh's sharp eyes picked up a fascinating detail, which she immediately passed on to Ah Cheng Mm. 'The girl wears no jewellery and covers up that fabulous jade bangle with a handkerchief whenever she is with the young Mr Tong. Haven't you noticed?'

The two women thought they might find out from her mother.

'Don't ask me anything about my difficult daughter!' Ah Oon Soh said. 'The young nowadays think they can do as they wish!' and repulsed all further attempts.

She broke through the girl's defiant silence. 'Just what do you think you are doing? Doesn't he know you are engaged to be married?' She was amazed at the extent of duplicitous cunning that was involved in successfully keeping the two cars apart. Each time one called, she trembled at the thought of the other making a sudden appearance and hovered around in the greatest of anxieties, marvelling at her daughter's cool indifference.

'What will he say when he finds out?' Annoyance with the interloper merged with fear of the awesome benefactor to raise Ah Oon Soh's voice to a sharp shriek and fix her eyes with angry desperation upon her daughter's.

'I am not married to him yet,' the girl said wilfully. 'He does not own me yet.'

Ah Oon Soh appealed for help to its least likely source. Big Older Brother let out a loud laugh and slapped his thighs in a demonstration of glee at the unfolding drama. 'Let her.' He chuckled. 'Let Little Sister have her way. I'm going to watch!'

His resentment of Old Yoong, who brought gifts to reduce all of them into stammering timidity, was equalled only by his hatred of Austin Tong, who was dazzling his sister with his connections in the white man's world, in particular his white man's restaurant boasting special white man's food. One evening she had come home with a container of roast beef, potatoes and green peas and casually left it on the kitchen table, presumably for him, but he had disdained to touch it. He had no idea about his sister's intentions and no wish to know, being contented at present to watch the two detested men making fools of themselves.

Three cheers for Little Sister! Big Older Brother laughed, raising his glass of Guinness stout. Of the two, he decided he disliked Austin Tong the more. A means of getting back at him – for the humiliation of their fight over the toy train, for the sheer contrast between his degrading dependence on his mother even for paltry spending money, and the other's dazzling ownership of the biggest, best restaurant in Luping and whatever else his father had left him – very soon presented itself.

On one of his visits, Austin Tong, who apparently had no recollection of the boyhood incident, had offered Big Older Brother a position in the running of his restaurant. The proposition was made with a brief description of the duties and a quick, precise statement of salary. Big Older Brother responded slowly, deliberately, savouring the deliciousness of a rare situation that could be turned to advantage. People did him favours or gave him gifts because of his sister and this caused him pain. But he meant to spin as much pleasure as possible out of this offer, beginning with that of seeing the enemy wince under the barb of obvious insult: 'Thank you for your kind offer. Very kind of you. But I shall have to consider it. I shall let you know in due course.' With secret satisfaction he watched a hot angry flush spread over Austin Tong's pale face.

'He wants me to manage his restaurant,' he told his mother, 'and I told him, "Let me think first,"' and it was a second savouring of sweet satisfaction to watch his mother's eyes widen and her mouth open to protest.

Anger against his mother, to whom he regularly stretched out a hand for money, was not easily discharged. It grew dangerously and festered upon a single remark he overheard her make to Pig Auntie when she thought he was not at home: 'Why can't he be a road-sweeper or a rubbish-collector or a lorry attendant? Then he won't have to depend on others!' His dream was to catch her unawares one evening as she sat drinking her cheap coffee in her cheap enamel mug at the kitchen table, slap down a huge wad of money on the table and say, 'This is enough for a house. Or any amount of jewellery at Tin Ping Goldsmith. Now throw out all the eaters and mah-jong players.'

Now he waited for her to say, 'What? A manager's job at the Britannia eating-house and you turned it down?' So that he might repair with biting coolness, 'Yes, as I will turn down the job of Luping's most important man, Mr T. C. Williams. Or of the Governor of Penang.'

Among his friends at the coffee-shop he liked to frequent, he said, 'Work at the Britannia eating-house? I will have to eat my own shit first before I smell the white man's!' and for good measure added, with a guffaw of pure delight, 'What a name! It is not enough that he calls his restaurant after the white man, he must call himself after the white man's car! So, what will be the name of First Son? Make a guess. Ford Tong. Name of Second Son? Morris Minor Tong. Does white man's shit have a name? That will be Daughter's name.'

'You watch it,' Ah Oon Soh said angrily. 'You watch what you are doing – two months to your marriage, the neighbours are talking –'

But Mei Kwei was already out of the house and sitting in the waiting black car.

CHAPTER TWENTY-TWO

'Don't look yet. That's the big man in Luping, Mr T. C. Williams,' said Austin, as the swing door of the Britannia eating-house was pushed open and a tall, brown-haired man in khaki with a blonde woman in a yellow sun-dress came in. 'The chief of operations. Most powerful man in Luping. The terrorists want to get him. They have their own price for his head.'

Smiling, Mei Kwei listened as his voice lowered to a whisper, saw his features animated by the whole novelty of admitting her into the world of men's talk and indulging her with town gossip.

'That's his wife with him. They say she's not happy here. The marriage is in trouble. Ah Hoy of the Luping Club says they quarrel all the time.

'That's Gray, junior officer but their good friend.' A young, worried-looking man with sandy hair and pale eyelashes entered and sat with the Williamses.

Brown, Mitten, Fitzgerald, McDonald, Jameson, Roberts. Austin's familiarity with the élite world of the British ruling class and those locals who moved with ease among them and spoke their language was impressive. Mei Kwei looked at the nest of framed British Royal Family portraits on the wall opposite.

'My father put them there. King George the Fifth and Queen Mary,

King George the Sixth and Queen Elizabeth, Princess Elizabeth and Princess Margaret Rose.' Austin stopped, changing the subject, for he did not like to talk about his father and the shame.

He spoke enthusiastically, however, about the terrorists and their activities about which he knew a great deal, since he liked to sit sometimes with his British patrons at the bar in his restaurant and have a drink with them. He told her about the savagery of the terrorists dedicated to the setting up of a Communist state in Malaya. The other day a dozen rubber-tappers had been found with their throats slit under the trees, presumably to spread fear among other rubber-tappers. The terrorists were brutal and had no qualms about slicing open the stomachs of pregnant women, replaying the atrocities of the Japanese occupation. The Japanese had been routed; once the terrorists were defeated, Malaya would become a happy, prosperous country again. The government punished severely anyone found helping terrorists in any way. The priest, Father François Martin, was almost certainly in trouble for creating a scene in the market-place one morning where dead terrorists had been exhibited. The chief of operations, Mr T. C. Williams, was known to be ruthless with Communist sympathisers. But he was a friendly, unassuming man, despite his status. He had come up to Austin once and congratulated him on the excellent food in his restaurant. 'My wife likes the pork chops and the puddings. Just like home.'

Mei Kwei realised, with a little tremor of pleasure, that for the first time, face to face with a man, she had not lowered her eyes in embarrassment or confusion, or looked away in disgust or fear.

'You may look now.' She entered into the playfulness and turned quickly to regard the threesome eating steak amid the small polite clatter of knives and forks.

The piquancy of their delicious peeping conspiracy in the intimacy of the restaurant's dark, cool interior could not but be sharpened by the larger conspiracy against fate itself, in the form of the stern visage of an old man framed in the window of a gleaming white car. The imminence of the marriage hung in the air, palpable but unspoken. Like two children drawn together in a hostile world, Mei Kwei and Austin faced the world with bold insouciance, and drew strength from each other – he from her growing ardour, the continuing proof of divine ordinance, and she from his unshakeable determination to stand by her in the face of the fearful opposition of her family and of an even more fearful threat from an old man, already shaping in the distance, like storm clouds, ready to break upon their heads.

He must really love me, Mei Kwei thought. They talked of everything except the approaching marriage, or anything remotely connected with it. The jade bangle, hidden from sight but conspicuous by its hard shape under the twisted handkerchief, provoked no question. Its unremitting hardness had sunk into her soft flesh and become one with her body.

I am not married yet she thought in a leap of daring. I will snatch at laughter and happiness as long as I can.

And Austin Tong thought, Nothing stands in the way now. Certainly not wealthy old men presumptuously snatching at girls younger than their own daughters. He thought of one more obstacle before the final fulfilment of his dream: the fact of her still being outside his Church and showing no inclination to enter.

It was part of this girl's rarity that, while still under the influence of her pagan ancestors, she was demonstrating that eminent Christian virtue of love for the poor and despised of the earth, so important to him since his own conversion not too long ago. He smiled with genuine pleasure as he turned to look at her beside him in the car and saw her eyes light up at the sight of Tee Tee, waiting at the prearranged spot under a tree beside a path, wearing a clean shirt, shorts and slippers, his face wiped clean of customary dirt, his hair combed and creamed for the occasion.

Mei Kwei helped the boy into the back of the car, complimenting him on his appearance. Between the excitement of the promised treat and the immediate one of sitting in a car for the first time, Tee Tee was not quite sure how to behave, so his small thin face grew tight, his arms stiff and his large eyes larger, as he looked silently from Mei Kwei to Austin and back to her. He kept timidly to his apportioned place on the back seat throughout the drive, not daring to shift even an inch. In the Britannia eating-house, the timidity continued, despite much coaxing from Mei Kwei to eat. She cut the roast beef into small pieces for him and, impatient to see his enjoyment, began to feed him with a fork. He opened his mouth obediently and, while savouring the taste of beef, potatoes and green peas, continued to look silently at Mei Kwei and Austin.

'Ice-cream afterwards,' said Austin generously. As a treat from his mother, the boy had once been given money for a small lollipop when the ice-cream man came round with his ice-box on the pillion of his bicycle, and he now stared at the rich, smooth, creamy, colourful scoops in a glass dish in front of him.

'Go on, try it,' said Mei Kwei, putting a spoon in his hand.

An Englishman with a small curly-haired boy came into the restaurant.

'Good afternoon, Mr Robinson,' said Austin. 'Hello, Bruce, how are you?'

But the small boy, who was holding a toy aeroplane in one hand, immediately broke away from his father's side, ran up to Tee Tee and began to run the aeroplane up and down his arm, making tremendous hissing and swooshing sounds.

Tee Tee maintained stoic immobility to the sensation of four small wheels whirring up and down his arms. Everyone laughed to see his silent consternation.

'Stop it, Bruce,' said Mr Robinson, and pulled away the child, now intent upon extending the plane's territory to Tee Tee's face.

Mei Kwei laughed and Austin, glancing sideways at her as he always found himself doing, thought, I like her more and more.

The Christian precept of caring for the lowliest of the earth could not have been more warmly manifested. Once more the car slowed down at Mei Kwei's request, a short distance from the Kek Lok Temple and she got out with a packet of the good food for which the Britannia eating-house was famous and for which the lowly would always yearn in vain. Mad Temple Auntie came running out to its aroma, and with her two others who were always at hand for a share of bounty.

'There's enough for all,' said Mei Kwei, to forestall a fight, for the temple vagrants were not above shoving and pushing like small children over her gifts of food.

She returned to the car, smiling from the pleasure of Mad Temple Auntie's joy, before she realised, with a little start of alarm that beef was forbidden in the temple. But the joyousness of the day refused to admit the thought that her small act of kindness was in effect a desecration, nor the fear that something terrible was about to happen; something which took the contours of a severe old face in the cool dark interior of a white car.

'Just what do you think you are doing?' her mother said again, and she replied, with a spirit that belied the growing fear, 'I am not married yet. Nobody owns me yet.'

But her boldness failed her when, on the way home in Austin Tong's car, she saw the familiar white one parked in front of her house and was confronted by a fearful vision of the censuring figure in the impeccable Mao suit, his gold watch held up to time the precise moment of her entrance. Either he or she had got the date of the next visit wrong. Or, working on a suspicion, he had come on a checking mission.

'Stop here,' she said to Austin Tong, in the middle of the dirt road that would from now onwards have to be the stopping place. Like other secret meeting or parting places, it would have its share of guilt. She got down and walked slowly to the house, hating the sight of the white car as much as she dreaded to face its owner. She saw the uniformed chauffeur sitting inside. She worried that he had seen her getting down from the black car and would, at the first opportunity, whisper to his employer.

Stepping into the house, Mei Kwei saw two elderly women whom she had never seen before and whom she immediately connected, through their fine clothes and jewellery, with Old Yoong's privileged world. Probably, she thought, they were part of the long retinue of female relatives who lived in that large stone house that she had glimpsed during one of their leisurely drives through Penang.

Another thought struck her: he had sent them to convey a message that his male dignity would not allow him to deliver personally. Yet another flashed: he had found out about the black car and was terminating the engagement. It was proper that only female emis-saries be assigned the delicate task of divesting her person of all the jewellery and taking it back. Her mother's frowning timidity seemed to confirm her surmises. She was aware that while fears raced through her mind, making her temples throb feverishly, her heart remained calm and detached. She sat quietly with the visitors while they sipped tea and engaged in polite small-talk with her mother, noting that both cast frequent furtive glances at her, as if to glean and store up information about her appearance and demeanour which they would later share with each other in the back of the car on their return home.

She was impatient for the end of their visit, and as soon as the white car finally rolled away, she turned to her mother: 'So? What was that all about?'

It had nothing to do with any change of heart about the forthcoming marriage; if anything, it emphasised the old man's eagerness for the event, which demanded an assurance to be provided by the mother of the bride-to-be herself. This was a customary practice, the two genteel visitors had stressed. 'It is easily done,' said

Ah Oon Soh to her daughter, meaning that she would be able to provide, within days, the ceremonial long white cotton trousers to be used by the bride on her wedding night, for the proving of her pristineness. Unstained, the trousers would be the greatest stain on her reputation. Ah Oon Soh said, 'You are a grown woman now. You should know,' and proceeded, the next day, to go shopping for white cotton cloth.

Old Yoong must have made a similar demand with regard to each of the three wives and pulled out from under each body the vital crimson proof to relieve and gladden his heart. On his next visit, he beamed at his young bride-to-be. He would protect her intactness for the wedding night, even from himself. Thus while his mouth and hands roamed freely and a month before the marriage, felt entitled, to slip past the restraining barriers of clothes and underclothes, they checked themselves and remained respectfully outside the gate to the inner sanctum of her virtue.

'I love you so much,' he said. 'I do not think I have ever loved any woman so much,' confusing love with desire in the back seat of a slowly moving car on a languorous afternoon. Confusing it, too, with the victory of an incomparable gift as he remembered Old Tang's humiliating defeat.

'I shall never forget the expression on his face that day.' Old Yoong paused, in the middle of a slow exploration with his mouth, to look up and chuckle his triumph.

CHAPTER TWENTY-THREE

Mad Temple Auntie would still take her time with the temple tortoises, feeding them and attending to a leg wound she saw on one of them, while Mei Kwei, squatting on the floor of the room, waited for her return. At last the feeding and tending were over, and the woman came in and ran straight to her, eyes dilated with concern. Uttering little cries of affection, she cradled the girl's head in her arms, and rocked to and fro. Like a child fretful with fever, Mei Kwei gradually quietened to the the gentle rhythms of the embrace. The silent whispering of the dead grandmother in the cold earth was not enough; she needed the touch of arms still warm with life and loving to sooth away the torment in her heart.

Then Mei Kwei told her story. She told it in a luxury of racking sobs while the vagrant listened, her forehead and lips puckered in lines of deepest concern. There was to be no response to the telling; if the rumours were true, of the divine gift of sudden speech in a moment of illumination or crisis, her friend from the temple might have found it now to ease her pain.

Instead the woman left her side, stood up, paused, then began to dance. She moved her arms and legs with graceful ease, tracing slow arcs in the air. Then, as if responding to some inward urging, she clenched her hands and punched the air in pugilistic fury. Mei Kwei watched, fascinated, as Mad Temple Auntie circled an imaginary adversary with sinister power. Once, twice, three times, then she had him cowering in fear as she moved in for the kill. Still she would not let him die, but glided and leaped round him. At last she stopped, opened her mouth wide, a silent cavern of savage intent and drove in a long spear. She stood still for a moment, breathing heavily, savouring her victory.

Then in a swift change of mood, Mad Temple Auntie pranced to a corner of her shed where a spread of newspapers hid something on the floor, but only imperfectly for Mei Kwei saw its colours glinting and gasped at the audacity of the theft. With the gleefulness of a wayward child, Mad Temple Auntie pulled off the newspaper covering to reveal the full resplendence of the God-Kings headdress and the Moon Maiden's diadem, stolen, with whatever ingenuity, from whatever place the opera troupe kept their costumes after each performance in the temple grounds. In the silence of night, the vagrant must have awakened suddenly, to the sound of a gong or a clash of cymbals still reverberating upon a fading dream, slipped out into the darkness in search of the riches glimpsed in her dream, and gone straight to the storing room to pull out the richest prize of all. Now, she picked up the God-King's head-dress carefully, causing its magnificent side wings to quiver like a giant butterfly, and put it on her head, laughing. She skipped about, as happy as a child, calling for attention and applause. Then it was the turn of the Moon-Maiden's diadem to grace the despised lice-infested head, its delicate strings of pearls and gold beads falling gracefully over despised, sun-roughened face. She continued to dance for joy. Through her tears, Mei Kwei smiled at her.

148

CHAPTER TWENTY-FOUR

'**B**ig Older Brother will take care of you. Have no fear.'
He had heard Mei Kwei crying in her room and was by her side on the bed in an instant. From the time of her first blood and her subsequent sharing of a bed with their mother, he had hovered on the edges of her privacy, impelled by the same need for closeness with her that had brought both the frustration and the joy of his boyhood years. *Little Sister*. Both the thought and the utterance brought to him a secret, inexplicable thrill. 'Little Sister, do you remember the time when –' But he had realised with dismay that she had changed and was lost to him. Each attempt by her to repulse him, though wordless, had been a far greater wound than either his mother or father could inflict.

Now, sitting beside her on the bed, he watched, with secret exultation, the racking anguish that was making her compliant and willing to be drawn into his arms. It was a delight impossible to hide and unwise to show, so he tried to distance himself from it by an explosion of hatred against the perpetrator of the anguish. There was now a common enemy; the thought quickened Big Older Brother's heart even as it darkened his face and put a savagery into his voice. 'You won't have to marry him. I'll see to that.'

He was galvanised into energetic activity as, carefully, he planned the rescue of his sister. It was to be effected in clear precise stages, leaving no room for uncertainty. First he went to his mother and told her bluntly, 'The engagement is off. Little Sister is not happy to marry him,' disdaining to name the man, and stopping the protests that immediately came forth in a stream of small, startled, bewildered sounds, by saying, in a voice charged with emotion, 'It's a horrible sacrifice. Don't you see she is doing it for all of us? Don't you have eyes?'

His mother disposed of, he went to his father. Standing outside the locked door, he announced, in the crisp, efficient manner of the official messenger, his voice raised to reach everyone: 'As of today, the engagement between Little Sister and Old Yoong is off.'

But no sound came from the dark interior.

Then he launched himself upon the most important stage of the rescue. 'Bring me his photo.' Old Yoong's likeness was propped up against a vase on a nearby table. He could easily have leaned over to take it himself, but he wanted the touch of his sister's renouncing hand upon it to erase her earlier acceptance and admiration, which had pained him.

Mei Kwei looked wonderingly at him.

'Bring me that photo,' he repeated. 'Also, the one on the table outside,' meaning the engagement photograph, framed and prominently displayed. She obeyed. He cast both photos carelessly by his side.

'Bring me all of it. Do not leave anything out,' he commanded, and she knew he meant the jewellery. Hating both giver and gift, he could not bear to name either.

Mei Kwei got up, opened drawers, and returned silently, with an armful of small red boxes that she laid before him on the bed.

'Sit down,' he said and proceeded to divest her of the gifts still on her person, unclasping an ear-ring from one ear-lobe, then the other, lifting a gold chain from around her neck, pulling off rings from two fingers.

'Now this,' he said, and untied the twisted handkerchief from around her jade bangle.

He would personally take the entire haul of gifts back to their owner, together with the photographs. 'Here you are, Old One. Don't think that because we are poor we can be bought by you.' An old man's injured pride and need for revenge might unleash upon him the many ferocious watchdogs supposedly kept in every mansion, but he would brave all for his sister. Mauled and maimed, he would shout to the heavens, 'I did it all for my sister!' He tugged and pulled at the bracelet.

Tears of pain sprang to Mei Kwei's eyes as she felt her bones crushed once more. All gifts to her were crying gifts, destined by the teardrop mole.

'Come,' Big Older Brother said, and took her into the kitchen. But no amount of lathering with soap would budge the band of stone. It gleamed, a magnificent green, mocking them. The most illustrious piece among the gifts, it had claimed possession of her and would never relinquish that claim. Big Older Brother, his face red and hot with effort, continued the struggle.

'Please,' gasped Mei Kwei.' Please stop.'

It was the same prompt protectiveness that had chased away the intruder in the cemetery which now pushed Big Older Brother roughly aside. Austin Tong's act would have developed into a fury of punches and kicks if another look at the girl had warned of danger. But there was none. Mei Kwei was sitting quietly on a stool, nursing the crushed hand, while her brother stood nearby, protective custodian, and glared at him.

'She is not going to marry the old man,' said Big Older Brother, with a sneer intended to clothe the second, silent part of the utterance: 'And not you, either, you contemptible white man's shit-eater.'

'Stop it! Don't you see it's hurting her?' cried Austin angrily, and bent to look at the bruised hand.

'She has to return it. It cost the old man ten thousand dollars,' snarled Big Older Brother. The sum had only been whispered by his mother and Pig Auntie, but he had caught it, as he had caught other small fragments of talk about his sister and her suitor, to stoke further the secret fires of his resentment. Pre-empting any interference in his scheme of rescue, he remarked darkly, 'I am personally going to Penang to return everything. It is my responsibility as her brother.'

Austin Tong said, suddenly and authoritatively, 'Nobody is to touch that cursed thing on her wrist till I come back.'

So now there were two rescuers. Mei Kwei longed to run away from the raucous world of men and remembered, with a sharp onset of tears, the time when she crept into Second Grandmother's arms and was soothed into a long, deep peace.

'What do you plan to do?' jeered Big Older Brother, but Austin was gone.

He returned and, in the manner of one claiming silent but indisputable victory, casually placed the instrument of triumph on the table. Always, the feelings of the men who loved and fought for her, raging around her like ominous thunderclouds, would condense into hard packets of jewels or money, which they cast at each other in a final show of strength. Austin Tong had brought his money in a large brown envelope. His refinement would not allow him to tear it open in case the bundles of large notes neatly tied in rubber bands – probably the takings of his restaurant over a period of time – spilled out. But the size and bulge of the envelope suggested an adequate amount not only to buy off the jade bangle but also to redeem the assortment of smaller items from the pawn-shop.

The intensity on Austin's pale, lean face said, 'You are free.'

CHAPTER TWENTY-FIVE

'Out! I say get out this instant!'

Walking into the house, Austin Tong swallowed his greeting and jerked his body to one side in self-protection as if the shrieks were so many barbs flying at him. The imprecations were meant to stick in his conscience and ruin his peace. 'Interloper! Intruder! How dare you come along and ruin everything for my daughter? She was about to get married to one of the richest men in Penang. She was about to save us all.'

Pig Auntie might have consoled Ah Oon Soh thus. 'It may not be a bad thing after all. The father left him a lot of money, besides that restaurant. There is a good job for your son there. Not as rich as Old Yoong, but rich enough. And younger. There will be children. Whereas with Old Yoong –'

But Ah Oon Soh, a day after being casually informed by her daughter that the engagement was off and all the jewellery returned, was in no mood for consolation. 'It's done, there's no more to be said,' said her daughter and, from that instant, Ah Oon Soh looked upon Austin Tong as the greatest villain, deserving the greatest abomination.

'Get out, or I'll throw faeces in your face.' Ah Oon Soh offered food for God's blessings and threatened its foulness upon hateful fellow humans.

Swallowing back some placatory words, Austin again stood uncertainly before her and made a few weak gestures with his hands while, in his heart, resolution hardened into grim determination: he would save the girl as soon as possible from her execrable family.

He looked at the door in the hope of seeing Mei Kwei or Big Older Brother; a third presence would surely defuse the violence building up so dangerously in the small, taut, work-hardened body of the pathetic woman perched upon a stool at the table. Her hands were clasped tightly round an enamel tea mug which he expected, any moment, to be flung at his face. In one unguarded moment, he turned his head aside, and felt a rush of energy from the table. He looked back abruptly to see the end of the broom coming directly at his face. Ah Oon Soh must have had that instrument of revenge, second only to faeces in the discharge of hate, next to her all the time she was drinking coffee and brooding, otherwise he could have stopped her getting up and reaching for it in its customary place behind the door. He managed to intercept it – a mere inch from his face – aware, with a sickening sensation deep in the stomach, of an anger so intense it would have rubbed his face in the broom's foulness. For it was the lowest of low brooms, being used only for sweeping the chicken yard.

'Mother, how dare you –' It was Mei Kwei's turn to show anger. She snatched away the offensive insrument and flung it upon the floor. 'Mother, how could you? Are you mad?'

She turned to Austin Tong and their mutual shock threw them together in a first, shuddering embrace, ignominious broom at their feet.

CHAPTER TWENTY-SIX

From the moment that Old Yoong stepped out of his white car, Ah Kum Soh and Ah Cheng Mm, peeping from their windows, could tell that this was not one of his usual visits. In the first place, he did not go into the house but stood resolutely by the car. Besides, his whole demeanour, down to the last detail of flaring nostrils and hand firmly grasping the flap of his suit pocket, intimated some portentous judgement to be delivered on the Oon family.

'White Car is on the rampage. Black Car is to blame,' whispered the peeping women.

The chauffeur, who had gone into the house, came out followed by Ah Oon Soh, pathetic in the pure terror in her eyes as she fixed them on the visitor. Old Yoong ignored her greeting, which came out in pitiful gulps, and said haughtily to the chauffeur, 'I want to speak to the father. Tell the father to come out this instant.'

Ah Oon Koh had no choice but to come out, the power of wealth having spoken. Blinking stupidly, in his pyjama trousers, he stood before the awesome personage and, like his wife, submitted to a brusque dismissal of his greeting. He kept his head lowered and sheepishly scratched an armpit as Old Yoong launched into the urgent business of his visit.

Old Yoong might have been a magistrate in a court of law or a priestly custodian of proper behaviour anointed by the gods. Unable to express the private hurt of his rejection – it was worse than rejection for her brother had returned the gifts and photo in the most insulting fashion, thrusting them into the hands of one of the servants – he resorted to public censure. While it would have been beneath his dignity to resort to women's curses and call down the wrath of the Lightning God, and certainly against his inclination to summon the girl and the odious brother for an explanation, he felt it incumbent upon a person of his position to pour upon her father's head all the anger of his insulted position: Teach your children manners.

No flash of lightning appeared in the sky but an approving sign from the gods presented itself immediately for there came drops of rain, which made the chauffeur quickly hold up an umbrella over Old Yoong while the other remained bare-headed. The drops of rain grew larger and fell more heavily, plopping noisily upon the umbrella and the bare head. And still Old Yoong spoke and still Ah Oon Koh stood in silent shame as if both were compelled to act out an ancient tableau for the benefit of the watching gods.

'Father, come.'

Old Yoong's heart quickened with sharp interest, then pain, at the sight of the girl. For a moment he thought, as he saw her grab her father's arm to draw him under the protection of her umbrella and then lead him back into the house, that he might soften enough to call her name, even beg to hear from her own lips a disavowal of that outrageous deed. If the girl could turn to him and say, with a look in those wondrously expressive eyes of hers, 'They made me do it, I had no part in it,' the pain would have been somewhat assuaged. But Mei Kwei did not look at him once, and the sight of her retreating figure as she led her father back into the house, blurred by the pelting rain and a quick smear of tears, hardened his heart once more. He got back into the car and ordered the chauffeur to drive away.

She dreamed she was in a large building, which could have been the Penang British Club for she saw couples at distant tables in cool splendour, sipping cool drinks under great whirring ceiling fans, and heard snatches of a Doris Day song on a record-player. Or it could have been a shop, for she saw row upon row of glittering necklaces, bracelets, bangles and rings in glass cases. Old Yoong came up to her

154

and she thought, with a start, Why, he is no longer old. He looks exactly like his photo. His dark hair gleamed with hair-cream, his fingers with rings.

'Choose!' he said to her, laughing, and swept a magnanimous hand across the rows of sparkling jewels in their glass cases.

She laughed back and said, 'Enough! You have given me enough already.'

'Choose.' The invitation had become menacing command, and she looked up to see no longer a smiling young man but a glowering old one. 'Choose!' the voice rasped, an old man's voice, and it might well have said, 'You have no choice, it is my wish,' for the next moment he picked up a hammer, smashed the glass cases and picked up fistfuls of jewellery, which he began to drape upon her.

'No!' she cried, as she felt the weight of ropes of gold round her neck, massive gold pendants in the shape of grape clusters and flowers and tortoises on her chest, enormous ear-rings dragging down her ear-lobes, rings with diamonds as large as pigeon's eggs locking up her fingers.

'No!' she sobbed, and sank down upon the floor under the weight.

But still he continued to load her body, drawing her attention to the exquisite design of this or that piece. 'Now for this one!' he cried joyfully, and she looked up in horror to see his nakedness, for at the same time that he pulled a jade bangle from his trousers, he stepped out of them.

Even as she stared at him as he exhibited a young man's throbbing, virulent power in an old body, she was able to remind herself calmly to spit three times in a drain, in expunction of the obscenity. He was down upon her in an instant, at the same time that the bangle, as if infused with a life of its own, pressed upon her wrist. As his body struggled to enter hers, the bangle pulsated with menacing energy, enclosing her fingers in a tight grip, crushing and crunching bones.

'Help! Help!' she cried, and looked around to see dimly flitting shadows in the distance, amid a desolation of tombstones. 'Help me, Second Grandmother,' she wept. For Second Grandmother sat on a low stool, looking at her with tears brimming in pity. But they were tears for herself – for her feet which, with their toes bent inwards to grow into soft flesh, were like a child's balled fists.

'Help me, Father and Mother. Help me, Big Older Brother.' Mei Kwei could not see them but she could hear their voices, coming from some distant darkness, raised in argument. They were talking about her. She heard her name mentioned several times, and struggled to hear what they were saying but their words came to her ears only as faint, incoherent fragments, like the charred bits of ghost money floating about in a current of air.

She felt a final savage thrust, of both the old body and gleaming jade, and a sensation of burning wetness on her thighs and hand, and looked to see a mingling of blood, from broken pristineness and broken finger-bones, on her white cotton trousers. Still naked, Old Yoong pulled the trousers from beneath her body, and looked from the triumphant stain on it to another, much smaller but no less triumphant one on the tip of his penis.

'I knew it,' he said. 'I knew I had no reason to doubt you.' He brought his face close to hers and she could almost smell the old man's stale breath and feel his dry, hard lips on her face. 'Yet I doubted,' he went on. 'I kept seeing that black car in front of your house.' She felt a great, searing pain in her private body and curled up, like an insect, to hide her shame.

'Help,' she said weakly. She heard a shout of anger and saw one of the dimly flitting shadows detach itself and move quickly forward, assuming the solidity of a powerful rescuer.

'I will save you!' he said loudly, and leaped across tombstones to hurl himself upon the attacker. Old Yoong fell to the ground, blubbering.

'That will teach you!' cried the rescuer. He was a blur in the fast movements of his assault of the old man on the ground.

When he had finally finished and came to stand before her, she said, 'Thank you. You will need to take me to your restaurant for medicine for these wounds.' She held up her bruised wrist with the jade bangle clamped round it. 'This, too,' she said tearfully. 'I can't bear it any more.' Her rescuer bent down and gently touched her wrist.

What kind hands, she thought, and looked up to see not Austin Tong but Father François Martin.

He helped her up gently, and watched her smooth down her clothes over her nakedness. 'At last we have met,' he said. 'Why did you run away from me that morning in church?'

'Run,' she whispered urgently, for she saw her mother in the distance come charging at them, with a broom that had been dipped in a bucket of faeces. 'My mother does things like that when she is very angry.'

They ran panting across a vast expanse of space as the wind rose in a wail and the rain fell.

PART THREE

第三章

CHAPTER TWENTY-SEVEN

Austin Tong remembered that even as a boy, he asked God for signs to help him out of the confusion of his childhood. He was then of course not yet a Christian, but the use of signs to speak to faltering mortals was no god's monopoly. He remembered a relative whose life was almost entirely regulated by the number of prayer sticks that fell out of a shaken temple urn, the markings on the shell of a temple tortoise, the small whisperings of gods and goddesses from behind clouds of incense smoke, a dream of food or its opposite, faeces.

His mother lay ill in bed once, her body racked by coughing. 'Will you die, Mother?' Austin had asked tearfully.

She had smiled weakly, stroked his face and said, 'No, I won't die, son. I'll always be here to protect you,' whereupon he had wriggled into the warmth of her blanket to lie close to her fevered body, impelled by relief as much as by the fear of that someone she promised always to protect him against, for his father's strong, rough hands were as likely to pull him out from under the blanket as to tear off the little crucifix that his mother made him wear under his shirt.

'God, give me a sign that Mother will not die.' His mother's promise was not enough; he wanted assurance from the highest authority. The God he prayed to lived somewhere in the sky, high above in the clouds, higher than any bird could fly. This God had a long white beard, a golden halo and a deep frown between his thick, white eyebrows. From his fingers darted great beams of light and sometimes even roaring flames to reduce the wicked to a heap of ashes in an instant. But his parents' gods lived in houses, in each case so small that he wondered if the divine power might be sadly circumscribed by his tiny box-like residence. His mother had once taken him to her church when his father was away on business, and had pointed to what must have been no more than a doll's house behind small embroidered curtains on a large stone table, in the midst of flowers and candles. 'God is inside there,' she told him.

To his shock, he saw God's house shrunk further, to a tiny round white wafer, which the priest laid on his mother's tongue and which she swallowed. 'God is now in me.'

His father's god's abode was no bigger, being a little yellow rectangular box, like a pigeon's house, perched on a wooden stand, in the back garden under a tree. It was decorated with gold filigree and had a tiny door through which the resident spirit, made its exits and entrances. His father lit small red candles and stood them along a ledge that ran round the box, and sometimes swung a censer in front of it, covering it in huge billows of fragrant smoke. His father told him that the spirit was an especially powerful one, given to him by a monk in Thailand, and could grant any wish. 'My son,' his father had said, 'I am a rich man today and can afford to support your mother's family and send you to school in a car because of the power of this spirit. I am one of its chosen ones.'

The fact that each parent took him to visit his or her god only in the absence of the other and, moreover, warned him not to speak of it, had made him aware that the two gods were enemies and had to be kept apart. His mother spoke with horror about his father's god, but only in whispers and only to members of her own family when they came on visits, all wearing tiny crucifixes on their chests, as if to ward off the evil influence of that alien yellow house spirit in the garden. Austin would listen to their hushed conversation and try to understand what was going on. He came to the conclusion that his mother was very unhappy but it was too late to do anything since she was already married to his father. He once saw his father stretch out an arm to sweep an entire array of holy objects – statues, bottles of holy water, blessed medals – off a little altar that his mother had set up in his room, and heard his mother gasp and raise both hands to her mouth at the sacrilege.

'It is enough that you belong to that useless, foreign religion! No son of mine will come under its influence,' his father had shouted. Yet he sent his son to a Christian school, and practised a strict selectivity. 'You will learn the white man's language and pick up his knowledge and skills,' he said to Austin. 'But you will not be persuaded by those Christian Brothers to be baptised in their religion. We do not need their religion, son. We have our own.'

One evening, Austin was in his room, in bed – he must have been about seven – when he saw his mother come in softly and sit on a chair opposite his bed. Keeping very still, he listened to her silent weeping in the darkness and the voices coming from the room opposite his, distinctly those of his father and a woman whom he had mentally nicknamed Auntie Forehead Mole, for that was her most distinguishing feature, a rough irregular growth on an otherwise pretty face. He had seen her several times with his father, but this was the first time he had brought her home. The injustice to his mother, chased out of her own bedroom to wait in his while they did their shameful deed – at seven, he had an idea of what men and women did together in a locked room – struck him cruelly. He would have leaped out of bed to console his mother except that he knew she preferred him not to know. He continued to lie very still in the darkness, listening, with violently thumping heart, to his mother's anguish and his father's brute, insensitive laughter, and the little tight knot of pain and loathing deep inside grew tighter.

'Look,' said Austin's father, and showed him a gleaming watch with a black-leather strap.

Austin had seen it in a shop and wanted it badly. His face broke into a smile and he leaped up for the dazzling gift, dangled tantalisingly in the air.

But his father jerked it away. 'It's not yours, my boy, I'm sorry to say. It's a gift for –' and he mentioned the name of an obscure cousin and watched a flush of jealousy spread slowly on the boy's face.

The boy withdrew his hand and looked away sullenly. 'But I'll show you how you can get one,' said the father, 'this very night. Come with me.'

Austin followed him to a remote corner of the house where his mother had, in defiance of her husband, set up her Christian altar. There was a small statue of the Blessed Virgin Mary, flanked by two kneeling angels and white candles. A picture of the Holy Family was propped up against one of the candles. The boy, expecting to see the brutal arm raise itself once more in the act of desecration, was surprised by the conciliatory tone. 'Now I want you to kneel down and pray to your mother's gods for the watch.' The boy hesitated, staring at the father.

'Kneel,' he repeated. 'Look, I'll kneel with you. We'll pray together.' They prayed together for the watch.

'Now tonight when you go to sleep, repeat the prayer, then look under your pillow. The watch will be there.'

Austin found no watch.

'What?' exclaimed his father, scratching his head. 'How can that be? Your mother's gods are supposed to be all-powerful. Never mind, son, let's see what we can do next to get you that watch.'

He took the boy out of the house to the yellow house where his god was domiciled, fed supposedly with animal and human blood to sustain its gift-bestowing power.

'Now say the same prayer,' instructed his father. 'Tell him you believe he will grant your wish.'

But Austin found no watch under his pillow.

'What?' said his father, again scratching his head. 'Are you sure you've looked carefully? Try one more time.'

The boy looked again, and pulled out a gleaming new watch, with exactly the same handsome black-leather strap, from under the pillow.

'See, I told you!' cried his father, and helped the boy put on the watch. 'Now go to the spirit and ask him to make you a strong, fearless boy.'

Austin waited for his mother to leave the house on a shopping trip in town, then ran breathlessly to the yellow spirit house.

'Please, god,' he prayed, 'make my father respect and love my mother.' It was an all-encompassing prayer and he did not need to add, 'Don't let Father bring Auntie Forehead Mole here again to do shameful things with her,' remembering the one, anguished sob that his mother had allowed to escape from her lips in the despairing wait in the chair.

Austin's father hated his wife's gifts to her son and once – he must have been about ten years old – emptied a whole box of his favourite toys at the feet of a stranger, a rough boy who had come to sell eggs and tried to steal his toy train. After he had fought the egg boy, his father was so pleased that he beamed and said, 'Son, get your mother to clean you up. We're going shopping. I've got a reward for your bravery today. I'm proud of you, son!' It was the first time his father had clapped him on the shoulder.

But the reward turned out to be a punishment. His father drove him all the way to Penang and scoured the shops to find his gift – a pair of boxing gloves which he made Austin put on immediately for a few minutes of playful sparring. The second stage of the reward was enrolment in a boxing class for boys, where sturdy lads from

Thailand were brought to be opponents to force some fibre into the soft bodies of local boys made useless by their pampering mothers. It was a disastrous experiment and Austin came home bruised, bleeding and in a state of shock. He was ill for a week and his mother wept over him. His father, his coarse face an apoplectic purple, cursed loudly and said that, from henceforth, he was washing his hands of his son. He flung the gloves out of the window.

Austin's excellent school report cards brought at first only grudging acknowledgement, and his father signed his name with curt perfunctoriness, muttering, 'Still beancurd. What's the use.'

But his son's dazzling academic performance could not be totally ignored and Tong found himself one evening, in the middle of a drinking bout, saying in a flush of pleasure, 'Always among the top three in class. From his first year in school. Boey's boy has never got anywhere near!' He decided to groom his son to take over his various businesses and, in particular, the restaurant he was planning to set up in the heart of town to cater exclusively to the British community. It would be the biggest, the best restaurant in Luping.

'Come here.' He called to his wife and son, while he drank beer or brandy. 'Let me tell you, Mary, that without my money, your family would starve, your consumptive father would not have the good food he needs to fight the disease. And let me tell you, my boy, that without my money, you would not be able to have all these good things for school. You would have to walk there or go in a trishaw! What? You don't want to hear about the Britannia eating-house which will be yours one day?'

Mother and son sustained each other as they endured the stale breath upon their faces, the brutal grip of their shoulders.

They turned away, too, from the strange men and women who popped up now and again from the murky shadows of Tong's business world, like insects scuttling out from the dank, dark undersides of rotting wood. They were men and women whose very looks betrayed their shoddiness, prompting neighbours to whisper to one another, 'The police will always look the other way. Tong knows how to grease palms.'

'Mother, why did you marry Father?' Austin asked, after witnessing another bout of anguished crying.

'It's God's will,' sniffed his mother.

'I hate Father!' Austin shouted, and his anger lit up the pale intensity of his face.

His mother turned to him and said sharply, 'Stop that! You're never to say that again, do you hear?' Then she drew him into her arms. 'Promise me that you will never do anything to upset your father.' The boy hesitated, frowning. His mother held up his chin and made him look straight into her eyes. 'Promise me.' The boy promised.

Except for Auntie Forehead Mole and a few other women, his father never allowed his friends into the house, but talked to them in the garden or drove off with them in his car. I will have nothing to do with Father's world, thought the boy.

'Come,' said his father, 'it is time,' meaning that it was time for his son to be introduced to the world. Austin was seventeen. He was tall and handsome, but retained the delicacy of features that his father so detested.

The introduction comprised a whirl of visits to places, both alien and alienating to him, though he maintained a polite silence so as not to annoy his father. The cabaret halls, the open air *ronggeng* grounds, the drinking and gambling parlours, the horse-racing clubs bored him thoroughly. He came back from each visit shaking the dust of corruption from his shoes before venturing into the presence of his sainted mother, dwindling away in her silent martyrdom. Once he saw her staring at a photograph of herself, which she had taken out of a drawer. He peeped over her shoulder and saw a beautiful young woman, with a soft white veil over her head, her eyes downcast, her hands clasped in prayer. 'Mother,' he said feelingly, for he saw a glistening of tears in her eyes, a sorrowful farewell to lost innocence.

The youthful beauty of his mother made him recoil at the coarseness of the women his father exposed him to. 'Go on,' urged his father, in an exuberance of spirits brought on by drink and the presence of a half a dozen *ronggeng* girls. 'Go on, dance!'

But Austin shook his head and stayed determinedly in his seat, cautiously sipping his first beer and trying to ignore a girl with long hair, heavy makeup and a tight pink satin blouse that pushed up her breasts. He had come to accept his father for what he was and was glad to be at hand when he made a fool of himself or slipped and fell and had to be taken home. Once his father fell into a drain outside a brothel. Somebody ran to tell Austin and he came in time to take his father home, his heart swelling in shame as he pushed his way through a small crowd that had gathered round the drunken man stretched out ridiculously on the pavement.

Then his father began to be fearful of one person from his shady world: Auntie Forehead Mole. He stopped bringing her home and refused to see her whenever she appeared at their gate. Each time the woman, who had grown grossly fat and was clearly no longer in full control of herself, would shout abuse and ask for money to support herself and a child she described as sickly. 'Your son,' the demented woman wailed, 'your bad seed, a useless sickly child, a ghost child. Bad seed.'

'Is she gone yet?' his father would ask timidly, and send Austin to give her some money. The unruliness of his father's world terrified Austin; it no longer collided with his mother's world of gentleness and goodness, and he, shuttling between the two, felt exhausted in body and spirit.

Then his father said once more, 'Come, it's time,' meaning the induction into manhood itself which would turn his world upside down and create a turbulence that would leave no place for gentle, quiet dreams.

'Father, please –' Austin said in polite remonstration, but he knew it was no use. He had allowed himself to be taken into his father's world stage by ignominious stage; this was the next inevitable stage and he knew his father was bent on it.

'Son, I had already done it by the time I was fifteen.' At fifteen, his father boasted, he had bedded a servant girl and at sixteen, had had his first prostitute.

'You are nineteen, and already a man, and yet not a man,' he said, clucking his tongue in doleful commiseration. And Austin sat silently through the whole range of hateful theatrics – the head-shaking, the laughter, the conspiratorial winking.

'Here, show that you are a man,' his father ordered, pushing him unceremoniously into a room with an ugly, tawdry bead curtain, then closed the door upon him. Austin did not dare look at the girl reclining on the bed but continued to stand awkwardly, listening to the fading sounds of his father's footsteps and laughter along the corridor. The girl – a closer look revealed her to be a woman, perhaps in her thirties – looked steadily at him and laughed, guessing his predicament. He blushed deeply, feeling a slow heat spread through his entire body, as he waited to hear the taunting question, surely even more humiliating coming from a woman than any of his father's rough drinking and gambling friends. 'What? Nineteen and still a virgin?'

Austin turned away from her and shrank into himself in an undisguised revulsion of her presence, of the gaudily appointed room with the cheap bead curtains and plastic flowers. The revulsion swelled to include her entire clientele, in particular his father, probably now in another locked room, sweatily lunging at some woman as grotesquely made up as this one, or drinking beer in the small bar downstairs and boasting about his resturaurant for the *ang mohs*.

'I will pay you and leave,' he said miserably. But the woman appeared to have taken a liking to him.

'Don't go away,' she said in all sincerity. 'Don't worry. Your father has paid me already.' She looked steadily at him and repeated, 'Don't worry, you don't have to do anything. He need not know.' She would concoct, if asked, a story of the manly leap from inexperience to lustful expertise, all in a matter of an hour.

'Thank you, that's very kind of you,' Austin stammered.

She adjusted her clothes and went to take a cigarette from a pack on a small table beside the bed. 'Cigarette?'

He shook his head.

'Tell me about yourself.' To her delight, he allowed himself to be led to the bed. Her dressing gown fell from her shoulders, exposing her breasts, large, round and white. He stared at them. 'Come,' she said and drew him to herself.

And then he thought of the multitude of hands that had reached for those breasts, of legs that had pushed those legs wide apart. Once again, he felt the hot odour of his father's world in his nostrils, and he got up abruptly and murmured something about not feeling well.

'Here, let me rub this on you.' She had a bottle of Tiger Balm at hand for the soothing of her own body in between the satisfying of a multitude of appetites. She rubbed the balm on his temples, his forehead, his neck, her large breasts brushing lightly against him.

'So,' said his father later, beaming at him. 'So? How did you like it? She told me you were a real man. Here's to my son, man at last!'

He held up a glass to toast his son's entry into manhood. Austin smiled sheepishly, then looked up in puzzlement as his father's expression changed suddenly to one of harsh contempt. 'Don't pretend! I saw it all! What sort of thing are you? You have a beancurd for a penis too!' And he laughed uproariously.

The thought of the coarse man and his companion stealing out of their room to peep, giggling, into his, sickened Austin.

'Your father does not have long to live,' the doctor told Austin. 'That is a great mercy, considering his terrible suffering.'

Austin's father's illness was the kind that was said to catch up with every hardened sinner and corrupter of innocence, punishing each part of the body that had sinned so that the flesh fell away from venal fingers that had grasped at forbidden money, the tongue swelled and filled the mouth for its deception and lies, and the penis rotted for its wanton despoliation of young bodies. It was a punishment reserved for the specially depraved so that even while still above ground, the body began to shed itself, bit by bit.

Lying in bed, waiting for death, Austin's father was a grotesque sight, despite the covering bandages, and struck fear in every visitor, who went away silent with horror. The strong man whose brutal arms swung against both gods and fellow mortals was as helpless as a child and wept constantly in self-pity. His wife was always by the bedside, the illness rousing her to an unaccustomed level of activity that put back the alertness in her eyes and the strength of purpose in her frail body. She took tireless care of her sick husband, feeding him porridge carefully from a bowl, cleaning the terrible sores on his body, soothing his cries of pain in the middle of the night.

He still had hopes of a cure from the potent being in the yellow house in the garden, and begged his son to burn red candles on his behalf. 'Your mother cannot do it because she is a Christian, so you must,' he pleaded.

His mother clung to one hope, for which she was prepared, with the help of her family and fellow Church members, to storm heaven. 'Will you get baptised?' she asked her husband. She left unsaid her belief that dying pagans recovered after baptism and went on to live their remaining years as exemplary Christians.

'My god didn't cure me, so yours must,' he said tearfully. He did not care about any promised heaven: all he wanted was to be spared the hell of his present sufferings that made him scream out loud and, when there was no more strength left, to groan and twist in silent agony.

Fearful in her husband's robust presence, the gentle woman had suddenly become energetic and purposeful in his helplessness, and herself went to dismiss the crazy ex-mistress with the forehead mole who stood by the gate demanding entry and money for herself and her sickly child, now more a ghost child than ever for want of proper food.

'Go away,' said Austin's mother and made sure the gate was padlocked.

'Bad seed,' shouted the mad woman after her. 'Tell him it is his bad seed!'

'Your father wants to see you.'

In his last days, Austin's father was beyond speech and made signs, intelligible only to his wife who rushed to satisfy every wish. But his father's last wish was not clear, for tears swelled in his eyes amid the struggles to form words with his dried, broken lips.

Finally Austin gazed silently at the corpse, upon which no mortician's skill could hope to bestow anything resembling the peace and serenity of death, and then looked away abruptly. He repeated the promise he had made to himself. I dissociate myself completely from your world, he thought. I will have nothing to do with the businesses you have left behind. The only business he would take over was the Britannia eating-house. He would make a success of it for his mother's sake, and take care of her for the rest of his life.

He was twenty years old.

In the Britannia eating-house, her wrist encircled by the jade gift of another man, Mei Kwei leaned across the table and touched Austin Tong's arm. He turned to look at her with the pale intensity with which she was now familiar.

'You know,' he said, 'after my mother died and I had converted to Christianity in accordance with her last wishes, I asked God for a sign. "Send me a sign," I pleaded, "so that I might know that there is hope for the future, and that I am not alone." I was in the Catholic church. I felt full of anger and despair, and considered ending my life. And then I looked up and saw you.'

Austin covered Mei Kwei's hands with his. Only she, he told her, could rescue him from his inner torments; from his terrible memories which, even now, pressed down upon him, threatening to overshadow everything he did.

CHAPTER TWENTY-EIGHT

S
he would slip out of the greedy grasp of men all her life – why did men love her with a greedy love? – and seek solace where none would go, the abodes of the dead and the insane. Having sat quietly upon the ground next to Second Grandmother's grave, she got up and rode her bicycle straight to the Kek Lok Temple. Mad Temple Auntie was not in her shed, or outside with the beloved temple tortoises, so Mei Kwei rode home. She might have explained to Tee Tee that her decision to take the unfamiliar route was once again the work of the demon prankster residing in her bicycle wheels. It took her past the children's playground, meriting that name on the basis of one stone bench and a row of three swings, two sadly out of use with broken chains and smashed wooden seats. A number of children, all studiously ignoring the swings, went about their own improvised amusements. Mei Kwei smiled as she watched some playing hopscotch – pushing pieces of broken tiles across neatly drawn patterns of lines with their toes as she had loved to do – and some squatting in a circle to engage in noisy transactions, involving swift exchanges of cigarette-cards, rubber-bands and rubber seeds. Two neat little girls were standing hand in hand, looking on and eating buns.

She saw someone pass by on his bicycle and also slow down to watch. His face lit up in a smile too. Father François Martin did not make the mistake of invading the children's territory and scattering them in flight; he kept a reassuring distance on the boundaries of their happy, noisy world but signalled friendliness by toying idly with a small bright red rubber ball in one hand and patting tantalisingly a bulging pocket with the other. He was patient, waiting for the children's invitation.

It came at last when a little boy, who had been eyeing the red ball for some time, boldly ran to stand before him and to reach out for the coveted object. The priest held it above him, high in the air for all to see, and soon the little boy's frantic leaps to reach it attracted the attention of the rest who came running to test their own skills. There were prizes galore as grubby hands invaded the deep hidden side pockets of the priestly robe and pulled out an assortment of small objects which they were allowed to keep. But curiosity about the foreigner soon superseded interest in the new possessions; a dozen little boys and girls were prepared to forget newly acquired pencils and erasers, rubber-bands and bottle-caps, beads and marbles to surround the priest, gaze at him and wait for interesting developments promised by the brilliant blue eyes, bushy beard, hairy arms and booming voice.

Father Martin rolled up his long sleeve to demonstrate the power of his biceps and invited a shy little boy to hang on to his arm as long as he liked. Clinging on for dear life, the child was lifted two feet off the ground, to general applause. The bold boy who had been the first to approach him, now planted himself self-consciously before the priest and demanded to be lifted up too. Father Martin obliged immediately, making a great show of the difficulty involved, so as not to disappoint the fellow, who had grown red-faced with the tremendous effort of fixing his short stout legs very resolutely on the ground. At last, with a fine display of grimaces, gasps and grunts very agreeable to his admiring spectators, Father Martin lifted him off his feet and held him aloft in the air, for the entire duration of twenty counts, made in a deep, sonorous voice in which the children joyfully and noisily joined, before setting the boy back on the ground and pushing him off with a slap on the buttocks.

There was a rush for the same test of strength, and it soon took on the aspect of a well-organised exercise, with the participants ranged in order of size, ending with the tallest, stoutest boy in the group, who was about ten and who shouted lustily that not even his strong uncle could lift him, much less hold him up like that. The priest obliged, succeeded easily once again, and laughed to see the boy, smiling sheepishly, jeered at by his friends. A look of sly intent came into the child's eyes, and he began to look around for someone even taller and heavier, not wishing to give up his theory that adult strength was exhaustible.

To her consternation, Mei Kwei saw a finger pointed directly at her, and heard the boy shout something to the priest. The gesture, the shout were almost accusatory, as was the priest's determined approach. She would have turned and fled if he had not flashed a bright smile at her and boomed out his pleasure in the instant of recognition. 'Ah, we meet again! And now you are not allowed to run away.'

In one swift movement, he swept her up and carried her, in triumph, back to the playground where the children stood, watching and cheering. He strode into their midst and raised her above his head. 'Count to thirty,' he roared.

For a while, Mei Kwei felt not just the novel sensation of being suspended in the air above a sea of wide-eyed, upturned little faces but the keen thrill of his strong warm hands, which had once held hers in that reassuring clasp when she had sought refuge in his church, now pressing upon her back, sending their warmth through her entire body.

'Again! Again!' screamed the children, seeing him about to put her down.

He obliged, lifting her up again and shouting, 'Forty! Forty this time!' For good measure, he did a dramatic twirl of her suspended body before setting her down.

The children applauded and laughed loudly, the two little bun-eating girls leaning against each other and covering their mouths with their hands to hold back an explosion of giggles.

Father Martin was suddenly all profuse apology. 'Forgive me,' he said. 'The children commanded, and I obeyed.' He looked at Mei Kwei with a pleasure that would not have been proper in the midst of saying Mass in church, but was in place now in the general exuberance of the children's happy world. And she looked back at him, smiling too, and startled him by a sudden onset of tears, which said, 'Thank you for the saving of a sad day.'

CHAPTER TWENTY-NINE

The chief of operations was not particularly looking forward to his meeting with the French priest. Indeed, he groaned inwardly that it had to be held at all. He made himself a drink of whisky and water to fortify himself against any unpleasantness. There had been enough unpleasantness at home in the morning; another dose would be just too much. His Chinese cook and his Malay gardener were quarrelling again, and Jill said she was terrified that their animosities would explode into tragedy.

Jill's querulousness increased, as it always did, with the humidity, the tropical storms which she said affected her menstrual cycle, the mosquito net and the sleepless nights inside it, a nasty box of trapped, stale air. Inside the net, she dreamed of the cool touch of spring, and winter flakes on her nose during a long walk home to the blazing logs and marshmallows.

Complaining of slush and cold only a year ago, bright-eyed with the prospect of perpetual sunshine, exotic palm trees and cute native children, she had sailed into disappointment, and was now agitating to be sailing back.

Williams envied Frank Griffiths, whose wife Elizabeth had, from day one, taken everything in her stride – heat, mosquitoes, stupidity of servants, the tension of living in one of the nastiest, Communist-infested towns in Malaya. Elizabeth learned the local dialect and delighted the servants. Once, while shopping in the market-place ('You mean you actually go to that dirty, smelly place?' one of her friends had gasped), she overheard a cluster of locals talking about white men in the most derogatory of terms, and sweetly turned to respond to them in the same dialect. She poked about in the quaint Chinese medicine shops and found the most effective pills and ointments for stomach-aches, diarrhoea, cramps, vomiting and snake-bites. She had discovered a medicine, in the form of tiny red pellets, which was an unfailing cure for any stomach complaint and she always carried a good supply with her wherever she and the family travelled in Malaya, as the best safeguard against the unreliable drinking water and the oily Chinese food that poor Frank had to eat to avoid offending his Chinese hosts. Elizabeth loved her life in Luping. Her dream, she said, was to be equipped with a rifle, to shoot down one or two of the Commie bastards who were making life so difficult for everyone in the country.

'Why can't you be like Elizabeth?' Williams said irritably to Jill. And her reply was to flounce out of the room and to sulk for the rest of the day. He was grateful for the presence of Gray. Young Gray, nervous, timid and capable of absorbing any amount of female ire, was ideally suited to form a third in the house, to help keep the peace. And Jill trusted him.

'Come over right away,' Williams called one evening. 'Chilli Padi's at it again.' The secret nickname, based on a particularly virulent kind of dwarf chilli that could sting the unsuspecting mouth into a flaming wound, was most apt to describe the intense, fiery, petite Jill and gave both men, equal sufferers, a sense of warm brotherly solidarity as they sat in the Luping Club huddled over their gins.

T. C. Williams waved Father Martin to a chair in front of his desk, and offered him a whisky.

'No, thank you,' said the priest, and sat down stiffly.

The olive-green uniform of the chief of operations and the white cassock of the priest demarcated their respective domains.

There was very little danger of the chief straying into the priest's territory of souls. But the priest could be carried by his over-zealousness into what did not concern him. It could only be over-zealousness, concluded the chief, looking at the intense, honest blue eyes searching his, the earnest hands grasping the arm-rests of the chair. Sent to foreign lands to save souls for Christ, some of these missionaries went overboard, thinking that the sheer power of prayer, penance and faith could transform the heathen's landscape of superstition and ignorance. They should know that these went too deep for eradication. It amused him to think that these dedicated men of God believed they could hoist up the statues of the Blessed Virgin Mary and the saints as easily as you did the Union Flag to replace the entire pantheon of temple and shrine deities – Sky God, the Monkey God, the Goddess of Mercy, the Kitchen God, the Lightning God of Revenge – and put crucifixes and rosaries into hands that had held joss-sticks and ancestral spirit tablets for generations.

The field is white with harvest! The rallying cry of the Church Militant had sent her ardent sons to all corners of the globe. T. C. Williams wondered, again with some amusement, at the appropriateness of the colour imagery for the teeming yellow and black populations of these vast continents that were the special target of missionary enterprise.

'Father Martin,' said Williams, going straight to the point. 'I understand that –' Even the most severe warning began with a declaration of understanding. He understood that, on a certain day, the priest had been seen in the market-place praying for dead terrorists. He had originally decided to ignore the several complaints about the priest, particularly the one from Evans. Evans had been a fool, exposing the breast of the dead woman terrorist with his foot, and had been roundly rebuked for the histrionics. But he decided he could no longer ignore the many reports coming in of this Catholic priest's apparent sympathy for the Communist terrorists.

Williams knew that Luping was one of the reddest, most dangerous little Chinese town in Malaya, infested with Communism's sympathisers in their secret enclaves, acting either out of fear or conviction. A rice wholesaler's lorry, laden with full sacks, plied between Luping and neighbouring towns. It was noticed that as the vehicle rumbled along a lonely stretch of road close to the jungle, a sack would shake loose from the pile and tumble out on the road. Within minutes it was gone. When pulled up by the authorities for questioning, the terrified rice-dealer denied he had been supplying food to the terrorists.

'They fell out accidentally.'

'Four times?' asked his interrogator.

The decision to exhibit the dead terrorists in the market-place might be seen as brutal and barbaric, but no measure could be too harsh to bring the Communists to heel. It was easy for these namby-pamby idealists and humanists to talk, T. C. Williams reflected, but let them get out of their ivory towers to view the carnage in the field. Let them see the rubber-tappers with the slit throats, and the sliced-off head of that poor Chinese bloke on the platter. And now this meddling priest was making it a practice to kneel down and pray for dead terrorists in a public place.

The chief of operations listened patiently to Father Martin's explanation, looking intently into the priest's face and nodding in step with each pause in the exposition, not to show agreement but to hurry it along to its conclusion.

The preciousness of souls. Souls, even of terrorists, are immortal and precious in the eyes of God. Souls have no colour or political ideology. The duty of a priest is to save souls. Immortality. Love. Salvation.

'Father Martin, I understand all of what you are saying,' the chief of operations said. 'But I must warn you that we are dealing with a very difficult and sensitive situation in this country. A war is going on, although we call it an Emergency so as not to alarm the people too much. The Communist terrorists are ruthless, and mean to destroy the government and set up a Communist state. They will go to any length to achieve their goal. Even during the brief time you have been here – eight, nine months? – you must have heard of their atrocities. They blow up railway lines, ambush cars, shoot our soldiers, throw grenades into police stations, kill innocent men and women. They will stop at nothing. Before the people can be mobilised to help us in our struggle against them, they must first be made to see the utter ruthlessness, to recognise and distrust the terrorists totally.'

Father Martin thought of the dead woman, her hair cut short like a boy's, her small frame no bigger than a child's, strapped to the plank of wood on the ground, her mud-caked khaki shirt ripped open to expose a large bullet-hole in her left breast. He thought, too, with a resurgence of anger, of the ugly brutal boot. She certainly did not fit the picture of ruthless aggression painted by the chief. He had heard of young girls being kidnapped from their villages by terrorists and taken to the hide-outs in the jungles where they served the men by cooking and cleaning for them, and sleeping with those in the higher ranks of power. The brighter ones eventually became comrades in arms. Father Martin wondered about the age of the woman terrorist, but you could never tell with the Chinese.

'You were seen kneeling down and praying for the enemy,' the chief continued. 'In full public view, you demonstrated sympathy. Where do you think that puts us, in our work of convincing the people?'

Father Martin felt his anger rising dangerously. In such situations, he would pray silently to the gentle St Francis to curb wrath, a sin as deadly as any, as Uncle Jean Claude had taught him to do from a young age. But now he gave full vent to his exasperation, becoming red in the face and waving both arms about.

His anger was directed not only against the chief of operations but against the heartless world of government laws and bureaucracy, which made no exception for young girls, dragged from their homes, enslaved and shot to death. It was bad enough to expose the dead men; it was the height of barbarity to exhibit a dead woman, half naked. He quivered with indignation at this violation of woman's dignity.

'Don't be misled, Father,' said Williams. 'One of the most dangerous terrorists in our experience was a young woman of nineteen, petite, pretty, hardly four feet ten. She looked no different from those innocent native girls you see everywhere, with their sweet round faces and friendly smiles, drawing water from the well or buying vegetables in the market. But put a gun or grenade in her hand and she became your deadliest killer. She masterminded an ambush in which three of our men were blown up in their Jeep.'

But Father Martin was not interested in the world of guns, Jeeps and ambushes. Evil was everywhere and was part of the divine mystery. Men would go on killing each other. But beyond the

175

violence of the ripped body was the soul's thirst for God. *I thirst.* It was the cry of mutual need: both God and man needed to slake their thirst in the spring of love and grace. He saw Uncle Jean Claude's face and heard his voice: 'Love above everything.' In China, Uncle Jean Claude had embraced condemned murderers and brigands, and was once knocked senseless by the club of a prison warden.

Father Martin did not care which side of the war he was on. He would comfort a dying terrorist and cross over to offer the same solace to the young British soldier weeping in the pain and terror of his first killing.

'Praying for the enemy's soul?' sneered the chief of operations.

Suddenly Father Martin's anger exploded. 'What do you know of the souls of the people here?' he shouted. 'You come here, live in big houses, drive your big cars, drink your whisky, have your parties at the Club.' He was aware that he was echoing the sentiments of some of the natives with whom he talked and ate. 'You live in luxury. What do you know and care about the souls of the people?'

'We do our job,' said the chief, 'and do it well, because we know our limits. You don't know yours. You overstep your boundaries, and blunder into other people's territory that you don't understand. From now onwards, Father, remember that the Communist terrorists are off limits.'

The shouting was over as quickly as it had begun, overtaken by the consciousness not to show a bad example to the native clerks who were going about their work diligently but listening intently. The chief of operations downed the rest of his whisky; Father Martin stared silently ahead of him.

Separated by their different functions, they were still united by that sense of affinity that links those who choose to leave home to live and labour among alien people. The chief had heard of the selfless work of the priest not only among the town's Catholics but among its poor and destitute; and the priest had heard of the chief's sincere and unstinting efforts to improve the security in the town and protect the people against the worst abuses by the terrorists. He was invariably described by his subordinates as fair and hard-working. Besides, he flaunted none of the perks of position and privilege, preferring to drive around in a battered van. Each had had his share of the initial trauma of adapting to the heat, the humidity, the malarial mosquitoes, the homesickness. Each, too, at the end of the day, wanted to leave the world of the natives better than they had found it.

But their worlds remained apart, and both men hoped that another meeting would be unnecessary.

'Cigarette?' asked the chief. And he lit the priest's cigarette with his lighter.

CHAPTER THIRTY

'I'm listening to the hum of the night insects outside.'

Father François Martin liked to begin each letter home to Léonie with a description of his surroundings. There was very little to describe about the drab little room that he called home, attached to the back of the church almost as an afterthought, a mere box of an annexe with its four walls and holes punched in for windows. Two and a half pages of his close, neat handwriting had exhausted the description of the church, a modest wooden building that Father Martin's secret ambitions would regard only as God's temporary dwelling, to be replaced, possibly in the near future, by a worthier edifice suited to Luping's growing Catholic population. But the surroundings – now he could go on and on describing the astonishing tropical plants and flowers, the myriad butterflies whose appearance, in delightful clouds of shimmering yellow or white, followed the patterns of rainy or hot seasons, the strange, lizard-like creatures lurking in the underbrush with their ugly scaly skins, long tails and flicking tongues, the night insects that set up a rhythmic moaning after sunset. Léonie loved flowers, so he described the hibiscus, which he loved for its bold red, so vividly contrasted with the shrieking green of its leaves, a yellow flower called the Trumpet Flower, which showed the local people's curious conception of the trumpet's shape, the white frangipani, which his Chinese cleaning woman had convinced him was sinister, being the flower of ghosts and mourning. There was a bloom that had no name but which was the most exotic flower he had ever seen, like a miniature flamingo in flight, which the Chinese called the New Year Flower because it bloomed just before the start of their festival.

Frangipani bad, balsam good. Bamboo bad, pomegranate good. The Chinese had an engaging way of placing even the most innocent things of God's creation in categories of good and evil, which invariably meant money, good, and death, evil. All bad plants were connected with ghosts and haunting, all good plants with prosperity and lottery money. His cleaning woman, who lived in a tiny cubicle in one of the meanest streets in Luping, carefully nurtured a pomegranate plant in a small kerosene tin on a window-ledge, beside an urn of joss-sticks, which had been placed there by her mother. She was a Catholic convert, who kept the traditional beliefs of her girlhood including that of the special luck-bringing properties of pomegranate, but drew a firm line at joss-sticks. She would have nothing to do with the urn, a few inches away from her plant. In their small cubicle, each stayed on her side of the great religious divide, in the form of a sarong curtain, while the smoke wisps from blessed church candle and temple joss-sticks sometimes came together in peaceful commingling. Her mother once attributed a lottery win of fifty dollars to the joss-sticks, she a win of twice that amount from her pomegranate plants, working in conjunction with St Joseph, her favourite saint.

The Chinese!!! Father Martin sometimes expressed his amused astonishment in an extravagance of exclamation marks.

There was a Chinese cemetery on a hill near the church, he wrote, where he could see families arriving from early dawn on special festival days, to pay respects at their ancestors' graves.

From ancestors, it was an easy step to food and here Father Martin wrote copiously to tantalise his sister, who ever reproached him for his fondness of eating, about the exotic Chinese dishes he had tasted since coming to Malaya. His pen flowed in sensuous ease, in the description of duck and salted cabbage soup, lotus root and pork-bones soup, mushroom and chicken entrails (he could see Léonie grimace: 'Chicken entrails!') a marvellous, no-name vegetable fried with what the Chinese were too bashful to reveal to their foreign visitors as, perhaps, some species of snake or slug (he could hear Léonie shrieking, 'Stop it, François!' with that violent shaking of her head which, even as a small boy, he had liked to provoke). His parishioners sometimes left generous gifts of food at his doorstep, and if he had stomach-ache from eating too much, there were always the ubiquitous Chinese stomach pills called *po chai yin*, which his kind cleaning woman made him take with a cup of warm water. It was amazing, he told his sister, how the Chinese preoccupation with food permeated all their dealings with each other, both in this life and beyond. Their greetings and blessings were of food – 'Have you eaten?' 'May you eat till a ripe old age!' – and their devotion to dead ancestors was expressed through rich feasts at which the ancestors indicated their presence by leaving unequivocal evidence of foot-prints or handprints in trays of ash placed beside the food.

Recently, Father Martin wrote, with a self-congratulatory flourish, 'I saved an entire Chinese family from death.' One morning after a rainstorm, he had woken up, taken a walk in an expanse of wasteground between the church and the cemetery and had come upon an amazing patch of mushrooms that must have proliferated in the night. They were beautiful, creamy-white, luscious, but his admiration turned to alarm when he saw an elderly Chinese woman walk up eagerly, begin gathering them and putting them into a tin bucket, presumably for a meal for her family. 'Stop! Stop!' he cried. She looked at him in puzzlement, then decided to ignore him. She gathered a large amount and got ready to leave.

'Please don't. They are poisonous,' he begged, but she continued to ignore him.

He followed her all the way back to her house, a ramshackle little hut nestling among dozens of others, in a rubber plantation. He saw a large family inside, including some small children. The elderly woman waved him away, as if he were a buzzing insect pest. He remonstrated once again, noisily, and she shrieked back. Then he knocked the bucket of mushrooms off her arm and trod vigorously on them, squelching them into a mess on the floor. The woman made angry little noises, shaking her fists at him. He went into a ridiculous mime of eating with great enjoyment, smacking his lips and cocking up his thumb, then of great suffering, clutching his stomach and grimacing horribly before finally choking and falling dead upon the floor. The buffoonery did the trick, and some members of the family showed enough understanding to explain the message to the elderly woman who, however, remained unmollified, staring in anguish at the ruined mushrooms.

'You never know what to expect in this strange country,' wrote Father Martin, and he set down the incident of the dead terrorist woman and her comrades in the market-place and the subsequent encounter with the chief of operations, but spared Léonie the gruesome details of the bared, bullet-riddled breast and the brutal boot above it. In his previous letter he had described the terrible scourge of Communism and the atrocities of the terrorists. 'My heart aches,' he had written, 'for the many innocent young girls misled into joining the movement or simply abducted from their homes to serve the men in their jungle hide-outs.'

He thought once again of the dead young woman exhibited in the market-place and, curiously, the dead face softened, took colour, and came alive in a reconfiguration of most exquisite, vibrant features, of the most beautiful and troubled eyes he ever saw, with a small black mole in the outer corner of the right eye. It was astonishing how he had caught that detail in the one fleeting moment when he had turned his head to look at the spectators in the market-place and seen that staring, intense, stricken face. It was not the first time he had seen the girl. She had been in his church one morning, kneeling and making the sign of the Cross though she carried a bag of temple joss-sticks. Then he had found her loitering outside a classroom in St Margaret's school and had stupidly mistaken her for a bicycle thief. On both occasions, he had come close enough to notice the mole for he had shaken her hand outside the church and grasped the handle-bars of her bicycle.

Then there was the last occasion when he had caught her up and swung her in the air to amuse a group of children in a playground: in putting her down upon the ground, his face had almost touched hers. But, strangely, he had observed the mole only in the market-place. In the uproar of that eventful day, he had registered every detail of her face. The local people had a belief about a certain category of spirit, usually female, who spent whatever time they were allowed on earth in following men and bursting in upon their dreams at night and their activities by day until the men grew pale, fell ill and begged them to leave. If he were superstitious, he might begin to believe that this young Chinese girl, who had appeared in his life on four separate occasions, was one of these ethereal beings. But the girl was no ghost. The solidity of her existence was clear enough, in the warmth of the hands that he had held, of the lithe body he had lifted into the air and spun round.

Suddenly Father Martin stopped writing, feeling a flush spread on his neck and cheeks. Three-quarters of his letter had been devoted to a girl he did not know, who was not even a member of the Church. He tore up the letter. Uncle Jean Claude would not have approved. He always imagined Uncle Jean Claude, in heaven at last after a life of true service and devotion to God, peeping over Léonie's shoulders to read his letters home, much as he had during those years when he had bent over to rid François' homework of spelling and grammar mistakes.

'What would you like to be when you grow up?'

Other little boys wanted to be firemen or policemen or doctors, but he would always shout, 'To be like Uncle Jean Claude!' in lusty demonstration of his great attachment to the uncle who had taken care of him since his father's death, when he was only two. If Uncle Jean Claude had been a bee-keeper or a circus clown, he would have wanted to be that too, his mother would say, smiling, to friends.

'And what does your uncle Jean Claude do?'

The little boy, quivering with eagerness to proclaim the nobility of his uncle's position in the world of God and men, would shout, even more lustily, 'My uncle Jean Claude is a missionary in China. He has gone there to save souls for God!'

He remembered how he would accompany his mother, even in the coldest winter weather, to the post office in their village in Provence to pick up letters; immediately, his eyes would pick out the envelope that bore Uncle's handwriting, with the special stamps which he was allowed to have. He remembered his mother reading excerpts of Uncle's letter to him, her face glowing with pride, her eyes glistening with tears, as she read, slowly and carefully, descriptions of the privations in China, which Uncle tried to play down – not so much of cold, poor food and lack of medicines but of a callous bureaucracy that always sought to obstruct him in bringing the faith to the people he had come to live among. He loved them dearly and would die for them: 'The Chinese are a special people,' Uncle wrote fervently. There was a picture which he had sent back of himself – tall, ascetic, stern-eyed and hollow-cheeked – with a Chinese family in a small village, two children in quilted jackets perched upon his knees.

'Your uncle is a saint,' his mother had told François. Poor Maman's greatest cross was not her poor health, which gave her terrible coughs and fevers at night, but Uncle's, because it had cost him his beloved mission in China. Uncle Jean Claude had returned to France, his health and spirit utterly broken, and she had wept in the silence of the night in a sharing of the aching loss. She knew that under the calm surface of his new persona as a parish priest burned the fires of an undying dream to return to that vast country, which must already have been in the divine mind when He had spoken of the great fields white with harvest. It was part of the divine wisdom to test even the few labourers there and send upon them trials and tribulations, as He had with Job of old. Jean Claude had Job's patience, and one day, he hoped, the divine will being at last satisfied, he might have a miraculous return of good health and be sent to that distant shore again. He spent hours on his knees, body proudly erect, the pride derived solely from the profound satisfaction of doing God's will. 'Thy will be done.' That had been Uncle's most heroic prayer in the greatest pain of his lost dream.

François Martin's earliest recollection was of his uncle on his knees in the dim light of the altar-lamp in church, or in his room, a sparse cell with no more than a rough bed and a chair by its side, dominated by a large crucifix on the wall. By the austerity of his looks, garb and habits, Uncle Jean Claude might have stepped out of a medieval monastery or the pages of a tome on the lives of the saints.

'Come here, François.' To determine the mood of his uncle, the little boy looked at a special feature on his face: two small vertical lines between the heavy eyebrows, just above the nose, which deepened when Uncle was angry and vanished magically when he smiled. He saw no lines and rushed forward, squealing with delight to see a candy bar held up in one hand. Uncle had never given out candy bars. The boy cast about in his mind for any recent good deed to a neighbour or a special act of obedience for which Maman and Léonie had praised him and about which they had later told Uncle.

'Just a moment, François.' Uncle put the bar out of his reach.

Then, with a severity of mien that silenced him immediately, Uncle Jean Claude said to him, 'Today, François, I am going to see how strong you can be.' The priest was talking of spiritual strength and he was going to use the candy bar to test the five-year-old's possession of that virtue. The candy bar was put on the kitchen table for the entire duration of the Lenten period, when good Catholics fasted and denied themselves all kinds of bodily pleasure in memory of the sufferings of Christ. On Fridays during Lent, Maman had only dry bread and water during meals. Uncle Jean Claude's self-imposed deprivations were so severe that his doctor ordered him to end them at once.

'You, François,' said Uncle Jean Claude, 'will prove your spiritual worth if you can refrain from touching the candy bar. The temptation will always be there, for the Evil One will whisper in your ear, "Taste it, it's the most delicious thing in the world," which, indeed, it is. Each time that happens, my boy, pray for strength and declare to the Evil One, "I am not of thy camp. Begone, Satan!"'

The temptation scene of snake and apple in the garden of Eden was replayed every day in Maman's neat, scrubbed kitchen where François sat at table with his plain soup and bread, while the candy, rich in promise of chocolate and nuts under its bright red wrapper, lay nearby, tugging at every fibre of his eager, robust body.

On the last day of Lent, Uncle Jean Claude came up to him, beaming, for the candy bar lay intact on the table. And then, a very short while later, he went into a towering rage as he picked up the bar and discovered it to be a small block of wood, cleverly covered over. His eyes red with the hot tears of angry disappointment, Uncle said that the sin of deceitfulness was much worse than that of gluttony.

'He's only a child, don't be too hard on him.' His mother came quickly to François' aid while Léonie had run in fright to hide behind a curtain. Uncle Jean Claude never raised a hand to hit him but his words could cut to the bone. In the end, François sobbed in Uncle's arms, thoroughly ashamed and repentant, for he was convinced that it was greedy, lying boys like himself who went on crucifying the Divine Master. A tender-hearted lad, he cried to see others in pain, and even more if he had caused that pain. Uncle had once shown him a picture of Christ, half naked, being whipped by brutal-looking soldiers. Uncle said that the sins of men, women and children continued to be the cruel whip on the divine flesh, making it bleed anew. It was much later that François realised the candy-bar test was the first of a stringent series, designed with a special purpose.

His dream seemingly lost for ever, Uncle Jean Claude had risen from his knees late one night captivated by a sudden vision of its recovery: he would groom his nephew to take his place. The more he thought and prayed about it, the more he was convinced that it was part of a divine scheme only now fully revealed to him. He spoke about it to his sister, and she wept with joy at the thought of her son being marked out for the supreme honour. The boy was strong, bright, generous, loving, exuberant: these qualities, if properly nurtured, would equip body and soul admirably for the arduous work of a labourer for the Lord's harvest in strange, distant lands.

François had a sensitive mind and absorbed instruction well, listening hard to his uncle as he spoke of God, told stories of the saints and urged the development of this virtue and the subjugation of that vice. Uncle saw the body as a potential enemy, warranting the greatest vigilance if it was not to subvert the soul; it was the coarse Brother Ass, as that greatest of saints, Francis of Assisi, had called it.

His uncle worried that the boy's natural liveliness and zest, his sensuous enjoyment of everything around him, would slip into something regrettably like vulgar sensuality, if not properly chan- nelled. Through a strict, conscientious regime of prayer, instruction and example, he succeeded in excising the boy's character of its rougher qualities, succeeded indeed beyond his dreams for, from the age of twelve, the boy became pious, prayed longer, shouted less, and read more from the devotional books that his uncle scattered in the house for him.

One evening, Jean Claude saw him kneeling in rapt prayer before a statue of the Blessed Virgin Mary that had been in the family for generations, then rise to tell him, 'Uncle, I'm going to be a missionary.' He was fourteen years old.

François' mother and sister offered a Mass of thanksgiving for his vocation which he was sometimes tempted to relinquish on their account. They needed him. The alternative life was certainly a pleasurable prospect and could by no means be displeasing to God: he saw himself as growing rich – but not rich to the extent of being Mammon's slave: Uncle Jean Claude never tired of telling his parishioners the story of the foolish young man who could not heed the call of the Lord because he had too much wealth, thereby provoking the Lord to make that drastic comment about it being easier for a camel to go through a needle's eye than for a rich man to enter heaven. No, he would not forfeit Heaven under any circumstances. He would want just enough wealth to take Maman to live in a warmer part of France, where the hateful coughing at night would disappear forever, and for Léonie to keep house for them, own pretty things that all girls liked, and be happy.

But his announcement, 'I'm going to be a missionary,' had had the thrilling aspect of a covenant with God, with his uncle as witness, and from that day he was irrevocably committed to the exalted calling. The prospect of never sleeping on a comfortable bed again (in China, Uncle Jean Claude slept on a plank bed with a straw mat and a thin coverlet), of never eating the good food he enjoyed ('How could you eat well, when you see hungry people around, especially children?'), of never romping in his beloved hills and meadows and streams ('God gave us the beauties of nature to enjoy, but for the true labourer in His field of souls, even that pleasure must be sacrificed') was for a while daunting to a fourteen-year-old.

But there was another pleasure, of a secret kind, that could never have been confided, not to shy, delicate Maman and Léonie, who would have been painfully embarrassed, and certainly not to Uncle Jean Claude, who would have been deeply shocked.

One day, François could no longer contain his curiosity and did what he knew the other boys in his school were doing with elaborate secrecy – and, if caught, with elaborate pretence at nonchalance – so that they would not be teased by friends or reprimanded by teachers. Finding himself alone in the school library one afternoon, he went to the shelf that held the school's collection of magazines and journals and made straight for a copy of the *National Geographic*, easily the best-thumbed magazine in the collection. The cover showed a tribe in a remote part of equatorial Africa, magnificent in full regalia of feathered headdresses, beads, body paint and decorative quills piercing noses; inside, a full page showed a young girl, even more magnificent in her gleaming, vibrant, full-fleshed nudity. François remembered a warm flush spreading slowly over his face and neck as he gazed upon the smiling African girl, her breasts a pair of perfect cones, the nipples small and hard and erect in proud proclamation of youth's beauty and vitality. Light and shadow played upon the sun-warmed body to accentuate its contours and confer upon it a certain palpability that must have compelled curious, eager, boyish fingers to touch and feel. In boyish dreams, the printed page must have melted away and surrendered a live, breathing female into the eager boyish arms. The first time he had had such a dream, François had woken up with a guilty start and rushed to the bathroom, hoping that neither Maman nor Léonie would hear. The next day, he confessed his sin of concupiscence to Father Henriot, an old priest helping Uncle in his parish. Father Henriot gave him as penance the recitation of the entire rosary. Even in the dimness of the confessional, François could see the severity on the priest's face.

The boy was troubled and confused. The same energy and zest for the beauty and fragrance of the hedgerow flowers in summer, the whirling stars, the sunshine washing over his skin like pure honey, the delicious sandwiches and puddings that Maman spoilt him with, the hills and meadows that reverberated with his yodelling, was turning inwards and brimming along guilty, secret channels that filled him with embarrassment. His body, which had given so much pleasure in its celebration of the sights, tastes, smells and touch of God's world, now gave deep, secret shame. For a while he wanted to be alone, avoiding Maman and Léonie.

Uncle Jean Claude spoke to him at length about this most insidious of sins, the chosen weapon by which the devil had the greatest chance of trapping a priest, whose work required him to move freely among men and women in the world. 'Pray,' he urged, sensing the boy's inward struggles, which he was too shy to talk about. 'Pray to the

Blessed Virgin Mary, who will help you in fighting the devil and all his works and pomp.'

The problem came to be known, between them, as the Devil's Pomp, and the boy thereafter had language to describe his trouble in its various aspects of onset and frequency, its accompaniment by sinful thoughts. His mother gave him a little plaster statue of Our Lady of Lourdes, which he kept by his bed and implored for help on his knees whenever he felt the coming of the Devil's Pomp.

The little museum in town conspired with the *National Geographic* to make him sin.

'François, come and look at this.' He and Uncle Jean Claude were visiting the museum and Uncle was drawing his attention to something. Whatever it was, it could not have been more compelling than the small piece of statuary he was looking at in surreptitious fascination, which showed a naked man and woman embracing, their legs intertwined. Likely to be removed once it came to the notice of an outraged parent or teacher, it now stood inconspicuously among a cluster of other figures and must have elicited glances more daring than those from young François Martin. The boy felt the hot spreading flush, the hot coursing in his veins that he noted, with growing dismay, was occurring more frequently. He turned away abruptly and strode off. He hoped his sharp-eyed uncle had not noticed anything.

For a while, the constant blandishments of the devil were ignored in the urgent task of taking care of Maman, who had been caught in a heavy downpour and was now confined to her bed. There was nothing he would not do for Maman. He read to her for hours from her favourite books, and scoured the countryside to pick her favourite flowers.

She touched his face gently with her thin, frail fingers. 'My son, the missionary,' she said proudly, and might have added, 'My brother, his wish fulfilled in my son.' For Uncle Jean Claude daily grew more saintly. François saw old peasant women kissing his uncle's hand as if their parish priest were already a canonised saint in their midst.

The true extent of his uncle's saintliness had dawned upon François when he was about twelve, shocking instead of edifying him.

'Uncle,' he had called softly, outside the austere cell that was Uncle's room in the loft of his church. There was no answer so he pushed open the door softly and peeped in. Uncle was kneeling on the floor, facing the crucifix on the wall, and scourging his bare back with a whip made of small lengths of rope tied together. *Whip, whip.* The boy watched in a mixture of horror and fascination as the lashes of rope descended, with vicious force and regularity, upon the exposed flesh. *Whip, whip.* He watched red streaks appear on the flesh, saw them multiply, cross each other, and break out in tiny rivulets of blood.

He ran away.

Back in his room, he tried to fit this shocking bit of new knowledge into the overall picture of Uncle Jean Claude's saintliness. He remembered his uncle telling him that the closest resemblance to Christ could be gained by taking on the sins of others, as He had done. Uncle was sinless, so his whip was a voluntary punishment on behalf of others. There were some dark whispers about an errant priest in a neighbouring town: was Uncle asking God's forgiveness with his own blood for the wretched man? After all, the Lamb of God understood the language of blood.

That Uncle was human, after all, and might actually have stepped into the dark world of human failings occurred to François one day when they were walking together through a part of town that was preparing for some carnival. There were open-air stalls, bright with bunting, ribbons and summer flowers, and children ran around eagerly, bright-faced with the anticipation of treats galore, dragging their parents to see the puppets or sample the candy-floss. A group of gypsies was looking on from their van, decorated with balloons and streamers, parked in a corner. A young woman detached herself from the group and walked up to them. She made straight for Uncle Jean Claude, ignoring the young François. She exuded pure sensuality in her every feature and movement: her hair was a mass of coal-black curls that tumbled extravagantly on to her bare shoulders, her blouse was pulled down to bare not only her shoulders but half her ample bosom, her eyes were black and sparkling like some exotic jewel, and her lips were a vivid scarlet, parted to show gleaming white teeth which, in their turn, parted, ever so provocatively, to show a tiny protuberance of moist pink tongue, while her skin gleamed like burnished copper. She moved with the dangerous ease and grace of the preying feline, stood boldly in front of Uncle Jean Claude and said something to him, in a suggestive drawl. The cliché of the scarlet, gaudy temptress was no cliché but a real presence, mocking the consecrated purity of the Catholic priest. She was the harlot of stern biblical warnings come alive.

Uncle ignored her and made to move on; she grabbed his arm and was gently but firmly brushed aside. At a safe distance from her, Uncle muttered, 'She's drunk, let's not pay any attention,' and indeed the gypsy woman must have been dreadfully intoxicated, for she suddenly squatted down on the ground and shouted some imprecations in a strange tongue before being led away.

Female beauty, sensuality, desire. In their excessive forms – as in the case of the wretched drunk gypsy woman trying to seduce a priest in a public place – they could repel, as they did Uncle Jean Claude. But who could tell what would happen if they took a subtler form, even that of innocence, and gently led their object into a hushed den of hidden pleasures? Had Uncle ever been led into such a snare and scrambled out to do penance for his sins? He had spoken admiringly of those saints who had fought the lust of the flesh through a range of amazing strategies. One rolled through briar bushes, another always kept by his side the skull of the city's most beautiful woman to remind himself that all female beauty was in reality no more than worm-corrupted bone. Yet a third, who was a bishop, punished himself for the pleasure of a woman's kiss on his hand by cutting off that hand.

'Stop it, Uncle! Stop it!' François had rushed into Uncle's cell and snatched the whip from his hand. Uncle, still kneeling on the cold, hard floor, his back bare, turned and looked sorrowfully at him.

The boy stamped on the instrument of self-punishment, now lying on the floor, crying in his anguish that he had not been in time to prevent its cruel infliction of a hundred lashes on the thin, fragile body. He could find no towel or napkin to wipe the blood, so he took off his own shirt, and laid it gently on his uncle's back, still crying. 'Uncle, it wasn't your fault!' he almost shouted. 'She came to you and tried to make you commit the sin of concupiscence, but you did nothing. I saw everything. You need not punish yourself for her sins!'

Uncle had embraced his nephew and said, 'Indeed I have sinned.' For the Lord had warned that a man could sin in his head as in his body: the struggle against Brother Ass must go on, and flagellation was but one of the means.

The boy hated the whip. He would have flung it into the air if Uncle had let him.

François was by himself on the bank of a stream – he was fifteen – his fishing rod by his side, a book on the life of St Francis of Assisi lying open on the grass, his mind in that gentle, contented state that, on a warm summer's day, was pure heaven. He was startled out of his reverie by the sound of splashing water and laughter and, looking upstream, saw a young girl swimming in the river. She saw him and waved. He remained where he was, staring at her as she swam towards him, the sunlight bouncing off her dark wet hair and strong shining skin in playful flecks of pure light. When she reached him, she stood up and the water fell off her body to reveal the fullness of her dark naked beauty. She was probably a gypsy and looked not much older than he. She stood perfectly still, as if allowing his eyes to take in every detail of her startling beauty. He gazed at her: his eyes had become a separate organ, with a life of their own, so that not even the greatest act of will could wrench them away from the object of their fascination. Somewhere, at the back of his mind, the severity of Uncle's voice and Father Henriot's mien sounded the alarm bells, but they rang in vain for he was in a paralysis of shock and wonderment as his eyes roamed over the girl's breasts, the curve of her shoulders, the slight swell of her belly, the gleam of her thighs, the dark wet gleam between her thighs. Somewhere, too, from a secret recess of memory floated the picture of the African girl, to merge with this one of the bathing gypsy girl. It remained a picture – he could have been in the school library, his fingers gripping a page of the *National Geographic* – until the girl scrambled up the river in a burst of joyous noise and walked towards him. Her movement and her laughter, which was like full-throated birdsong, had a tangibility outside picture or dream and demanded a response on his part. But he was incapable of response, still in the paralysis of wonderment.

The girl sat down, wet and slippery, on the grass beside him. She spoke in a tongue not familiar to him but his whole being vibrated to its message of the pure joy of being alive and young and beautiful. She sat so close to him that one breast brushed against him. He held his breath.

'Listen.' She put a finger to her lips and he heard the whistle of a bird somewhere in the distant trees. 'See.' She pointed to a kingfisher rising from the sparkling water, and he caught a flash of vibrant red and green before it disappeared. Child of nature, with the child's innocent eagerness to show off nature's bounty, she was directing his attention to this or that sound, this or that sight, on a beautiful summer's day by a river. It turned out to be a sly ploy: in seemingly distracting his eyes from the beauty of her body, she was compelling even greater attention to it, for the eyes would only be diverted momentarily from the sight before they fixed themselves again on her beauty. She looked at him, simpering, then caught hold of his hand

and laid it upon one breast. The little spasm of rapture exactly coincided with a shudder of horror, as the sound of a church bell suddenly burst upon the air, making him scramble up in a hurry.

'Wait, wait,' the girl gestured, but he was already running away, panting in his terror.

Maman and Léonie wondered about François' unusual reticence in the ensuing days, and a restiveness that their anxious eyes could not miss. But he could tell neither of the encounter, and certainly not Uncle Jean Claude.

'François, is something the matter?'

He shook his head and continued to keep to himself. He yearned to see the gypsy girl again. He made two more secret trips to the river, with fishing rod and the devotional book on St Francis, and came away disappointed.

He was lucky on the third trip. His heart quickened to the flash of the burnished body in the sparkling water and the sounds of the splashing, each a celebration of the brimming life and joy in the body. The girl saw him and waved with both arms. He waved back. To his delight, she swam towards him. There was the same mesmerising sight of her scrambling up the riverbank, an agile, long-limbed animal. She stood before him, shining, brimful of vitality, and motioned to him to take off his clothes and join her in the river. This could have been the moment for breaking out of the spell and bolting to safety, since no church bell sounded this time, but even as he protested and resisted her laughing efforts to unbutton his shirt and trousers, he knew that he was completely under the spell, was being carried along by a tide of feeling, as powerful as it was indefinable. It was taking him somewhere and, with the overpowering curiosity of someone being led into a world that he knows he could never have ventured into on his own, he wanted to see where that would be.

The gypsy girl, looking at his nakedness, said something that could have been a compliment for the adult robustness of frame that he had already acquired at fifteen. Laughing, she took his hand and tried to pull him into the water. And still he resisted, shaking his head, and she left him and returned to the river. He stood on the bank and watched her cavort in the water, like some playful water-creature, and struggled with the last vestiges of embarrassment. They vanished in an instant, and he plunged into the water.

And now all was the joy of pure animality – something he had never known before – as they swam together, splashed water on each other, came close enough for limbs to touch. In the later years, he would remember most vividly the laughter and the playfulness, the thrill of the sight of that young shining body rising out of the water, like a magic maiden in an oriental tale, a promise of eternal youth and joy.

Exhausted, they lay side by side on the grass under a tree, close to the river. Sighing with pleasure they turned to look at each other and smiled. And then he was covered with a confusion that only later, in quiet reflection, he would see as the product of a whole range of feelings crowding in upon each other: fear, shame, guilt, delight, pure exultation. As he felt her lips on his, her body pressing upon his, only the exultation remained, blinding white, reckless. He turned to face her fully with something like a grunt.

He would always remember the moment of his shame or, as Uncle Jean Claude would later convince him, of his redemption. God sent angels or comets or natural disasters to intercept sin. In his case it was his saintly Uncle Jean Claude who came upon him, in the ignominy of his nakedness with a gypsy girl upon a riverbank on a hot summer's day, just in time to save his purity and his vocation. The girl fled, plunging back into the river, and he put on his clothes slowly, and wished for the earth to open up and swallow him.

Maman and Léonie would never know about this, Uncle Jean Claude promised, otherwise they would die from shame and sorrow. A priest served God with his entire soul, heart, mind and body.

'You were ever weak in the flesh, François,' said Uncle sorrowfully, and perhaps he was thinking of that time, so many years ago, when a candy bar had come before his love of God. But prayer and penance could strengthen even the frailest flesh. Prayer and penance could turn the greatest sinner into the greatest saint.

'You what?' cried Uncle incredulously.

The boy repeated that, yes, he had been once more to the riverbank. Actually, it was not so much to look for the gypsy girl as to soothe the turmoil in his soul. He wanted to lie on the long, soft grass, close his eyes and surrender himself to the peace of sky and clouds and trees. There was no more peace in the presence of Uncle Jean Claude. He wanted to be all alone, by himself. His defiance, the unravelling of years of hard work, frightened Uncle Jean Claude. The boy said sulkily that he was not repentant – how could one repent the joyousness of the body? – and looked up to see tears in Uncle's eyes.

He stepped into his uncle's room one evening, for no other reason than to obey Maman who wanted him to apologise and kneel down for his blessing, gave a start and stepped back, his eyes filling with tears of rage. For his uncle was once more on his knees on the floor with the hateful whip, and he knew that the flagellation this time was on his account. His proud heart recoiled at the thought, and he almost rushed forward to snatch the odious instrument and cast it upon the floor once more. Instead he ran away, dashing the angry tears from his eyes with his fist.

For his benefit, Uncle Jean Claude, in his next sermon in church, spoke of the great battle in heaven between the good and the bad angels, led respectively by St Michael and Lucifer, and how the battle was replayed every day in the secret lives of men and women, boys and girls as they went quietly about their duties. Would they join forces with St Michael and defeat the forces of evil, or would they succumb and fall from grace?

The boy, sitting between Maman and Léonie, squirmed inwardly, refusing to see the relevance of that cosmic battle – aeons ago, even before Creation – to his life, or to denounce the encounter, so joyful, so brimful of youth's energy and beauty, as a force of evil.

'My son.' Maman said little but spoke much. She went to him one evening as he lay troubled on his bed and held him tightly in her arms. His eyes asked, 'Do you know, then?' and hers replied, 'Yes, but it makes no difference. You are still my own precious François,' and she held him even more tightly and pressed her lips to his forehead.

They stayed thus for a long time and then he said, 'Maman, will you pray with me?'

They knelt before the small chipped statue of Our Lady of Lourdes and prayed together. He rose from his knees with the heaviness of heart gone. He would always remember that moment of ineffable joy and peace when he felt with a certainty that God loved him, despite all that had happened, and would connect it, in the later years, with the most mundane, everyday details – the specks of dust dancing in the beam of sunlight through his window, the sounds of children playing in the distance, the smile on the face of Our Lady of Lourdes and the missing two fingers on her right hand, the pattern of grey and blue flowers on his mother's shawl, the flecks of grey in her hair.

Maman's last days were horrible; she did not deserve such a painful death. Léonie went about tirelessly, pale as a ghost, to make her feel comfortable. Uncle Jean Claude was devotion itself, spending whatever time he could spare beside her bed, comforting her. 'Your mother is a saint,' he said to the son and daughter.

François would not be denied the treasure of her last words, her last touch and stayed possessively by her bedside till the end. 'My son, priest and missionary,' she said, smiling, and it was the precise moment when his vocation, blurred and tattered, shook into a clear, bright promise to her and entrenched itself solidly in his consciousness. The greatest joy of the ordination ceremony would be the thought of Maman looking down from heaven and smiling, in the fulfilment of her dearest wish. 'Maman,' he whispered, as her hand fell away from his. He kissed her brow and watched her eyes close.

About a week later, Uncle Jean Claude found him in his room, sobbing as if his heart would break, and went up to touch him gently on the shoulder and hold him until the sobs subsided.

Throughout the years of François' training in the seminary, the memory of Maman on her death-bed and her last loving words were a gentle, tempering influence, guiding his life into quiet rhythms that would be disrupted no longer by the unruliness of youth's feelings. He had renounced for ever the call of a summer day's desire by a river.

When he said goodbye to the young Father François Martin, ready to set sail for a distant country called Malaya, Uncle Jean Claude was visibly fading away. But his eyes, dark and sunken, brimmed with tears of purest pride and joy. He had a gift for François. 'My most precious possession,' he said, and François knew what the brown-paper parcel contained.

He also knew that it was the last time he would see Uncle Jean Claude. Léonie wrote, not much later, to say that Uncle had died peacefully in the night, his last words being that he had run a good race and fought a good fight. It was only upon Uncle's death that François opened his gift, and gazed at the whip of ropes, fingering each separate strand in deep thought and noticing that the end of one still bore the penitential blood of that horrifying day.

'You wouldn't believe how charming the little native children are,' he wrote. Léonie loved children. She had never married and chose to be a teacher in a kindergarten, among small children about whom she wrote to him endlessly. He knew little Pierre, who had the face of an angel but was the terror of all the little girls, Marie, who was a tomboy, the twins, Claudette and Juliette, whose mother made sure they were dressed identically every day, down to the last detail of shade of hair-ribbon, and Jean Claude, her favourite, by the double recommendation of his name and his daily gift of a flower placed shyly on her table whenever she was not looking. 'Let me tell you of *my* children,' he wrote, and described a ragged urchin called Tee Tee, with an intense, peaked face like an elf and a great store of cunning, who followed him everywhere and once came up to test the hairiness of his hands. He went on to write about the delightful children he met in the playground, but his pen began to falter, for the girl's face once again intruded upon his consciousness and he saw her, saw the engaging mole, and felt something like an ache of longing to see her again.

CHAPTER THIRTY-ONE

In the rising fury of the wind, Big Older Brother and his two companions for the night's adventure found the grave at last and shone their torches on it. It was a mere mound, unmarked, as were all the graves of terrorists, beggars, derelicts, abandoned babies, the unwanted and unclaimed of the earth, who had been hauled from the town's hospital mortuary and dumped into holes in unhallowed ground, for ever separated from the rest of the neatly tended, regularly visited tombs in the cemetery.

They squatted around it and shivered in silent collective realisation of almost intimate proximity to the dead woman lying below: she of the boy's haircut and the naked breast. An urn of joss-sticks and a plate of oranges had mysteriously appeared on the precise spot where her body had lain in the market-place barely a month ago; a gesture of appeasement not extended to her three dead male comrades. The appeaser must have come in the silence of night, then fled. The town's cleaners coming with their long-handled brooms every morning, swept around the offerings, refusing to remove them. The joss-sticks and oranges mouldered in the heat and rain, and in the end the authorities got a Malay cleaner to do the job.

Big Older Brother and his companions were less interested in appeasement than petition. From a basket, they brought out two candles, which they stuck in the ground, a cluster of joss-sticks, a meat chopper wrapped in a towel, and a cockerel, pure white, with not a tinge of colour in its feathers, its legs tied together with string, its beak with a piece of rag. Out of the basket, the bird began to flop about with desperate energy, and was pressed to the ground to be quietened.

The wind blew out the candle each time it was lit. They had not bargained for bad weather: it was said that the most potent of spirits rode on wind and storm. A dome of cupped hands finally allowed the appearance of a flame, an abatement of wind its bright and steady growth to illuminate the entire scene of the conjuration. The dead woman, more powerful in death than she could ever have been in life, might be enticed to appear. The three men each lit a joss-stick, held it in both hands, bowed reverently, then stuck it on the mound.

'I'll do it,' said Big Older Brother, referring to the most difficult part of the ceremony. He held the cockerel's head down on the ground with one hand and with the other brought down the chopper on its neck. The head came off neatly and noiselessly; the headless bird leaped into the air, spurting blood furiously. It came down clumsily, managed a few feeble flaps, then lay still at last. Big Older Brother picked up the dead bird with both hands and dragged it a few times across the mound for a more even spread of precious ritual blood. Blood appeased blood.

'Now you,' said Big Older Brother, not caring whether it was Tua Bah or Tua Poon who would take them on to the next stage of the supplication. 'Hurry up.'

Tua Bah brought a small wooden canister with a sheaf of numbered sticks from his trouser pocket, and handed it to Tua Poon. But the man was growing more frightened by the minute, and his hands were trembling too much for him to shake the canister over the blood-soaked earth to allow the favoured numbers to drop out. For through such means did the dead, once properly propitiated, grant lucky lottery numbers to the living. An inveterate gambler, Tua Poon had on countless occasions shaken out lucky numbers, on sticks or little rolls of paper, at coffins and ancestral altars. But this was his first time at an actual grave in the open. In the midst of a rising storm that could carry a whole legion of unquiet souls, he lost his nerve.

'Here, let me do it,' said Tua Bah, his own fear forgotten in an overpowering need to get the thing done and go home before the storm broke. He tried to wrest the canister from Tua Poon, who clutched it to his chest, saying, 'No! No! No!' in a voice of rising terror.

In what was later explained as temporary possession by the spirit of the woman terrorist or some other spirit that happened to be wandering that night, Tua Poon dropped the canister to the ground and ran hither and thither, uttering little shrieks and clutching his head.

Tua Bah stood by helplessly, but when a sudden invasion of chill in his body coincided with a screaming blast of wind, he, too, began to run.

'You fools! People will hear us,' cried Big Older Brother, concerned that the night's expedition might yield nothing, even as he felt a tremor of fear all over his body.

Tua Poon had fallen on his knees and was knocking his forehead on the ground in a frenzy of pleading.

Big Older Brother went to pull him up, saying, with the stern ferocity reserved for the abject insane, 'Stop that! Stop that, I say!'

'Don't let them get me! Please don't let them get me!' Tua Poon pleaded, his teeth chattering.

In later ruminations on the matter, Big Older Brother remained unsure about whether the sensation of cold wet fingers on his cheeks or the sudden tugging of a tuft of hair on his head was the work of wind or spirit. Now he, too, lost all nerve and shouted, 'Run! Run!' dragging Tua Poon with him. He looked around for Tua Bah, who was nowhere to be seen, but just before they left the cemetery, the man appeared, paler than a ghost and blubbering with fear.

The rain came down in torrents and together the three men ran along the only footpath leading out of the cemetery, Tua Poon still beseeching, 'Please don't let them get me.' Drenched and shivering, they stopped at the first building they saw, which was the Church of the Sacred Heart of Jesus.

Inside it, silently, gratefully, the three men stood close together, not daring to sit down or touch anything. At the far end of the darkness flickered the light of a lamp – eye of the watchful alien god.

Tua Poon pointed a trembling finger in its direction. 'They're here, they've followed me here,' he whimpered, and clung to Big Older Brother, like a terrified child.

They all looked. A white shape had detached itself from the light and was coming towards them. 'No! No! No!' shrieked Tua Poon, covering his face with his hands, while Tua Bah followed up the cries with his own pleas, as the white shape drew nearer, 'Please don't harm me. I've never done harm to anybody. Please –'

Big Older Brother was about to turn and run when a voice said,

'What's the matter? What are you all doing here?'

With tremendous relief, they saw that it was the foreign priest.

CHAPTER THIRTY-TWO

'See if it's ready,' Ah Oon Soh said to Mei Kwei, indicating the herbal brew bubbling in its earthen pot on the kitchen stove. She turned back to Big Older Brother, lying on his bed, his eyes closed, a long arm flung across them. 'Lift your arm. Further down. Turn over.'

Seldom spoken to in the imperative, Big Older Brother submitted his body like an obedient child to her expert ministering hands as they kneaded, rubbed and soothed with special coconut oil.

When Mei Kwei brought in the brew in a large bowl, Ah Oon Soh said, 'Sit up. Drink.'

His eyes still closed, Big Older Brother sat up, and, with his mother holding the bowl to his lips and his sister looking on, he sipped the hot, pungent mixture. Grimacing, he turned away and gestured that he wanted no more.

'You must,' said his mother anxiously, looking into the bowl: only half of its healing power had been ingested. But he made another gesture, for her to be gone, lay down on the bed again and remained still, his eyes closed resolutely.

In the night when Mei Kwei heard him groaning, she went to him and laid thin slices of potato on his brow. They turned black, showing that they had absorbed the vileness of his fever, for the plant world, like the animal world, could be depended on to show compassion for humans by taking over fevers, aches, swellings, mumps. She sat by his side, remembering a time when she had lain ill with a fever and he had wandered in, an ice-ball in his hand. The sight of his sister's pale face and parched lips must have moved him, for he removed some ice flakes and put them on her lips. They melted instantly, and she remembered the immense relief of the cool contact. He watched intently, and generously laid more on her lips until they were parched no longer. The brother of her childhood could be kind: Mei Kwei

197

needed to remember past kindness to stem present rage. She could touch and nurse, in sickness, the massive swarthy limbs from which, in health, she shrank.

'Why doesn't he see a doctor?' Austin said. 'I could make the arrangements.' Engaged to Mei Kwei, he still felt the antagonism of her family. Loving her, he was prepared, with all his resources of time, energy and money, to overcome this antagonism. The job at the Britannia eating-house was her brother's, if he wanted it.

In two other households, women attended sick men because the men had become ill on their account.

Big Older Brother, Tua Bah and Tua Poon had gone on that ill-fated expedition to win money for their women. Their spirits and bodies broken by the misadventure, they now lay whimpering on their beds, while the women hovered around with palliative brews, soothing oils and supplicating joss-sticks to stick in urns before the ancestral portraits on the altars. The soul's dark terrors, which in the first days had emerged as bad dreams, were beyond the helping touch of the women who watched and were themselves afraid. Big Older Brother moaned and tossed in his sleep, banging on the wooden walls separating the bedrooms. Tua Bah woke his old mother each time he sat up screaming that he heard voices in his ears. The voices disappeared as soon as he opened his eyes but returned with greater force the moment he fell asleep again. Tua Poon suffered the most, recollecting in every vivid detail the onslaught of the avenging spirits who crowded his dreams, the benign white solidity of the foreign priest's robe completely submerged by a horde of hostile, shrouded women who surrounded him, hissing.

Tua Poon's wife, eighteen years old, woke up to his groans and the shrill cries of their small child at the foot of the bed, startled out of an infant's light sleep. Rocking the child in her arms, she stared in awe at her husband in the thrashing throes of nights gone mad. There were now two for her to soothe out of fretfulness for Tua Poon, opening his eyes and seeing his wife by the bed looking at him, became tearful and indicated with the sobbing urgency of a frightened child that he, too, wanted to be held.

For days, the houses smelt of the pungency of herbs bubbling in pots and oils released from bottles and flasks, of the acidity of urine and vomit in chamberpots quickly brought out from under beds for emptying into lavatory buckets.

Austin said, in an exasperation he could hardly control, 'Your brother's illness is making you ill. I've never seen you so tired and listless. Why don't you call the doctor? Why don't you let me?' He continued to watch, with each visit, her devoted attention to her brother. 'You smile less, you pay less attention to me.'

A mother's indifference was equally painful to the generous male heart. Tua Bah wanted enough money to send his mother back to China. Her dream of returning to the ancestral country to die and be buried among family had become central to her existence, permeating her every thought and action, so that on the few occasions when she got lost in town and kind strangers offered to take her home, she invariably gave them the address of a house in a small village in China, adding, with tears in her eyes, that it had a large courtyard where she used to play as a child.

Of the three, Tua Poon claimed that his need was greatest, because he loved most of all. Tua Poon had married his wife when she was seventeen because she was six months pregnant with his child. She was no more than a child herself; to sexual delight was added the genuine satisfaction of having rescued an innocent girl from a brutal father. It was now the responsibility of Tua Poon, twenty years older, to provide her with a secure and happy life.

Tua Poon wanted to be able to buy a car and drive her past her father's house to make the old man choke on his words: 'Give her a good life? She should thank God for three meals a day.' But if the big dream was distant, small ones could be secured, and he came home sometimes, from his cold-drinks stall near the town's movie-house, with packets of her favourite fried noodles, a small bottle of perfume or a bead necklace. After the birth of her child, her young body fleshed out, and it was said, with much ribald laughter, that if Tua Poon's drinks stall was closed for an hour every afternoon, it was because he was at home enjoying his young wife's voluptuousness.

A month after the misadventure, about which the three men had agreed to an oath of secrecy, they met in a coffee-shop, much recovered in health and spirits. It had gone wrong for whatever reason, and now, before putting their minds together for a second collaborative venture in pursuit of a common aim, they thought to expunge every vestige of doubt and fear, to put the matter behind them. Big Older Brother was all for rational thinking and bore down, with much authority, on all the assertions of the other two.

'I wasn't imagining,' said Tua Poon earnestly. 'They were coming at me. I saw them distinctly.'

'I heard their voices for days afterwards. How can that be imagining?' asked Tua Bah, with equal gravity.

But Big Older Brother, being the youngest, most intelligent and most articulate, convinced them that it had been only the combined effect of cemetery and storm, expectation and fear, not to mention the eerie presence in the darkness of the white-robed foreign priest.

CHAPTER THIRTY-THREE

The news of the terrorists' attempted assassination of Old Yoong, Penang millionaire and philanthropist, was suppressed by the police for his protection, but it found its way quickly to Luping. Pig Auntie came breathlessly to tell Ah Oon Soh. Since the engagement of Mei Kwei to Austin Tong, Old Yoong had been cast out of their lives and any news of him was matter for private, whispered, speculative talk only. The terrorists' favourite targets were those openly supporting the armed enemy, the British authorities: Old Yoong, with his generous donations to white men's hospitals and schools and charities, was a secondary target, but his turn had come. Luckily, the story went, the grenade had destroyed his car without killing him or his chauffeur.

'Should I tell her?' Pig Auntie made a gesture in the direction of Mei Kwei, who was in her room getting ready to go out with Austin, but Ah Oon Soh shook her head, frowning.

Even if the assassination attempt on Old Yoong had been successful, it would not have created the same consternation as Mr Aw's murder. Mr Aw was Luping's best physician and one of the most prominent members of the Chinese community. His assassination had all the marks of defiance and challenge. At about six thirty in the evening, when the town's streets were still full of people and traffic, a terrorist had stopped outside his house and thrown in a grenade. Mr Aw was killed instantly; his wife and daughter escaped. Hubris had brought about its own destruction. Having escaped two previous assassination attempts, the physician strutted his invincibility and was quoted in a Chinese newspaper as saying that he would rather empty into the river the entire stock of medicines in his dispensary than give a single dose to save the life of a Communist terrorist.

David Parry, one of the planters living in a remote area, was rushing his pregnant wife to the nearest hospital, fifteen miles away, when he was fired at. He knew at least half a dozen of them were hiding in the undergrowth. He, his wife and their baby survived only because he had recently decided to armour his Ford V8, replacing the windows with steel plates and erecting a metal shield with eye slits that could be lowered over the windscreen by pulling a cord.

The terrorists were getting bolder. A curfew was imposed, which reduced Luping to a ghost town after six o'clock in the evening. Anyone found outside his home after that hour would be hauled off to the town police station.

What had caused T. C. Williams, chief of operations, to hit the roof and slap on the curfew immediately had very much to do with personal anguish. A boyhood friend of his – they had been at boarding school together in Scotland, had been best man at each other's weddings and godfather to each other's children, had remained in touch from different ends of the earth – was shot dead one morning while shooting birds on the edge of a palm-oil plantation. A witness to Duncan Bryce's murder said that he saw a man in khaki shorts run up, shout, 'Die! Die!' then flee into the plantation, an imprecation hurled at Empire itself, not just at one more Englishman.

As Williams gazed upon his friend's body on a cold cement slab in the town hospital mortuary, the face a gaping hole, and put a comforting arm around his friend's wife, who was bravely keeping back tears for the sake of her little boys, he felt enraged. The bastards! He would get them. And he would make it impossible for their secret helpers in the town to slip out under cover of darkness with their food or medicine or secret information.

One of the secret helpers, a shop assistant, was caught and forced to get off his bicycle. Inside the tyres were small packets of rice. Some terrorist, sick of eating wild tapioca or yam, must have put the grain at the top of his list of requests. It was truly amazing, the central role of this commodity in the lives of the locals. Not surprising, really, said T. C. Williams to his friends, in his expatiations on local peculiarities, considering their origins in a wet rice culture in the ancestral country. At the first hint of trouble the women rushed to the shops with their bags, sacks, pots, kerosene tins, every possible kind of container, and filled them to the brim with the precious stuff.

Williams wanted to use the case of the bicycle rice smuggler to serve as the strongest possible deterrent. He had the man severely flogged and fined, and his whole family put under strict surveillance. Whitehall had put a stop to the practice of market-place exhibitions of dead terrorists after a journalist wrote about it in the London *Times* and caused several Members of Parliament to wince at the savagery and lodge a strong protest. But Whitehall had better not interfere too much.

'What do they know, with their fat comfortable arses never out of their armchairs?' growled Williams. He made arrangements for Duncan Bryce's wife and boys to fly home and thereafter mourned in private the loss of his best friend.

There was a memorial Mass for Duncan, a devout Catholic, in the town's Catholic church. He went, together with Jill and Gray whose eyes were red throughout the ceremony. He held Duncan's wife's hand comfortingly and, later, Jill held Gray's outside the church. The priest, Father François Martin, shook hands with them all and offered his sympathies.

That evening T. C. Williams shut himself up in his room and got drunk.

CHAPTER THIRTY-FOUR

She had never been to Penang on her own. Ordinarily her mother would have been alarmed at the prospect of her going by herself, first on a two-stage journey by bus, then by ferry across a strip of water. The alarm would have been greater if her mother had known the purpose of the visit.

But nowadays Ah Oon Soh refused to have anything to do with the wilful daughter: 'You do as you like. Why bother to tell me at all?' Like her husband, she had withdrawn from the turbulent worlds of both son and daughter. The damage that her daughter's actions, encouraged by the young upstart Tong, had done to her sensibilities of all that was right and proper had left her, initially with a bitter resentment and then, after the bitterness was swallowed like the countless disappointments in her life, with a numbing weariness.

An Oon Soh was convinced that it all boiled down to the discharging of a debt: the wrong-doings of a previous life were being paid for in this one, through the pain inflicted on her by her entire family. 'My fate,' she summed it all up to Pig Auntie. She emerged from her numbness to do this or that for the husband, son or daughter, without joy or hope, no longer praying to ancestors who seemed unable, or unwilling, to help. So it was with a quiet dispiritedness that Ah Oon Soh had helped her daughter prepare a gift – a brew of bird's nest soup.

It was a long and arduous task which involved soaking the bird's nest overnight in cold water, clearing it of the impurities floating at the top which included the tiniest bits of feathers, brewing it over a slow fire in an earthen pot and keeping a watchful eye on the different stages of the simmering.

'Mother, aren't you going to ask me who it is for?' her daughter asked. And when Ah Oon Soh remained silent, she said, 'It is for Old Yoong. I'm going to Penang to take it to him.'

Without looking at her, Ah Oon Soh said once more, 'Why do you bother to tell me?' She helped the daughter put the soup, simmered to perfection, in a deep tin container, which she covered carefully then lowered into a basket. She would not give her daughter the satisfaction of seeing her curiosity about the purpose of the visit and the gift.

In the bus and in the ferry, Mei Kwei felt the hardness of male stares on her face and body. Her hands grasped the handle of the basket on her lap and she looked studiously out of the bus window upon white sky and, from the ferry, upon murky water. Even in the position of a claimed woman, as when sitting with Old Yoong in his car or walking with Austin along a street, she was not free from the stares of men. Throughout her life, she fled from men or ran to men. Now she was running to a man she had fled from with a gift. On her wrist, she wore a gift, once his, now another's, because Austin had bought it with money. Jade grew greener and brighter through lucky touch; her jade bangle, if it gleamed more brightly now, must have thrived on fear.

The servant who came to the large wrought-iron gate, accompanied by two barking dogs, said, 'Who are you?' adding curtly, 'The master is resting. He does not receive visitors.'

Mei Kwei gave her name. 'Tell him I have come to see him.'

The servant reappeared with a woman in a blue blouse and brown sarong, accompanied by another whom Mei Kwei recognised as one of the two emissaries who had come in the white car to request the white trousers for the wedding-night ritual from her mother. The women conferred quickly together, never taking their eyes off her.

'You can't see him,' said the woman in the sarong, who must be Second Wife, allegedly the most loyal one, in charge of his recuperation after the attempted assassination. 'He is resting. He does not receive visitors.'

'I have a gift for him.'

'He does not receive gifts either.'

But Mei Kwei was adamant. 'I have to see him. Please tell him I'm here.'

The two women went back into the house. After what seemed a long time, the servant reappeared. 'The master says he does not want to see you.'

She knew it was not the two women's doing for, without lifting her head, she had seen the curtain of an upstairs window, just above a side entrance, move a little, to show, fleetingly, part of a familiar face that could be saying, 'Don't even dream of it. Not after what you have done to me.' And she thought she heard a sharp, gleeful laugh.

Mei Kwei turned to go and was half-way down the drive when the same servant came running after her to say, no less curtly, 'The master says to wait in the hall for him.'

She entered the house and followed the servant into the cool, dark interior of a large room, replete with antique furniture, heavy brocade curtains, huge lamps, enormous portraits on the walls among which was one, in an ornate gift frame, of the younger Yoong, handsome and imposing, that had been sent to her in the early days of the negotiations. She stood near a table, her basket on the floor beside her, and saw again slight movements behind curtains and screens, probably of wives and their servants stationing themselves for a full witnessing of her humiliation. When Old Yoong came in with a walking stick, helped along by a male servant, she was shocked by his appearance. The expensive silk robe over the expensive silk pyjamas did nothing to hide the depredation of age, aggravated by the trauma of the assassination attempt: he looked far thinner, older and more haggard than she had ever seen him or imagined he could be. The servant helped him into a chair, and he imperiously waved Mei Kwei to another, facing him, a short distance away. There were a few minutes of silence, during which he surveyed her with none of the benevolent pleasure he had shown in the days of courtship.

Having recovered from the shock of the announcement of her presence at his gate, he had abruptly sent the message of refusal through Second Wife, then retracted it just as abruptly and sent the servant after the girl. While he waited for her, a delicious chance of restoring his grievously wounded pride had presented itself to him, and had enlarged into a scheme of grand revenge to erase the pain of that last meeting, when she had come out in the rain with an umbrella for her father and had ignored him completely.

But he had not bargained for the power of simplicity of gesture and authenticity of feeling. As soon as Mei Kwei saw him, she made an involuntary movement towards him and her face lit up in unmistakable pleasure at seeing him again. Gratified, he decided to show no sign of being so. 'Why have you come?' he asked tersely.

The girl was covered with confusion, but managed to deliver her message. If she had rehearsed it at home, its smooth coherence now fragmented into a faltering speech. It was a strange message of self-reproach for ingratitude. She was sorry she had been ungrateful to him despite his kindness. She spoke feelingly of his generosity, which had, on so many occasions, saved her and her family. She had regretted their last meeting, when she should have thanked him. The news of his attempted assassination had jolted everything back, painfully, into her consciousness and she had not been able to sleep, thinking of his misfortune and wanting only to see him again, to express sorrow for her bad behaviour and gratitude, long overdue, for his kindness.

She would have told him, if it had not made for greater agitation in her voice, that, given the chance, she would seek out the Indian labourer who had rescued her, as a child, from a ditch and then been rudely dismissed by her mother and brother, and a Mr Satosan, who did not speak her language but had spoken comfort and healing words when he put her on his knee and wiped away her tears. Kindness from strangers or from friends – until it was returned, she felt unease in her heart. She pointed to the basket at her feet on the floor, with a little nervous laugh, to distract herself from the tears beginning to spring into her eyes: 'A small gift from my mother and me, which we hope you will accept.'

The hardness of purpose with which Old Yoong had steeled himself for the meeting was fast evaporating and into its place had crept a new thought, creating new hope. Greater than the gratification of soothed pride was the thrill of the conviction that the girl had come to ask to be taken back.

A small smile played on Old Yoong's face as he looked at her. There was no guile about her expression of gratitude – she was capable of foolhardiness, but not guile. It was all of a piece with her regret for her folly and the change of heart towards him. The pain of her rejection had been greater than that from any assassin's weapon for he had never stopped loving her and desiring her. The keenness of the loss had surprised even him and for a while he had sought assuagement in the company of other women. He came to the conclusion that she was one of those rare women, very like the demon women of folklore, whom men could not forget but for whom they ever pined, tragically, beneath the smooth surface of their continuing lives. Mercifully for the men, such women destroyed themselves in the end. It was said that the distinguishing mark of these fatal women was a teardrop mole; they would cause men to shed tears before they did so themselves in a last act of self-immolation.

He looked at the girl's mole and remembered kissing it once, remembered, too, as he looked at her face, her eyes, her mouth, her body, his joyous taste of her beauty and his bitterness at the denial of that last private beauty, reserved for the wedding night alone.

Suddenly Old Yoong felt a resurgence of the old fire. He said to Mei Kwei, 'You have come. That is the most important thing. You have come back to me – it is not too late –' and realised he had made a dreadful mistake.

He would have got up to her and taken her in his arms, if she had not looked down suddenly and said, 'I am engaged to be married.' He caught the glint of the engagement ring on her finger. Her hand was clenched and pressed tightly upon her thigh, but it was as if she had waved and flashed in his face the hard taunt of her betrothal to another. It must be to that young man he had heard about, who had forked out the cash for the jade bangle. It was still on her wrist, rich and gleaming.

If the girl had faltered in the announcement, had shown even the slightest indication of distress, he would have once again jumped to the rescue and plucked her out of that wretched world in which she was trapped. But there was a finality in her voice.

Suddenly Old Yoong felt very angry. He got up, his face flushed, his eyes blazing. 'There's nothing more to be said on the matter.' In the space of ten minutes, his heart, hardly recovered from the terror of the grenade incident, had palpitated through the wild oscillations of anger, hope, love and despair. He trembled visibly and the concerned servant made a quick movement towards him.

Mei Kwei rose slowly. She had hoped, for her own peace of mind, to carry away memories of understanding and forgiveness.

Old Yoong paused in a doorway. 'I see you are still wearing my gift,' he said. 'As long as it rests on your wrist, you will always be coming back to me.'

Alighting from the ferry, she caught sight of Austin's black car parked some distance away and of Austin himself hurrying towards her.

'You look very pale,' he said 'Your mother told me – I was worried – why didn't you ask me?' He had guessed the purpose of her visit: 'I would have been glad to take you. You could have got into trouble, going all by yourself. And the ferry's no place for a girl like you.'

Mei Kwei told him about her unpleasant encounter, and Austin's solicitousness surged afresh, expressing itself in an elaborate flutter of small intimate actions he enjoyed if only because they presaged the consummate thrill of the wedding night: the smoothing back of the wisps of hair fallen on the forehead, the gentle wiping away of the remnants of tears under her eyes, the cupping of his hands to the contours of her face. She was growing more precious by the day, this strange, beautiful, rare girl delivered to him, like manna, for the assuagement of the hunger of his body and soul.

'Why didn't you ask me?'

But she seemed to be drifting slowly away from him as she carried the burdens of her untidy, confusing world, the vengeful ire of a repudiated fiancé and the incessant demands of a brutish brother alone.

'Why can't we get married soon?' Austin realised he was becoming querulous with his demands, and checked himself. For a moment he experienced a little thrill of terror, deep inside, that she did not want to get married to him after all, that it was not compassion for an old man suffering the double blow of a rejection and an attempted murder that had prompted the strange visit to his mansion in Penang, but a change of heart on her part.

The quiver of terror bubbled to the surface in a slow, taut question. 'What did you tell him?'

But he was reassured once more, for she said directly, 'I told him I was going to be married to you.'

CHAPTER THIRTY-FIVE

'The curfew. Don't forget the curfew,' said Ah Oon Soh anxiously, fearing that her son, completely bewitched by the *ronggeng* girl from Thailand with whom he spent his nights in the town's boarding-houses, would stumble drunkenly out into a deserted street one evening and be nabbed by a policeman.

There was another worry. The girls from Thailand came well equipped with charms, which they put into the men's food or drink and enslaved them. They had learned from their mothers, who had learned from *their* mothers, the secret of making potions from the secret discharges of women's bodies to compel males into unstinting devotion and lifelong fidelity. One man, it was said, had sold his business and handed over the entire proceeds to the enchantress, finally abandoning his wife and four children to follow her back to Thailand. Ah Oon Soh knew about the large wad of lottery money in her son's pocket. One evening, while he was in the lavatory, she stole into his room, looked quickly into the pockets of his trousers lying on the bed and saw her suspicion confirmed: the wad was down to a mere handful of notes. That Thai whore Nee Nee was behind it all. While vowing to have nothing more to do with recalcitrant offspring, Ah Oon Soh worried endlessly about her son.

Big Older Brother was with Nee Nee in a room on the upper floor of a shop-house, one of two let occasionally to couples in urgent need of overnight accommodation. He sat up on the bed, amid a squalid entanglement of unwashed sheets, pillows and bolsters, and would have pulled down the luscious Nee Nee once more upon himself if she had not eluded his grasp and slipped out of bed. He demanded a drink and she passed him a half-finished bottle of beer.

'Come here,' he murmured, and was asleep again in two minutes.

When he woke up, in growing darkness, she was gone. His first thought was to establish the state of his finances. Dragging himself out of bed, he staggered to his trousers, hung over the back of a chair, and searched its pockets. He pulled out a few fistfuls of small notes and coins, counted them, and looked around disconsolately. Then, putting on his trousers and shirt, he staggered out of the shop-house and into the street. Its eerie silence and emptiness stirred no memory, struck no warning, as he lurched along, with some vague purpose of going to the girls' boarding-house. He heard a shout behind him, and stared stupidly as two policemen came up, positioned themselves on each side of him and handcuffed his wrists behind his back.

'Come with us,' said one severely. They had let off the wife-beating Indian drunk with a warning and a smack across his head, and had ignored the town idiot, a shock-headed, gibbering youth with a low, simian forehead and dangling arms, but they had to punish this strong, swarthy young man, whose drunken stagger might be only a ruse.

As soon as news reached her of her son being in the lock-up in the town's police station, Ah Oon Soh ran crying to Mei Kwei, who was stirring soup in the kitchen, then into her husband's room.

'The fool, the fool,' muttered Ah Oon Koh.

He got up, put on his trousers and shirt, got on his bicycle and rode to the police station to see what he could do. Only a threat to his son's safety could rouse him from his opium-induced torpor and bring him out of the darkness of his room.

'Would you do the same, Father, to save my life?' Mei Kwei might have asked bitterly. The anxieties of her new life forced a chilling thought: she knew how any trouble in the family would end and how she would be ensnared more than ever, a small creature struggling feebly against the ever-tightening ropes of its ensnarement and finally giving up in exhaustion.

Ah Oon Koh, wizened, stained and bent with opium, wearing an old, unbuttoned shirt that flapped around his singlet and rasping out a stream of protests in rough dialect, was ignored by the officers and clerks in the police station who continued to go about their work in cool disdain. A middle-aged Indian officer with a trim moustache was walking in and out of rooms with sheafs of papers and simply waved him to a row of three chairs lined against a wall.

Ah Oon Koh looked around with a baleful glare and decided to go home. He mounted his bicycle and pedalled away furiously, muttering to himself. Back home, muttering grew to vehement ranting, as he paced the floor and flung his thin arms about, watched by his pale-faced wife and daughter. The ranting was solely against the arrogant police; of his son, whose errant ways had always been tolerated because he was a son and first-born, he only growled, once again, 'The fool, the fool.'

The ordeal of Big Older Brother ended as abruptly as it had begun. The familiar black car rolled to the front door, and out came Big Older Brother, dishevelled, squinting sullenly in the bright afternoon sun, followed by Austin Tong. The beneficence of power and influence became apparent at once to father, mother and sister gathered anxiously in the doorway. 'Why didn't you tell me?' Austin asked. He had found out by accident from one of the cooks in his restaurant and had immediately swung into action, driving straight from the Britannia eating-house to the police station. Here the consummate value of an English education was immediately apparent for, speaking the foreign language throughout with quiet and polite urbanity, he had cleared all obstacles. He had first obtained permission to see the prisoner, and then to see the superior officer in charge to explain and plead the case. He had commended the two policemen highly for doing their duty and hinted, lowering his voice, that the prisoner was basically a good, decent person, who had lately fallen into bad company and got involved with the *ronggeng* girls to the distress of his parents. Austin had then casually let drop the names of Mr Robinson, Mr Robert and T. C. Williams, and finally agreed, with friendly alacrity, to sign an undertaking as guarantor that the prisoner would in future respect the curfew. The visit to the police station had ended with Austin Tong passing cigarettes all round and inviting the officers to come by and try the good food at the Britannia eating-house at a substantial discount.

But there was to be yet one more event that pulled even tighter the ropes of the snare round Mei Kwei's struggling heart.

Barely a month later, Big Older Brother was severely beaten as he was walking home. Two youths with handkerchiefs over their faces had leaped upon him from behind some bushes and assaulted him with sticks and bricks. He was left sprawled on the dirt track, his face, neck and arms a raw, red mess. Tee Tee found him, and ran yelping all the way to the house. The whole family rushed out and carried him home.

Drumming her fists on her chest in abject remonstration with the gods, Aah Oon Soh repeated, 'Why is all this happening? What have I done to deserve it?'

Ah Oon Koh paced the floor, muttering ferociously, shaking his head as his son groaned in pain.

Mei Kwei hated it all – the histrionics of their helplessness directed at her with the one shameless unspoken plea, 'You know what to do.

Get Austin Tong to come at once,' which was all the more shameless for their avowed hatred of him.

Big Older Brother was taken to hospital and placed in a good ward with a proper bed, and was attended by a doctor whom Austin Tong knew personally. A proper report, written and signed by Austin on Big Older Brother's behalf, was filed at the police station; a sum of money was surreptitiously pushed into Ah Oon Soh's hand, with the quick words, 'You may need this,' and a quick finger at the lips to forestall any reaction by the bewildered woman.

The culprits were never caught and after Big Older Brother was discharged from hospital, he withdrew into greater reticence and, in the end, stopped co-operating with the police. For, although his unruly world had, at one time, overlapped with the dark alleys and dens of hoodlums, gamblers, secret-society gangs and pimps, he now chose to remain tight-lipped about them all.

'We have to talk,' Austin said, his face taut with anger.

Their meal in the Britannia eating-house remained untouched as he and Mei Kwei faced each other across the narrow table.

He held her hands with a ferocity that frightened her. 'You have to tell me the truth,' he said. 'It is agony not to know.'

'I have already told you the truth,' Mei Kwei said quietly.

But the single shake of her head to his question had not been sufficient: he wanted a far stronger denial, a denial shouted out, followed by a whole-hearted attempt at reassurance, to quell the unspeakable torment of his question, 'Have you slept with your brother?' The suspicion, starting as a tiny, teasing thought, like a small insect's buzzing in the ear, had swelled into a mighty roar that rocked the foundation of his being. That ravenous, green-eyed monster, having been continuously nourished on the rotting heap of suspicion's secret discharges, now reared its head.

'This something I have seen between you and your brother is not natural. The day after the curfew, when I brought him home, I was watching you – that day in the hospital, too, I could not help noticing – even the nurses noticed – you seemed so frightened of him – is it possible that –'

Austin recalled their close proximity, side by side, on a wooden bench against the wall in the police station; Mei Kwei's tender spooning of food into her brother's mouth; the gentle laying of his tear-stained face upon her shoulder. And the single, culminating image, still that of conjecture but eliciting pain's loudest cry, was that of Mei Kwei's quiet submission to her brother's body, and of her going to her husband's bed on their wedding night bereft of her gift.

The interrogator broke down, overcome by the weight of his own questioning while his subject continued to sit still and look down calmly.

'Swear,' he said, 'swear upon this Bible that you have never slept with your brother.' He whipped out the sacred book from under the table.

Mei Kwei had never seen a more savage expression on his face. While kindness softened her, savagery stung her into reckless defiance, so that she now looked up at him, her face white, her hands visibly trembling. 'There is no need to swear,' she told him. 'Besides I am not a Christian.'

'Then swear by your grandmother's grave, your ancestral altars, the whole damnable range of your temple gods.' He had never raised his voice at her before, much less uttered an imprecation.

The swing door of the restaurant swung open suddenly to admit Mrs T. C. Williams and Gray. As soon as she recognised Austin, Mrs Williams waved to him and said brightly, 'Good afternoon.'

But the effort to return her greeting produced no more than a small, constricted smile and a feeble lifting of a hand. In an instant, Austin was submerged once more in the wet abjectness of his misery, which prompted Mei Kwei, ever awed by the sight of strong men crying, to go in search of a cup of hot water and place it before him.

'Drink,' her eyes said, and the gentle hand that brought the cup to his lips might have added, 'I'm sorry.'

Austin ignored the cup and grabbed the hand, laying it pathetically against his cheek. 'Please don't leave me,' he begged. 'I love you so much.'

Men told her they loved her, but each time she thought she could love them back, her heart whispered its most urgent message: 'Run, before it is too late.'

Austin made a movement towards her and, with a little strangled sob, Mei Kwei took his anguished face and laid it against her breast.

CHAPTER THIRTY-SIX

'Father.' She could not remember how many times since childhood she had stood outside his door, in anger or confusion, despair or hope, listening to the small sounds from within and smelling the opium fumes through the cracks. The room was always closed to her, like his heart. One of these days, she thought, before she got married and left her home for ever, she would storm both, and scream, 'Father, hear me, talk to me.'

Yet she had sensed a relenting, since the day she had led him back into the house under an umbrella in the rain. The humiliation of the public chastisement by Old Yoong might have turned him more bitterly against her, but he had meekly submitted to the protection of the umbrella and had said not a word. Quickly, she had brought him a large towel to dry himself. Her mother would have said, 'You are a good daughter,' by way of gratitude; there was the merest hint of this when Ah Oon Koh took the towel from her and went back to his room.

'Father, can I get you your cough medicine?' She listened for his answer. The coughing had stopped. 'No need. I took it a short while ago,' he replied, and she knew the ties of blood had not been sundered.

Towards her mother, her heart had no need to beat in trepidation. Ah Oon Soh maintained a tight-lipped incuriosity about the coming marriage but softened into a state of true, smiling amity if Mei Kwei offered to massage her back or legs, which ached in rainy weather.

'Mother, talk to me,' Mei Kwei said, carefully pouring some oil from a bottle on to her palm and spreading it on her mother's leg. The night wind howled outside their room and the first drops of rain fell on the roof.

'What is there to talk about?'

What is there to do? What is there to feel? What is there to be happy about? These days, her mother's responses fell into the weary resignation of a listless code. But Ah Oon Soh smiled as her daughter rubbed and kneaded, tugged and pulled expertly, and the aching vanished. 'You were a strange child,' she answered. 'You haven't changed.'

'Mother,' Mei Kwei said earnestly, and now she was fighting tears. 'After my marriage, Big Older Brother will have a job in the Britannia eating-house.' She had her plans for the entire family laid out; those for her father, who was assured a monthly sum for his opium, were best left unmentioned.

'Let's not talk about it,' replaced her mother. 'You are a good daughter. The rest we shall leave to fate.'

After the massage her mother settled into a deep, peaceful sleep but Mei Kwei lay awake, listening to the wind and rain and letting her thoughts take her wherever they would. They veered, zigzagged, spiralled, so that images of past, present and future came together crazily. In a half-dream when the faces of Second Grandmother, Sister St Elizabeth, Polly, Old Yoong, Austin, her own, shimmered and floated around, and their voices, fragmented echoes from a distance, combined to form a faint hum, she suddenly felt a solidity of touch and an urgency of voice that did not belong.

'Little Sister, I'm cold. Take care of me.' Big Older Brother was lying beside her, curled up against her back in the dark warmth of the blanket, while on the other side of the bed, her mother slept, snoring gently.

Mei Kwei stiffened and lay very still, while he pressed closer like a small child burrowing into the arms of its mother, fearful of being pulled away. 'Nobody loves me but my little sister.'

Very slowly, he turned her round; when she was fully facing him, he let out a little sob. 'Little Sister.'

Mei Kwei's whole body, clasped in his, burned with a new horror. 'Get back to your room,' she hissed.

Her mother turned in the darkness, flung out an arm, said something and was silent once more.

'Get back,' she repeated, and began to disengage the clinging arms.

'I've come to say goodbye. Tomorrow I'll be dead, Little Sister. You'll wake up in the morning and find me gone.' A few days before, she had seen him drag a length of rope into his room. The image of Big Older Brother suspended from the ceiling, tongue hanging out, limp arms dangling by his sides brought a chilling terror. A heavy sadness descended on her; the burden of blood ties would never be lifted from her.

'Don't die. I don't wish you to die.' Her gentle tone induced a fresh spasm of sobbing, which she muted by pressing a hand across his mouth as one would with a crying child in a temple or a public place: Sssh, sssh. People will hear.

After a while, his sobs subsided and he lay quietly against her, like a fretful child lulled to sleep at last.

'Now go back,' she said, 'and go to sleep.' But the horror of the night and its wounding had only just begun, for in the darkness his mouth was groping to find hers, and his hand, with feverish energy, had worked itself up, under her pyjama top, to clasp a breast. She gasped, and felt the hardness of his desire press against her, then shift to adjust itself to her body's centre.

'Little Sister, you are the only one I care for in the whole world.'

In the darkness, her mother stirred again, moaned and slipped back into the oblivion of sleep. Mei Kwei tried to wriggle out of the tight embrace, hot tears searing her eyes.

'Little Sister, please. I will not hurt you. I *know*.' Big Older Brother knew the precise limits of his lust; she would still be passed on intact to her husband. A woman's body was for men's pillaging as long as they agreed among themselves on their territorial limits. Strangers exposed and waved their penises from a distance, brothers came close but stopped short of the rupture, husbands claimed right of full invasion and checked white bridal trousers for proof. The woman could cry out in protest, but it was no use. Her fate had been ordained from the beginning of time.

Mei Kwei shrank into herself, curled up tightly like a small jungle creature caught by its predator. 'Please go away,' she sobbed.

'Little Sister, you know that your brother will never hurt you.'

CHAPTER THIRTY-SEVEN

The first morning Mass at the Church of the Sacred Heart of Jesus was at six o'clock, to allow the devout to attend the service and have time for a quick breakfast before the start of their busy day. Sometimes confession preceded the Mass, which meant that Father François Martin had to be up before dawn for his own private prayers before going into the church and sitting in the confessional box to await the penitents.

In the dawn darkness, the priest struggled to shake sleep from his eyes. 'I am ashamed,' he wrote to his sister, 'about how frequently I doze off in the confessional. I'd like to put the blame on the strange tropical weather, especially the thunderstorms that supposedly affect people in all kinds of ways. But, Léonie, your brother has only himself to blame, for the rich food that he allows himself to be spoilt with.'

But his drowsiness could also be produced by the monotony of the confessed sins. Devout women, leading saintly lives of total service to husbands and children, unburdened themselves of sins of astonishing veniality. 'Bless me, Father, for I have sinned. I had an unkind thought about my neighbour. I felt angry with my husband. I lost my temper with my son. I felt tired and rested instead of finishing the housework. I gambled in a lottery, on a number given by my sister-in-law, who got it from a ghost. I gossiped with a neighbour. I ate some roasted pork at a relative's house on Friday.'

He jerked up to the sound of someone entering the confessional, sheepishly rubbed his eyes, cleared his throat and adjusted his vestments, in readiness for the start of another day of God's work. He heard the sounds of fumbling and uncertainty and gave a slight cough to signal his presence and the start of the business. In the dimness of the heavily curtained enclosure, through the fine wire netting of the grille, he saw a bent head, pressed upon clasped hands, and heard anguished sobbing. His first thought was of the wondrous power of a sacrament that could melt even the most hardened sinners in a wash of contrition; his second, as he peered through the netting and saw a young girl, was of alarm. The sinned against, not the sinner, had come to confess.

The kneeling girl, distraught, raised her face from her clasped hands and tried to say something. In the dimness, he saw the mole at the corner of her right eye and almost started up in the shock of recognition. The girl was crying and talking at the same time, incoherent in her distress.

'My child, talk to me. I am listening. Talk to me, my child.' His voice, when modulated for counsel or comfort, had a soothing quality and immediately toned down the hysteria. The girl subsided into quiet weeping and kept her eyes down.

'My child.' He was speaking to her as spiritual father, but mixed into the voice of the anointed priest were dangerous human elements. Only a short while ago, as he lit a lamp in the cold dawn darkness of the church and prepared to go into the confessional, he had thought of the girl – or, rather, into the blankness of mind that sometimes accompanied the first routine act of the day had floated a fragment of a startled face bobbing up from a sea of laughing children's faces in a playground. 'Won't you talk to me?'

The girl had stopped crying now and was very still as she knelt before him, their faces separated by the grille. The silence and the stillness were deceptive, hiding a struggle that was evident in her three fingers, stark white, which pressed upon the window-ledge through a small tear in a corner of the netting. The priest, remembering that he had given instructions to a carpenter to repair the tear, was suddenly glad of it. He pushed his hand through the opening and laid it reassuringly upon the girl's.

'Here, take this.' He pulled out a white handkerchief and gave it to her. She clutched it in her fingers, then withdrew and stood up.

'Wait,' said the priest, and he rushed out of the confessional. In his hurry, he did not bother to retrieve his chasuble that had caught on a nail or a hook and slid off his shoulders on to the floor. He saw, to his relief, that the girl had not run away but was standing uncertainly nearby, still holding his handkerchief.

For the rest of the day, Father François Martin was perturbed by that strange incident, which distilled into a compelling image that would haunt him in both his dreams and waking hours, and make him go down on his knees to beseech his God for help. The image even intruded upon his consciousness in the saying of Mass. Again and again, he re-enacted it in his mind even as he struggled against it: the spontaneous rushing towards each other outside the confessional, the pure embrace, less of caring shepherd-priest and distressed lost sheep than of protective man and crying woman. A man and a woman who had met as strangers on four separate occasions in the most unlikely of circumstances, who had never spoken a word to each other, met again for a fifth time in a church, in the still darkness of a dawning world and locked, again wordlessly, into an embrace. The image gathered around it an aura of shimmering possibility, which both horrified and excited him.

CHAPTER THIRTY-EIGHT

On his round of visits to the priests in his diocese, the Bishop tried to be as gentle as possible, despite the irritability caused by a persistent toothache for which his helpful housekeeper had provided a mulch of some jungle leaves. He had received mixed reports of the new French priest in Luping, which worried him somewhat. An innate graciousness and kindness had clothed the priest's blunders – yes, they were nothing but blunders – but in the end, the Bishop, who did not have much time to spare and whose toothache was getting worse, came straight to the point. 'Father, all these incidents must stop. I've had adverse reports.'

Father François Martin coloured and said, with a small edge to his voice, 'Incidents, my lord?' But he knew already. The first he had already labelled 'The Coffin Incident' and had written to Léonie about it with much gusto before he sensed the Bishop's displeasure. He had been riding his bicycle on his way to visit a family when Tee Tee appeared – the boy had the ability to materialise from nowhere – and indicated, with a flurry of agitated sounds and gestures, that Father Martin was needed more urgently somewhere else. Tee Tee had pointed excitedly to a wooden hut, visible in the distance among other dilapidated huts, in the midst of what appeared to be a great junk yard.

Immediately he had changed course and had ridden quickly towards the hut, imagining a scene of great disorder and hoping to be in time to save a frightened wife from her drunken husband, or to where a dying sinner on his death-bed had at last turned contrite and asked for a priest. He parked his bicycle beside a pile of rotting timber, stepped over mounds of rubbish and went inside the hut. Four men were gathered round a square table, playing mah-jong. Oblivious to everything around, they concentrated on the game, smoking and drinking coffee from large porcelain mugs to aid their concentration. Father Martin looked around, looked into the dark recesses of the hut, and saw the reason for the child's agitation. A dead body lay unattended on a rough wooden bench pushed against a wall. Moving closer, Father Martin saw that it was an old man, his bare feet caked with mud. The presence of mud on his clothes and some dried leaves caught in his hair, as well as a small dark gash across his cheek, pointed to an accident: he must have fallen into a ditch, died there and been pulled out later.

Father Martin was later to regret the impetuosity of his action, but now, as he stood looking upon the bizarre scene, he was struck by its gross indecency. An old man lay dead and all that his friends – or family – were concerned about was the continuing indulgence of their vice.

He approached the gamblers and asked about the dead man. They ignored him and went on with their game. He raised his voice and they continued to ignore him. He stretched out a hand to touch one of the gamblers on the shoulder, and was astonished when the man swung round suddenly with a savage snarl. This was better than being ignored, and the priest pointed to the dead body and fired off, in rapid succession, a series of sharp questions and demands.

'None of your business, you foreign devil! Get out this minute!' the man shouted. And then all was pandemonium as the priest, in a surge of wrath, overturned the table and sent all the tiles clattering to the ground.

The men shouted and sprang up, their chairs falling backwards and crashing to the floor, and would have laid their hands on him if he had not done something, which, in the quiet of later reflection, he decided had been divinely inspired. He had calmly walked over to the corpse, knelt down beside it and prayed. His alliance with the dead had saved him: his action stayed the menacing advance of the four men, one of whom, he noticed through the corner of his eye, had pulled out a knife.

But it seemed the incident had not gone down well with the local community. 'I understand your shock,' the Bishop said. 'But we must be extremely careful in relation to the local people's sensitivities. We can't be seen as meddling with their culture. The incident could have ended very nastily.'

He had also written to Léonie about the second incident. He had been in the market-place one morning – he liked to go there to mingle with the people and talk to them – when he accepted the invitation of the friendly roast pork noodles lady to sit down and have a bowl of noodles. She always made a great fuss when he insisted on paying, and they invariably engaged in an elaborate ritual of pushing the money to and from each other across the surface of the rough wooden table, sometimes upsetting a bottle of sauce or a canister of chopsticks. He always won and she took her revenge by giving him six pieces of delicious roast pork instead of the usual four. He was shaking his head over the largesse when he looked up to see five female faces turned towards him from the next table, smiling and nodding in cheerful greeting. The *ronggeng* girls often came to the open-air eating stalls in the market-place for a meal; away from the bright lights and loud music of the *ronggeng* stage, out of their hideous makeup and gaudy clothes, they looked no different from the town's girls. But their unabashed smiling and waving at the priest immediately set them as a group apart, and invited stares and grins as well as murmurs of disapproval. One had a camera and immediately got up to take a picture of the priest. He posed good-naturedly and the next moment was surrounded by the rest of the girls who giggled as they adjusted clothes, hair and ear-rings and shouted noisy instructions to their picture-taking friend. Then it was the friend's turn to be included; she passed the camera to a passer-by, gave instructions, and bounced over to face the camera with a brazen arm around his shoulder while the others cheered.

Various versions of the scandalous incident of the *ronggeng* girls must have found their way to the Bishop's ears.

'We must be ever so careful,' said the Bishop, 'ever so careful in a society that can be extremely conservative in its views about what constitutes proper behaviour. Especially for a priest.'

The Bishop had also heard about the strange incident of Father Martin and the dead woman terrorist in the market-place but decided not to bring it up. The French priest was evidently a bit of a maverick, an eccentric, as most idealists tended to become; give him a year and he would learn to tone down some of this idealism in proper accommodation to the society to which he had come to do God's work. The Bishop, looking at the priest's open countenance and the bright honesty of his clear blue eyes, decided he liked him, after all.

'I hope you will be very happy in Luping, Father,' he said kindly. 'Is there anything – a problem – you would like to talk about?'

The image of the crying embrace floated into Father Martin's mind, and again a small tremor ran through his body. 'Thank you, my lord, there is nothing,' he replied.

CHAPTER THIRTY-NINE

The soft, urgent knocking on his door must have gone on for some time. As Father Martin got up from his bed and turned on the light, he pushed out of his mind an expectation – born of wild, senseless hope – that, since his strange encounter in the confessional, had followed every knock upon his door, every scratching at his window.

'Who is it?' he asked, opening a window and peering into the darkness. He saw the shape of a man slumped on his doorstep, obviously injured.

The mud-caked shirt, the gun by his side, the extreme pallor of years spent in the dense jungle out of reach of the sun – all marked the man as no ordinary night intruder. T. C. Williams's stern warning rang in Father Martin's ears. But the terrorist was clearly in need of help; he lay groaning, his last ounce of energy spent in crawling to the doorstep of the priest's room in the Church of the Sacred Heart of Jesus.

Father Martin helped him up and into the house and put him on his bed, where the man lay still for a while, groaning softly, one arm flung over his eyes. He could not have been more than twenty. Contrary to first impressions, his injuries were minor, and were confined to a gash on his forehead and a multitude of scratches on his arms.

After he had managed to sit up and drink a bowl of hot soup that the priest had brought, the terrorist took from his pocket a tattered photograph, which showed a smiling girl holding a plump baby. 'My wife and son,' he whimpered. 'I think of them all the time. I will carry their picture to my grave.'

The priest thought, After the exhibition in the market-place your grave could be that dumping hole. Then another thought occurred to him, and his heart quickened to the possible import of the night's happening. He had heard of the various circumstances in which terrorists surrendered themselves and returned to civil life, sometimes under the greatest risk of being betrayed and executed by comrades.

But he was wrong. The young terrorist had not the slightest intention of surrendering. He broke into angry invective against the foreign, white-skinned devils overrunning the country – 'I will not include you priests among them, for you come to do good' – and swore he would continue the struggle to drive them out. 'Father,' he said with a savage smile which made the priest wince, 'I took part in an ambush which killed two of the devils.'

'You're a murderer, then,' said Father Martin. 'Get out at once.'

The young terrorist ignored him. 'I need some money, medicine, food.' He looked around the priest's meagre store and said, 'Give me whatever you have.'

'Take whatever you need and get out,' said the priest.

'I like you, Father,' said the terrorist. He continued, with a smile, 'I went to a Christian school once – just for a few years,' and he began to recite the Lord's Prayer. Any hint of mockery would have angered the priest, but the tone was respectful – indeed, almost wistful – and spoke of nostalgia for lost innocence. 'My wife went to a Christian school, too,' he added, 'and wore one of those around her neck,' pointing to some small crucifixes on a table, with holy medals and pictures, that the priest had brought from home for dispensing to the faithful.

'Would you like one?' said Father Martin.

Only after the terrorist had left did the priest realise that he, Father François Martin, had just committed a crime for which the Emergency laws prescribed no less than long incarceration in Luping's top-security prison.

T. C. Williams would have snarled, 'You thought you were above the law, didn't you, Father?' and the Bishop would have lamented, 'I warned you, Father, don't tell me I didn't warn you.'

CHAPTER FORTY

The curfew had eased somewhat and, in the hour before its imposition, people hurried to the scene of a great commotion.

In a part of the town that, by day, saw a small gathering of hawkers and pedlars, Tua Poon had tied his wife, half naked and shivering in the night air, to an old tree-stump and was yelling to all to come and see. With his dishevelled hair, ferociously staring eyes and wildly waving arms, he was almost unrecognisable as the mild-mannered cold-drinks seller near the Luping Odeon. Her hands tightly bound with ropes behind her back, his wife made no attempt to break free but stood silently in the desolation of her terror. Her breasts, startlingly round and white in the shadows cast by the street-lamps, were exposed to view, unhidden by the tangles of hair hanging over her drooping face or by – the grotesque sight gave those who were gathering to watch the first inkling of the cause of this outrage – a pair of men's boots, black, mud-caked, tied round her neck by their laces. The woman wore yet more evidence of her guilty liaison: a man's blue-striped, long-sleeved shirt was draped around her waist, the sleeves tied together, the shirt front barely covering her shame.

The crowd massed quickly. Eyes moved with mounting curiosity from the woman to her husband, then back again to the woman: two compelling figures in a sordid drama dragged from the bedroom into a public place. They strained to hear the demented man's words, to piece together his story, and to pass it on quickly to those who did not happen to catch it. They shifted, jostled, stood on tiptoe, peered over shoulders, to see her nakedness. In widening ripples of excitement in the hot night air, the man's tale of betrayal and torment floated out to chasten, caution, warn.

He had caught his wife in the act of adultery. The lover had made a quick exit through the window, leaving behind his shirt and shoes. Tua Poon had caught only a fleeting glimpse of a disappearing back.

'I know who he is!' shrieked Tua Poon, and waved about, for all to see, a fistful of small objects he had found in the man's shirt pocket. 'I will have the police throw him into prison for fucking other men's wives!' He looked around in defiant challenge.

'Next time,' he yelled, the veins on his throat and forehead pulsating fearfully, 'I will strew broken glass on the floor to catch the bastard, hang knives at the window!' But his anger was concentrated on the adulterous wife. He threatened to throw her into the sea, squeezed into one of those tight, round baskets used for transporting pigs in carts over long distances. The ancestors would have nodded their approval.

By now the crowd had thickened and still more people kept coming. Mei Kwei was standing at a spot where she could see the girl clearly. She was aware of a gathering whirlpool of feelings, making her almost giddy, that had nothing to do with the wild hoots coming from some men in the crowd, the titters and hushed whispers of the women, the undisguised fascination of all at the sight of those perfectly shaped, white, unblemished breasts.

Mei Kwei looked intently at the woman who moved her head to ease the strain. The thick curtain of hair parted for an instant to allow her to peep out at the crowd massed around her. Her eyes did a quick sweep of the rows of tight faces, then suddenly stopped to meet Mei Kwei's. Mei Kwei saw a bright wetness that was quickly hidden once more behind the masses of tumbled hair but not before it said to her, ever so distinctly: 'He got away. I am not allowed to do so.' A similar brightness of gathering tears in Mei Kwei's eyes replied: 'I know.'

A man pushed himself through the crowd and began taking pictures of the naked woman. He was the reporter–photographer from the Chinese daily paper who specialised in naked women. Now, to his photographs of the dead woman terrorist in the market-place and of Pearly Chong, the strip-tease dancer, would be added this one of a woman taken in adultery and publicly shamed by her husband. *Click. Click.* He moved around expertly, coolly considering angles.

Tua Poon at first stared at him open-mouthed, then shouted, waving both arms, 'Take all you want! Put them in your newspaper tomorrow! I want my beautiful wife to be on the front page!'

His reference to her beauty triggered another round of explosive anger during which he slapped her across the face with such force that her long thick hair flew with his hand and the ugly boots round her neck bobbed up and down on her breasts.

Then Mei Kwei was aware of somebody pushing through the crowd with purposeful energy, of people deferentially moving aside to allow him to carve a path straight to the girl tied to the tree-stump.

Father Martin took off his robe and threw it around the girl's shoulders to cover her breasts, so that he stood almost naked, his broad chest bare and heaving above a pair of cotton trousers. He flung a look of withering rage upon the crowd before turning back to the girl to untie the ropes at her wrists. Tua Poon's fury had worked them into a number of vicious knots that bit into her flesh. Father Martin brought out a small penknife from his trouser pocket and slashed at the ropes. When the last one fell, the girl collapsed heavily in a faint into his arms. The laces round her neck unfastened at the same time and the heavy boots dropped to the ground with a loud clunk.

The spectacle was mesmerising. With murmurs of heightening excitement, the crowd gasped as the tall priest, his eyes flashing fire, his beard bristling with a savage energy, held the limp girl in his arms and shouted out his contempt at their cowardice.

'Not one, but not one of you thought to come to the rescue of this poor girl! How long has she been subjected to this public humiliation? An hour? Two? She could have died, for all you cared. What sort of human beings are you?' He flung their hypocrisy into their faces. 'Who has not committed worse sins in the boarding-houses and dens of pleasure? How many wives in Luping have not wept and grieved privately over their husbands' infidelities?'

Father Martin swung upon Tua Poon who was staring at him, open-mouthed. 'And you. Can you claim you were never unfaithful to your wife?' he asked. It seemed that the glittering eyes of the priest fastened upon every sinner and burrowed into the most secret chambers of their hearts.

As she gazed at the priest and felt the power of his words wash slowly over her, then gather to weave a hypnotic net around her, Mei Kwei was again aware of the rising whirlpool of her feelings. Shock pulled strongest: here was the God-King himself, descended from heaven, to rescue the Moon Maiden from the depths of her humiliation and despair. Amid a roll of drums, he would vanquish her enemy and invest her with power to drive away all the fire demons of the underworld. Then the vision of splendour faded and she saw a man, an ordinary man, who used an ordinary man's power to lift not crush a woman. Her heart went out to him in a swelling of gratitude and love.

She gazed, pale with the shock of recognition, at naked priest and naked girl – for the robe had fallen off her shoulders – his strong arms around her, her breasts crushed against him. She thought that she saw him, for a very brief moment, bend to touch his lips to the girl's bowed head pressed on his shoulder. The image, like a hot iron, seared itself into her memory; years later, she could remember every detail of the blaze of his eyes, the ripple of muscles, the strong protective arm around the girl's bare shoulders, the contact of nipples.

She felt a dryness of throat and constriction of muscles that she recognised with mounting trepidation as desire, an overpowering desire for the man himself. She knew from that moment that her heart, already restive, would grow more restive in the coming months and every future encounter with the priest would bear the imprint of this one shaking moment.

'Before you condemn this girl, look into your own hearts,' the

225

priest declared. 'You who infest the vice dens, you who gamble away the money that should be spent on your children's food and schoolbooks.' His voice, Uncle Jean Claude's, Father Henriot's – all came together in ultimate ferocious condemnation of all that was ignoble in the human soul.

Gradually, one by one, the spectators slunk away.

The priest turned his head for a brief instant and caught Mei Kwei's eyes. They looked at each other, then stared with an intensity that swallowed up the space between them and pulled them towards each other – as close as on that day in the children's playground, as on that day at the confessional when they were separated only by the wire netting, their breath almost on each other's faces.

In the intense embrace of their eyes, all else fell away and disappeared – the remaining onlookers, the reporter–photographer, the naked girl herself. The thrilling disquietude of the earlier encounters, the secret gusts and squalls that had swirled around their hearts, was now settling into a deeper disquietude of a simmering storm. He feared its coming; she wanted it. His eyes, burning with the night's turmoil, said, 'I know now,' and were afraid. And hers, always bright with the onset of tears, sparkled with electrifying new purpose and replied, 'I am not afraid.'

PART FOUR

第四章

CHAPTER FORTY-ONE

'Thank you,' Father François Martin said, as he took the tiffin-carrier of food from Mei Kwei. His whole being quivered at the thrill of seeing her again. A knock, a tap, a footfall, a moving shadow glanced from his seat in the confessional, a fragment of a voice in the distance, the flash of a girl on a speeding bicycle, had stirred foolish expectations that left him shamefaced.

'You fool! Just what are you thinking about?' The priest in Father Martin reproached the man: he had split into two, the easier to cope with the folly. 'You idiot! Say a rosary as penance.' The man confessed to the priest in the secret tribunal of his heart, and was rebuked roundly.

'Please come in.'

It was the man's invitation. The priest would have been more circumspect, would have thanked the female gift-bearer briefly but politely and closed the door once again. In a foreign country, the priest should have developed a whole code of conduct, translated into clear and specific guidelines, for dealing with friendly local women. One salacious glance could mean ostracism: one act of indiscretion the deadly *parang*. But the man, delighted by the sight of the pretty face and even more by its look of intense eagerness, distanced himself. 'Please come in,' he repeated.

Father Martin watched as Mei Kwei walked into his house as if this were part of an unfolding plan. This girl, whom he had met in the most unexpected circumstances on five separate occasions, had come to see him, to talk to him in the quiet and calm not allowed by earlier circumstances. There was no mistake about it: the food was the excuse. There she was, standing near him and communicating a sense of urgent expectancy. Or perhaps – and he did not particularly like the sudden intrusion of the prosaic banality into the brightness of his mounting joy – she was simply waiting for him to take out the food and return the tiffin-carrier. Hope fought banality and vanquished it. Instead of saying, 'Would you sit down while I find something to put all this good food in?' he said, 'Please join me.'

This second invitation was far more daring. More clearly than the brightness in his eyes and the deep flush on his neck and face, it implied, 'I can't bear you to go away as soon as you have come. I want you to stay as long as possible.'

On each occasion that they had met, Mei Kwei had slipped away as suddenly as she had appeared, elusive as a darting fish in a pond, as a fairy maiden in one of their enchanting Chinese legends who slides down a moonbeam and is seen no more. Now his invitation would pin down her presence to the duration of a meal.

Father Martin allowed himself to be carried along on a wave of exuberance which made him do things that even now, in the midst of all the headiness, he knew he would have to confront some time in the quiet of future reflection. The future was the future, he thought, with a dash of insouciance, as he watched the girl spoon out a large dollop of something, probably beancurd, from one of the tiffin-carrier containers into his bowl. He would not allow the future to intrude upon either the present or the past, for as soon as he saw Uncle Jean Claude's face loom in his mind and heard Father Henriot's voice, he dismissed them. How happy I am, he thought, as he watched the girl take out a small dish of chilli-and-prawn paste. 'In this country, they eat everything with chilli-and-prawn paste,' he would remember to tell Léonie in his next letter. 'I have come to like the strange stuff, but the first time, my tongue burned and I saw smoke coming out of my ears!'

He felt quiveringly alive as he concentrated on every moment of a joyous present – constrained by the duration of a Chinese meal, which was sometimes eaten so quickly that the moving chopsticks became a blur. And there was a further constraint: he had an appointment with a Catholic Indian family living in a rubber plantation some distance away, and would have to allow at least half an hour's bicycling time.

The concessions thus made to the demands of duty, Father Martin settled down to the full enjoyment of a simple afternoon meal transformed suddenly into a glittering banquet. The pleasure of braised beancurd and snowpeas, duck with pickled cabbage, pig's shank in vinegar combined with the greater pleasure of a staggering realisation: that each of these items had come into contact with her hands at various stages of the preparation and cooking, that each had been selected in advance, with a thoughtful view to his preferences.

'That is exactly my favourite dish. How did you know?'

But Father Martin's greatest pleasure was independent of the food. He thought he had never seen a more beautiful girl in his life. In the church, in the market-place, the confessional, the children's playground he had had little time or opportunity to look closely at her. Now he was astonished at how much he was able to absorb of Mei Kwei's beauty. In the future, he would remember the stray strands of hair that had become disengaged from the smooth, neat bun at the back of her head, and which floated, like tiny tendrils on a vine, on her forehead and neck; the astonishingly translucent skin; the large expressive eyes with their inner dark fires and hint of tears that always gave the lie to any bright smile, any bright burst of laughter. She spoke little, but every feature, every small movement of head, neck, hands, body seemed to gather to a peak of intensity that spoke everything.

He suddenly thought – stray thoughts darted in and out of his mind with amazing speed and energy – of a Christmas tableau he had once seen as a boy in a church pageant at which he had stared in wonder at the face of the young girl who was playing the part of the Virgin Mary. It was a beauty that defied conventional description, that was not reducible to separate items of lip or cheek or eyes. It was a beauty of rare spirit that shone from within and startled the observer. This Chinese girl had that beauty. If ever he needed to stage a similar tableau in Luping for his parishioners, she would be first choice for the Virgin.

In surreptitious glances, Father Martin watched Mei Kwei eat, watched the movements of her mouth, the slow sensuousness of biting, chewing, swallowing, and registered the small, sluicing sounds of her enjoyment. A new image floated into his mind of a picture of the Magdalene, which he had once seen in a museum, breaking an alabaster bottle of finest perfume for the sweetening of her contrite tears on the feet of her Beloved. He imagined Mei Kwei's smooth, tightly combed hair, loosened of its restraining combs and pins, shaken into similar abundance and passion in one dazzling moment; saw a flash of her beautiful white throat

231

in the small spasms of swallowing – and was overcome with embarrassment.

Deciding to pull his dangerously soaring imagination down to a sobering level, he thought he would ask the girl, in a frank and forthright manner, why she was not taking instruction for baptism into the Church since she was soon to be married to a Catholic? He decided to begin with innocuous questions about herself and her family, and immediately saw his mistake. Mei Kwei shrank into herself, as if his questions were invading barbs. A tiny frown appeared between her eyebrows. He saw something of the distress he had witnessed that day in the confessional and, alarmed at the enormity of his mistake and the prospect of her leaving, tried to repair it by embarking upon a lengthy story of his cleaning woman. He had often reproached himself for making a good-hearted, well-meaning but thoroughly superstitious woman the object of fun in his letters home, but now the poor woman was blown into a caricature to make a pretty girl smile.

The frown disappeared, Mei Kwei appeared to relax once more, and he heaved an inner sigh of relief. He resolved never to refer to her family again, or to her approaching marriage. But the aura of intriguing possibilities surrounding the girl increased, deepening both his fear and his joy. Fear's alarm bells rang shrilly: This girl who comes to you with her unabashed shining eyes is dangerous. She is doubly so because of her impending marriage.

'That was the best lunch I've ever had,' Father Martin said. 'You Chinese are such marvellous cooks.'

Mei Kwei, speaking with spirited defiance for the first time that afternoon, said, 'Let me help you with the washing up.'

Father Martin perceived that, although the meal had come to an end, their pleasure could be extended, deliciously, by the clearing of bowls and plates from the table, the scraping of food remnants into bins, the washing at the sink, which would allow for a side-by-side proximity not possible at the table.

'Yes, but –' He put forward objections, which he knew would be borne down: she ought not to be put to work; the cleaning lady could easily do the job the next morning; he ought not to keep her longer. His thrilling suspicion was confirmed: Mei Kwei meant to stay. She demolished each objection and got ready for the task of washing dirty dishes at a sink, a small domestic chore that now shimmered with promise.

A soapy bowl slipped from his hand and fell to the floor. Father

Martin was all apology. She picked up the broken halves, but did not throw them into the bin. Why did the thought that she would take them home with her and treasure them in sweet, secret remembrance bear down upon him suddenly as a certainty? He blushed at his presumptuousness, as later he blushed, shuddered, thrilled, winced to a hundred unwonted thoughts and feelings of that wondrous day. And why, when she finally got ready to go, the containers properly washed and reassembled in the tiffin-carrier, did he suddenly say, 'Wait, I should have thought of it earlier. Forgive me for being rude.'

He looked around for something to give as a return gift. He admired the Chinese custom of meeting gift with gift, even if it were only a lump of lucky rock sugar or two eggs placed in the returned container. His eyes fell on the crucifixes. He picked one up and gave it to the girl. A fleeting picture of pagan joss-sticks in a paper bag came into his mind, as well as their distinctive smell. For a moment he thought the girl, who had already made the decision to retain the religion of her ancestors in opposition to her husband's, would reject his gift. But she took it smilingly, even eagerly.

Will I see you again? It was a question that he wanted to ask but did not dare.

As soon as she was gone, the disquiet set in as he had known it would. The man stood shamefaced before the priest and worked himself into a state of bitterest self-reproach: for the last two hours, the poor Indian family in the rubber plantation had been waiting for him.

'Oh, no! Oh, no!' cried Father Martin, genuinely stricken, as he prepared to get on to his bicycle. 'It must never happen again.'

CHAPTER FORTY-TWO

'I'll fetch you in an hour,' Austin Tong said, the hour being the duration of Mrs Solomon's English language lesson. Three times a week he drove Mei Kwei to the private tutor's home, a neat little wooden house on the edge of town. His generosity went beyond need to aspiration: having taken care of everyone in her family, he listened for the tiniest whispers of her secret dreams and jumped to fulfil them. 'Tell me,' he had urged. 'Tell me your dearest wishes and I will grant them.' Husband-to-be, he meant to be the fairy king, dispenser of golden dreams. 'You don't talk to me enough. You are always deep in your own thoughts.'

She had come out of her thoughts to tell him about the unbearable pain of having her education at St Margaret's convent school abruptly terminated; of never having had the full benefit of Sister St Elizabeth's teaching of reading and writing. Then she told him of the bitter bonfire of her dreams that miserable evening when she had become a woman.

'Recite to me the poems you remember,' he urged, just to hear her voice. He loved her with an aching love already; he would love her even more after their marriage. Exactly two days later, he told her to get ready, he was taking her to have lessons with the best English language tutor in Luping: a Eurasian lady and former teacher who spoke and wrote impeccable English. They would be lessons especially tailored to her needs. Her education would be saved, after all.

Mrs Solomon took her through the entire routine of jaw-breaking and mind-numbing oral practice. Peering above severe glasses perched on her nose, the good lady supervised her pronunciation of English vowels, consonants and diphthongs, and her proper under-standing of English grammar, writing model sentences on a small green blackboard hung on the wall for Mei Kwei to read and copy. She had to learn to define a noun, a verb, a phrase, a compound sentence.

'Mrs Solomon, please tell me stories.' Mei Kwei broke through the sterility of grammar to its rich narrative sources, which she had greedily and surreptitiously absorbed from her secret place at the window outside Sister St Elizabeth's classroom. 'Love stories of men and women.'

The lady was nonplussed and, in the end, compromised by agreeing to read an abridged version of *Romeo and Juliet* if Mei Kwei would do a dictation exercise based on an excerpt later.

Mei Kwei was glad when the lesson was finished, and even more glad when Austin's time with her was over and he was ready to leave. His kiss said, 'Only a few weeks more.' He spoke movingly of the supreme joy of the wedding-night gift of herself to him. But in her mind, the picture had no romantic radiance. Indeed, it collapsed into a mere wash of sexual plunder and gluttony, which both depressed and revolted her.

She decided that if she could not stave off that dark day, she could gird herself for it. If her life moved inexorably through its prescribed stages of daughterhood, dreary marriage and motherhood, she could try to save some of her dreams and smuggle them in somehow. She could then spin the dreams into stories for her own private enjoyment. Life is made bearable by the stories we save and tell.

Mei Kwei remembered that when she was a little girl, a friend of Second Grandmother, whom she called Por Por – an old woman, almost blind and bent double – saved every bit of cloth and begged tailors to save their remnants for her, amassing over the years, a veritable mountain. Sorting out the pieces, cutting them into precise shapes to sew together, she turned out the most beautiful patchwork blankets. No cloth remnant was too small for her. Tiny pieces, the size of a baby's fist, could be cut into perfect triangles, squares or hexagons for piecing together, stitch by stitch, to form the loveliest blanket for a child's cot or the loveliest cover for an ancestral altar.

Por Por gave her a blanket that thrilled her with its perfection of design and riot of colours: there was not a single colour that was not represented. But the greatest thrill of Por Por's patchwork blanket was its richness as a source of stories. The old woman pointed to a tiny triangle of cotton cloth with small blue flowers against a yellow background somewhere in the middle of the blanket and said, in her quavering voice, 'Now there's a story there. Let me tell you the story.' And she told the true story of a girl named Swee Choo, who went mad when her fiancé's family decided to break off her engagement on the advice of an astrologer. The seamstress, who had been helping her to prepare her trousseau had sewn four *samfoos* for her, only to find later that the demented girl had set fire to them. The cotton piece with the blue flowers came from a remnant of one of the *samfoos* and thereafter stood out from the other pieces in the blanket in the vividness of its tragic connection.

Mei Kwei determined to make her own patchwork blanket of secret stories. Indeed, her saving of precious secrets had already begun. Her five encounters with Father Martin yielded rich, tender memories for that drear time in her future when she would be cut off from the rest of the world in the dark tomb of a passionless marriage. She would call forth these memories again and again and lay them, a fabric threaded with her dreams, against her cheek, and press them to her heart.

Mei Kwei went about her work in a systematic manner. Into her treasure chest would first be laid, like a bride's rich dower of silk and lace and doll's shoes, the memories of the first four encounters, each more dear than the last; next were the memories of their meal together; the last and most precious of all was still to be striven for.

The treasure chest in her heart had a tangible parallel – a solid wooden box that she intended to keep in an obscure part of her new home. Eventually it would be dragged out into the light.

'What's this? Why haven't I seen this before?' her husband would demand. 'What have you got in here?' And she would be forced to reveal its contents. He would remember the Moon Maiden's diadem and the God-King's crown as some gift from her crazy temple friend, but he would be puzzled by the other items: 'What is a broken rice bowl doing in there? Whose white handkerchief is this?'

But there would be no need, even then, to tell him her stories. She would turn a cool, impassive face to his enquiries and watch the uncoiling of that monster of jealousy, more terrifying to behold in a man than a woman. She would save her mementoes at great personal risk; years later, if the dreams should fade into faint wisps and disappear altogether, she could still lay her face against the white handkerchief and recall the warm touch of his hand upon hers in the dimness of the confessional that anguished morning, and move her fingers slowly over the jagged edges of the broken rice bowl to summon up that moment of wordless connection by a square cement sink full of dirty dishwater one magical afternoon.

CHAPTER FORTY-THREE

'I have made arrangements.'

With his money, his energy, his purposefulness, his immense love for her, Austin was always making arrangements to clear this or that obstacle from Mei Kwei's path, to make possible this or that secret wish. He told her that she would no longer have to bother going to the poor parish priest to give him a hot, home-cooked meal, for he had made arrangements for food to be sent regularly from the Britannia eating-house.

'I have given instructions for your brother to take the food,' said Austin, adding, in a casual tone, 'He doesn't have nearly enough work in the restaurant.'

Mei Kwei knew of the complaints by the other employees about her brother's laziness and insolence. He was always running off to attend temple seances and on one occasion had brought Mad Temple Auntie and a temple medium, after the restaurant had closed, to perform some secret ritual in a back room; an employee had found incriminatory joss-sticks, candles and chopper in the morning. The sacrilege – the restaurant had been blessed by a Catholic priest in a ceremony some months previously – had seriously depleted Austin's reserves of patience. But once again he thought of Mei Kwei and contented himself with issuing a grim warning to her brother: 'Any more misdemeanours and . . .'

There were times when Mei Kwei hated Austin, when his largesse was no compensation for the turbulence of feelings he aroused in her. She hated him now, for she thought she would never see Father Martin again. She was sure that one or two more meals together would have provided her with evidence of his love, which she needed – oh, so badly! – to take away with her.

'You are very quiet. What are you thinking about?' Austin asked.

She resented his constant intrusion into her privacy. She hated even more his greedy anticipation of their wedding night as if her body were a fruit on a tree, ripe for plucking, or a fowl in a farmyard, ready for slaughter.

'Three more weeks,' said Austin, and once again anticipation's warming glow moved him to take her into his arms and press his lips tenderly upon her face. He picked up a straying wisp of hair on her forehead to smooth it back into place, and wiped an imaginary speck of dirt from her cheek.

'I have made a decision.' The gravity of Mei Kwei's tone made him look sharply at her.

She told him that she had decided to be baptised after all. She would be a Catholic, like him.

Austin looked keenly at her, then took her into his arms once again. His reaction was one of overwhelming gratitude to his God. For some time now, he had ceased to ask for signs. This sign, unasked – undreamt of – was one more endorsement of his coming marriage.

Taking her hand, he pressed it to his lips. Now she would truly be one with his world.

'I am ready to begin the instruction for baptism straight away,' she said, and hoped he did not hear the tremor in her voice. Catechism lessons, she thought, would do as well as food for the opportunity and comfort of each other's company. Father Martin would instruct her in the articles and the practice of the faith, the immediate duties of the holy state of matrimony, the eternal verities of heaven and hell. His presence, his attentiveness, the sheer fact of being in the same place, even if in the presence of other catechumens, would be sufficient for her.

Second Grandmother's voice, 'Beloved granddaughter, you cannot do this to me,' might be muted for a while. Mei Kwei might even calm it into acquiescence. For Second Grandmother, she of the passionate nature and wild dreams, would surely understand that love was the greater imperative.

Suppose, suppose. Nowadays, Mei Kwei's thoughts and feelings swung wildly with hope. Suppose the catechism instructions, to be effective, had to be conducted over a period of time and hence entailed a postponement of the marriage?

'Get ready now,' Austin said the next day. 'I'm taking you for your first catechism lesson. I've made all the arrangements.'

In the car, Mei Kwei wondered if Father Martin was thinking the same thoughts and sharing the same feelings: how wonderful to have the chance to be together again. In the same way that the table at which they had sat, the cement sink by which they had stood, were becoming dear objects of saved memory, the lone rough bench in the church on which she would sit with other catechumens, the little instructional book she would hold in her hand would, in time, be invested with a consecrating grace.

Who made you? God made me. Why did God make you? To love and serve Him with my whole heart, soul and body in this world and to be happy with Him for ever in the next.

She had recast the hallowed text to apply to themselves. Her heart and soul were already his; her body, promised to another, yearned for him too.

With growing unease, Mei Kwei noticed that the car was going in an unfamiliar direction. After what seemed to be an extremely long time, it stopped in front of an unfamiliar church, slightly bigger than the Church of the Sacred Heart of Jesus.

'The Church of Our Lady of Lourdes,' said Austin. He had taken the trouble to make arrangements for Mei Kwei's instruction with the parish priest of the neighbouring town of Udong.

CHAPTER FORTY-FOUR

Father Martin wiped the perspiration from his brow and neck with an already soaked handkerchief. In this country, it was said that the heat could kill, searing your eyeballs, seeping into the capillaries in your body, bringing the blood to a boil. It was supposed to be cooler in the rubber plantations, where the tops of the tall trees absorbed the sunlight and provided a cool canopy, but, as he rode his bicycle along a narrow path between the great silent trees, their trunks bearing white diagonal gashes for the rubber milk to ooze and trickle into attached cups, he felt a great oppressiveness of soul and body.

This was his second visit to the Indian family. The first had been disastrous: they had waited a full two hours and had not shown the least offence when he arrived, quickly bringing out a tin mug of warm tea and milk. He had been supremely humbled and had decided that he would pay them another visit as soon as he could. His self-reproach was the greater for making the grandmother in the family, a frail old lady of eighty-five, wait for him. If the oppressiveness of the heat had increased ten-fold, if a swarm of jungle insects had come out to bite him all over, he would have welcomed them as part of the penance for his dreadful remissness.

The family fussed around him, eager to share whatever little they had, including the tea with milk. They were one of the few Catholic Indian families in the rubber plantation who kept the faith, and proudly displayed framed pictures of the Sacred Heart of Jesus and the Blessed Virgin Mary in a community where pictures and statues of multi-armed gods and goddesses with heavy garlands round their necks proliferated on door fronts and in shrines.

Father Martin liked the two boys in the family. They were bright-eyed, intelligent lads who looked dreadfully undernourished. But he was less fond of their father who drank most of his wages, despite the priestly scolding. At least he had stopped beating his wife.

The younger of the boys took the priest by the hand and said they ought to go to poor Letchmy and give her some food or money. When he saw her, Father Martin gasped but managed to steady himself. He was looking upon a monstrosity that even priests would have difficulty in reconciling with a Creator whose love of beauty was evident everywhere in His universe. He stared at her and the woman stared back. She was used to onlookers' shocked reactions and allowed them to gaze for a full half-minute on her right leg before she stretched out a hand and demanded money. Her leg was no longer a leg but a monster attached to her body. The disease had blown up the normal contours of thigh, knee, calf, ankle and foot into a mountain of amorphous flesh, like a huge, wounded, beached leviathan.

'Letchmy', Father Martin said weakly, glad of his ability to address a fellow human being, a creature made in the image of the Creator none the less. She said something in a shrieking voice and stretched out her hand again. He gave her everything he had in his pocket. He found out from the boy that the woman was a derelict, abandoned by her family who lived only a few huts away and salved their conscience by bringing her food twice a day. The boy said Letchmy begged her family to take her out for a visit, but they always refused.

'See?' said the boy excitedly, pointing to a large, crudely constructed cart on four wheels, hidden in long grass by the side of the hut. 'They made this to try to take her around. But she is too heavy. And she smells.' And the boy pinched his nose with thumb and forefingers, and grimaced.

Father Martin prayed for Letchmy that evening. Unsure as to what to ask for on her behalf, he ended his prayer with a simple plea, 'Dear God, bless Letchmy.' It was little comfort to her that such a horrendous disfigurement could be a blessing in disguise; a preparation for the reward of heaven. Of the spiritual value to himself of the encounter, however, he had not the slightest doubt. God was pulling him back from the false world of his foolish dreams to the harsh realities of the world in which he had pledged himself to work with dedication, truth and love all his days. The shepherd was unworthy of his vocation if he tended only the loveliest of his sheep and ignored the maimed and ugly. He had noticed that many times in the past, when his feet wandered off the path of duty in response to the seductive beckoning of delight and pleasure, there would come a divine intervention, in the most unexpected way, to chasten him and direct his feet firmly back again. He knelt and tried to concentrate his thoughts on God but his dreams kept insinuating themselves into the very texture of his prayer, so that in the midst of his fervent 'Our Father' her face rose into view, like a carefree sea-bird on the crest of a wave, like a bright child's kite soaring into the blue sky.

'Help me to forget this girl.' His voice was steady but his inner state was not. Who was he to presume that she might not be part of God's plan for him in his work in Luping? She was not a Catholic but was going to be married to one: suppose God had made him the instrument to bring about a change of heart in her – to lead her to Him? There must be many like her in Luping, still in the darkness of their old beliefs, needing the gentle warmth of friendship, not the severity of censure, to lead them into the light.

The gentle warmth of friendship. He himself was in greatest need of that and, in the hours of solitude and creeping doubt about his vocation, would have gladly turned from the friends in heaven to a fellow human being. The foreign missionary's cross was never the oppressive climate, harsh terrain, inhospitable customs. It was loneliness. He yearned for the sound of a familiar voice, the touch of a familiar hand.

For a while he feared that his letters home would distress Léonie – and indeed they did, for she wrote back to console him in page after page of her neat handwriting: 'Dear, dear François, you are doing well in God's vineyard. This night of the soul will be over soon. Mother and Uncle Jean Claude would have been so proud of you. I am so proud of you. I say a prayer for you every morning and every night.'

Father Martin knew that every man and woman dedicated to the service of God went through the dark night of the soul; he never thought his would come in a little town in a strange tropical country, barely a year after his arrival, and that it would crush him and send him stumbling from his bed and on to his knees on the cold hard floor in the darkness, his face pressed into his hands, his heart beseeching God and His Blessed Mother to take pity on him.

'Help me,' he said simply. 'Take this heaviness from me so that I can work well among the dear people in Luping whom I have come to love.' It was a heaviness that he could not describe, except in its effects. I do not laugh so much anymore. I do not sing. I am not sure I even like or trust myself any more. Then the girl had appeared with her gift of food and dispersed the heaviness. He had seen the change in himself immediately, and become alarmed: his smile was brighter, his step lighter. Uncle Jean Claude and Father Henriot would have said that the brightness and lightness were not wrong in themselves, but in their source; they should have come from his sense of duty, not from a woman.

'Beware,' said Uncle Jean Claude, in exactly the same severe tone that he had used, so many years ago, when he sensed the boy's yearning for beauty on a patch of warm summer grass, beside a sparkling river.

'Dear God, please save me from concupiscence.' The word stuck in Father Martin's throat and he rejected its connotation of coarseness of appetite. The girl's beauty had afforded him immense delight and was surely part of a celebration of the beauty of God's creation. It could not be incompatible with his duty, for what good was a dry, dusty, joyless priest?

Startled by the way his prayer was turning into an inner debate, Father Martin gathered his thoughts into a tight knot of ardent concentration. 'Dear God, help me to do your will. Your will, God, never mine, be done.' It was the best prayer, the purest surrender. For a time he felt at peace with himself.

The intrusion of his fears and yearnings was far worse at night when sleep melted away the day's resistance. But his horror was in the guilt of waking after his dreams, never in their content for they were always so joyous. There was always so much laughter and brightness as they sat and talked or walked together, in a street, in the market-place, along a riverbank. In one, he asked her a question he had never dared ask in reality: 'Why do you always cover up that bangle on your wrist?' He had caught a glimpse of the translucence under a twisted handkerchief and was curious to know. Laughing, she pulled off the handkerchief from her wrist and he gazed at the bangle in all its dazzling beauty.

'It's the most beautiful thing I've ever seen,' he said, and took her hand to lay the cool translucence against his cheek. He drew it, gently, tenderly, to his lips, and then he was reaching for the other hand and drawing the girl to himself.

CHAPTER FORTY-FIVE

I t was a most eerie sensation, Father Martin said to himself, but his thinking of the girl as he sat at his desk writing a letter, seemed to have materialised her. He felt her presence, then saw her shadow outside his door – not the vaporous substance of dreams, but the reality of a moving shadow that betrayed its presence by the small sounds of moving feet and the scuff of a pebble dislodged from somewhere. He sat still and listened, wondering if he should go to open the door or wait for the rap that was sure to come. Through a window, he had a quick glimpse of her face, and a distinct perception of urgency and distress.

He opened the door and saw, to his surprise, that there was nobody around. A shuffling sound made him move towards a bench placed against the side of the building. In the darkness, he saw a woman sitting in the slumped posture of utter dejection.

'Mei Kwei,' he began, but the face that turned up to look at him was not Mei Kwei's. It was much thinner and the hair that had fallen over her face on that night of humiliation was now combed back into a neat pony-tail. He remembered her naked. Now, she was fully clothed in a blouse and trousers. She stood up and faced him. In her hands was a large bundle, wrapped in newspaper and string.

'I've never thanked you for coming to my rescue that night,' she said. 'And I want to return this.' He took the parcel from her, undid it and held up the black robe that he had given her that night to cover her nakedness. It was freshly laundered and ironed.

'I came to say thank you and to return your robe,' said the girl again. But the straightforwardness of her intention was belied by her furtive air. Her eyes shifted here and there, and her movements indicated that she wanted very much to be allowed into his house.

Father Martin kept resolutely to the innocuous space around the bench; entirely distrusting the girl's motives, he led her into the openness of the church compound and to the gate, speaking in as businesslike a tone as he could muster. Putting himself in the safe position of the rescuer receiving the gratitude of the rescued, he

enquired about her well-being and reminded her of her respon-
sibilities. 'How are you now?' he asked. 'Is your husband treating you
well? I hope you will not commit any more sins and bring shame to
your family –'

'There was a bad tear in your robe, and I've sewn it up for you,
see?' the girl said quickly, taking back the garment, and moving
closer to him. 'Here it is.' She showed him a row of fine, neat stitches.

He did not remember a tear in his robe. He watched her uneasily as
she continued to hold it lingeringly, suggestively, like an object for
magical reconnection. 'You needn't have bothered to come all this
way to return it,' he told her.

The collapse from brightness to abjection was instant; between
sobs, the girl related her misery. Her husband beat her constantly, he
locked her up in the house frequently, he threatened to cut off her hair
or slash her face with a razor, he never gave her any money. She had
put her child in the care of a relative in another town. She was in
desperate need of money. Could Father Martin give her a job as his
housekeeper? She could cook, wash, mend. She would ask for very
little.

Father Martin was aware of the woman obtruding her charms
upon his notice; she kept moving closer, undaunted by his stepping
backwards, she touched his hand lightly, she undid her hair which
tumbled luxuriantly around her shoulders. 'I already have a
housekeeper,' he said coldly. Contrary to his belief that he had
successfully developed an immunity to female tears, he was softened
by pity when the woman, abandoning the seductress's role, began to
sob once more. She appeared to slip in and out of moods in response
to the changes of tone in his voice. But this had an authenticity and
finality that moved him deeply. It was the prolonged, convulsive
sobbing of darkest despair.

'Wait a moment,' he said, and hurried back into the house. He
returned with an envelope in his hand. 'Here,' he said gently, 'it's not
very much, but it will be useful.'

The woman hesitated, then took the money gratefully. She lingered
for a while and the priest stayed with her, unafraid now, for the
seductress's need to test her power was gone, replaced by a greater
human need for understanding and sympathy.

'Please find me some work, Father. I must earn money. I must take
care of my baby.' The contrite Magdalene, who heeded the Divine
Master's call to sin no more, stood before him weeping, and he
promised to help her. As he watched her slip away into the darkness,

he wondered about the darkness of deceit and falsehood that had engulfed her young life: she could not be more than twenty.

He walked back slowly into the house, and was aware of a peculiar feeling that had been pushed into the background all this while, but was now rushing to the fore with overpowering force – the feeling of intense disappointment that the visitor had not been Mei Kwei.

'Mei Kwei –' He thought of the time she had presented herself, smiling joyously, on his doorstep with a gift of food, and now found himself superimposing her face – oh! much-loved, he had to admit that now – upon the other's. Even if she had not come but just left another tiffin-carrier to signal a continuity of their connection, even if there had been no signal, just the merest hint of one – he wanted so much to see her again.

With something of a grunt to recall his foolish self to reality, Father Martin returned to his unfinished letter.

CHAPTER FOURTY-SIX

The illness had come slowly, then suddenly burst out in a virulence that defied all medicine and signalled the onset of the end. All his life Ah Oon Koh had disliked the fuss of women. He disliked it even more on his death-bed and used the remaining energy in his dried, shrunken body to snap at his wife and daughter as they bustled about with medicine, towel, hot water, chamberpot. Austin had made, then immediately retracted, the offer to take his future father-in-law to the hospital. Ah Oon Koh's only contact with the outside world for the last fifteen years had been the weekly bicycle ride to an old decaying building in town to procure his weekly supply of opium; his only contact with his family had been the few ventures out of his room to eat, go to the toilet, go to the bathroom, watch out for the envelope of money on the small table outside his room. It was to be expected that he would choose to die in his bed, in the familiar dimness of his room, in the familiar presence of the instruments of his addiction. On a hospital bed, exposed to the sight of doctors and nurses he distrusted, among strangers he disliked, unease would kill him before disease.

Her father was dying. When she was told about it, Mei Kwei's first thought was whether this would mean a postponement of her marriage. Her heart leaped with hope at the possibility. Weddings and deaths clashed ominously; weddings had to give way.

'Mei Kwei's father wants to see you.' Ah Oon Soh never referred to her husband by name. Austin looked up, startled, then got up from the table where he had been sitting and walked into the room.

It turned out that the dying man had an urgent last wish. 'Don't let my illness and death stand in the way of your marriage plans,' he said to Austin. 'Go ahead as planned.' Dying parents strove to confer benisons upon surviving offspring, even struggling to avoid unpropitious hours of death such as dusk when they were deemed to have consumed all the meals of the day, leaving none of life's good things for posterity. Instead they chose to close their eyes at dawn, well before the first meal was eaten, so that they could say to their family, at parting, 'See, everything is left intact for you.'

But Ah Oon Koh seemed more concerned with the immediate effect of his funeral upon the young people's plans. 'Do not mourn for me,' he instructed, and told Austin that when they were married they could dispense with the traditional deep black of bereavement. Perhaps it was simple gratitude for the countless envelopes of money left on the table, or a last expression of concern for the well-being of the daughter he had never loved.

In the last days of his life, Mei Kwei wanted to probe her father's thoughts to see if she could pull out a remnant of present kindness to help wipe out the pain of past rejection. She stole into his room when everyone was asleep and was startled to see Big Older Brother sitting, head bowed, on a stool beside the bed, in silent, sad vigil. Their father's approaching end had galvanised him into a frenzy of attentive care, for he would not leave his bedside, sometimes blubbering out his sorrow and dashing tears from his eyes with the back of his hand, like a child.

'Father, forgive me,' he had wept loudly at one point, and had to be led away by his mother.

Mei Kwei raised him gently, saying in a low voice so as not to disturb their father, who seemed to be asleep, 'Go and take a rest now. I'll take care of Father.' By herself, she sat quietly on the stool and listened to Ah Oon Koh's laboured breathing and occasional groans as he turned and tossed in the last ravages of disease. She pressed her hands tightly together, then raised them to her eyes to turn back the sharp, hot tears springing up in them.

'Father,' she said softly in the darkness, close to the dying man's ears. 'Did you ever love me?' She felt a rising, exhilarating recklessness. The howling demons in her needed to be exorcised, and this was her last chance.

Mei Kwei knew he had heard, for the groaning stopped suddenly and the breathing grew more laboured. A small sound, a tiny movement of head or hand to signal affirmation would have been sufficient for her. An explicit utterance would have given her unspeakable joy. But he remained silent and still. Her recklessness mounted, dangerously.

'Father,' she said, and found it hard to continue, her tears now flowing freely. 'I believe you never loved me.' Pressing her ice-cold hands together once more she began, in distinct tones, to tell him of those times in her childhood when she had gone to him, crying with need, and he had turned her away. The incidents that she thought she had locked out for ever now broke through in brutal replay.

'Father,' she pleaded. He turned his head away from her, and she stifled a sob.

'Father, you loved only Big Older Brother. You never loved me,' she said and, in between racking gasps and wheezes, she heard his reply, 'You never made it easy for me.'

CHAPTER FORTY-SEVEN

'Second Grandmother, I have come again.'

There was no need to apologise for the real purpose of her visit. Other ghosts might be offended by the audacity of making use of a visit to the dead for the purpose of a secret rendezvous with the living, but Mei Kwei knew that Second Grandmother would understand. She sat on the ground beside the tombstone and spoke to her, lying in the earth, overgrown with long grass, lashed by wind and storm but still the beloved grandmother of her childhood, with the sharp eyes, bright smile and dainty doll's shoes. In her memory Second Grandmother would lie ever thus,

247

fresh, uncorrupted. Had the tiny feet once borne her, too, on a daring mission of love's need, just as the defiant energy had cut a daring path through society's censures and earned her the name the Crazy Old One? Had Second Grandmother woven a way around the obstacles set up by rival wives and concubines to slip, tantalising in her pink silk doll's shoes, into the room of the man she loved and who loved her? Women passed their defiant spirit to their daughters and granddaughters through milk and blood; as she lifted her face to meet the coolness of an approaching breeze and the promise of a coming joy, Mei Kwei felt its singing in her veins.

He would come. She knew he would come. Lovers, it was said, were connected by invisible threads tied to the bones of their ribcages, so that the tiniest tug could alert one to the approach of the other. Lovers, like some strange species of insect, developed a hundred antennae for the purpose of responding to a single caller. In a room filled with sound, they caught each other's faintest whispers; in a room of continuous activity, each noted the other's smallest movements of head, eye, lip. Lovers claimed their own universe, a cosmology of two.

He came, walking briskly up a curve of hill, and waved to her. She waved back. He had probably come on a lie, as she had. Had a catechumen been dismissed, on the excuse that another priestly duty awaited, as soon as he sensed her presence on the hillside? she wondered.

Her own lie had been to her husband-to-be. 'Would you like me to get you some candles and flowers for your father's grave?' Austin had asked. But she had no feelings for her father, lying in fresh, recently dug earth, some distance from her grandmother.

Poised giddily on the peril of a conspiracy of lies, they stood facing each other. Perilous but precious, their meeting had been achieved at great cost and could well be the last. Their world, shrunk to a little bit of space in a cemetery on a wind-swept hill, to a tiny slice of time marked by the harmonious ticking of seconds and minutes of the watches on their wrists, shrank further as they concentrated on a solitary insect struggling up a thin stalk of grass growing by Second Grandmother's tombstone. It was a small black beetle and for a while it was the absorbing centre of their universe.

'Look at this brave little fellow,' he said pointing to it.

She moved nearer to him, and they were thus as close together as they had been that afternoon by the cement sink. In later years, she would remember most vividly a small part of the scene – or, rather, a tiny part of the small part – as her eyes rested on a square inch of priestly sleeve. Love's attentiveness cherished details: a small mole on his left ear-lobe, a right eyebrow that lifted quizzically, the worn-out soles of plain sandals that had not been replaced for some time.

It could have been a bird, a passing cloud, a fallen leaf – any of these would have served their need to avoid looking at each other in order for the overbrimming joy on both their faces to settle into proper composure. He whittled at a stick; she plucked up small blades of grass and crushed them between her fingers.

Then they began to talk, purposefully, and to tell each other stories. Stories were safe, free of the insinuations of past, present and future; stories were innocuous, free of the encroachments of passion. Their different worlds brushed against each other joyfully; sky gods and goddesses streamed across the heavens in a blaze of light, the Lightning God striking dead the unfilial with his thunderbolts, the Monkey God, ever playful, entering human bodies in a cloud of joss smoke, making them prance about and scratch their underarms; the Moon Maiden and the God-King, united at last after their travails, met and jostled with Christian saints who banished snakes for ever, hermits who lived in deserts and performed miracles, and holy men and women who had the stigmata of Christ and whose bodies remained incorruptible after their death.

'Tell me again of your grandmother's doll's shoes,' he asked. And the tiger sign written in indigo on a swollen cheek; and the lessons learned in secret outside a classroom window; and the love of the child Tee Tee.

'Describe a snowflake,' she said. And the pig called Lottie who smelt out mushrooms from deep inside the ground which could be eaten without fear; and an apple tree.

'I'll walk you to your bicycle,' he said, as she got up to go. He would have liked, but did not dare, to take her hand, although he had touched it three times. He saw his hand clasped over hers outside the church, and again in the confessional and yet again in their wonderful encounter in the children's playground when he had held her arms and lifted her up in the air. Each occasion had presented itself and he had responded spontaneously, exuberantly.

Now he led her by a different path that ended in a small, rocky slope. She would need assistance and he offered it, glowing with the sheer pleasure of holding her hand again as he helped her over the jagged rocks. He would not have minded a whole path littered with treacherous rocks, for the joy of the warmth in the necessary negotiations to a safe end.

'Will I see you again?' It was a lover's question, and he had asked it.

'Yes,' she replied. Both knew one more line had been crossed towards perilous horizons where, overhead, the storm clouds were gathering.

A few days later, at almost precisely the moment she anticipated, Mei Kwei saw him coming over the curve of the hill. She rose from her place beside Second Grandmother's tombstone, a patch of cleared stones and flattened grass that would henceforth be touched by memory's hallowing power. They stood facing each other, wind blowing hair and rustling clothes, a man and a woman among the dead in a cemetery on a hill, the tiny life of their love stirring.

A meeting as effortless as a chance encounter at a street corner, in the market-place, a children's playground, it belied the manipulative power of the planned lie, his to his housekeeper, who had asked where he was going, and hers to her husband-to-be, who had asked the same question. A meeting with all the appearance of calm and restraint, it was fraught with inward upheaval, as the swirling, restless energy of a river banks up where it is strongest. The bank breaks, but the swirling energy still submits to be regulated and, for a while, they stood together calmly, saying nothing.

Then she made a slight movement towards him; perhaps it was no more than an impulse to touch the sleeve of his cassock. It prompted his own movement towards her, and, while the suspicion of anyone's presence in that vast cemetery that late afternoon – even the sound of distant voices – would have stayed their advance, the wind's desolate moan and the plaintive cawing of a bird allowed them to rush towards each other. He held her, not as the playful priest in the playground, or the anxious pastor of souls in the confessional, but as the man who loved her. To his dying day, he would remember the supreme moment of his release as he took her trembling body in his arms. Their faces pressed together, then shifted in one swift movement for their lips to touch.

'I am afraid,' Father Martin had implied on that strange night of the rescue of the adulterous woman in the market-place, and Mei Kwei had responded wordlessly, 'I am not afraid.'

Now, as the storm in his soul threatened to engulf him, he broke free from her eager clasp. 'We must never see each other again,' he told her. Then he turned and almost ran down the hill.

CHAPTER FORTY-EIGHT

'**Y**ou must be tired,' Father Martin said to old Mary Fong. 'Why don't you go home for a rest now?'

But the old lady, nodding vigorously and smiling broadly to reveal a single gleaming gold tooth among decaying stumps, insisted on continuing with her work of cleaning the altar, polishing the candlesticks and removing dead flower petals and candle droppings from the feet of the statue of the Virgin. She performed each task with meticulous care, after which – her neat, starched blouse and trousers as immaculately uncreased as when she started – she took out her rosary beads and prayed quietly in a corner of the dimly lit church. Twice a week her grandson brought her to the Church of the Sacred Heart of Jesus for a ritual that had become the centre of her simple existence and which prepared her for its end, when she would rise into celestial clouds to meet the Virgin, the rosary beads entwined in her old, gnarled fingers, just as an ancestor must have risen, with holy temple beads, to meet the goddess Kuan Yin.

Mary Fong had grown very fond as well as very respectful of the *si fu*. Her fondness was shown in the amount of cooking she was prepared to do of his favourite food, which included rice dumplings, her respectfulness in a reverential clasp of his hands in both her own each time they met, and in going down on her fragile, crumbling knees for his blessing. In great alarm, he would protest and try to pull her up from the ground.

'No, no, Madam Fong, you mustn't do that.' In deference to her age, he never called her Mary. Mary Fong believed, with all the fervour of her simple soul, that the saintly *si fu*'s blessing banished every evil, from threatening illness to the presence of Satan himself. She told everybody that, until the priest came to her humble little wooden house with cleansing holy water and prayers, she had felt the disturbing presence of an evil spirit that lurked in the rafters of the ceiling and even under her bed, giving bad dreams.

'Go away,' she said to Joseph Arumugam, the Indian man from the

251

rubber plantation and grimaced at the sight of the vivid red *ceray* mouth and the smell of cheap toddy. The man had come, she knew, not to pray in the church but to make a nuisance of himself. She thought the priest was being too kind to this worthless fellow, who beat his wife and spent all his money on drink. '*Keleng kooi*,' she muttered to herself, the charity of her religion failing to expunge from her blood the ancestral prejudices that made devils of other races. Soon the old Chinese woman and the Indian rubber-tapper, neither of whom spoke English, were quarrelling in Malay.

'*Busu!*' said old Mary Fong with a fierce sparkle of her gold tooth.

And Joseph Arumugam, with a lurch forward, growled, '*Gila!*'

Father Martin came out to see what the noise was about, and groaned to see the familiar quarrelling pair. They turned to him, noisily accusing each other, and, with another inward groan, he set about restoring peace all round. Old Mary Fong looked at him with her sunken, wistful eyes and once again reverently grasped his hands, while Joseph Arumugam, repeatedly touching his forehead in a great show of docility, departed.

'Dear God,' Father Martin prayed on his knees in the quiet of his room. Neither needed God's help as much as he did, for their faults were trivial, involving no falsehood. His self-reproach was greatest in the presence of parishioners like old Mary Fong who worshipped their *si fu* and draped sainthood's mantle around his shoulders. He looked at the good, trusting women of Luping, living their simple, honest lives, and recoiled at the depth of his betrayal of their trust.

His self-reproach was no less severe when he stood up in the pulpit for the Sunday sermon and looked upon a sea of calm, gentle faces turned upwards to his. No matter what the theme of the sermon, at some point, a sentence, a phrase, a word would rebound upon his ears in a singing of self-mockery. He preached the virtue of charity and felt a shuddering realisation of how little of that he was practising towards Austin Tong. He spoke about the wondrously radiant life of this or that saint, and saw, by comparison, how his was engulfed by darkest, most sinister shadows. He spoke about God's forgiveness, which was boundless: the prodigal son could have been prodigal seventy times seven and would still have been forgiven. But were there sins at which even the divine bounty balked?

He spent long hours on his knees, storming heaven for help, yet unable to articulate the nature of the help beyond an anguished, 'Lord, have pity on me.' The precise nature of the help he required would have to be expressed in the rawness of passion's language, not suitable for divine hearing: 'God, I desire a woman and think of her all the time. I desire her so much in my waking and sleeping hours that I carry a fire in my loins.'

Pray, pray, pray. When he was in the seminary, his spiritual adviser had said that prayer was the most effective way to resist temptation. Ask and you will be given. Knock and it will be opened to you. Seek and you will find. God had cast the invitation in myriad forms – such as when He had told the story of the importunate widow and the exasperated judge who gave in at last to her pleas just to stop her badgering him day and night. Be shameless, God had hinted. Make a nuisance of yourself until I give in.

Suddenly Father Martin thought, with heightening emotion, of the time Uncle Jean Claude had turned the exhilarating taste of chocolate on his tongue to the bitterness of shame and guilt, the celebration of young life and love by a riverbank on a summer's day to a funereal gloom of loss and sadness. He remembered how, as a seminarian, when he was walking by himself one day in the garden, he had looked down to see the first crocuses pushing through the earth and up to see a flock of birds in the top of an elm tree. His heart had lifted to the vibrant promise of spring and he had begun to whistle. Uncle Jean Claude had always frowned on whistling. He had indulged himself fully then, delighting in the pure notes that came in a rich stream from his tightly rounded lips, and thought he heard a response from an appreciative bird.

Then he saw Father Monet, his spiritual adviser, coming from the opposite direction, breviary in hand. 'You should not whistle,' Father Monet told him sternly. 'Bird-whistling is a mating call; whistling encourages concupiscence, therefore it should be assiduously avoided.'

Father Martin never whistled again. Nature, sunshine, flowers, Maman's delicious food, chocolate, singing, a girl's beauty by a river – if they were concupiscence, then concupiscence was natural and could not be sinful. God made the earth, and saw that it was good. Surely this goodness included birdsong, a girl's beauty, a man's body, the five senses, and an appreciation of the beauty. Guilt was unnatural and bad, a lacerating thing, whip-lashing the body into whimpering submission. The body, rebelling against the tyranny of the soul, had come up with its own logic

Tired out by his thoughts, he fell asleep. In the unfettered world of dreams, his body broke away from his soul's domination and carved its own wondrous landscape. He saw himself in a large meadow filled with flowers, bursting in the vivid generosity of spring. He saw the girl on the top of a hill in the distance and waved to her. She waved back, with both arms, signalling her joy in seeing him. Without the effort of a single forward movement, they were facing each other.

'Come,' he said, and again, effortlessly, they were in a different place, sitting beside a river and looking upon sparkling water, while from somewhere in the distance came the peal of bells mixed with children's laughter. Then they were in the water. He took off his robe and draped it round her to cover her nakedness, then took her into his arms. They stood pressed against each other, knee-deep in river water, the warm spring sunshine bringing every muscle in their bodies to a tingling vibrancy; and it was at precisely the moment when the robe fell off that he awoke and felt ashamed.

Pray. Pray against the temptation of both the waking and the sleeping hour. The devil, like a roaring lion, goes forth.

Father Martin looked at the small alarm clock by his bedside. It was four thirty. Outside, in the darkness, came the sound of a rising wind and the plaintive cry of some night bird in the cemetery. He got down on his knees and prayed, and did not rise again until the first rays of light appeared in the sky.

CHAPTER FORTY-NINE

Mrs Solomon saw that the lessons in English language, which had begun so well, were taking a disturbing turn. The girl was increasingly restive. She fidgeted. Her eyes darted about, reflecting the agitation of her mind and heart. Mrs Solomon hoped that her wild oscillations of mood, expressed in strange outpourings of need and longing on paper and couched in alien imagery of summer sunshine, meadow flowers and apple trees, had nothing to do with her impending marriage. She observed how, in Mei Kwei's hands, the English language had turned into a private cry of the heart; pages of her exercise book, which should have contained the innocuous practice of the intricacies of English syntax, were now covered in a sheaf of love letters.

'Should I turn these over to her husband-to-be? After all, he's paying for the lessons,' Mrs Solomon asked herself, but decided not to.

'I want to write a special letter. Help me,' Mei Kwei asked, and Mrs Solomon knew that, unlike the previous letters, this one had an immediate purpose and a new urgency.

'Please,' pleaded the girl.

It was a heart-rending letter, which worried Mrs Solomon who thought, with grim resolution, if he asks, I will say that I was only doing what she insisted.

Helping Mei Kwei put her feelings in writing, she could not help wondering about the secret world of the young while, at the same time, feeling a deep gratification as a teacher that her pupil appeared to care about correct grammar, spelling and punctuation even in a distressing letter of farewell.

CHAPTER FIFTY

As soon as Father Martin recognised the messenger on the bicycle, his heart gave a little leap of fear. He remembered the unpleasant meeting in the office of the chief of operations many months ago. The messenger who was getting down from his bicycle had the same gravity of mien and intimated the same kind of unpleasantness.

'Mr T. C. Williams would like to see you immediately,' he said.

I knew it would come some time, the priest thought. The young terrorist who had crawled to his doorstep one evening, and gone away fed and supplied with medicine and money, must have been caught and, under interrogation or torture, had blurted out the names of secret sympathisers and supporters.

'Father Martin,' he could hear the chief of operations saying, in his clear, well-modulated voice, 'I let you off the first time. This is just one time too many.' He could hear the Bishop too, 'Father, I thought I had warned you in no uncertain terms,' and could see the Bishop's natural generosity tighten into a cold knot of severity: 'Father, you leave me with no choice but to send you back to France –'

Suddenly Father Martin saw himself as a failed priest and missionary. Uncle Jean Claude's return home from China had been due to a failure of health; his would be the result of a deplorable weakness of judgement.

The chief of operations was pacing the narrow corridor outside a hospital ward that looked out on to a row of frangipani trees, and smoking furiously. As soon as he heard Father Martin's bicycle wheels on the gravel, he turned, a grim expression on his face. The priest felt an immediate surge of relief. His fears had been unfounded. For it was a grimness largely unfocused, related to some larger, more intractable trouble.

'Here you are,' said the chief of operations. 'I'm glad you could come. I apologise for the haste.' He made an unconvincing attempt at a half-smile. 'Come with me.'

The purpose of the chief's request became clear as soon as they walked into the hospital ward and entered a makeshift room, screened off by improvised curtains, in which the young terrorist of that night's adventure lay groaning on a bed. The priest recognised him instantly. On one side of the man stood a policeman on guard duty. The man's head and bare chest were in blood-soaked bandages; he was clearly dying.

The priest's eyes fell upon the small object, lying lightly on the man's chest, that must have triggered the evening's mission of mercy. He saw the crucifix he had given the intruder, a strange gift to an enemy who could have killed him.

It was part of the chief of operations' magnanimity not to ask questions about the source of the gift but only to respond to its cry on behalf of its dying owner. He said, matter-of-factly, 'Father, your territory, you take over here,' and withdrew.

Father Martin immediately went to the dying man's side. He saw, with a little shudder, that the tiny, naked figure nailed on the Cross had taken on some of the blood of the mortally wounded terrorist. The dying man, gasping and tossing about in wild-eyed terror, saw him, made some choking sound and attempted to grasp his hand. The poignancy of this act brought tears to the priest's eyes: God's mercy was touching all three of them, each being made the agent of redemption for the others. Just when he was resigned to the despair of a life gutted by God's withdrawal, the divine mercy was reminding him, through this Communist terrorist who had come into and gone out of his life in the course of one evening, of a love larger than he could ever have thought possible; a love that embraced all, beside which the anguished loves of men and women sank into insignificance. It was a love that broke through the false bonds of race, culture and creed, through the selfish bonds of sex. It was the love of universal creation itself. And if the woman whom he loved so much were there, he could tell her, in all the truthfulness of a heart that was made to see at last, 'Not that I love you less, but I love my God more.'

The terrorist was dying fast. Unable to remember whether he had said he was a Catholic, but assuming he had the desire to be one, Father Martin administered conditional baptism and then Extreme Unction. Then he knelt to pray for the dead man and to thank God for holding a light to his darkness.

'Father, let's go for a drink at the Club,' said T. C. Williams afterwards. 'The Lord knows, we both need one.' The priest thought, I'm beginning to like the chief of operations very much, and T. C. Williams thought, A good chap. I don't mind him at all.

'You have lost much weight, Father.' By now, the chief of operations had had several beers and his severity had melted into something close to gentle melancholy. 'I hope you haven't found it too rough here.'

Father Martin felt a slight easing of his heart as he explained how sometimes loneliness in a foreign land could drive even a dedicated man of God to fall into temptation.

'Father, you don't mean . . .' began T. C. Williams anxiously, and through his mind flitted the image of the young seductress whom the priest had rescued so spectacularly in the market-place. He had seen the young woman once or twice and had been startled by the seductive glances she cast at him. He stopped immediately, aware that the priest looked pained and confused.

The two men fell silent for a while, drinking their beer, lost in thought. The urge to unburden himself came over Father Martin again, and if there was awkwardness in talking about the girl, there was none in recounting some of the other strange happenings of his life in Luping, such as the incident of the mah-jong players and the dead man lying unattended on a bench. He told his story eagerly, ending with a humble acknowledgement. 'You were right, Mr Williams. We priests think we know everything and go blundering like fools into situations we can never understand.'

The chief of operations turned to him, his face suddenly creased in a smile. 'You know what I think, Father?' He chuckled. 'That was the craftiest thing I ever heard. The next time I want to escape a *parang*-wielding man, I shall go right up to the corpse of his grandmother or his uncle and befriend it. Ha! Ha!'

Father Martin said, 'I had thought it was divine inspiration. But you're probably right. It was the pure cunning of survival.' They laughed heartily, each thinking, I like the chap more and more.

Unable to breathe a word of a growing disgruntlement to any of his friends in his small, intimate circle, the chief now spoke freely to the priest. The beer dissolving whatever reserve was left, he told him with childlike candour of his sexual frustrations: how his wife had made a permanent bedroom for herself on a sofa outside their room and, if approached, was liable to fly into a rage and blame him for her wretched life in Malaya.

'It's either the thunderstorms or me – we both get the blame,' T. C. Williams complained. 'I go home needing a woman's soft touch and I have the pillow thrown in my face. You know what she says? "You don't satisfy me at all! Why don't you just accept that and leave me alone?" The thunderstorms fare worse. They get the full brunt of her curses which, considering her Irish ancestry, are no small thing.' He gave a short, sharp laugh.

As he called for one replenishment of beer after another, his mood swung from tearful self-pity to exuberant self-mockery. 'Here!' he cried, raising his glass. 'Here's to T. C. Williams, best chief there ever was – competent, dedicated, showed an enlightened approach in the war against Communism, improved security appreciably since he took over, blah, blah, blah. Do you know, these will be the exact words in their citation for promotion? Well, here's to the great T. C. Williams, greatest sexual failure!'

He drank down his beer in one long gulp and pushed his glass along the counter to the attendant for a refill. 'Look at you,' he said to the priest, putting an affectionate arm around his shoulder. 'Look at you, committed to the vow of chastity. Doesn't that make life simpler, Father? Eh, Father?' He brought his face closer to the priest's and gave a lewd wink.

'You know, there is a girl –' Father Martin said.

T. C. Williams looked at him, wide-eyed with surprise and slapped him on the back. 'You don't say, Father! Good for you!'

'I love her dearly.' The confession gave him a shuddering frisson. He felt suddenly reckless with the need to confess. He heard his own voice, coming from a distance, and it filled him, not with the sickening sense of falseness, as during his sermons, but a secret exultation in honesty at last, a luxurious feeling of relief. He was aware of a tingling glow that radiated out to embrace his Maker, the chief of operations, the dead terrorist, the officer who had stood guard over the terrorist, and the girl Mei Kwei. The radiance spread out further, like the welcoming waters of a flood over a large expanse of parched earth, and touched the man the girl was going to marry, the dead opium-addict father, the dead grandmother under that desolate tombstone, the child Tee Tee, skinny but very much alive and alert, old Mary Fong, possessive and quarrelsome on his account, the useless Joseph Arumugam, the pathetic Indian woman cursed by elephantiasis, the young dead terrorist woman exposed in the market-place, the young live woman exposed naked in the same place. It spread out still further, across vast stretches of land and water, across great chasms of time, to touch the father he was too young to remember, the mother he remembered with an ache of longing, Uncle Jean Claude, Father Henriot, dear Léonie, the bathing gypsy girl.

When he stopped talking at last, he became aware of the voice of the chief of operations, as indistinct as in a dream, coming in small bursts of surprise or approbation. 'You don't say, Father!' 'My word, Father, who would have thought!' 'Good for you, Father Martin! You're my kind of bloke!'

'I must go,' Father Martin said.

'Sit down, for Christ's sake,' T. C. Williams insisted and called for another round of drinks. 'Let's sing,' he shouted, and launched into a song that had become a favourite with the locals, possibly because it spoke about the impossibility of a meeting of East and West, even between ardent lovers:

Rose Rose I love you
With an aching heart
What is the future
Now we have to part
East is East and West is West
Our worlds are far apart
I must leave you now
But I leave my heart!

When he finished, T. C. Williams applauded himself loudly, calling upon the bartender, a young man conscientiously drying glasses, to join him. Then, as if drink could no longer ward off the pain of the day, he sat very still, hunched over his drink.

'Mr Williams,' said Father Martin anxiously, for he thought he saw the glint of tears.

The chief of operations turned to face him, his face twisted like a child's. 'Father, my wife is having an affair with that bastard Gray,' and, surrendering himself to the release of his secret torment, he wept like a child in the priest's arms.

CHAPTER FIFTY-ONE

He had said, 'We must never see each other again,' but Mei Kwei knew they would. Waiting beside the grey tombstone and idly watching a trail of ants emerge from a hole in the ground, she knew she would look up at the precise moment he strode into view over the crest of the hill – a familiar loved figure in a long black or white robe. Lovers need proof of their love and hers was clutched tightly in her hand: the letter, so laboriously written under the watchful eye of her English language teacher to ensure that no grammatical error detracted from the import of its message.

She saw him at last, coming over the hill, and dropped the blade of grass with which she had been teasing the ants. As she rose from the ground to meet him, still managing in the rising tumult of her feelings to wipe the dust from the back of her trousers, she realised that the stern set of his face presaged no reassurance, could bring no joy. The sky had turned grey and the wind had risen ominously. In later years they would remember a roll of desolate clouds and distant thunder and a swell of sobbing wind as they met that evening in the cemetery. Each of them would remember, too, the other's struggle to clothe the pain of hard decision in the calm tones of an ordinary transaction.

Father Martin's struggle had begun many hours before. By the time he walked out of the church and made his way to the appointed place, the priest had wrestled the man to the ground and stood over him, panting and claiming victory. From henceforth, he would meet and speak to the girl only as a priest. His mind was clear. God had intervened, acting through the humble intermediary of a dying Communist to save his soul; now he would be God's intermediary, to save the girl's.

Clinging to the clear lines of his resolution, he went straight to the task of the rescue, aware of a trembling in his voice. 'I met Father Pang recently and he told me –' Father Pang, gentle, well-meaning, fretful, had confided that his new catechumen had not shown the least interest in the catechism instruction.

'I don't know why I was chosen to be her instructor in the first place. You are the parish priest,' he had told Father Martin unhappily. 'Now I don't know whether I can consent to her baptism. I pray a lot about it, you know.'

The recollection of Father Pang's distress strengthened his resolve and enabled him to look straight into Mei Kwei's eyes and speak in a more steady voice. 'You must be sincere about becoming a Catholic. The Church cannot accept you if you have no real intention. No baptism can be allowed under a pretext.' The sternness of his tone was matched by the severity of his brow and eyes. 'Baptism is a sacrament. Once given, the soul is marked for ever.' They were no longer man and woman, but priest and charge, father and prodigal daughter who had to be rescued.

She cut through his peroration with the abruptness of a declaration that could no longer remain unuttered. 'I did it all for you.'

Through the weeks, she had sat on a bench in the Church of Our Lady of Lourdes, catechism book in hand, listening to Father Pang, repeating the tenets of the Holy Roman Catholic church after him, in the presence of God Himself, at His tabernacle on the altar, and all the while, her heart had remained solidly committed to her old gods. She would receive the water of baptism on her forehead and be admitted to the sacrament of Holy Communion during which the consecrated flesh of God Himself would be laid on her tongue and swallowed by a body which was still tied to pagan rituals of amulets, charms and joss-sticks.

'Have you no idea –' he began, then saw in the eyes of this strange, mysterious girl the irrelevance of his remonstrations. She would have gone to a Hindu temple for initiation, would have subjected herself to a hundred alien rituals for his sake.

The magnitude of her love descended upon him slowly. A woman loved him. A woman loved him for the first time, magnificently, unconditionally.

'I did it for you,' said Mei Kwei. 'I will leave this on a table for him. Austin will see it as soon as he comes in, and then I'll come out of my room and talk to him.' She had reduced the magnitude of love's risk to a simple plan, which would unroll in a few neat, clear steps.

Betrayal, rupture, shock, rage – they were as nothing to her, only so many doors to walk through on her way from an old love to a new.

Mei Kwei continued to face Father Martin, letter in hand. Her love reduced him to awe-stricken silence. In its immensity, it made his for her shrink into a pitiable point.

'I will come to you as soon as I can.' She turned to walk away quickly, down the side of the hill.

He raised his arm. 'Wait, you can't –' he called after her, and stopped, his arm falling back feebly to his side.

'Oh, my God –' He reeled under the threat of the looming danger, a runaway carriage on crushing wheels, a virulent disease on the rampage, determined to run its frightful course.

CHAPTER FIFTY-TWO

He had no business to be going to the Britannia eating-house, but as soon as he caught a glimpse of T. C. Williams, making a hurried entry past the swing doors into the restaurant, Father Martin felt an urge to speak to him. It would, he felt, be the greatest of incongruities: a Catholic priest hurrying to a police chief to say, 'Wait. I need to talk to you. I need you, in this time of my soul's crisis, more than I need my bishop or fellow priests.' But the talking might not even be necessary: all he really wanted was the solace of sitting beside the chief of operations over a glass of beer or a plate of food.

He was delayed at the restaurant entrance by Tee Tee, ragged as usual, and a dirty beggarwoman who lived in the Chinese temple and was well known in Luping. His first impulse was to dip his hand into his pocket and pull out some money for both child and vagrant. Their pinched faces spoke of hunger; a hot meal in the market-place would be the best thing in the world for each of them.

Tee Tee and the woman received the gift joyfully, but the boy's mother, who seemed to have appeared from nowhere, swept down upon him and demanded that he return the money. The boy's fingers closed tightly over the coin. Pig Auntie, who had been in a shop opposite, intently watching her son for any signs of bad behaviour, began to scold him for daring to take money from the *si fu*. She caught hold of his hand and, for good measure, gave him a smack on the head. Tee Tee cried, the coin fell out and rolled to the feet of the vagrant, who not only picked it up to return to the priest but gave back her own. She began making little noises of agitation, to add to Pig Auntie's scolding and Tee Tee's bawling. Here was a ridiculous little tableau indeed, thought Father Martin and he had started it all! He muttered something and went quickly into the Britannia eating-house, glad to leave the messy scene outside.

T. C. Williams was sitting by himself at the bar, one hand round a glass of beer. But there was no enthusiasm in his return of the priest's greeting; and his curtness repulsed any attempt at a resumption of the previous evening's intimacy. While the priest's overtures said, 'Let us be friends,' the chief's whole demeanour, as he turned back to his beer and continued to gaze dully at it, said, 'No, let us keep our distance.' For T. C. Williams had recollected, in the clear light of morning, the shocking scene of the night before: of himself crying, stupid and sodden with drink, in the arms of the Catholic priest. He had sworn that such a thing would never happen again and hoped fervently that no one, apart from the young bartender, had witnessed it. He looked up briefly from his glass and was glad to see that the priest had gone.

In the quiet of his room, Father Martin thought of a lecture that Father Monet had given him and his fellow seminarians on the need for detachment. 'Be in the world but not of the world,' the wise old spiritual director had said. 'Be among men and women, for that is your work, but beware of human attachments.'

In Luping, he was forming too many human attachments, he decided, which was why the rejection by the chief of operations and the rejection by the girl were combining to inflict the greatest pain he could remember. It was mainly the girl. Long after the picture of the chief turning away from him had subsided into an inconsequential blur, the image of Mei Kwei during their last meeting in the cemetery remained in his mind.

'I will come to you as soon as I can,' she had said, having told him of her plan to give the letter to the man she was leaving for him. But three whole days had passed, and he had not seen her.

He had been ready with a response which he had rehearsed endlessly in his mind, 'It's no use. It cannot be. We must not see each other again,' but his resolution had melted into a great wretchedness of uncertainty. He had gone to the cemetery three times to look for her, but the familiar patch of dry grass next to the grey tombstone was empty of the dear presence.

As Father Martin walked back down the hill, something very like panic gripped him – suppose something had happened to her? – followed by a despairing cry that no amount of meticulous rationalising, no recourse to any defensive strategy could suppress. He loved, needed and wanted her. His cry shook the nebulousness of his dreams at night into a tangible shape. He felt her breathing beside him, moved a hand to touch her face on the pillow and waited to hear the words, 'I did it all for you.'

CHAPTER FIFTY-THREE

Joseph Arumugam's bright boy watched the priest intently, puzzled about his intention but certain that, whatever it was, it promised a great deal of excitement. Nobody ever paid a visit to Letchmy, not even her family who came to leave food and other necessities then departed hurriedly. The Catholic priest had come on his bicycle, panting with the heat of the long ride through the rubber plantation, and was sitting beside her, making gestures with his hands and talking to her in the few broken Tamil sentences he had managed to pick up. Letchmy nodded vigorously, reciprocating his friendliness. Monstrous in appearance, even without the unruly mountain of her leg, her long, unkempt hair was streaked with white and floated in a stiff mane around her face, and her face – a dense blackness relieved only by the whites of her eyes and the vivid moist red of her *ceray* mouth – was puckered in a grotesquerie of lumps, blotches and wrinkles.

Father Martin soon asked the boy to help him pull out, from a tangle of roots and tall grass beside the hut, the low, four-wheeled cart, which was lying abandoned and upside down. Instantly the boy understood his intention and pointed out the impossibility of the task ahead. For even if Letchmy could be placed in the cart, it would be impossible to transport her across the very narrow passages between the rubber trees to her destination which lay at the other end of the plantation. Her family had tried once, failed, given up and thrown away the cart.

But, once she understood the purpose of the priest's visit, Letchmy would not hear of his abandoning it. Like an excitable child handed a gift only to have it snatched away, she screeched her distress, flinging out her arms and tugging at her hair. The huge monster attached to her body shook, too, menacingly. In her desperation she caught hold of the priest's arm, shouting something that had to do with her dream, nursed during the long months in the squalor of her disease and isolation.

'Go and get your father to come and help,' Father Martin said and, while each bodily sense recoiled from the horror of the misshapen woman clinging to him, his spirit gathered itself for the strength of his promise: 'I will help her achieve her dream.'

As a boy, he had listened to Uncle Jean Claude tell the story of a saint who came upon a leper and was so revolted by the man's appearance that he retched, turned and ran away. The Indian woman was possibly more revolting; he had to overcome his revulsion in order to prove his love for God, who had promised that any act of kindness to the least of His creatures would be an act of kindness to Himself. The saint had run back and pressed his lips to the horrible, rotting flesh, and lo and behold, in place of the leper, stood the resplendent, shining figure of Christ Himself. His own visit to Letchmy, however, had been motivated not by saintly love but by the need for distraction. Yet it would be punishment of flesh as well. For, more than Uncle Jean Claude's flagellating whip, this physical encounter with an unspeakably ugly woman would lash into exhaustion his raging desire for a beautiful one.

When he finally arrived, Joseph Arumugam would have nothing to do with the foul leg, and insisted on limiting his help to the undiseased part of Letchmy's body. He put his hands under her arms while Father Martin held her leg, a bloated, bleached monster from the deep, and together they dragged the woman towards the cart. The Arumugam boy helped, too, heaving and puffing. As long as he lived, Father Martin would never forget the recoil of his body as it brushed against the mound of diseased flesh. The nausea distilled into a stream of pure bile that rose threateningly up his throat and was swallowed down again. The woman, shrieking throughout, was at last put into the cart. Her face shone and her voice rose in an excited stream of chatter as her dream neared its realisation.

The manoeuvring of the cart and its passenger through the narrow lanes between the rows of rubber trees was not as difficult as the boy had made it out to be. His exuberance took a sadistic turn: he said he saw a tiger lurking behind a rubber tree and watched to enjoy Letchmy's reaction. In her excitable state, she shrieked at every provocation. Cowed and silent in the presence of his father – Joseph Arumugam had run off as soon as Letchmy had been successfully put in the cart – the boy became mischievous once he was sure the man's battering fists were at a safe distance. A tiger, two tigers, a cobra, a rhinoceros, a terrorist with a gun pointed at them, a horde of terrorists in a bush – he was enjoying himself immensely. Father Martin ignored him; Letchmy, unable to contain her excitement as they neared their destination, became oblivious to everything else.

The surreality of the experience that afternoon would dawn fully on Father Martin only after it was over, and he had, with the Arumugam boy's help, got Letchmy back. Now he watched her weep with joy as, still sitting in the cart, she was brought face to face with her favourite goddess in a derelict shrine in a remote part of the plantation. The purple paint on the face of the goddess had faded but the dark kohl of her large eyes and the vivid red of her mouth were surprisingly intact. Her breasts, large and round, were sadly chipped, but her arms, raised either in blessing or dance, were still graceful. The remnants of a garland around her neck and of broken coconut and dried flower-petals at her bare feet testified to a continuing though erratic devotion.

With a sharp intake of breath, Letchmy brought together her palms in a reverential clasp of greeting. She gazed upon her goddess spellbound, her eyes shining with joy. Then she prostrated herself several times, with immense difficulty, before the statue and raised herself, eyes sparkling with purpose and hope, to pour forth a prayer that could only be a plea for a cure for her horrible disease. Make me whole again. Take away this curse from my body. Or perhaps it was simply a prayer of joy, for a reunion with her beloved goddess whom she had not seen since she had been afflicted.

Watching her, Father Martin saw a young Indian girl, almost pretty, in a bright sari with flowers entwined in the long coil of hair down her back, draping a garland of sweet jasmine and tinsel around the neck of the goddess, then holding up a dainty earthen bowl from which clouds of fragrant smoke billowed to purify the air of the goddess's abode on earth.

'Here, take these.' While Letchmy prostrated herself, he had picked a handful of red hibiscus flowers from a bush a short distance away. Letchmy took them eagerly and gratefully, tore off the petals and scattered them joyfully at the goddess's feet. He watched tears fill her eyes and splatter her cheeks and felt his own, welling up slowly, blurring his sight, so that for a few moments the goddess's face shimmered, floated and melted into a smile.

That night Father Martin wrote a letter to the Bishop. 'I humbly and earnestly request your help with regard to a problem I have been having for some time. May I beg your permission . . .' Long leave in France was what he needed where, in beloved surroundings, his spirits, so sorely tested, would have the benefit of quiet and reflection; or even a posting out of Luping to some other place in Malaya. Only flight could save his vocation.

CHAPTER FIFTY-FOUR

The brown envelope containing the letter – a single white sheet, carefully folded – bore only the simple inscription 'To Austin' in her neat handwriting. Mei Kwei put it on the table at which he sat on every visit while waiting for her to come out of her room. She sat on her bed, tense with expectation, although he was not due for several hours. She was glad there was nobody in the house on what would surely be the most fateful day in her life. A few minutes after placing the letter on the table, she retrieved it and expanded the inscription. 'To Mr Austin Tong Kiat Wai,' she wrote carefully, and below that 'From Miss Oon Mei Kwei'.

'I am not afraid,' she had said. But fear had followed her at each stage of the perilous enterprise, from the writing of the letter under the watchful eyes of Mrs Solomon, to the declaration of her intention to her lover, who might already have pledged allegiance to his jealous God and be preparing to renounce her for ever, to the laying of the letter on the table for her fiancé to read. Love has a recklessness that overrides fear and carries its own special fire, and Mei Kwei's eyes never lost their brilliance and her hands, although icy cold and clasped tightly together, were ready to strike down any opposing force along the way.

All her life, her body's purity had been a gift for others, not for herself. Old Yoong had slavered at the prospect of plundering her body, and Austin was drooling now, their love for her reduced to brutal satisfaction upon her rupture. Even her own brother claimed his share. 'I will not take all of it,' he had promised, as he pressed himself against her in the stillness of the night, expecting gratitude for his show of consideration.

'It's only for your husband. Remember that,' her mother had insisted. 'I will give it to whomever I like,' Mei Kwei had said defiantly, without at that time knowing what it meant. Now she knew. She had known it when Tua Poon's wife was rescued in the market-place; when her eyes and his had met and locked in a blinding-white moment of truth and desire. It had grown and taken hold of her – a consuming madness that Second Grandmother, the Crazy Old One, could no doubt have matched if she had been forcibly separated from the man she loved.

'My gift to you,' she would say to him; a gift freely given, not bought with money or a priceless jade bangle. In the anxiety of the long wait, Mei Kwei got up, walked out of the room and paused as she looked up at the picture of her dead father framed and hung on the wall over a small altar where two cups of tea and a plate of oranges had been placed. She turned away abruptly. Until the knot of anger loosened and melted into forgiveness, she would not look at it again. She returned desultorily to her room.

In her growing anxiety, Mei Kwei's eyes grew heavy and she fell asleep and had a dream. But the dream brought no comfort; it was a jumble of disquieting images and sounds: Tee Tee crying from a ditch into which he had fallen; Mad Temple Auntie, who had also fallen into the ditch, whimpering piteously as she scrambled up its side and slipped down again; a brutal fist; a child's suppressed choking; an old man's angry face and mouth opening and shutting wordlessly, while the veins throbbed fearsomely on his neck; a dead bird; a girl being pushed from a ferry and falling, with a scream, into churning waters.

She got up with a headache and looked at the small clock on the wall. Austin should be in the house at any moment now. She heard a sound, peeped through a slit in the door and saw, with a start, that he was already there, sitting at the table and reading the letter. His back was turned towards her, but she could sense his deep distress. She sat on her bed, her body numb with an invading chill. Her meticulous preparations had not taken into account the shock and guilt that a woman feels when confronted with her heartlessness and its devastating effect on a good, kind man. For Austin had been kind to her; now she was rewarding his kindness with the cruelty of rejection and betrayal.

Mei Kwei opened the door softly. As soon as he heard her, Austin leaped up from his chair and rushed to her. He held her tightly and pressed his face, taut with fear and distress, against hers, whispering, 'Thank God I can have you with me now. You were sleeping and I did not want to wake you.'

He led her to the table and said, 'I've bad news, very bad news.' He showed her a letter, one of several spread out on the table, and she could see that it was not hers, and that there had been a mistake.

'Read it,' he said, in the strangled voice of the terror-stricken, and as she stretched out her hand to take the letter, she could see her own, still in its brown envelope, untouched, unopened, lying on the floor close to a table leg where it must have fallen. Quietly, she laid a foot on the brown envelope, meaning to retrieve it at the first opportunity.

Scrawled in a crude hand, this letter screamed abuse.

Running dog. You who stoop to lick the white man's arse. You who serve food to the white skins and look down on your own people. King George and Queen Elizabeth. Princess Elizabeth and Princess Margaret. Licker of royal arses.

The letter-writer clearly had an observant eye and a sharp memory. 'On such and such a day,' Mei Kwei read, 'Mr T.C. Williams went to your restaurant. Your men fawned on him. On such and such a day, Mr Currie went to your bar and got drunk. You did nothing, but when an Indian man got drunk, your men threw him out. Mr Robert owes money to your restaurant, but you smile and say, "Never mind." Would you have shown the same generosity to your own people?'

In a crescendo of virulence, the letter screeched, 'Why don't you go all the way and share your beautiful woman with the white arses, beginning with the white priest?'

It wound down into a snarled warning:

Beware! Those who turn their backs on their own people, beware! Those who aid and abet the white man and have no regard for the brave patriots in the jungle, making supreme sacrifices in their struggle against the hateful imperialists, know what is in store for you. Remember the fate of Hock Seng whose traitorous head was chopped off with a *parang*. Remember the fate of Mr Aw whose evil heart was blown out by a grenade. Remember the grenade that blew up Mr Yoong's car. He may not be so lucky the second time.

269

The letter came with a pink leaflet, one of thousands dropped periodically by government planes over the jungles, exhorting terrorists to surrender and return to normal life. It was relevant to the writer's purpose only in so far as it allowed him to express his hate in an obscene scrawl across the entire sheet and include Austin Tong's name in the obscenity. The envelope also contained a bullet. Austin showed it to Mei Kwei.

He slumped back in his chair. 'I want you to listen carefully to me,' Austin said. 'Should anything happen to me – you can never tell what will happen in this crazy town – I want to make sure –' In the deadening chill of his terror, he thought only of her. 'I don't want you to worry,' he said, tears appearing in his eyes, for the onslaught of so many feelings all at once, shock, fear, anger, self-pity, love, concern, was too much even for a strong man. 'A man about to be married ought not to contend with so much,' he concluded bitterly.

'Can I get you a hot drink?' Mei Kwei's first impulse towards healing was always dependent on this most basic offer. She stood close to him and put her arms around him as he drank, deeply and gratefully, the tea she brought him. To comfort him was her immediate concern; she could do no less.

Austin Tong took the letter and the bullet to the police. Some of the warning letters from the Communist terrorists carried drawings only of guns or grenades; this one, dispensing live ammunition, would be taken seriously.

From threat, the adversary moved swiftly to action.

The cook in the Britannia eating-house, who slept in a room at the back, got up early when a frightful odour pervaded the building. He went to investigate and discovered that the front part of the restaurant facing the road had been splashed with human faeces. At least two large buckets had been used.

In great consternation, the cook ran to Austin Tong's house in the dawn darkness to alert him. Austin stared in shock at the vandalism, and realised with greater shock the extreme hate that must have prompted it. Then, surprised at his outward calm, he set about the task of organising a thorough cleaning before the rest of the town woke up. He found some early road-sweepers, who had come with their long-handled brooms, and prevailed upon them to do the work for an attractive sum of money. Meanwhile the cook had pleaded illness and left the scene. By the time the shops began opening their doors and women with baskets on their arms were on their way to the market, the vileness had been removed.

But the malodorous intent lingered for a long time afterwards, imparting a sense of foreboding to all the employees of the Britannia eating-house, except Big Older Brother who, with grim relish, saw it as a fit punishment of the arrogant owner who had once humiliated him in front of the other staff. The humiliation of knowing that each sly glance of his fellow workers in the restaurant bore the taunt of his abject dependence on his brother-in-law was daily growing more painful, and he wondered how much longer he could take it. The spectacular incident of the dawn ablution of the restaurant was guaranteed to keep the fires of his hatred stoked for some time. Big Older Brother let out a loud guffaw and slapped both thighs. 'The gods are just,' he roared.

I don't understand what is happening, thought Austin. But he understood what he had to do. Nothing would make him postpone his marriage; indeed, he decided to hurry it in order to put an end to the string of misfortunes which had lately beset him. He had a plan, which he would not as yet share with his wife-to-be: after their marriage he would sell his businesses in Luping and move with her to live in Penang, or Kuala Lumpur, or even Singapore. He was beginning to hate Luping. He wanted to sever ties completely with the town of his birth, upbringing and present problems.

Then his robust constitution, which had defied the threat of the terrorist letter and the vandalism, crumbled under their combined stress. He complained of chest pains and was confined to bed.

'I see it all now,' he said grimly, as he sipped the nourishing soups and brews that Mei Kwei and her mother prepared for him. He had had no idea when he embraced the Catholic religion that he was also embracing a temperamental God who delighted in testing His mortal creatures. Like the gods of his ancestors, this God had gifts in plenty, but sent thunderbolts to terrify and chasten. Recovering from his illness and looking forward to his marriage, which under no condition must be postponed, Austin decided that there was no choice but to play up to the divine caprice. No matter what happened, he decided, he would be a winner because he was going to marry the woman he loved and prized. For this, he would always be grateful to his God.

He woke up to see Mei Kwei sitting at his side, ready with her medicine and gentle care. The long vigils by his bed had taken a toll on her spirits and beauty; she looked wan and sad as she moved towards him.

Gratitude and love welled in his heart, together with the tears in his eyes. He held her hand and said, 'As long as I have you . . .'

And she said, putting her hand on his, 'I will never leave you,' and knew then that she would be uttering, for his benefit, one falsehood after another. Love, in the presence of a greater imperative, hides itself behind a hundred untruths.

CHAPTER FIFTY-FIVE

'Come,' Tee Tee said with mounting excitement. 'Come, she asked for you.'

When they arrived in the temple grounds, he pulled her away from the familiar shed at the back and towards the temple itself. 'She's in there,' he said, 'and she wants to see you.'

Tee Tee enjoyed provoking curiosity and watching its shocked reaction. He liked to store up, for his own private enjoyment, details of raised eyebrows, rounded eyes, dropping jaws, the sharp intake of breath. He now watched Mei Kwei closely as she looked at Mad Temple Auntie cross-legged in prayer before a statue of the goddess Kuan Yin.

In the dim light of the temple interior, Mei Kwei saw the transformation of the vagrant and for a while she could not believe that the quiet figure in a grey robe, with a clean-shaven head, no different from any of the venerable nuns in the Lok Si nunnery, was the dirty, unwashed, beggar woman with the wild matted hair, who only a short while ago was roaming the streets of Luping in search of a free meal in the market-place. She stared at the limbs, once restless and ready to dance to raucous opera or *ronggeng* music, now locked into a discipline of prayer and meditation, at the face, once contorted by the imbecile's display of extravagant emotion, now smoothed into a tranquillity not unlike that of the Goddess of Mercy herself. The most intriguing feature of the transformation was the cleanly shaven head which marked her as one of the goddess's chosen ones.

Mad Temple Auntie must have heard them enter the temple, must have felt their presence as they stood waiting near by. But she did not move and continued to pray to the goddess, eyes closed, hands clasped, legs crossed.

The waiting became long and intolerable. Tee Tee squatted, then curled up on the cool, tiled floor and fell asleep. Mei Kwei herself tried to shake off the drowsiness of the afternoon heat and the joss fumes from her eyes. But Mad Temple Auntie went on praying. At last, Mei Kwei walked up to the perfectly still figure, touched her lightly on the shoulder and whispered, 'Mad Temple Auntie, you asked for me. I'm here,' and saw her fall forward, swiftly and noiselessly, to rest on the ground, forehead pressed upon a cool tile.

Mei Kwei would later recall no feeling of shock or fear, as she searched the body for signs of life, and then ran to get help. She would have no part in the excitement that gathered quickly around the remarkable death of the vagrant. Stories spread of someone's dream the night before that corresponded with the spectacle of a flock of white doves appearing mysteriously in the sky over the temple roof; or of the temple tortoises that had committed mass suicide, having been found in a heap in their cement enclosure on the day of Mad Temple Auntie's burial.

'I'm sorry to hear of her death,' Austin said kindly, knowing Mei Kwei had cared very much for the temple vagrant and remembering the time they had given her a meal from his restaurant. But Mei Kwei felt no grief, only a sense of peace that all at last was well with the strange, despised woman she had known and loved from childhood.

But always, in her dreams of her friend, she saw, not the saintly woman with the venerable shaven head and grey robe, but the earthy, unkempt, shaggy-haired woman, raising one leg, then both arms in a triumphant dance, the diadem of the God-King perched on her head. And as Mei Kwei sat watching spell-bound, she saw, advancing towards her, the Moon-Maiden with her diadem glittering like a hundred stars.

CHAPTER FIFTY-SIX

Some days before his wedding, Austin Tong decided to ingratiate himself with his God by an act of charity. For a long time he had thought about his half-brother, the sickly ghost-child borne by his father's mistress, Auntie Forehead Mole. He remembered distinctly the woman's distraught appearance at the gate during his father's illness, and his mother's grim determination to ignore her and send her away with nothing. He remembered the woman, bloated, unkempt, bemoaning her fate and cursing his father for the wretched, sickly child he had left on her hands. *Bad seed*. As a boy, Austin had wondered about the meaning of her accusation. In his mind, he saw crinkly, hard, malformed seeds giving rise to malformed plants. *Bad seed*. He was good seed so the fault lay not in his father, but in the mistress.

His mother's Christian kindness had not extended to her husband's mistress and child but he, on the threshold of a new life that he hoped would be blessed by God, decided to pay them a visit. He had heard that his half-brother was still alive, living in a rented room with his mother in some squalid part of the town, his sickness leaving him so frail and timid that he could not even step outside the room. He would search them out and without exactly bringing them into his circle, he would ensure that they would never again be in want. His father had committed a sin and caused to be brought into the world one who would suffer grievously for the rest of his miserable existence. His mother, saintly person though she had been, had compounded that sin by her indifference to the victim's plight. It would be up to him to rectify that and remove whatever vestiges of anger God might still have with regard to this pathetic piece of family history.

But the clean lines of Austin Tong's deliberations were sundered by the reality that confronted him as soon as he stepped into their rented room. The blackened walls and broken furniture, the meagreness of possessions exemplified by a jumble of dented tin mugs, flasks and chipped bowls on a table, the desperation of a solitary joss-stick stuck in an empty cigarette tin by the window – even the sight of the mother's thin, pinched body shrunk to half its remembered size – was nothing compared to the horror of the devastation visited upon his half-brother. He was sitting in a chair in the darkest corner of the dark room, a mere ghost, a slip of a ghost, fleshless, colourless. It was impossible that this pale, fragile, shell of a body could still be alive. When it blinked, or moved its head, Austin had an impression of a corpse come to life. Then the wraith smiled and spoke. Its voice was soft and gentle. It expressed warm greetings to Austin and made courteous enquiries about his health, his business. It asked, too, about Austin's late parents, showing detailed knowledge of the circumstances of their deaths. Slowly, it turned its large skull-head, covered with thin wisps of hair, in the direction of the miserable woman, sitting in another corner, and requested her to make a drink for the guest. The woman had the numbed look of unrelieved despair. Throughout the visit she said hardly a word. The acts of screaming defiance at the gate, so many years ago, must have consumed all her physical and mental powers, leaving her drained and bewildered.

His half-brother. In his veins flowed the same blood. A little spasm of horror ran through Austin. He brought out a large wad of money from his pocket. He could not remember what he said to the woman but he would remember, long afterwards, the feelings of acute embarrassment accompanying the words.

'Thank you very much,' his half-brother said, still in the soft and gentle voice. 'You are very kind. But we do not need it.' The broken furniture, the ugly dented mugs and chipped bowls, the dirty torn curtains and solitary joss-stick, the woman's desperate eyes all screamed, 'Of course we need it!' But his half-brother was adamant. He said once again, 'We thank you for your kindness,' and then gave the signal that he wanted the visit to be over, shrinking deeper into his shadows until he was no longer visible.

At least I tried, Austin thought, as he left, and was determined, after his marriage, to make another visit, and another, in the months to come. Pity overwhelmed and choked him as he stumbled out into the bright sunshine and made for his car.

Austin's self-control was once more in evidence, however, when a few days before their wedding, he said to Mei Kwei, 'For your sake, I will, as usual, forgive your brother.'

She looked up sharply at him, the tightness in his voice and face portending danger. Then he told her, in calm, measured tones, that the police had found the perpetrator of the two crimes against him. Big Older Brother had left his fingerprints all over the threatening letter and even on the bullet, as well as on the bucket from which the excrement had been flung upon the front door of the Britannia eating-house. Both were serious crimes and carried jail sentences.

'Thank you', she said. 'I'm deeply grateful.' But her heart swelled with anger and hatred. You mean me to carry this burden for the rest of my life, she thought.

'Your brother could be in jail for ten years,' Austin told her, still holding her in his arms. 'There are men serving longer sentences for lesser crimes, Inspector Maniam told me. But I said, "Let's forget about it. I forgive him because he is my future wife's brother."'

He wondered about the glitter in Mei Kwei's eyes, and was relieved to see it melt in a wash of soft tears, unaware that the weeping was precipitated by a different sadness. For, in the midst of a lengthy expatiation on the need for forgiveness prior to the reception of the most joyous of the sacraments, he had said casually, 'By the way, Father Martin will be leaving for France on long leave. Our marriage will be his last official duty.'

CHAPTER FIFTY-SEVEN

Years later, each of the three principal persons in the ceremony that morning in the Church of the Sacred Heart of Jesus – the bride, the bridegroom, the priest who married them – would vividly recollect the strangeness of it all and experience again the pervading sense of unreality. There was nothing abnormal about the outward appearance of the event: the bride, in a simple, white silk dress with a veil and carrying a bunch of lilies, the groom in his best suit, the priest in his vestments, the prayers, the organ music, the exchange of rings, the final blessing to go forth and multiply. The abnormality might have been in the bride's recalcitrance.

'No,' she had said, 'I will not become a Catholic,' thereby violating a cherished tradition in the town's Catholic community by which pagan wives converted unquestioningly to the religion of their husbands. 'I will not become a Catholic – yet.'

Her husband, in the generosity of his heart, had moderated the hard pronouncement with a softening qualification: it was only her lack of readiness. After her marriage, she would have more time and incentive to be drawn to his faith and finally weaned from her own.

Standing close to her – his wife at last in the eyes of God – he would not let any disquieting thoughts cloud his happiness, not even the observation, as he looked at her face behind the veil, that it was shadowed with sadness. For a brief instant, as bride and groom stood before priest, her sadness broke through the sonorousness of the sacramental blessings in a flash of acrimony perceptible only to the priest as he kept his head bowed.

'Your fault, if your church claims one member less. You know I would have become a Catholic if –'

And Father Martin, flushed with pique, had flashed back, 'What manner of woman are you that you have no qualms about making a mockery of the Church?'

Their rancour cut through the gentleness of sacramental music and prayer, shredding them into pathetic little ribbons that rained down like a poisonous shower, hushing everyone into a sense of foreboding. It was perhaps this sense that, years later, the husband would remember and identify as the first of a number of warning signals. 'I should have known even then,' he would say. Now, tremulous bridegroom, he waited patiently for the ceremony to be over, to carry home the great prize of his life's long and arduous search.

As the ring was slipped on her finger, the bride's anger turned to despair and was felt, shudderingly, by the priest, every fibre of his consciousness being attuned to every fibre of hers. 'You are going away,' she mourned. 'This separation will be a little death, preparing me for the final one. I may never see you again.'

And, as he made the sign of the Cross over the bride and groom's heads, his charged heart shouted back, 'This is the saddest moment of my life.'

Bride and groom knelt for the final blessing and still Mei Kwei's and Father Martin's hearts shouted to each other. Perhaps it was the intrusion in the closing ceremony of the thought of a rapturous encounter behind closed doors on a soft bed and pillows, that lifted their hearts swiftly from the depths of despair to a moment of daring hope and back again to despair.

If only – the priest tried to shake off the image – sacrilege of sacrileges, in a church itself! – of joyous copulation, and the vividness of long, sun-warmed, glistening limbs. The bride thought, if only – meaning that, even as her husband was leading her down the aisle in triumph at the close of the ceremony, she would gladly have seized the chance to turn away from him, to offer the first gift of her body to the other man, and then return to her husband to say: 'Now my life is made bearable by a precious story I have saved for telling secretly to myself.'

Each small movement of preparation for the night – the brushing of his teeth, the washing of his face, the changing into pyjamas, even the opening and closing of drawers and doors – became a self-conscious ritual, precisely measured out and executed, to impose a regulating rhythm on the roaring energy of his body's eager anticipation, so as not to frighten his innocent bride trembling on the threshold of experience. As Austin came out of the bathroom and gently closed the door behind him, he saw her sitting in a chair in a corner of the room, still in her bride's clothes.

'Would you like to use the bathroom now?' he asked.

She was determinedly silent, her eyes fixed on her hands lying on her lap.

He was going to say, 'Don't be afraid, I will be gentle,' remembering his disgust, whenever he heard stories of brute ancestors throwing their coarse bodies upon their brides or concubines lying terrified in the darkness. He decided that a promise of gentleness for an essentially rough act would only reinforce the roughness for the frightened girl, so refrained from more talk as he prepared to get into bed.

Suddenly, Austin Tong felt a great wave of happiness and peace break over him. The consummation of the night would not merely put the seal on the sacrament of the morning, it would be a healing; he would rise from the body of this pure girl, completely cleansed of his father's corruption.

He woke up in the middle of the night with a start, and found, to his immense delight, his bride curled up beside him in sleep, a shoulder touching his. He listened to her soft breathing, enchanted by the prospect of such warm, close physicality for the rest of his days. He turned slowly to face her and gather her into his arms, dispensing with gentleness, claiming the happy bridegroom's privilege of disrupting sleep for love. She stirred and then sat up suddenly; it was her turn to greet with a start the newness of the surroundings including the novelty of a breathing, heaving man beside her. Austin's joy, postponed too long, dispensed with the solicitousnes of enquiry and offer. He could have tried to calm her fear, now rising rapidly in the darkness, making her shrink into herself and away from him. Instead, with a grunt, he pulled her to him to feel the rising power of his desire. He had never touched her breasts; now his hands and lips were loosed in a frenzy of exploration, incredulous at the soft rich beauty of her body. As he pulled off his trousers and helped her out of hers, he had the exhilarating thought that the supreme pleasure of this night was his to repeat over a successive one hundred, one thousand nights. He would have liked, on this special night, for his pleasure to be complete; for him to fall back upon the bed in the full satiety of a sleep made possible only by love's fulfilment. But her sharp cry would not allow the completion of the act, and he withdrew from her in concern. She lay crying softly.

Suddenly Austin felt ashamed. He had promised gentleness but had been carried away by the savagery of his lust. He hovered over her, kissing her gently and saying, 'I'm sorry.' Then, as he soothed her back to sleep, he became aware of a deeper, more exhilarating pleasure: he had proof of the purity of her body, and assurance of the husband's claim of first gift. He would wait patiently to make his claim and then the gift of her fragile beauty, broken into at last, would be all the more precious.

CHAPTER FIFTY-EIGHT

The news of the assassination of T. C. Williams, chief of operations, spread like wildfire through the town and countryside. Fear gripped Luping. If the Communist terrorists could kill the chief himself, people whispered, who was safe? Rumours multiplied and swirled. It seemed that he had been trapped in an ambush but the two officers with him had survived. Another story had it that he had saved their lives by offering his own; a third that he was alone in the jungle and had simply got out of his Jeep and walked straight into enemy fire.

'Oh, no! Oh, no!' Father Martin exclaimed, when a parishioner told him the bad news. Thinking selfishly of his own pain, he saw it as yet another terrible loss. He pedalled furiously to the hospital, dropped his bicycle on the ground and ran to the mortuary. Policemen barred his entry. He argued with them, and they were about to turn him away when Jill appeared and said that he could see her husband's body. It was the first time he had met T. C. Williams's wife and he found it hard to reconcile her tired, childlike face, her blonde hair tied in a pony-tail and her petite body with the image of a shrieking wife who locked her husband out of their bedroom and was having an affair with a brother officer.

'You must be Father Martin,' Jill said. 'Timothy thought highly of you.'

Timothy. He wondered what the C stood for. His friend had told him the most intimate secrets but not this. Now he was dead.

He stared at the body lying on the cold cement slab, and sensed the expectation among the small group of people looking on that he would go down on his knees and pray. Priests in houses of death did precisely that. Somewhere in the stale, acrid air of the mortuary hung the whiff of a shocking doubt. 'Oh, no! Oh, no!' Father Martin repeated, not in protest against the senseless assassination, but against the dawning certainty of a terrible truth. He could see the chief of operations, unable to bear the pain of the betrayal by his wife and trusted colleague, and unable to relieve his anguish through drink swerve his Jeep in the direction of enemy territory, then, with grim determination, walk straight into enemy fire.

At last, Father Martin knelt beside the body and wept.

He rose to a great commotion, as someone – a woman – tried to force her way into the mortuary, screaming abuse at those who were restraining her. She was dressed in deep mourning black, in contrast to the light, lemon-yellow dress that Jill was wearing.

'Get out, you slut,' Jill hissed. Father Martin recognised her at once. On the night that she visited him to return him his robe, she had had her hair tied up and looked different. But her beautiful young sensuous face, deeply imprinted in the minds of all those who had seen her that terrible night of her exhibition in the market-place, would always be recognisable.

Tua Poon's wife broke free of the restraining hands and made a rush for the body, screaming something in her dialect. It could have been, 'Let me touch him for the last time. He was the only one who was kind to me.'

Jill stopped her, shrieking back, 'Get out, you Chinese slut!' And the girl was dragged away, sobbing hysterically.

Father Martin tried to shake from his mind the images of T. C. Williams's terrible, self-willed death in the jungle, and of his desperate liaison with a local woman, probably in some squalid rooming-house in a dimly lit part of town where her husband was not likely to find her. Had the chief, in his desperation, been careless and left his Jeep parked outside for a dozen pairs of curious eyes to peer at?

'An eye for an eye, a tooth for a tooth,' T. C. Williams might have snarled, for he quoted the Holy Book liberally. 'An affair with a local Chinese slut for your treachery with Gray right under my nose!'

When the two men had met for the last time in the bar of the Britannia eating-house, each carried his secret pain, each cried to be understood and comforted. In a foreign country, both men had stumbled and fallen.

'I hate this country. I hate everything that has happened here.' As he took a last look at the corpse, its eyes serenely closed, its face perfectly composed, Father Martin's tears were bitter.

CHAPTER FIFTY-NINE

Used to curfews, Luping shivered under this one. The faces of the townspeople as they moved quickly about their business in the hours before the shop shutters came down and the streets emptied, were pinched with tension. Every British Jeep that roared by seemed driven by the need for revenge; every scowling *ang moh* face that met a local's seemed to say, 'We'll get you for this.' The circumstances surrounding the death of T. C. Williams would be matter for future enquiry; for the present, the most important thing was that their chief had been murdered by Communist terrorists, and the bastards, as well as their secret informers, would have to pay. A drag-net was cast through the town and all suspects were thrown into interrogation centres and lock-ups.

But for his illness, Big Older Brother might have been among those taken away in handcuffs. His fear, as he lay writhing on his bed and shouting incoherently, was no longer of earthly forces but those whose touch was more deadly. He pleaded with the ghost of Mad Temple Auntie not to torment him; his eyes wide with terror, his face ashen white, he shrieked as he tried to fend off her blows. Or perhaps it was the ghost of the young woman terrorist whose grave he had once disturbed for gain, for he looked up suddenly and said, 'Forgive me, forgive me, I did not mean to disturb your rest.'

Ah Oon Soh waited by the back door of her daughter's new home like a servant or fugitive, not daring to go in. She wanted to make clear to her daughter, now even more painfully distanced by marriage, the absolute necessity of her visit. 'You are a new bride. You should not be disturbed like this. Forgive your mother for disturbing you,' she pleaded, when Mei Kwei came to the door.

'Stop it, Mother. What's all this? What has happened?' Thoroughly alarmed, Mei Kwei grasped her mother's trembling hands and led her to a chair.

Big Older Brother had gone raving mad and was calling for her, Ah Oon Soh told her. If she did not come, he would kill himself. In great fear, Pig Auntie, who had been most helpful throughout the family troubles, had hidden all the knives, choppers and sharp instruments in the house.

'Will you come?' Ah Oon Soh lifted a tear-stained face to her daughter. Under normal circumstances, even the mention of illness and madness would not be tolerated in the presence of a new bride. But circumstances were not normal.

'One trouble after another,' Ah Oon Soh moaned. 'If it is not my daughter, it is my son. My children will be the death of me.' Then, once again, she slipped into the abject role of desperate supplicant: 'Your mother begs your forgiveness for daring to disturb you.'

'Don't talk nonsense, Mother, of course I will come to see Big Older Brother,' Mei Kwei said impatiently.

'What about your husband?' quavered Ah Oon Soh.

'My brother is dying, he will understand.'

But when they arrived, they found Pig Auntie on the doorstep in great agitation. 'He's left the house,' she cried. 'I went into his room with the porridge and he was gone.'

As she made her way up the slope to the cemetery, Mei Kwei thought how strange it was that this isolated home of the dead should draw her back again and again. It was as if its grey tombstones, the tall grass that sprang up after each thunderstorm, the remains of food, joss-sticks and money offerings washed into the earth or blown about in mournful eddies of wind, were destined to be the backdrop against which the story of her life would be played out.

She sat down wearily near Second Grandmother's tombstone and looked around. Guilt had driven Big Older Brother, as a boy, to the cemetery on a visit to his poor little sister. Since then neither guilt nor duty had prompted him to visit his dead grandmother or father: he woke up resting spirits only for gain. Yet Mei Kwei was sure that this time his visit had to do with their appeasement. The young terrorist woman who had never stopped tormenting him was now joined by Mad Temple Auntie; Big Older Brother had two female ghosts on his back, and no amount of his pleading with them could stay their avenging hands.

Then she saw him, sitting disconsolately on a mound of earth, holding a placatory joss-stick. She was shocked by his emaciated and wild appearance. He was wearing only his pyjama trousers and his shoulders and arms bore the cuts and bruises that he must have inflicted upon himself in a moment of frenzy. He turned round and stared quizzically at her, frowning.

'Big Older Brother, Mother told me that you wanted to see me. Here I am.' He continued to stare at her. 'Big Older Brother, I've come to take you home. Please come with me,' she continued gently.

Big Older Brother shrank into himself and shook his head vigorously, like a distressed child. Mei Kwei realised that all the resources of her persuasion were called for as the sky darkened and the curfew hour approached.

'Go away! Don't bother me!' he said petulantly and began to clear a little space near the mound, as if preparing for a ritual of prayer and offering. He muttered to himself and looked around in search of something; it could not have been for lottery number sticks to shake before a spirit, for he was clearly past that and seemed to want only to appease the dead. He knelt on the earth with the joss-stick clasped in his hands, and knocked his forehead on the ground.

Mei Kwei watched him wearily. Then she went up to him and took him by the shoulders. 'Big Older Brother, let's go now. They're all waiting anxiously for you at home.'

Suddenly he sprang upon her snarling, 'Go away!' His was a face that no longer belonged to this world but looked and smelt of the desolation and decay of the graveyard. Considering that he had not eaten for days, his reserves of energy were amazing. He ran hither and thither like a frenzied animal, and picked up a sharp-edged rock with which he began to cut his forehead.

'Oh, for God's sake, stop!' Mei Kwei screamed.

'You all want to see Big Older Brother dead,' he cried in a return to lucidity. 'I know you want to get rid of me!'

Then there arose a tremendous noise of shouting and screaming as she struggled to snatch from his hand a piece of jagged, rusty metal more vicious than the rock.

'Stop. Don't hurt her!'

Mei Kwei turned and saw Father Martin. He came running up with great urgency and pushed away her brother, who fell heavily to the ground.

'Are you hurt? Did he hurt you?' he asked anxiously.

Big Older Brother sat on the ground, panting heavily, while a trickle of blood flowed from his forehead.

'We'll have to get him out of here. Quick,' said Father Martin. He dragged Big Older Brother along the small footpath leading to the church with Mei Kwei walking alongside. The hour of curfew had come and he offered them the use of his house until Big Older Brother could be taken safely to hospital, for he was certainly in need of medical attention.

Soon the wretched man was cleaned of blood and dirt, given a hot drink and put to bed. Delirious, he still talked wildly about peace-offerings to the dead. It was a long while before Father Martin and Mei Kwei, anxiously watching by his side, heard his voice trail into a murmur and saw his eyes close in sleep.

CHAPTER SIXTY

They had avoided looking at each other till then. So much had happened since they had last seen each other – so much pain from deaths and loss. If their situations had been different, he might have shared with her his grief at the assassination of T. C. Williams and she might have shared with him her great sadness at the sudden death of Mad Temple Auntie. But the loss and death that most concerned them were their own: how could they tell each other, just three days after she had become irrevocably bound in marriage to another man, and just one day before the priest's departure for his home country from which he might never return to Luping, about the loss of hope and the foreclosing of their dreams?

Father Martin beat down the turbulence of his feelings by playing the correct, generous host: 'This blanket is for your brother. There is a cold wind rising, would you like a hot drink? I will be outside if I am needed.' He put at their disposal his humble bedroom – a screened-off area with a bed, a small table and a chair. He intended to lie on a small couch pushed against the wall near the kitchen sink. Then he bade her goodnight and was gone.

Mei Kwei sat staring at her brother, now deep in sleep and snoring gently, and thought only of the priest. Partings were like deaths, she thought; this would be the combined pain of all the deaths in the cemetery that she had ever mourned and if, in some future time, she sat on the hilltop and mourned once more, it would be for herself, for her long death since the moment of his departure.

The presence of her sleeping brother began to oppress her spirits. Quickly, she left the house and went out into the still night where, for a while, she stood under the dark sky and lifted her face to a softly blowing wind. She walked for a little distance and sat on a small wooden bench placed against a side of the building. A sense of peace slowly permeated her whole being.

A small frog hopped towards her and stopped by her feet. Averse to cold, moist creatures since childhood, she welcomed its presence in the darkness, and linked it with the night insect somewhere around, whose low, mournful hum brought her a small measure of comfort.

She heard steps upon the gravel and looked up to see Father Martin standing before her.

'You must be cold,' he said, and handed her something soft and warm. It was a woollen cardigan; he would have come with a blanket, but there was only one in the house and it was being used by her brother.

She took it silently and, while she waited to see what he would say or do next, her mind marvelled, as it had so many times in the past, about how wish could materialise presence. Never once, as she waited in the cemetery on the hill, had she wished and he failed to appear.

'Put it on,' he said, and sat down on the bench beside her.

If she were asked, years later, of the exact space between them on the hard wooden seat in the darkness of that night, she could have given the precise measurement of three spans of her hand. They sat together saying nothing, absorbing the small sounds of the night: the mournful hum of the insect, the faint bark of a dog somewhere in the distant town, the caw of some night bird in a far-off tree, the crackle – possibly of gunfire – in a remote part of the jungle.

'I'm leaving for France tomorrow evening,' he said simply.

It had the effect of a spontaneous movement of his hand towards hers on the bench, and of a sudden sob rising dangerously in her throat. He was close by her side in a moment clasping both hands and then dropping them to clasp her to him as he felt the full weight of her pain and heard the sobs, irrepressible, burst forth. It was the crying of an impossibly racked heart.

As she clung to the priest in the darkness and he pressed her to him with greater tenderness and ardour than he had ever given, or she had ever received, Mei Kwei felt the luxury of consummate release and, quietened at last, lay contentedly in his arms.

Father Martin laid his face against hers and tried to convince himself that he was only comforting a distressed woman. This was the ardour of innocence, not desire. But his desire, inflamed by hers as she shifted ever closer into the warmth of his embrace and let out a gasp that was absorbed into the small sounds of the night, gave up the lie. He was kissing her with a fervour he had never known in himself, an intensity of joy he had never thought possible.

'Let's go in, out of the cold,' he said, and led her, still holding her close to his side, into the house.

CHAPTER SIXTY-ONE

In the early hours of the morning, as soon as the curfew was lifted, Austin Tong rushed in panic to the cemetery where he saw his wife, pale as a ghost, her clothes and hair horribly dishevelled. She was running after her sick brother among the tombstones.

'Please –' she implored faintly in her distress, but the miserable man, wearing only his pyjama trousers, his arms and chest bearing horrible cuts and bruises, his face that of one completely insane, kept eluding her.

'For God's sake!' gasped Austin, and dashed towards her. She gave a little cry when she saw him, then clung to him crying. He took her to the safety of his car, then went to get her wild brother. His soul seethed with anger and hatred as he saw the man on his knees on the ground. He pulled him up roughly. 'I'm taking you straight to the hospital,' he said.

Inside the car, he looked at his pale, distraught wife, worried that she was going to be ill from the horror of her experience. 'Didn't you think to get help?' he asked. 'The Church of the Sacred Heart of Jesus is just down the hill. Father Martin would have helped.' But, unknown to Austin, the priest was on his knees, his face buried in his hands in bitterest shame, in front of the statue of Our Lady of Lourdes that his mother had given him. And if Austin had gone to his house a little later, he would have stared in horror at the shocking sight of Father Martin, bare to his waist, kneeling on the cold, hard floor and scourging his back with a small whip of vicious cords.

In the little room adjoining the bedroom where he had left his wife asleep, Austin Tong lay in bed and heaved in the agitation caused by the morning's events. There was not the slightest uncertainty about what he was going to do now. As soon as Mei Kwei's brother was discharged from hospital, he would make arrangements for him to take a job in another town and to have his mother go with him. The situation was becoming untenable. If the brother refused to budge, then he would leave Luping and take Mei Kwei with him – any place would be preferable to one that entailed proximity to her hateful family. He would wait for his wife to recover fully from her ordeal before breaking the news of his plan to her.

He could hear her stirring in her sleep in the room next door, and was about to get up and see what he could do to ease her distress when he saw her standing by the door. She was still looking pale, and in her eyes was an intensity he had never seen before.

'Mei Kwei!' he cried out and with an anguished little sob, she was with him on the bed.

His need for her was immense and swelled urgently. 'I will not hurt you. I will be gentle,' he said, his voice constricted into a hoarse whisper by the power of the passion sweeping over him and bearing him aloft on a wave of relief and joy. He took his bride, and, in heightening wonderment, saw, as he fell from her warm, soft body, the rich red trickle of her broken pristineness down her right thigh.

CHAPTER SIXTY-TWO

The passing of the months could be noted in any number of ways in Luping, but not by falling leaves or fading flowers or the availability of this or that fruit in the market-place, with the exception perhaps of the well-loved durian, which had its own calendar of growth and maturation so that its appearance in large gunny sacks or cane baskets in speeding lorries or trundling carts, sending whiffs of its powerful odour into the air and into eager nostrils, signalled the passing of another season.

For Ah Oon Soh, the measuring of time had no sentiment, only practical necessity, as she watched her daughter's growing pregnancy through each month and worried about its difficulty. For Mei Kwei had suffered right from the start from constant bouts of nausea, vomiting and faintness. Ah Oon Soh shuttled tirelessly between the invalid son at home – since his discharge from hospital, Big Older Brother had kept to his bed – and the pregnancy-racked daughter. Big with the coming child, she had become thin and pale, a wraith, her remarkable beauty reduced to a ghost-like insubstantiality that worried her husband.

There was nothing he would not do for her. He begged her mother to stay in his house to be with her as much as she could; the most nourishing bird's nest soup, ginseng and herbs that women knew about were to be procured for her, regardless of cost. He wanted, too, to bring a smile to her face, to distract her from her pain with gifts that were novel and whimsical enough to make her paleness light up and her eyes, large and listless, sparkle once more. Passing the Luping Club one evening, he saw a group of Englishwomen putting up a tree with pretty lights and ornaments, in preparation for the coming of Christmas, a foreign festival that would pass unnoticed and uncelebrated in the town. He drove immediately to Penang to look for such a tree and came home, full of excitement, to put it up for his wife and watch the interest and delight on her face. For a while, she seemed as happy as a child, draping the decorations on the tree and getting Tee Tee to help her. 'Come,' he said, gently drawing her away for a moment to drink the bird's nest soup or herbal brew that her mother had prepared for her, and watching to see she finished every drop.

'If my son-in-law has caused me any pain, I forgive him completely, for the love he bears my daughter,' Ah Oon Soh told her friends. She was also charged with the responsibility of procuring the best midwife, who lived in another town and who was to be ready for attendance as soon as she was called.

Each time Austin looked at Mei Kwei's growing belly, he experienced a little tremor of pure joy: therein, his seed had stirred into life and was being nurtured for triumphant entry into the world and the completion of his joy. He saw his wife sitting by the window one evening crying quietly, and went to her immediately, holding her in his arms and letting her rest her wet face on his shoulder. Later he went to his mother-in-law and gravely forbade her to bring any news of her ailing son into his house, even if Mei Kwei asked. She was to be cocooned against any upset, and if his money could prevent every spell of nausea or bout of vomiting, he would consider it put to the best use.

One morning, Ah Oon Soh went to Austin and wept: Big Older Brother was dying and would not last the week.

'He's asked to see his sister,' she whimpered.

But Austin was adamant. The child would be born very soon and he could not allow any risk. Mei Kwei was not to be told of her brother's death until she was well enough to deal with it.

It came well after the predicted week. Ah Oon Soh went to his room one morning and found him stiff and cold on his bed; he must have died in the night. The end that he had threatened to bring upon himself, with much drama and violence of hanging rope, sharp knives and kitchen detergents, had been peaceful enough.

'I have no tears left. I have done too much crying,' Ah Oon Soh would later tell her friends, as she went about, dry-eyed, getting his body ready for burial.

It was Tee Tee who told Mei Kwei. Once he had overcome his shyness about going to the big, important-looking house, he visited her regularly and went away with pocketfuls of coins and good things to eat. Austin was furious; he wanted to have the boy brought to him to be shaken and punished and forbidden to enter the house again. But his anger subsided when he saw the calm reaction of his wife. She sat quietly, saying nothing, although he found her later, looking at a photograph she had brought with her from her old home, showing a small grinning boy with an arm around his laughing baby sister seated in a cane chair.

'My dear, what are you doing?' he asked anxiously the next evening, when he found her on the kitchen floor, setting fire to the photograph as well as to a large white cotton handkerchief. She said nothing, but, despite the hugeness of her belly, continued to squat on the floor, watching the small flames consume first the photograph, then the handkerchief, and then staring, for a long time, at the small pile of ashes.

Austin was truly worried and feared for her mind. Some women, he had heard, sailed smoothly through a pregnancy; others suffered fearful mental and physical upheavals. His only consolation was that in a short while, a very short while now, all his troubles would be over. He pictured his baby son in christening white at the baptismal font, and his wife, also in white, about to receive the consecrating, healing waters of the Church as well. He thought he might persuade Father François Martin, who had returned from long leave in France and was staying briefly with the new parish priest, to extend his stay to conduct the baptism ceremony. 'You married us. It is appropriate that you baptise our first child,' he would say.

He found Mei Kwei, sitting by the window as she seemed to want to do, the Christmas tree in a corner of the room. Turning her face tenderly towards his, he told her his good news. 'Father Martin has come back from leave. He will be leaving soon for a new posting in Kuala Tiga. But he may just be in time to baptise our baby.'

That evening Mei Kwei went into labour.

CHAPTER SIXTY-THREE

Seldom speaking to each other at the best of times, Austin Tong and his mother-in-law were too preoccupied by the anxiety of the waiting to notice each other's presence. Ah Oon Soh sat on a chair, her hands folded on her lap, her eyes fixed on the floor, ready to spring into helpful action as soon as the midwife summoned her.

Austin Tong went into his bedroom and said the entire rosary on his knees. He had given money to Father Thomas, the new priest of the Church of the Sacred Heart of Jesus for a Mass to be said for the safety of mother and child; he would give much more, of course, for thanksgiving Masses after the delivery.

He lay quietly on his bed, thinking of his son – he was sure his first child would be male – and found himself spinning fond plans for his child's future. For he had kept alive, for his own private gratification, the dream that his son would be the first man from the humble town of Luping to win a national scholarship to a British university, alongside other bright young men from the bigger, better-known towns of Penang, Ipoh and Kuala Lumpur.

He lay on his bed, expecting at any moment a knock on his door from his mother-in-law to summon him to his wife's bedside to have a first look at his son.

Ah Oon Soh was also waiting to be summoned. She continued to sit silently in the chair outside the room and felt a drowsiness in her eyes and limbs so that it was necessary for the midwife to repeat, in a voice of heightened urgency, 'Ah Oon Soh, come.' The midwife looked frightened; her fear communicated itself in an instant and Ah Oon Soh, scrambling up, almost knocked over the chair. Her first thought was for her daughter, not for the child. 'Please God, don't let my daughter die.' The prayer, for efficacy, could have been multiplied three times over, to beseech her temple gods, the Christian God strung on a cross on the wall and the colourful, elephant-faced god in the Indian shrine.

Her daughter lay exhausted on the pillow, alive and well, and Ah Oon Soh would have rushed to her to wipe the perspiration from her brow and clear it of the strands of wet hair sticking to it, were it not that the midwife's frightened look directed her to the newborn baby, who was lying on a towel blood-splattered from the throes of birth, its tiny limbs waving about feebly. Ah Oon Soh stared at the baby and understood the cause of the midwife's shock. She stared again at its tiny white body, the soft golden down on its head, the small face puckered in a silent scream.

Ah Oon Soh felt weak and thought, once again, My children will be the death of me. Now, looking at her daughter, lying very still on the bed with her eyes closed, her hair in long dank streaks on her face, she could only stifle a sob and shake her head.

On the bed, her daughter stirred and opened her eyes. 'Let me hold the child,' she whispered. 'Call his father.'

Austin came hurrying in, his exuberance immediately checked by the tautness on the faces of both his mother-in-law and the midwife. He looked quickly at his wife, sensing tragedy, then turned to the child who was now laid on a towel by her side. In one brief moment, a multitude of thoughts sped through his mind, together with a rush of feelings. Mutilation, deformity, death. At the least, a girl. He could countenance a girl and not show too much disappointment. But, as he stared at the baby, he was aware of a strange numbness, as if all thoughts and feelings were being temporarily frozen to allow sufficient concentration on the skin, almost pure white, and the soft golden fluff on the tiny head. His strange numbness thawed to allow yet stranger thoughts: he observed that the child's long umbilical cord seemed out of proportion to its tiny body; and that his wife's hair was a mess and needed cutting.

Then Austin Tong picked up a chair and sent it crashing to the floor, swept flasks off a table, broke a lamp. As the three women watched in silent horror, he ran to a wall and banged on it with both fists. He never once looked at Mei Kwei, as if one glance would be sufficient to unleash yet more violence and force his strong hands to reach for her slender neck.

For a long time afterwards, the glint of the jade bangle on her arm casually resting on the pillow above her head returned to madden him.

He rushed out of the room.

It would be some time before his rage could settle into its separate strands; right now, it was a towering maelstrom which expressed itself in a senselessness of physical activity, such as running up and down the stairs, kicking furniture, breaking photographs in their glass frames, banging his fists and head on the wall. Nobody would have recognised the man who, only the day before – only hours before – had borne all the marks of domestic contentment and peace. His world had been turned upside down; his appearance, in fitting accommodation, was going through a total transformation so that his mother-in-law, approaching him timidly with a cup of hot water, was forced to look upon the savage brow, the ferocious eyes smouldering with the rage of betrayal, the vehement mouth pressed into the hardest, bitterest lines, and quailed. Physical exhaustion came at last, and he went into his room to fall heavily upon his bed. The veins in his temples and neck throbbed fearfully, but he was now able to view things with cool clarity. He was ready to do some thinking on the matter.

The centrepiece of the deliberations revolved around the betrayal by his wife and the priest, established beyond doubt. The evidence piled up as soon as he began to consider certain incidents, at the time puzzling, now so clear he wondered how he could have ever missed their significance. He thought of the strange scene he had come upon in the kitchen recently, when he had found Mei Kwei burning a man's white handkerchief. He ransacked his memory and thought of the visit with the gift of food to the priest, from which she had returned, he now remembered vividly, with a glow on her face she had never shown in his presence.

Oh, God, oh, God – Austin Tong felt a growing knot of pain somewhere deep inside his stomach, which contorted his face and twisted his limbs. He was losing his ability to think clearly and, wishing to concentrate his mind, he began to dwell on the injury to himself, feeling keenly its separate strands, like the lashes of a whip. Anger, self-pity, shame, hatred, despair – each, taking its turn to administer a lashing upon raw flesh, would have been sufficient for lifelong pain. Combined, they flung him into the depths of an abyss. All his achievements – his education, his prosperity, his marriage, his good standing in the town – were but a mockery, a dust-heap, and since these had always been attributed to a loving and caring divine Providence, Austin felt, for the first time, revulsion against the senseless cruelty of a God that only pretended to love and care. A false God, who was served by dastardly priests who guided your soul but corrupted your wife's body. How many more women would that French priest defile in his peregrinations through the country, packing up and leaving one town for another as soon as he was about to be exposed?

His wife stood the most condemned because no man had loved woman more, and no woman had reciprocated less. He had given her everything and she had flung it back, laughing, in his teeth. She had systematically deceived him, and all the while that she had submitted to him, she had been giving her body to the priest. He remembered, with a convulsion of rage, her postponement of conjugal duty. The reason was clear: she had meant the priest to have the first gift of her body. The actual settings of time and place of their guilty liaisons – the church? his house? her own? the Kek Lok Temple? the cemetery? the night of the curfew? – would be deliberated over in a calmer time. Right now, the screaming fact of their treachery demanded immediate action.

He ran back to the bedroom and saw his wife lying on the bed, staring at the ceiling. The midwife was carrying the baby, wrapped in a white towel. His mother-in-law was nowhere to be seen.

'You whore,' he hissed at last. 'How long has this been going on?' Mei Kwei said nothing.

'You whore,' he repeated. He moved towards her and raised his hand, which checked itself, tremblingly, a mere inch from her face.

CHAPTER SIXTY-FOUR

Father Martin was putting the final touches to a very lovely crib in the front part of the Church of the Sacred Heart of Jesus. Above him hung a banner proclaiming peace on earth, goodwill to men, in the Christmas colours of green and red, and another banner in white and blue, colours favoured by the Virgin Mother, proclaiming in gold letters, 'A child is born.' On this, possibly his last visit to his old parish, he would put his heart and soul into making the most beautiful crib to present to the little children on Christmas morning when they came to church in their festive best. He could see already the delight on their faces as they stared at the Baby Jesus in a pile of green grass (he would explain the difficulty of finding hay in Malaya), or at the three tiny cardboard boxes painted gold, placed beside the manger (he would describe the three gifts of the Magi and explain what each signified). If asked about the distinctly oriental features of the Christ Child (one of the parishioners had, at the last minute, contributed a Chinese porcelain doll that had belonged to her grandmother), he would explain that God, who made all men on earth in His image, could be just as validly represented by a black, yellow or brown baby.

Suddenly Father Martin felt happy. He had spent a good leave in France and was pleased to be back in Malaya; he was pleased, too, about his new posting to another town a hundred miles away. The restorative power of the few months in France when Léonie, sensing his trouble, had tiptoed round him with loving delicacy and understood his need to go into extended retreat in a monastery, had been precisely what his spirit had needed. God, in His mercy and goodness, sent ministering angels in human form to heal and restore. His healing continued in the monastery high in the mountains; from its pure air, he descended to the simple work of assisting old Father Trincant in his parish while waiting for the Bishop's decision for his new posting in Malaya. Everybody treated him with kindness and generosity, giving him a calmness of spirit he had not experienced in a long time.

One part of his life in the foreign mission had ended; another was beginning. He thought of Mei Kwei. He had experienced tremendous relief when, in his first few days back in Luping, he had not been forced into a face-to-face encounter with her. At some future time –

who could tell? – they might meet again and talk with the dispassion of two people who had gone through a terrible crisis together. He longed to tell her some day, if not now, 'We are friends. Don't you see we are the dearest of friends because we have loved and suffered much?' But the present still bore dangerous remnants of love's restiveness, and it was perhaps best that they should not see each other again for a long, long while.

He heard the sound of someone coming into the church and, in the dimness, discerned the outline of a man carrying something. The visitor walked rapidly and was now near enough to be recognised. Under normal circumstances, Father Martin would have stood up and said heartily, 'Good evening, Austin. How's everything?' except that the circumstances seemed far from normal, for the man had a savage intensity on his face and carried a bundle that whimpered and kicked in his arms.

'For God's sake!' exclaimed the priest, as the bundle was thrust roughly at him and he looked down to see the face of a tiny, newborn baby.

'Take back your bastard!' roared Austin, and struck the priest on the chest with his fist. The priest stumbled backwards, keeping his hold on the child, who was beginning to wail. 'Your bastard, I say!' thundered Austin. He continued to hit the priest. Father Martin fell to the ground; with one arm he tried to fend off the blows raining upon him, while, with the other, he kept the child safe, pressed to his side. Austin struck again and again in the extremity of his roaring pain.

'Wait!' cried the priest desperately. 'For God's sake, Austin, I can explain – it isn't true – there was nothing –' But his offer of explanation only had the effect of increasing the fury of his attacker who began to kick him too.

'No!' screamed the priest, as he saw Austin snatch up a large log from the Christmas tableau.

'No!' he screamed again, as he saw the log raised aloft, trailing a piece of red and green Christmas tinsel, then felt its rushing descent. In the crushing pain, he found himself, thinking, with curious calm, The child's safe, and again, What a pity, it's broken, for his last glimpse was of the Chinese porcelain Christ Child, which had fallen off its crib and split into two.

*

In later years, nobody could tell exactly what had happened, but what swept through the town in the next few days, with the awed certainty of a terrible truth, was the news that the foreign priest was seriously injured, the husband apprehended by the police, and the wife run away to nobody knew where. Some said the baby was dead, some that it was still alive but spirited away to an unknown place because of the shame. More shocking than the exposure by Tua Poon of his adulterous wife in the market-place, more shocking than the assassination of the chief of operations, which had begun to spawn its own rumours, the tumultuous event was matter for awed discussion and gossip in the coffee-shops, market-place and private homes in Luping for months to come. The news even crept into the dark, solitary room where the ghost half-brother of Austin Tong and his frail, embittered mother lived. The woman raised her pinched face and jabbed the air with a triumphant forefinger, hissing, 'The shame is his, not hers! Bad seed!' The news spread to Penang where Old Yoong, in the midst of a mah-jong game, let out a loud bark of gratification; in the privacy of his thoughts, however, he still felt the twinges of pain deep inside for the strange, rare, beautiful girl he had once courted and lost.

In the midst of the tumult, Ah Oon Soh, who had said she had no tears left, wept for the last time, quietly, calmly let down her hair which fell in long strands over her back, changed into a dress of deep mourning and walked up the hill to the cemetery where her mother, husband and son lay buried. Their graves were in separate parts of the cemetery, but by standing somewhere in its centre and raising her voice, Ah Oon Soh made sure they could hear her. Proudly erect, her loosed hair floating stiffly about in the wind, she shouted, for their hearing and for that of the entire population of spirits carried upon the wind that swept the wild hillside, 'From today, she is dead, she belongs to you. Do with her as you like.'

Then Ah Oon Soh walked down the hill and went home.

The child Tee Tee, understanding only that Mei Kwei had gone away and would never come back, refused to leave the house until he was pushed away by the servant who locked the gate after him. He stood outside it for some time in great bewilderment, then sat down on the ground and sobbed as if his heart would break.

PART FIVE

第五章

CHAPTER SIXTY-FIVE

In 1958, Luping and the surrounding district were officially declared a 'white area', almost the last in a whole swath of white areas where victory over the Communists was proclaimed. Along with the curfew, the rationing and the barbed-wire fences, a great miasma of fear and anxiety was lifted from its people. The memory of the exhibition of terrorist bodies in the market-place receded and became as much a part of their anguished past as the frantic rush by housewives to stock up with rice, oil and sugar.

But a year after Independence, when the Union Jack was lowered and the Malayan flag raised with much emotion, civil unrest continued. In Luping, Communists still held out in their jungle hideouts; and a surrendered terrorist and his wife, who had been earning a quiet living as food hawkers, were found with their throats slashed and their faces covered with a large piece of white cloth with 'traitor' painted across it in black ink. When the final victory came in 1960 and a magnificent parade in the capital announced a nation's joy, the inhabitants of Luping breathed a collective sigh of relief and went about their business quietly.

Yet, in a way, the tenor of their life had changed, as elements of a foreign culture were absorbed that would change it for ever. A younger generation was beginning to speak English with aplomb and had names like Jacky or Johnny, Rosie or Alice that tripped the tongues of their parents and grandparents. Young people used words derived from the English language, in particular from imported popular movies and songs from the United States and Great Britain, and turned on the radio to sing along with Doris Day and Guy Mitchell. They chanted the dialectal songs and rhymes of childhood only for the purpose of making fun of them.

'I lub you! I lub you belly much!' They mocked the inability of their Chinese-educated counterparts to pronounce unfamiliar consonant sounds.

Father François Martin noticed that, whereas when he had first come to Luping, his blue eyes and bushy beard had been stared at, now, on his return visit five years later, his appearance no longer provoked much attention. Nobody appeared to recognise him as he walked in the market-place. Perhaps, with his additional weight and newly greying beard – he was vain enough to regret the loss of the chestnut brown colour of the hair that still grew on his head – and in a short-sleeved cotton shirt and grey trousers rather than the familiar long white or black robe of the *si fu*, he should not expect to be acknowledged. He did not mind. He was enjoying his new status as a visitor as he moved freely among the people, observing changes as well as things that would never change.

He remembered seeing anxious, timid or suspicious looks when he first arrived in 1953. Now he noted a much more relaxed air: eyes appeared less shifty, voices louder, steps lighter. But it was probably his imagination that traced, in the features of a young man sitting on a stool by a coffee-stall, those of the little boy he remembered so well who had demanded to be lifted by him in the children's playground. He saw an elderly woman with a shopping bag on her arm turn back to have another look at him. He would have been glad to talk to her if she had not turned away again. A beggarwoman, dirty and smelly, came up to him and he gave her a coin; he thought that the existence of female vagrants must be a constant feature of the town's life, through war and peace.

Through a mist of startled tears, he saw the Church of the Sacred Heart of Jesus, derelict, silent, gloomy, amid a tangle of weeds and burnt creepers, and heard a swoosh of wind from the Chinese cemetery behind. Its dereliction marked progress, not decay, for a new building, bearing the same name but immeasurably removed from the old sparseness and deficiencies of its brick and steel surrounds, stained-glass windows and pews of solid wood, was to be found in a part of the town, which was more accessible to the growing Catholic population. Father Thomas had written to tell him, proudly and enthusiastically, of the new church, ending, as always, with the kind acknowledgement of his predecessor's invaluable contribution. 'Without your enthusiasm, hard work and unflagging energy, it would not have been possible.'

It was characteristic of Father Thomas's generosity to exaggerate his puny efforts, Father Martin thought. 'We pray for you to be in good health and spirits,' the letter had continued. There was, of course, no reference to his injuries, nor to the scandal that had rocked the town.

Father Martin walked among the ruins allowing his memory to run as freely as the tears down his cheeks. It was in this church – on the very spot where he was now standing – that he had blessed the young couple and linked them irrevocably in marriage; in this church too, in the secrecy of the confessional – a blackened enclosure was all that was left – that he had seen her great grief. He walked on and stopped in the area where his living quarters had been. An image of his bed, desk, couch, table and kitchen sink superimposed itself upon dreary remnants covered by weeds. Then he noticed something lying in the grass, sunk into the soil and discoloured by years of exposure to rain, heat and dust. He stooped to pick up a small remnant of a rosary, comprising just three beads that must once have been bright blue and translucent. Cleaning it with his handkerchief, he thought he would take it away for remembrance.

Places, had greater power to elicit tears than people; the two women he visited, one after the other, made him laugh and lifted his spirits immeasurably. His cleaning woman, who was still living in the tiny rented cubicle with her alert and cantankerous mother, was so happy to see him that for the first few minutes she was speechless. Then she began to talk unstoppably in a swift stream of dialect and broken English during which her old mother sat nodding and smiling toothlessly. She plied him with a wondrous amount of food and drink before settling down to tell him of her present situation and to ask him about his. She was now diabetic and incapable of working, but could support herself and her mother on the small savings she had. She resolutely refused the small cash gift he had for her, pushing it back with both hands, then clasping his with a warmth that delighted him and brought back his feelings for the simple, loyal woman who would have served him to the end.

There was not the slightest reference to the event that had so deeply upset her and her mother that they had spent two days crying about it and lamenting the injustice to the *si fu*. Now the *si fu* was among them again; he looked well and happy, and the past mattered not. The good woman reached to clasp his hands again. 'Do you remember ...?' She mentioned the roast pork noodles woman in the market-place.

Good God, thought Father Martin. How could I ... He had forgotten her and now, ashamed of his remissness, declared he would like to speak to her again.

The roast pork noodles woman almost dropped a bowl of hot soup when she saw him, standing in the sun outside the shaded area of her stall, smiling at her. 'Wa-ah, our *si fu!*' she cried, with great delight. 'Sit down, sit down!' And she promptly set about making him the largest, tastiest bowl of noodles.

'I have already eaten,' Father Martin protested, laughing, but she ignored his protests and, instructing her young assistant to see to her other customers, liberally heaped noodles and roast pork into his bowl until he pleaded with her to stop. They talked freely but, like the cleaning woman, she assiduously avoided any mention of the event in the church.

'He is well, he is happy, the past is the past, and who are we to say what was right and what was wrong,' the two women agreed when they next met. 'The *si fu* is a good man.' They felt proud that, when the ugly rumours were still flying about, they had stood by him, declaring stoutly, 'We believe no such thing. The *si fu* is a good man.'

CHAPTER SIXTY-SIX

'Sit down. Get Father Martin a beer. Or would you prefer something else?'

The something else could have been the most expensive wine or brandy in the world to match the sumptuousness of the house and its fixtures. It was probably the biggest and most luxuriously fitted house in Luping, Father Martin thought.

'Sit down. Make yourself comfortable.' Austin Tong apologised for the inadequacy of the large ceiling fan, then snapped his fingers for a maid, probably one of several in the house, to go and get a supplement; she returned within minutes with a portable fan, which she set up near him. 'Are you cool enough, Father? The heat these days is unbearable.'

Father Martin thanked him effusively. The exaggerated courtesies on both sides continued to hide the initial awkwardness. As the host, Austin was able to handle his better, resorting to a stream of instructions to maids to do this or that for the comfort of his guest, who felt overwhelmed by the generosity of one whom he had half expected to slam the door in his face.

During his years in France, Father Martin had sometimes thought bitterly, He could at least have written a letter to apologise for his wrongdoing. Surely he knew about my injuries. For a while, the doctors had feared that his hearing and the sight in one eye were permanently damaged, for Austin's attack had been concentrated on his head. Thankfully, he had rallied and recovered.

Saved by the fervent prayers of Léonie, who lit a candle for him every day in church, Father Martin's thoughts soon turned to forgiveness. He pictured Austin writhing under the execration of bad seed, raising his angry fist first to heaven against a God who was so unfairly punishing him and then lowering it to the earth to where his hated father lay, rightful object of the punishment. Not the foreign priest's child, after all, whispered the rumours, but a ghost-child, belonging more to the world of the dead than to the living for it cannot bear sunlight and must be in shadow all the time.

'Why have you come?' Sitting opposite the priest, Austin Tong bristled with aggressive confidence. His face flushed, his eyes shining with a hard brilliance, he began to tell his story.

I have never seen so much anger dressed up as pride, Father Martin thought. I do not like this man.

The basis of Austin Tong's awesome pride went beyond his worldly wealth, apparent in his splendid house, the two large, gleaming cars that could be seen in the driveway, and the very expensive watch gleaming on his wrist. It was grounded in a grand new philosophy that he had built upon the ruins of the old. To his immense gratification, he had discovered it to be precisely the right one for dealing with a perverse God who had treated him so ill, first leading him on with sweet promises then turning the sweetness into the bitterest gall for him to swallow. For, as if not satisfied with sending him one accursed ghost-child, God had struck again and sent him another. A year after he remarried, his wife gave birth to a son with the same bleached skin, hair, eyes. 'Bad seed,' God had taunted. 'Your father, you and your sons after you are cursed with bad seed.'

'How do you think I felt,' Austin cried vehemently, 'when I was cursed a second time, before I had recovered from the first? But still I said nothing. I only said, "You are my God. I have chosen you. I have to live with you."'

It would have been no use telling him that the little boy, pale white and pink, blinking painfully even in the mild light of the room, who now came and stood shyly before the visitor, was no curse. His smaller sister, robust and with an abundance of dark hair, also appeared and stood beside him, holding his hand. As he smiled at the little pale boy who smiled back, Father Martin thought that his birth, unattended by the terrible rage which had ripped his brother from the birth-bed and flung him upon the cold floor of a church, made him much the luckier of the two.

The priest stretched out his hand to the child who was overcome by shyness. He ran to his father, who took him in his arms and put him on his knees. The little girl toddled up, too, to claim her place and, while it was clear that fatherly tenderness would always be expended on the poor little son, fatherly pride was reserved for the daughter, whose keen dark eyes showed an alertness beyond her years.

A woman came in and led them away quietly.

'My wife,' said Austin Tong and the woman smiled briefly and murmured a word of greeting.

Then Father Martin became aware of another presence in the room. Involuntarily, he looked to Austin for the explanation of a pale, ghost-like man with thin wisps of white hair on his head, sitting down, looking at them and smiling with gentle wistfulness.

'My half-brother,' said Austin. After his second marriage, he had offered a home to his sickly half-brother as soon as he heard that the mother had died. Perhaps it was a last desperate act to nudge a hard God into looking upon him with favour once more, for he had braved the bitter censure of his new wife and her family, who told him that his responsibility for his half-brother ended with sums of money sent regularly. But, instead, God had cursed him again.

Father Martin stared at the apparition as once Austin had. The years had bleached whatever remaining colour there had been in skin, eyes and lips, giving him a spectral appearance. But the man's gentle smile was from a loving heart.

'I thought, That's it,' cried Austin with spirit. He had gone on a rampage of repudiation. The Christian icons had come down, and the spaces on the walls and altar-tables had remained empty ever since. His new religion was a religion of the heart – here he struck his chest dramatically: he would spend the rest of his life being good to the poor and oppressed. His various businesses had prospered marvellously, attesting to the soundness of his new stance. Having lost his position as a favourite of God, he had quickly become a favourite of men. He donated to the Kek Lok Temple liberally, more to feed the beggars than to beautify the building, and he had recently given a large sum to a committee of villagers who were trying to raise money for a new bridge over a stream, to replace an old, dangerously creaking one.

'They want me to officiate at the opening ceremony,' he told Father Martin, with a smile. 'They say that if they wait for government money, they will have to wait for ever or one of their children will drown first.' There would be bells and joss-sticks. The last time he had held a joss-stick must have been at least twenty years before. But he would do it to make them happy. Hindus, Buddhists, Muslims, Christians – all were welcome to his largesse. Rather than hitch his fortunes to one God, he now spread them comfortably over several. It was the never-failing strategy of multiple allegiance.

'Come again,' said Austin, who had not stopped talking throughout the duration of the visit. He looked at Father Martin as they shook hands. 'I know what you want to ask. But I can't help you. I don't know where she's gone. She took the child with her. It died. Or was given away for adoption.'

Father Martin took Ah Oon Soh's trembling hands in his. She pulled them away, less from rancour than from the embarrassed confusion into which his visit had thrown her. No, she did not know where her daughter was. No, she had no idea what had happened to her baby. She wept, clutching a handkerchief with both hands as he had once seen her do. Then she fell silent, and Father Martin was suddenly aware of the quietness of a house that had once teemed with noisy men and women, eating, spitting, playing mah-jong.

'Why don't you ask her husband?' she said peevishly. But it would have been no use telling her that he had just been to see Austin. He had left a man who had risen from the wreck of his suffering to shake a defiant fist at God; the woman sitting before him now could only blame herself.

'I am all alone,' she whimpered, and directed his eyes to two framed photographs – one of her husband, the other of her son – side by side on a table, propped against the wall and swathed in the deep melancholy of weak joss smoke and the faint odour of stale oranges, tea and flowers.

'Has Mei Kwei not come back at least once since?' Father Martin asked.

Ah Oon Soh said briefly, 'She has not come back, but she sends money. She sends money regularly.' In the stealth of one evening, Mei Kwei had, in fact, visited her mother. She had lit joss-sticks before the framed photographs, cleaned the table of old ash and flower petals, set up new, fresh offerings, and then gone away again.

Looking at her visitor, Ah Oon Soh was aware of a creeping resentment in herself. Convinced that the foreign priest was the ultimate cause of the family tragedy for the simple reason that all had been well before his arrival, she informed him that she had to go somewhere, so would he please leave?

Father Martin decided that he would consider his next action not as bribery but as charity. As Ah Oon Soh stood up, wiping the remnants of tears with her handkerchief, the priest offered her money.

CHAPTER SIXTY-SEVEN

He could have stayed at the parish house with Father Aloysius Chin, the only priest he knew in Singapore, but the special circumstances of his visit would warrant some explanation. So he checked into an hotel, an unusual choice for a priest, considering its general seedy character. One of the women there, heavily made-up and wearing a short, tight, satin dress had sidled up to him and been politely turned away. 'No money. No money, see?' he had said amiably, turning out empty trouser pockets.

'Hello,' said a small child's voice in response to his, amid a loud crackling sound on the telephone.

'Hello,' said Father Martin. 'May I speak to your mother?' There followed the frustrating incoherence that all adults must tolerate when a small child picks up the phone and insists on attempting a conversation.

'Hello, who are you? What do you want?' Another child, probably an older or brighter sibling, sounded more confident and assertive.

'I want to speak to Mei Kwei,' said Father Martin. 'Does Mei Kwei live here?'

'He means Mummy,' said the little girl excitedly to the other child, forgetting to cover the mouthpiece with her hand. 'Just hold on. I'll get her.'

'Tell her it's her friend Father Martin.'

The child came back to say her mother was not at home.

'Tell her it's very important. Please ask her to come to the phone.'

But the child came back once more to say that her mother was not in. Then she put down the phone.

There was only one telephone on the hotel reception desk and, for the next hour, Father Martin stood doggedly by it, trying desperately to get through, each time hearing the interminable ringing or the little girl's exasperated response, 'I told you, she's not at home!'

The house was modest but comfortable, a single-storeyed bungalow with a large garden in which stood a swing and near it a child's tricycle, fallen on its side. The gate was locked, as was the front door, but he hoped to catch a glimpse of her through an open window. He stood under a tree across from the house and watched. He had expected to see the children in the garden or hear the sounds of play from inside the house, but it was eerily silent. At one point he thought he saw a movement of a curtain, as if someone was peeping out at him. The discomfort of being watched in his turn by a neighbour and a passer-by, both of whom threw quick, suspicious glances at him, cut short the waiting. Frustrated, he went back to his hotel and once more made a call. This time, she picked up the phone.

'This is François. I need to see you. Please don't put down the phone, it's very urgent,' he said in a rush.

The voice was distant and detached. 'I have no wish to see you. Please don't call again.' He heard the click of closure.

He decided to go to the house again. From the less conspicuous position of a bus stop a short distance away and with some convenient intervening foliage, he saw a black car drive up and stop in front of the house. The impatient sound of the horn brought out an elderly woman, clearly a servant, who hurried to open the gate. The car rolled in and a man got out. From where he was, Father Martin saw that he was an elderly, stout Chinese man with dark skin and greying hair. A little girl – probably the same one who had spoken to him on the phone – ran out excitedly and skipped around the man as he walked into the house.

The next morning the car was no longer in the driveway and Father Martin rattled the iron gate in the hope of bringing her outside. Instead, the little girl appeared. She closed the door slowly behind her, as if carefully following instructions, and walked up to the priest with a gravity of expression that must have been difficult to impose upon features bright and vibrant as sparkling water.

'My mother says she will not see you,' she said. 'Please go away.' She lingered, looking at him wonderingly, and it was in her own capacity as curious observer that she asked, in her clear, little girl's voice, 'Why do you want to see my mother?'

Her curiosity gave him hope. 'Wait,' he said, and took out a notebook from his pocket, tore out a page and began to scribble on it, while she watched with great interest. He folded it. 'Here, take this to your mother.'

Thinking of a lovely face, radiant with laughter as it looked down upon him and the laughing children from the height of his outstretched arms, he added, 'What a very pretty girl you are. What's your name?' and wondered with a pang about her relationship to the stout, elderly man in the black car.

'Maria! My name's Maria!' shrieked the child. Pleased by the reference to her prettiness, she said, with the coyness of which even tiny budding beauties are capable, 'I've got a dimple. See? Just like my mother. I will marry Boy Boy when I grow up,'

His note said: *I am on my way to Vietnam. I have only three days left in Singapore. Please let me see you for the last time.*

He waited five minutes and the door opened again. It was Maria, subdued and unsmiling in the disconsolateness of a failed mission.

He turned to go, his heart seething with disappointment and anger. She could at least have agreed to see him. He was half-way down the lane when he heard footsteps behind him and turned to see Maria come running up and panting.

'Tomorrow, two o'clock. My mother says not to be late. And you must go away by four o'clock.'

CHAPTER SIXTY-EIGHT

S he said, 'Please sit down,' and waved him to a seat.
They faced each other with a tense awkwardness. He tugged at his beard and she made elaborate adjustments to a bracelet, which allowed her to keep her eyes lowered.

'Please sit down.' Mei Kwei's voice broke the silence again.

They sat on opposite seats, each carrying the burden of unasked questions and unspoken answers. Father Martin's self-consciousness made him perch precariously on the edge of his chair, and lean forward with his long arms dangling between his knees; hers took on a patina of defiance and allowed her to sit back comfortably – her arms laid carelessly on the arm-rests – and to cross her legs.

I've never seen her sit like this before, he thought.

They looked at each other silently across the heads of a dozen plastic lilies in an ornate blue vase. The flowers, the low glass table with a thoughtful ash-tray at each end, the carpet lately cleared of children's toys with the exception of a small rubber snake curled round a table leg, the cushions on the main sofa hurriedly shaken, plumped and set in a neat row for the visitor's benefit, the cups of tea brought in by the servant – all these combined to regulate the wild thumping of their hearts into the steady, measured rhythms of everyday discourse.

She smiled at him above the rim of her tea-cup. 'You have put on some weight.' He patted his belly with a laugh and said, 'People spoil me with food all the time. I must learn to say no,' and was immediately aware of the intrusion of a dear image: a four-tiered tiffin-carrier dismantled to display its rich offering, a laughing face and voice.

She said, 'Your beard's going grey,' and he replied, 'In our family, the men turn grey very quickly. First the beard, then the hair, and last the eyebrows. Always in that order.'

After a pause, he said, 'You look very well.' In fact, he had experienced a shock upon first seeing her, which he had not entirely got over. It was the shock of witnessing the total transformation of one kind of beauty into another. Of the quiet gentleness of face and manner, the austerity of hair swept back from the smooth young brow, the natural subdued colouring of cheeks and lips, he saw not a trace. She appeared before him in the brilliance of a new, defiant beauty: the kind, he thought with a frisson of tiny bumps all over his skin, that belonged to the world of pleasure – of clubs, cabarets or gambling halls.

He remembered once having heard of her resemblance to the stunning actress Pai Kuan. She was Pai Kuan now. She was the small, gentle, snow-white creature in the fairy-tale that had fatally crawled into Lamia's gaudy, iridescent snake-skin. He took in every detail of her transformation – her hair in its profligacy of tumbling curls, her eyes like a doll's, teased into a seductive brightness by pencil and mascara, her lips red and hard, her dress, of some soft, thin material which in Luping she would not have been caught dead in. There was a studied air of coquetry about her, which was linked to her large ear-rings and the jingling gold bracelets on her right wrist, at odds with the stark purity of the translucent jade bangle on the left.

But Mei Kwei's new beauty did not repel him; on the contrary, it had an intriguing quality because he sensed that it was worn over the real thing. It was a serviceable mask, something she would discard at the first opportunity. The priest had a fleeting picture of her huge assemblage of soft dresses, ornate jewellery, perfumes, rouge, paint and powder put to use for the delectation of a vain old man who liked to show off his mistress to friends and business associates. Home from a party or on her own, she probably cast off the clothes and trinkets and washed off the paint. He was convinced that she was in full regalia for his benefit and, with perverse relish, was enjoying his shock. The small bitter smile playing around her mouth said, 'You see I look different. That is because I tell different stories now.'

They both wanted to keep the meeting – so long thought about, so much despaired of – on an even keel. How long have you been – When did you – Where – These were safe questions.

Why have you come back after all these years? Why did you change your mind about seeing me just when I almost gave up hope? 'Why' was deadly. 'Why' had to wait.

He had been sent back to France to recuperate after the 'incident' – he used the word throughout. He was later given a position as assistant to the director of a seminary, doing a mixture of adminis-trative and counselling work in which he found some measure of relief from his – He swallowed the word 'pain' just in time, as he had swallowed 'tragedy' and also her name. His sister Léonie and his friends had given generous, loving support, throughout this difficult time, for which he would never be able to repay them adequately.

'One day was like another,' he said. 'There were long stretches of time when I moved about numbly.' Then God had answered his prayers and his spirits improved. The call of the foreign missions came again, even more insistently than the first time. Malaya, Vietnam, China. It was always the Far East. His director had been most understanding.

'Now, you tell me what you have been doing with yourself all these years.' His jocularity was well intentioned but ill-advised, for it made her defensive and she looked up sharply. But Father Martin's goodwill shone through his every feature, and when he coloured slightly and looked down in anguish at having caused her pain, she relaxed. She had never told her story to anyone, but now it came pouring out.

The priest's calm and measured voice had set the tone, but the story of her life in Singapore, even in its bare outlines, broke through the restraints and claimed its own language. Keeping her eyes fixed on her hands but occasionally glancing up to see his reaction, she told him of the time she had spent working in a cabaret. They had been hard years of learning to adjust to a new life and people. Father Martin's knowledge of the world of raucous pleasure, slight though it was and based mainly on what he remembered of the infamous *ronggeng* girls and dancing-halls in Luping, shaped a vivid picture of Mei Kwei, perfumed and painted, in one of her soft dresses, submitting to drunken embraces and turning away with revulsion from lust's fetid breath. His hands clenched as he suppressed an overwhelming urge to shout out his pain and anger.

'I had to work. There were the children to support,' Mei Kwei defended herself simply. 'See this?' She showed him the faint lines of a healed wound on her wrist. 'It happened one evening when I thought there was no point living any more. It was Maria's cry that saved me. Or perhaps it was Susie's.'

So she had wanted to die. In his darkest moments, Father Martin had never once thought of death; he had called to his God, struggling against the impenetrability of the soul's night, and He had taken pity on him and led him into the first faint glimmerings of dawn. She could call to no God.

'I think it was Maria. She came crying and tugged at my skirt. I let the razor fall from my hand into the kitchen sink.'

Upon hearing her name, Maria who had been standing in a corner, a forefinger deep in her mouth, rushed towards her mother and wedged herself between her knees.

'Where's Susie?' Mei Kwei asked, and like a small, energetic, uncontrollable animal, Maria ran to get her sister. She reappeared in a minute, dragging along a chubby little girl, who was in turn dragging along an enormous doll. At the sight of her mother, Susie abandoned the doll and made straight for her arms, which she used as a safe haven from which to taunt her older sister. Maria lunged at her and she screamed, shooting out a chubby little leg.

'Maria, leave Susie alone,' said Mei Kwei, pushing her away, then pulling her back to tie a sash that had come undone.

'Her name's Girl Girl,' said Maria. 'Papa calls her Girl Girl.'

Boy Boy. The priest wondered, with some amusement, at the strange parental habit of name-giving by which offspring were reminded, twice over, of their gender.

Crowded upon their mother's lap, the two little girls surveyed the priest with keen interest. As he smiled at them, he noticed, with a little start, their marked differences in skin colouring, shape of features, and texture and colour of hair, which pointed unmistakably to a sharing of only half their parentage. The younger girl's abundance of brownish hair and long curling eye-lashes would in Luping, have brought down opprobrium upon her mother's head. Father Martin imagined a shadowy succession of men rising from the beautiful body, bruised beyond its own description, and the quick exit when the dreaded words were whispered at last, 'I am pregnant.'

He screamed inwardly, 'Don't tell me any more! I can't bear it!'

In the solitariness of his retreat, high up in the mountain monastery, the bruising of his soul was nothing compared to this.

'Fortunately Old Yoong came back to me,' Mei Kwei continued. 'He has been very good to me and the children.' The goodness was evident in the surrounding comforts and, if it encompassed some measure of nobility in the rescue from squalor and the restoration to respectability, it was also present in the row of framed photographs on the wall.

In one of the photographs, which was in colour, Mei Kwei, with her hair piled up and decorated with a rose, was smiling radiantly and inclining affectionately towards the gentleman she called Old Yoong. 'He is kind to me,' she repeated.

Father Martin felt a rising bitterness that threatened to spill out in an angry flood and drown the lavish tributes. Kindness! The kindness would continue, no doubt, to put food on the table and clothes on the children, and might even include a promise to provide for their education if anything should happen. But the elderly gentleman he had seen in the black car was no fool and had probably exacted all he could in return. He had struck down Mei Kwei from her position of proud independence into one of abject grovelling at his feet.

'Old Yoong is honourable. He will keep his promise,' said Mei Kwei, as if she had read the priest's mind. 'You need not think he will abandon me and the children.' She could have told him, but chose not to, that she was depending more on an old man's obsession rather than his kindness for the future security of herself and her children. As soon as he left Penang for Singapore and found her, his love had expressed itself in a hundred concrete ways: he had pulled her and the children out of the squalor of their rented room and put them in an apartment. Later, he had bought, in her name, the house they were now living in, and provided her with ample money to buy furniture, the children's clothes, anything she needed. For his love for her, even after she had broken off their engagement, had remained strong. When the news of her tragedy reached him, he had first chortled and slapped his thigh in glee, exclaiming, 'The gods have eyes!' But, soon the old pain had begun to evolve into a new one, which was deeper, more intense, more unbearable. One evening, he simply announced to his three wives that he was going to Singapore to look for Mei Kwei. The grown-up sons and daughters were horrified, sensing the threat to the family fortune from an unscrupulous young woman who, according to rumours, was earning a living in the cabaret halls of Singapore. But the old man had been adamant. 'You shut your mouths,' he had roared, and then made preparations for his trip.

Father Martin felt his face flush and a rush of hot angry tears in his eyes. Maria ran over to him and presented, for his rectification, another small bow that had come untied, this time on her shoulder. He applied himself diligently to the task. If I hadn't suffered enough with her in the past, I am doing so now, he thought. When Susie, always alert to imitate her sister, came up too, he put his arms around them both and hid his tears in the abundance and softness of their hair. They began to quarrel and fight and he was glad of it as he restrained their fists and legs. His face was averted all the while from Mei Kwei.

She called loudly to the servant who appeared quickly and led away the children. The quiet that descended upon the room could have led to the final and long delayed discharge of the heart's burden but, strangely, both would have it further delayed. Instead, Mei Kwei told stories about Maria and Susie, light-hearted anecdotes of their naughtiness and delightful precocity. 'Maria's very like me,' she said. 'Her kindergarten teacher complains about her high-spiritedness and rebellious nature!' She didn't think to add, 'I hope her life will be happier than mine.'

'They're such beautiful children,' Father Martin replied, and would never have thought to ask, 'Who are their fathers?'

A tacit understanding had been reached: no questions, no raking up of the stories of the past. He had but two more days in Singapore, and these should not be frittered away on the past. Indeed, the past was the past and should not matter any more. They should rejoice in each other's present well-being: he was going on to head a mission in Vietnam, thereby achieving his boyhood dreams; she had found the peace and security that had eluded her for so long. The wheel had come full circle for both of them; why bother to talk about those times when they had almost been broken on its cruel racks?

Suddenly very happy, Mei Kwei said, 'I am really very glad to see you. Please have some more tea.'

The priest said, 'I could not have gone away without seeing you.'

She said, 'My untidy children –' and began to pick up small objects from the carpet, and he went down on his knees to help her, both savouring the small pleasures in the lives of ordinary men and women, drinking tea, talking about mundane things, rocking little children on their knees, clearing the carpet of toys, which would never be theirs.

'Why,' he exclaimed. 'Your mole's gone!' He remembered it so clearly, the engaging feature at the corner of her right eye.

She laughed. 'It was removed only last year. Old Yoong thought it would improve my looks.' In the old days, she would have fought off any violation of her body; now she submitted to it meekly, to please a vain old man who had suddenly decided he did not like teardrop moles on women's faces.

She raised her hand to touch the spot where the mole had been, and the jade bangle brushed against an ear-ring. 'You see I still have it,' she said. She had put on some weight, so the circlet of gleaming green stone pressed upon her flesh more possessively.

The door opened, and a tall, thin young man came in. He moved towards them deferentially, murmuring something that could have been a greeting.

'Don't you recognise Father Martin?' asked Mei Kwei, smiling.

314

The young man murmured something again, scratched the back of his neck and in a gush of awkwardness shifted the paper bags of books and notes in his hand.

'Don't you recognise him, François?'

The limbs had grown long and gangly, the dirt had disappeared from nose and feet and his inquisitiveness had been replaced by something like wariness. 'How are you, Tee Tee?' he enquired.

'His name is Chan Seng Tee,' said Mei Kwei, referring to the name by which he was now known to his teachers and class-mates. Tee Tee gave an uncomfortable, polite laugh and, at the first opportunity, left the room.

It was a simple story of love and need, Mei Kwei explained. Shortly after she had arrived in Singapore, she had thought of her little friend in Luping. She sent for him and he had come on his own by bus: a timid, clumsy boy with two plastic bags containing all his possessions in the world, including a pair of new shoes from his mother and two hard-boiled eggs to eat in the bus if he felt hungry.

He would soon have enough skills to earn a living. Old Yoong had been kind enough, Mei Kwei said, to agree to pay for the boy's education. But Tee Tee had given trouble lately, she confided. He had fallen into bad company and was neglecting his school work. She was dismayed by his report cards. Fortunately, she had managed to talk him round. But it had meant the loss of a whole school year and more money spent on his education. Fortunately again, Old Yoong had not complained too much.

The kind man was heard outside, sounding his car horn loudly. The servant rushed out to open the gate. Mei Kwei gave a start and looked at the clock on the wall.

'You must come again tomorrow,' she said, then inclined her body in the direction of the door while, at the same time, adjusting her features into a bland docility in preparation for Old Yoong's entrance.

He came in sullenly, having already noted the visitor's presence.

'This is Father Martin –' Mei Kwei began, but Old Yoong, muttered something and walked straight past the priest to his room, ignoring Maria who was clinging to his hand and shouting, 'Papa! Papa!' It dawned on him later that it was the same Catholic priest of the scandal; right now, he was just another objectionable male visitor.

'You must come again tomorrow,' Mei Kwei repeated, with resolution in her voice, defying danger. Father Martin could almost see her that evening, cajoling the old man out of his surliness and back into amiability, resorting not only to offerings of hot tea or ginseng, but to the soft dresses and trinkets of seduction.

Again the hot angry tears reddened his eyes. 'I leave for Vietnam tomorrow evening,' he said, with a sudden, urgent sense that tomorrow would be their last chance to unload their hearts and break the painful silence of the intervening years.

CHAPTER SIXTY-NINE

As she lay beside him in the darkness, she could hear his breathing. It was the heavy, laboured breathing of an old man's intense displeasure and it soon mixed with the darkness to form a thick, noxious miasma that filled the room and entered every pore of her body. She lay very still and waited for that small cough or sneeze, that small crick in his joints, which would provide the opening for the night's long ritual of appeasement and cajoling: 'Shall I get you some tea? Would you like a massage?' She had a whole array of restorative instruments at the ready: ginseng tea, ginger wine, tiger balm, dragon embrocation oil, powdered rhinoceros's horn.

No sound came from him; she could sense every line of anger etched deep on his brow and around his mouth, feel the simmering heat of jealousy that could give unexpected sharpness to the old tongue, unexpected strength to the old body.

He really is very angry with me, she thought. His rage seemed to be greater than on the occasion when she had, in an unguarded moment, mentioned Maria's – or perhaps it was Susie's – father. She had foolishly broken her own rule never to refer to the men in her past life, and had duly spent the whole of that night pacifying and reassuring him. By the time he had drunk her tea of peace and been calmed by the reassurance of her contrite body against his – still as desirable to him as during those rides in the back of his car in Luping so many years ago – the night was almost gone. She had lain awake till the first rays of dawn while he slept contentedly beside her.

If the mention of a man's name had called for so much appeasing, the physical presence of the foreign priest in his house would necessitate a ceremony of propitiation lasting many nights. Mei Kwei prepared herself for the the long task ahead.

She stretched out a hand to touch him gently on the shoulder to test the degree of his anger. She moved closer to him, and shrank immediately when he snarled with savage intensity, 'Don't touch me!' Then she raised herself on the bed and went to him, throwing herself at his mercy in a wondrous display of gentle tears, sweet kisses and diaphanous nightwear. This always had the effect of placating him. Although he continued to be stiff with lingering irritation, at least he had stopped snarling and was submitting to the caresses of her hands and lips.

When he had sufficiently calmed down, she said, 'I'll get you a drink,' and was gone in an instant, to reappear in a few minutes with a cup of his favourite ginseng tea, which she put on the table by his side. Then she made ready to spend the rest of the night in an adjoining room, her final caressing kiss saying, 'Not in spite, you understand, but in respect. For you are still angry with me and cannot bear my presence.'

She saw, as she knew she would, pride struggling with need. Need made an involuntary movement to keep her by his side. 'Don't go,' it pleaded, but pride checked it in time. He remained tight-lipped and made no attempt to stop her.

Lying alone in the room, she waited for the next step of the night's long ritual which she knew would not be long in coming. His need for her was overpowering and he soon stumbled out of the room in search of her. He stood almost abjectly at the doorway of the room, looking at her lying alone in her bed. He went to her eagerly, a besotted old man who would always be branded by his wives in Penang for the folly of his love. She has bewitched him, they told each other.

'Do you still love him?' He had wanted to know whether she still loved Maria's – or it could have been Susie's – father.

'No,' she had said.

'Did you ever love him?' His jealousy of the other men in her life was ravenous and savage, reaching into the past to stamp out all of them.

'Did you ever sleep with that foreign priest?' Now he was with her on the narrow single bed, his body pressed against hers in the mounting pain of his jealousy.

'No,' she said.

'Do you love that foreign priest?'

'No,' she said. 'Yes,' she had said to her husband, so many years ago, when he pranced in rage around her bed, which still reeked with the smells of childbirth.

'No,' she said now to Old Yoong, for she had learned since then to bury a private truth, as she had learned to bury a private joy.

But he was still not satisfied. He jerked her face towards his in the darkness and said, with brutal intent, 'If you even once –' He always left his threats unfinished, the better to convey their gravity. He would never say openly, 'Where can you go? Who will support you and your brood of bastard children?'

'Please, you're hurting me,' she said, for he was grasping her wrist where the jade bangle was, and pressing it deep into her flesh.

'Please promise me.' The old man's moods swung remarkably. He was now beginning to show much distress and to plead with her, like a frightened, fretful child.

Mei Kwei gave an inner sight of relief. The night's appeasement was over.

CHAPTER SEVENTY

She was shorn of all makeup, having in the few minutes left to her after seeing Old Yoong to his car, rushed to her room, removed her makeup, tied her hair in a pony-tail and put on a simple shift of indeterminate colour. Now, she stood before the priest and smiled, revelling once more in the startled look in his eyes.

I used to wonder at the swift change in her moods. She does that with clothes too, he thought.

'The servant has taken the girls to the playground,' she said. The black car was not in the driveway, Tee Tee was at school. The atmosphere, like her face, was shorn of all extraneousness.

'How could you –' he burst forth with angry energy, and for a while his hot tears, heroically checked yesterday, prevented him from speaking further. When he could speak again, his face was white with the intensity of his feelings. How could she do this to herself? To him?

For it was his pain to see her reduced to appalling servitude to an old man.

He imagined her recoiling from Old Yoong's brutal touch and his mind went back to that long line of shadowy men who, in a torpor of whisky fumes and malodorous breath, had been even more brutal. Love, anger, pity, jealousy combined into a spluttering incoherence. He was aware of words being forced out and choked them back. He paused, panting heavily, and slumped in his chair. She was silent, her face turned away from him. But he was not done yet; about to a confess his jealousy, in Luping, of her brother, the unruly men in her house, her husband – any man who came near enough to touch her – he was startled to see her turn round suddenly, eyes flashing.

How dare he talk this way, Mei Kwei demanded, when he was no better than any of the others who had abandoned her? Who cared for her in her moment of greatest need? Who would have cared if she *had* slashed her wrists that morning?

Her tears, too, came in a hot, angry surge. She exhausted herself quickly and fell back on the sofa, crying into her handkerchief. 'That's right, condemn me!' she sobbed. 'Spit on me. You abandoned me – you, whom I needed most of all.'

For Old Yoong's family had spat on her. All four of them, the third wife, the son, the daughter and a young granddaughter who must all have come to Singapore on a visit. She had met them accidentally in a shop and all together as in a rehearsed act, they had turned to face her, gathered the venom in their mouths and ejected it in her face, in full view of the shoppers.

'That's not fair!' he shouted. 'I was beaten to within an inch of my life. What could I do?' He had been a wreck when he returned to France, had had to use a walking stick for months and had kept knocking into things because of his impaired vision. One day Léonie had found him huddled in a corner of his room, crying. No soul could have been more abandoned by God or man. 'What about me? I, too, suffered. You seem to have forgotten that.'

What about me? What about you? The petty claims of egoistic vanity had to be made, for neither would let the other be the greater sufferer in love's bruising.

So the accusations flew to and fro, above the artificial lilies in their blue vase, above a carpet strewn with abandoned children's playthings, ringing violently against each other, hard and brutal. Breathing heavily, saying nothing, they sat back on their chairs. But the distance between them – that small stretch across a breadth of carpet – was too great. He got up, walked across and sat down beside her. It only needed a slight movement of his head towards hers for them to move closer together and clasp each other's hands like two frightened children, fearful of losing connection again in the dark woods.

'I have to tell you something,' she said. 'I could never leave him for anyone.'

And he felt a surge of irritation which made him look away for an instant and want to make his own declaration of intent: he could never leave his god for anyone. He might add, with the biting sarcasm he was capable of when annoyed: So both of us are safe from each other, you with your secure old man, I with my priestly vocation and new posting in Vietnam. He thought sadly, This is my last visit. I am not likely to see her again. We should not waste our time together in any foolish quarrel. To have gone on in this way would only stretch the tension-wire between them to a taut, purposeless antagonism.

He calmed down and said aloud, 'I understand,' and she looked relieved.

She could not stop talking about kindness. There was a special kindness that bound her irrevocably to the old man, Mei Kwei told him. Following her eyes, Father Martin saw a quick, darting movement behind the curtain of a tall side window.

'François, come here! Come out from there!' Mei Kwei got up, walked to the curtain and lifted it to reveal a boy, squatting on the floor, curled up tightly so that his face was not visible.

The priest recognised him at once. 'Oh, my God,' he breathed and walked over to the child, to join his mother in persuading him to come out of his hiding-place. He touched the soft white hair on the boy's head, wedged determinedly between the knees, touched, with extreme gentleness, the soft pale arms that shrank from him. He recalled, with exquisite pain, the tiny white baby in the blanket, who had rolled out on the floor in the attack of brutal energy on Christmas Eve. He remembered also seeing him still kicking in the throes of his birth and, nearby, the porcelain baby of the crib, broken into two.

'I decided to name him after you,' said Mei Kwei, and then signalled, by a forefinger to her lips, that they should leave the boy alone. They walked back to the sofa and sat close together, side by side. 'He's a very shy, sad child,' she continued. 'I can hardly remember seeing him smile or laugh like a normal child. I worry about him most of all.' Old Yoong had promised to take care of the boy all his life, and had shown her the money put aside specially for him in a bank account. She had studied the figure carefully. It was sufficient to take the boy into adulthood, if he should live that long. Love has its calculus.

Like a little animal curled safely into a ball against predators, the boy was inching his way – still with his head between his knees and encircled by his arms – towards them, stopping only when he felt their eyes upon him. It was an almost comical sight – the little tight ball rolling imperceptibly towards them on the carpet.

Father Martin wanted desperately to see the child lift up his head. He thought, almost with a ferocity of yearning, I cannot leave without seeing this boy smile. He resorted to the manoeuvres of adults, which sometimes work even with the shyest child. He made funny faces and sounds, he did a comical little prance. But it was no use. The child remained silent.

'He almost died at one stage,' said Mei Kwei. 'I went mad with fear. But luckily my little François survived. Look,' she whispered, and drew his attention to the child's accelerated progress in their direction, 'he likes you.' The priest waited, and true enough, the small pale face soon lifted cautiously in a quick upward glance.

'François,' Father Martin said softly. He got up and picked up the child from the floor. There was no resistance.

'Why –?' he asked, as he held the child in his arms and allowed his tears to flow. 'Why did you not tell the truth and spare the child all this pain?'

It would be too wearisome to tell her about the visit to the father a few days ago, about Austin's admitted shame and contrition when he knew the truth, too painful to tell her about the second pale son, the second curse. But he wanted to know, after eight years, why she had told this colossal untruth about themselves and the child? Or had allowed the untruth to go uncorrected?

'I told no lie,' Mei Kwei replied, with spirit. In his rage her husband had danced around her child-bed and screamed questions at her. 'Did you sleep with the priest? Is this his bastard? Did you have an affair with him?' She had remained silent throughout, strangely unafraid. But when he yelled, 'Do you love the priest?' she had turned a calm face to him and said, 'Yes.' And that was when he had picked up the baby and run screaming from the room and to the church.

'I had no idea what he was going to do. In any case I felt so tired and ill that I was not capable of the slightest movement. My mind was blank except for one thought: This is my story, they will never take it away from me.'

321

He put his arms around her, and she laid her head on his shoulder. He pressed his lips to her forehead and held her cold hands in his. 'You are the only woman I have ever loved,' he told her.

It was no mean happiness to come only after God in this good man's heart and soul, Mei Kwei said to herself. She had never loved anybody else and never would.

She settled contentedly in his arms and felt she had never been happier. If Old Yoong should see me now, she thought. Love, like everything, had its reckoning, but she did not care; she would not have cared if he had come in then and surprised them, or if the servant had seen them and was already on her way to tell him. She knew how to deal with the situation. 'There is nothing between us,' she would say truthfully. 'He came as a friend, and he left as a friend.'

Father Martin noticed that little François was no longer in the room.

'He'll be back,' said his mother. 'He likes you.'

She was right. He was back in a few minutes, staggering under the weight of an enormous burden, which he laid at the feet of the priest, as an affectionate dog might deposit a bone or rubber ball at the feet of a beloved master.

'Why, François, how did you find them?' cried Mei Kwei, as she searched the two headdresses – the God-King's and the Moon Maiden's – for any damage to beads and sequins in their forced journey from the secret cupboard across a stretch of floor. They had lost much of their lustre but were still recognisable; they were among the few things she had thought worthwhile to take with her from Luping.

The boy looked at them, his thin, pale face twitching and his sad eyes blinking in a shaft of afternoon light.

'Look at me.' Father Martin put on the God-King's headdress. He stood before François, shook the velvet and flapped the side wings. He made a silly grimace. The boy stared back, unsmiling. 'Here,' he said to Mei Kwei, pointing to the other headdress, 'you put that on.'

They faced the boy grinning, a pair of adults turned clowns for his amusement. He stared back, his little face as sad as ever.

The God-King and the Moon Maiden turned to each other. Their faces were grave, as befitted the solemnity of the occasion. They listened intently, as if to hear the opening sound of a gong or a drum. It came and they began to dance, at first very slowly, with heavy, languorous movements, then faster as they moved towards each other, their eyes fixed on each other's faces. They heard the drums

322

and gongs beating loudly. 'Dance,' said the drums. 'Dance,' said the gongs. They obeyed, adjusting the movements of their arms and legs to the rhythm of a hundred instruments filling the air with their music. They were close, yet never close enough to touch. Oh, how happy we are! they thought. At the point of touching, the drums boomed, 'Stop!' and the gongs said, 'No!' At the point of touching, their faces pale, their hearts beating, they swung apart, then began the dance again. 'Dance!' screamed the drums and gongs together. 'Stop!' A mighty clash of cymbals made them tremble in fear. Then there came through the din the sweet sounds of a flute. The flute said, 'Go on, dance,' and nudged them towards union. 'Go on,' said the flute, for they appeared reluctant. The flute played its sweetest note, which washed over them, like a sparkling flood, so that the God-King and the Moon Maiden came together at last in an embrace, laughing for joy. It was for a brief moment only, for the gongs, drums and cymbals would soon be starting again.

When it was over they looked shyly at each other then turned to see the pale, sad boy leaping up and down, laughing and clapping his hands. He made funny *Whoo! Whoo!* and *Hoi! Hoi!* sounds and never stopped clapping. He was joined by his two sisters, who had broken free of the servant as soon as they entered the house, and came to claim their share of whatever excitement was going on.

'Where's Vietnam?' asked Maria as they said their goodbyes; and it was a good thing, thought Father Martin, that the children's clamouring was distracting him from the pain, and a good thing, too, that the boy, overcome by confusion at the sudden arrival of his sisters, had retired to his hiding place behind the curtain. The little girls' faces before him were a blur through his tears as he bent down to kiss them. And, when he finally turned to Mei Kwei and pressed his wet face against hers, he thought, This is too much, too much.

Suddenly his whole soul rebelled. 'Let me come again, this afternoon, to see you. I have some time before departure,' he pleaded, and she knew, looking at the wild intensity in his eyes, listening to the hoarseness in his voice, that he was allowing passion its ascendancy at last, if only for a little while, and was pleading for its fulfilment. 'Let me see you in private. Let our love, so long suppressed, express itself.'

On the threshold of a new life in Vietnam, the priest was pleading to close the old one with an act of madness, as magnificent as hers had been that morning when she met him in the cemetery to show him the letter she was going to leave for her husband to be, and to tell him, 'I am not afraid.'

It would be a freak moment of blinding brilliance in the quiet drabness of their respectable lives, an iridescence in their greying rainbows. It would be the greatest story in the private storehouse of their sad hearts in the long years ahead.

Hunger had its own madness. He did not realise how hungry he had become for her face, her voice, the touch of her body, and the hunger, now consuming him, made him reckless. He held her hands so tightly she gave a little gasp and, for a moment, could not bear the intense grave yearning imprisoned in his eyes. 'Please.'

'No,' she said, and she meant, 'Too late. There is too much for me to lose. The spying servant is watching. She will have tales to tell the old man.'

CHAPTER SEVENTY-ONE

The child, strange little creature that he was, would sneak out of bed in the silence of night to bear witness to secret adult activities. This time, he followed his mother to the back of the house and outside to the yard, and squatted on the ground to watch her as she busied herself with a can of kerosene and a box of matches, preparatory to the immolation, once more, of her secret dreams.

'François, what are you doing here?' Mei Kwei turned round with a start and noticed his presence. But she did not tell him to go back to bed.

The child watched intently as she poured the kerosene over a jumbled heap on the ground, that was the two ornate headdresses, their glory long gone, but still capable of an impressive display of glitter and sparkle in the darkness, under the night sky. The child's eyes grew wide and his pale face seemed paler as he watched his mother light a match and throw it into the heap. The headdresses burst into flames instantly; the God-King's crown was the first to go, followed by the Moon Maiden's diadem. The lovely silken wings, baubles and bead-strings hissed and sizzled and finally fell silent, reduced to ashes and blackened wire frames, ghostly remains of past glory and joy.

The child said nothing but looked at his mother. She said, 'Come here,' and held him close to her side as together they watched the last pale afterglow sink into total darkness and heard, in the distance, the faint rumble of an oncoming storm.

CHAPTER SEVENTY-TWO

Father Martin had packed his bags and left them in a corner of the room, to be picked up by one of the hotel service boys. He lay on his bed and let his thoughts wander. They focused, quite unaccountably, on a small brown-paper parcel that had lain undisturbed in his luggage through his travels and which, again quite unaccountably, he took everywhere with him. Perhaps it was just habit. Or some vague sense of duty. He got up from the bed, opened the bag containing the parcel, took it out and stared at it. He removed the brown-paper wrapping and pulled out the little whip of ropes. He touched each of the ropes, slowly, reflectively. Uncle Jean Claude would have said, 'François, you can't do this!' and been outraged. But he had already made up his mind. He dropped the whip, together with the paper wrapping into a bin already full of discarded paper and boxes. By the next morning, the bin would have been removed by the hotel cleaning woman and emptied into the garbage dump.

Father Martin returned to his bed and let his thoughts stray again. This time they dwelt on the face he knew he would never see again. He had loved and would love only one woman in his life. If she had agreed to the urgent plea of his heart and body, he would not have been ashamed. He might even have worked up enough brazenness to defend himself to his jealous God thus: 'I worship you every day of my life. I loved this woman but once.' Over the years he would have recollected their act of passion and longing, and looked upon it as a precious secret to be endowed with joy rather than as a sin. But it was not to be, and he would have to be satisfied with lesser but no less precious secrets. 'I did it all for you,' she had said in Luping; in Singapore, she had told him the story of her love again. 'Do you love the priest?' her husband had roared. And she had turned a calm face to him and said, 'Yes.' He remembered, with an ache of longing, every syllable of her story; he would remember it all his life.

There was a knocking on the door and he got up to open it, getting ready a small tip for any of the hotel staff who were always knocking to ask if he needed this or that. He was speechless for a moment, staring at the visitor at the doorway.

'Come in.' His voice was a small hoarse whisper, while he held onto a nearby table to steady himself. 'Please sit down. Would you like some tea?'

She was in a simple dress and wore no makeup. She looked a little pale. 'I've come to be with you,' Mei Kwei said at last. 'I couldn't bear the thought of not seeing you again.'

He moved towards her, tentatively. She remained in her seat, not looking at him. Then she got up to ring the bell for one of the hotel attendants. He watched her wonderingly and thought he saw, with a thrill of joyous expectation, the look of wild defiance which she had had in her eyes during their fateful meeting in the cemetery.

She said to the young boy who appeared at the door, 'Please bring me a hammer.' The request being most unusual, she repeated it and stuffed a generous tip in his hands.

Father Martin continued to watch her in mounting fascination; this strange, rare, beautiful woman he would never stop loving. The boy appeared with the hammer. As soon as the door was closed upon them once more, and she took the tool in her hands, grasping it firmly, he knew what she was going to do. He gave a gasp as he watched her rest one hand on the table and raise the hammer with the other, bringing it crashing down upon the jade bangle, which broke, with a small dull crack, into three pieces. She laid the hammer down beside the broken pieces on the table and rubbed the freed flesh, slowly and lingeringly.

When it was all over, and the slow ticking of the clock on the table announced the approaching arrival of the hotel staff to take his bags they continued to lie together, not talking, preferring total silence for the full savouring of each other's warm presence. Mei Kwei remembered, after the joyous meeting in the cemetery, taking away the image – now grown so dear – of the precise woof and weft of a patch of priestly sleeve and saving it in her treasure chest of secret remembrances. Now, lying against him in the comfort of the bed, she was aware of a new yield of treasured pictures to be taken and stored away – the reflection of herself in his eyes, the feel of his beard on her face, the smoothness and paleness of his skin. She had wanted to give him the first gift of her body; now, her gift all gone and squandered, he was giving her his. It was a supreme love that would give a sublime rhythm to her life. The thought filled her with wonder and tears.

'I love you so much,' he said, and gathered her to himself once more. On his part, the treasures of memory would be rich beyond measure and centre on the way she was looking at him now, her eyes liquid with beseeching love, the white curve of a breast, the rich hair loosed upon the pillow, the sheets warm with her body.

Exhilarated by their daring, liberating embrace of life's totality, they would not and could not let each other go.

EPILOGUE

In 1992, long after little François had died at the age of sixteen of pneumonia and the grass had grown thickly around his grave, soon to be exhumed in an on-going government exercise of land reclamation to make way for industrial buildings; long after Uncle Yoong (they had stopped calling him Papa after childhood) had departed from their lives and become only a vague memory; long after Tee Tee had gone back to live in Malaya to take care of his mother, Maria and Susie, now grown women, would puzzle over their mother's last words as she lay dying. She had spoken, in a moment of lucidity in a long painful illness, of a dance, of a man and a woman in a burst of joy. Her words made no sense and were attributed to the deterioration of a mind much enfeebled by drugs. Maria had a vague recollection of her mother laughing with a man who was certainly not Uncle Yoong but, then, they had many memories of Mama, when she was young and lovely and wearing pretty clothes, laughing with men.

'Do you remember anything at all, Su?' said Maria.

'For goodness' sake, I must have been a baby then,' said Susie. They were both beautiful and, in the years before their mother's illness, when they took her out for a meal in a restaurant as a birthday treat or to celebrate Mother's Day and afterwards took her shopping for a present, they enjoyed the admiring glances they all drew. Somebody had even come up to Mei Kwei and said, 'They've got their looks from you.' Even in old age, she remained a beautiful woman.

'Do you remember anything about a priest?' asked Maria. 'I remember Mama talking of a priest once.'

'For goodness' sake,' said Susie again.

'Grandma would have known,' said Maria thoughtfully. But it

328

was no use talking about their strange grandmother who had agreed at last to live with them, and had died two years later. Ah Oon Soh had never been comfortable with her two spirited granddaughters who spoke a foreign language, and avoided them as much as possible. She was homesick to the last for Luping.

'Mama, is there anything you would like?' Maria had asked very gently, as their mother lay on her death-bed. 'She's having that strange hallucination again,' she later reported to her sister in a whisper. And, of course, since the priest was only part of the hallucination, nobody thought to try to find him to tell him of her death.

In 1994 Father François Martin lay dying, succumbing at last to a cancer that had developed several years earlier. He, too, spoke strange last words of a man and a woman together, and of a gift – a broken bangle. Léonie, tenderly holding his hand, knew it was no hallucination, but the surrendering of a secret connected with his years in Malaya that he had never fully shared with her.

'Dear, dear François,' she said, kissing his hand, and laying her worn cheek against it. It would have made more sense for him who had received the highest honours from the government as well as from the Church for his work in Vietnam, to talk of these, or of his visit to the Pope in 1992 when he had had the honour of being photographed with the Holy Father. But he spoke only about the secret woman.

'Dear François, is there anything you would like?' Léonie asked tenderly. She put her ear to his mouth, for he was now speaking only faintly. But the joy on his face was far from faint. It lit up his sunken, worn face ravaged by the cancer, as he spoke, for the last time, of a man and a woman dancing together, and of a pale, sad little boy called François who laughed for the first time.